The Bygone Archive

Joseph R. Lallo

Table Contents

ACKNOWLEDGMENTS

I would like to thank Nick Deligaris for his excellent cover illustration. I would also like to thank Tammy Salyer for going above and beyond to help make this story comprehensible. And most importantly, I would like to thank the readers for giving this new series a chance! Thanks for all your support!

Prologue

Always know who pulls the strings. It was a lesson he'd learned long ago, and moments like this made it painfully clear why. The man rubbed the scar on his temple and glared at the two brutes to either side of him.

"How much they paying you?" he growled. "Whatever it is, you aren't worth it. Paid to keep an eye on a man with his hands bound behind his back. Pitiful. Untie me and we'll see who the real man is."

The thugs didn't bother giving him a second glance. For all he knew, they didn't speak the language. But he'd been sent scurrying from Beffshire with his tail between his legs. After that, he'd spent weeks trying to avoid the Bolivans, who felt as though he owed them compensation for the priceless equipment he'd lost on his last mission. When he was finally cornered and subdued, it happened without giving him a chance to deliver so much as a black eye to his captors. The entire experience had left him spoiling for a fight. That even these muscle-headed dolts wouldn't offer him the dignity of a taunt in reply was downright torturous.

He gave each of them a sideways glance. They were big. Bigger than a human being ought to be. The fists wrapped around his upper arm were practically the size of his thigh. These boys had some mystic blood in them. Maybe, just this once, it was best if he didn't succeed in prompting a scuffle. Without a knife in his hand, he might not come out on top.

They half led, half carried him through an old hallway in a decrepit building up near the northern end of Quarr. Dust caked every surface. Windows without glass or curtains cast stark light through doorways that had been stripped of their doors. The only evidence this place had been used at all in the last decade was the floor of the hallway, which had been shuffled clean by no doubt countless similar instances of dragging captives through. Ahead, a single intact door seemed to be their destination.

His captors shoved the door open to reveal a small interior room. Compared to the rest of the house, it was black as pitch. No window, and only one small flame casting light. The room had been divided in two by a stout wooden screen. Intricate clover-shaped holes had been carved through it, and it completely blocked off the back half of the chamber such that there must have been another door on the opposite side to let people into the space behind the screen. They dropped him roughly into a wooden chair, the only bit of furniture on the near side of the screen, then shuffled out the door and slammed it behind.

Temple took stock of his surroundings. The room smelled of soot and lamp oil. The lamp on the other side of the screen projected the carved shapes faintly onto the walls around him. They were twisted and distorted in ways that seemed… wrong, somehow. He could see the shadows of their feet beneath the door. There would be no getting past them. He stood and struggled with his bound hands.

"I wouldn't waste your time," came a soft, calm voice from the other side of the screen. "My associates can be a trifle indelicate when someone misbehaves."

Temple froze and glared through the screen. Whoever spoke had done so at a whisper. It was difficult to determine even the gender of his captor. His short time in the darkness hadn't given his eyes much time to adjust, but he could just make out the curve of a big antique chair on the other side of the screen. The flame was positioned such that whoever sat in it was entirely swallowed by its shadow.

"You aren't Bolivan. I know who hired me, the kind of people they are. This doesn't strike me as Bolivan, so I don't owe you a duot."

"While I am tempted to challenge you on just how comprehensive a knowledge of the Bolivan organization you may have, as it happens, you are broadly correct. I am not, at this moment, acting as a representative of the Bolivan family. But that by no means implies that you do not owe me anything."

"I run one contract at a time, and I don't borrow money."

"This isn't about what you had planned, this is about what I had planned for you. And you botched it terribly."

"You don't get to make plans for me without paying my price."

"I admire the gumption of a man who would attempt to make financial demands while tied up in a house half a mountain away from the nearest person who might hear your screams."

"You can't get work out of a corpse, so if you're looking to deal, you're not going to kill me."

"I can't get work out of a recalcitrant wretch either, which makes you precisely as useful to me as a corpse, and a corpse would be less irritating. It would behoove you to be more agreeable."

"Fine. What's the job?"

"First, the price."

"I don't set a price without knowing what I'll be doing to earn it. You and me might have different ideas of what my time is worth."

"I'll negotiate and pay a price to appease the Bolivans so that you will no longer be hunted by them. As a matter of fact, I am quite confident I can smooth things sufficiently to put your purposes parallel with theirs once more. In addition, I will pay you ten thousand duots, plus expenses, up front and an additional twenty thousand upon a successful completion."

Temple settled down into the chair. "I'm listening."

"Prior to your embarrassing failure in Beffshire, a delicate plan had been laid out. The key to any plan of this sort is its subtlety. A victim cannot hold tight to his treasure if he is sleeping. But your bullheaded oafishness woke the mark and tightened their grip. Now light has been shed in corners I would have preferred remain dark."

"You sure use a lot of words to say nothing, whoever you are."

"Words are a specialty of mine. And as for who I am, for now you'll call me Lens. Now keep your mouth shut, and listen close. The instructions are voluminous, they are precise, and I don't intend to repeat them…"

Joseph R. Lallo

Chapter 1

Another day, another load of silver. Fel lugged a crate of assorted fine serving ware on one shoulder and whistled happily. Two months ago, hauling a heap of rich people's platters and spoons would have served to reinforce to him just how lowly his place was in this town. But a lot can happen in two months, and for Fel, the last few weeks had changed his outlook on life.

"Filthy, dirty rat monkey bird!" croaked a voice from a rooftop.

"Hey, Rudy! Looking good today," Fel said, fishing into his pocket without looking.

He pulled out a button and flipped it into the air. A lesser harpy dove from the rooftop and snagged it, warbling happily. Two more dropped down to hop along beside him.

"Toody, Moody, I didn't forget you two," he said. He bounced two more buttons off the cobbles, and they grabbed them and fluttered away. "Where's Judy?"

"Stupid *clod*!" squawked another harpy from the roof.

"There you are! Catch!"

He launched a button in the direction of the final harpy. It caught it neatly in its beak and fluttered off to join the others.

"Someone's going to have to teach you four the words 'thank you,'" he said.

"*Rat bird!*" the four called back in unison.

Fel reached the door of the family shop and tapped the chin of the mask on the sign before pushing the door open. For the first time in years, the shelves were stocked almost completely with new goods. Officially, the infusion of fresh inventory was thanks to Martin Masker, the patriarch of the family and its primary craftsperson. He'd developed some new repair techniques to breathe life into formerly worthless relics, or so the story went. And that was mostly true. That he'd "developed" those techniques by reading them in a book they'd rescued from the Greater Lands Wall, and that the repair parts came along with a few dozen contraptions that official assayers would have probably rejected if they'd known about them, simply wasn't worth mentioning. And the less said about the supernaturally animated bag of chains that had been helping with the repairs, the better.

"Fresh load of silver," Fel said to his sister, who was working the counter.

"Three folks weren't ready. It's all on the slip there."

"It's a weekly schedule. I don't understand how people can simply fail to have it ready. All they need to do is have things in a basket by the door."

"The richer you get, the less thinking you do," Fel said.

"Proof that you were born to be rich," Epiphany said.

"That's what I've been saying my whole life," he said. "Where's Mom?"

"Down in the dining room with Dad."

He paused. "Something big going on?"

"Would she be away from the counter at this time of day if there wasn't?" Epiphany said.

"Big good or big bad?"

"Depends on if you ask Mom or Dad."

The door chime rang again within the first moments of his stepping inside, and both Fel and Epiphany stifled the urge to roll their eyes. A few years of running a shop made it painfully clear when a customer's primary interest was looking at shelves and asking questions, and making a purchase was a distant second.

"You should get down there. Good or bad, it involves you," Epiphany whispered to him.

"When one of the options is 'bad,' it seems like I'm always involved."

"If it's any consolation, Mom blames me for the 'bad' option."

"That's a nice change of pace," Fel said.

Epiphany slipped into her customer-service tone of voice. Fel flipped up the hatch and opened the door to the stairs leading down to the dining room.

"Fel, good," said Martin as Fel emerged into the floor below. "Close the door behind you."

"Your father is insane," his mother, Vivian, said the moment the hatch clicked shut.

"Visionaries are always called insane."

"Most of the people claiming to have visions *are* insane."

"What's going on?" Fel asked.

"I've finished translating the book of door codes," Martin said. "And I've begun working on some of the ancillary text in the book."

"It's driven him mad," Vivian said.

"Mom, you can call Dad crazy some more when he's done talking," Fel said. "Dad, are we confident these codes will work?"

"I am at least as confident in these codes as I was in the ones that earned you access to the Greater Wall."

Fel clapped. "So that whole wall is our personal inventory."

"It could be much more than that, Fel," Martin said. "The external doors are marked with locations. The inner doors are a little harder to translate. They're labeled with descriptions. And this morning I translated this one."

He slid a page across the dining room table. Fel picked it up. It was typical of his father's scraps, covered with half-thoughts that were crossed out and replaced. But the final line, the full translation, read *Research Library*.

"Books, Dad?" he said. "Forgive me if I don't get excited about books. They don't sell for much."

"That's not *half* of what's wrong with his little scheme," Vivian said.

"Fel, our family has built its legacy on repairing and restoring contraptions. I've learned nearly as much from one of those books you brought back as I'd gleaned from decades of trial and error. I can fix things that have exhausted my capacities for *years*. But still something eludes me."

"You're never going to be able to fix *everything*, Dad."

Martin shook his head. "Incorrect. These are contraptions. They were built. If something can be made, it can be fixed. Even if it means making every bit of it from scratch again, it should be *possible* to make something work again so long as the techniques and materials are available. And so far I've yet to find anything in any of these contraptions, broken *or* functional, that was exotic. Rare, perhaps. Difficult to acquire. But nothing that isn't accessible to me for a price. So what's missing is *technique*."

"I don't follow."

"If one book can help me fix half the devices I'd been working on, imagine what two could achieve. Imagine what ten could achieve. Imagine what a research library would permit. I am convinced that a well-equipped library could provide us with the missing pieces that society has been dreaming of since the Bygone Era. Fel, I think we'll be able to create our own contraptions."

"Madness," Vivian said under her breath. "It's expressly forbidden."

"Selling the blunt dagger was forbidden," Fel said.

"Bygone dagger," Martin corrected.

"The Bygone dagger was harmless. It was a dull tool that deactivated contraptions. And half of the things we're discussing finding a seller for are things *we* know are harmless but the assayers disagree about. I don't *enjoy* the thought of sneaking things by the assayers, but so long as they're things that don't make sense to prohibit the sale of, I'll accept bending the rules if it means keeping this shop thriving. Forbidding the construction of new contraptions is something I *agree* with. And this is something that Fanny won't talk me out of."

"Viv, if we fully understand them, we can construct only contraptions that behave in ways that make sense to sell. We won't be beholden to finding troves of old contraptions and hoping they'll behave, we can actually manufacture our own."

"And what if you get it wrong?" Vivian said.

"I will take the utmost of care."

"You were taking the utmost of care when you reactivated that 'ice-manufacturing contraption' and ended up turning two-thirds of your workbench into some sort of crystal."

"That was because I couldn't know the function of the device before I activated it. If there is a library, and it is properly stocked, I won't have to speculate any longer."

She crossed her arms. "I don't like it."

"I've discussed it at length with Tome, and he agrees with me. Not to mention the added benefit that producing our own contraptions obviates the requirement of Fel risking his life in vaults and the like."

Vivian pointed a finger. "If I knew what a bad influence that boy would be on you, I wouldn't have given him Euphoria's old bedroom to sleep in. Maybe there's something wrong with that bed. Everyone who sleeps in it starts causing trouble."

Fel looked over the paper. "It doesn't say where it is," he said.

"No, I'm afraid not," Martin said. "The external doors are labeled by their location along the wall. The internal doors are labeled exclusively by their descriptions. I imagine there's a directory somewhere within the wall."

"It's a big wall, Dad. And most of it is underwater."

"But surely you understand the value of what that library represents."

Fel leaned on the table and drummed his fingers. Of course he understood the value of his father being able to make contraptions. It would be a dream come true. But having witnessed some of the more violent capacities of contraptions by way of the traps that vaults tended to have, he could absolutely understand his mother's view. For Fel, the question wasn't if he was afraid of doing damage. Doing damage was part of the job, as far as he was concerned. The question was how to persuade his mother to give his Dad enough slack to do something impressive enough to fully change her mind.

He ran through a dozen things that would persuade *him*, even if he wasn't already persuaded, but each fell well short of the sort of logic that would penetrate his mother's defenses.

Above him the door to the dumbwaiter opened and Fanny shouted down, "Do we have any music boxes?"

"Just what are on the shelves," Vivian shouted back.

Fel and Martin snapped their fingers at the same time. The dumbwaiter closed.

"That's it!" Fel said.

"What's it?" Vivian said.

"If Dad could figure out how to make music boxes, we'll never run out of music boxes."

"We both know that your father isn't talking about making music boxes. He's talking about making things that haven't been made before."

"But making music boxes, or puzzle boxes, or any other harmless item we already understand would be the first step," he said. "Imagine how much easier the shop would be to run if we knew precisely what our inventory would be month after month, year after year."

"But Martin wouldn't *stop* there. And it doesn't change the fact that constructing new contraptions is forbidden."

"Mom, we can fix boxes, right?" Fel said.

"Of course."

"And we can find broken ones, right?"

"Naturally."

"And making a few raids a year to vaults is allowed, right?"

"If you're working on a point, just get to it."

"How will the assayers *know* we're making them from scratch? If they knew what was in the Greater Lands Wall or the vaults—or if they could get to them—they would have cleaned them out before we got there."

The hatch to the next floor opened, and Tome emerged from below. "Forgive the intrusion on what is clearly a family matter."

"Tome, no. Never an intrusion. Come. I'm sure you'll have valuable insight," Martin said.

Fel and Vivian both glared at the paper mage as he pulled up a chair and sat at the table.

"I couldn't help but overhear the heated discussion."

"You'd have to be eavesdropping, Tome. I've lived in this house my whole life, remember? I know how loudly people have to talk to be overheard between floors," Fel said.

"… Well, be that as it may, I wondered, is there any official limit to how much repair something can receive?"

"No. Whatever repair is necessary to make it function," Vivian said flatly.

"And is there any prohibition for disassembling devices?"

"Contraptions, and no. Parting out malfunctioning contraptions is the primary way of getting spare parts to fix others."

"So there's your solution."

All three of the Maskers stared at him.

"We're not making the leap with you, boy," Vivian said.

"You take one of these music boxes. You take it apart piece by piece, until it is entirely disassembled. Then you start crafting new ones, and for each new one you craft, you use just one piece of the original. Now you haven't made new ones, you've simply repaired *very* badly broken ones."

Vivian furrowed her brow, mulling the words over. "How many parts are in a music box?"

"There are four hundred and seventeen components to a music box," said Martin. "I have been able to fabricate all but seventeen of them."

She patted the apron she wore and slipped a booklet from it. "We wouldn't part out all the boxes. The more intact a contraption is and the less repair work has been done, the greater the price… but if all the badly damaged boxes were broken down and rebuilt into handmade ones…"

Her eyes danced across the page as figures assembled themselves in her mind. The corner of her mouth almost imperceptibly twitched into a grin.

Again the dumbwaiter door opened and Epiphany called out. "Mom! The assayers are here for their monthly visit."

The grin vanished from her face. She snapped the book shut and tucked it away. "I will be up to help momentarily." She lowered her voice and addressed the others. "What we are discussing is a clear overextension of the word of the law and a willful misunderstanding of its intent… which has been the bread and butter of our shop for ages. We could do it freely and have very little risk of endangering the shop. Martin, are you confident you could do it, if you could learn how to make the missing parts?"

"I see no reason why not."

She huffed and said to Fel, "Then when you make your next trip to the Greater Lands Wall, you may as well put some effort into finding this library." She jabbed a finger at Martin. "But I will watch you like a hawk. I don't need you getting creative and accidentally re-creating whatever caused the Bygone Era to be bygone."

"I shall double my dedication to safety," Martin said.

"Fine then. Are we through? May I return to the shop?"

"I believe Fel and I can discuss the rest without you."

Vivian nodded and headed for the stairs. Martin revealed a booklet similar to the one his wife kept.

"I have transcribed all the door codes into this book. Twice, in fact. I burned the other in Wick's lantern, so he will have access to all the codes as well."

"I assume, with this in hand, I've got another trip to the wall in my future."

"In your near future. You and Tome will be—"

Fel raised a hand. "Tome is a part of this already?"

"I think you'll agree his help was crucial in the success of your last expedition. And he and I have been having some very interesting discussions regarding the possible intersections of contraptioneering and paper magic."

Fel glared at Tome. "I guess you can spend a lot of time musing about that stuff when you don't have a job to do."

Tome crossed his arms. "I'll have you know that some lucky games of grum and your family's very reasonable rates for room and board have afforded me a degree of leisure with my share of the earnings from our previous expedition. And my time has not been wasted. Come, I want to show you something."

Martin was nodding. "Oh, yes. You'll find this intriguing. I'll head back into the workshop and see if I can find a way to narrow down the location of the library or any other high-value chambers within the wall."

The trio headed for the stairs and went down one by one. Martin continued to the lowest level. Before they could reach the cramped hallway between Fel's and Tome's doors, a small curtain flipped open and a goat-sized creature with a single opalescent horn clopped out from inside, prancing happily and bleating. Parch, a lesser unicorn that had become rather attached to Fel after he showed it some kindness at the Greater Lands Wall, had become something of the family pet. This was much to the detriment of Fel's bedroom. The curtain Parch emerged from covered a splintered section of door surrounded by fragments of wood, which suggested the addition of the pet door was a choice made by Parch's strength and determination rather than Fel's affection. The beast sprang about for a bit and reared back. Fel slapped a hand right between Parch's eyes and horn and gave him a playful shove.

After three more iterations of the little game, Parch calmed down and gave Tome a decidedly dirty look before trotting back into Fel's room.

Fel gave Tome a remarkably similar look.

"What?" Tome said, reaching into his pocket and retrieving a slip of paper.

"I saw that look he gave you. What'd you do?"

"Please, Fel. He's an animal."

"What'd you do?" Fel repeated firmly.

Tome tore the end of the page and pressed it to his door. It rattled and swung open.

"I suppose he *may* have been displeased that I applied another taming spell to him—after a frustrating amount of chasing."

"Why did you do that? Was he causing trouble? Did he try eating another bedspread?"

"No. I required samples."

Tome stepped into his room and tore another page. Three lamps lit themselves at the behest of the spell, revealing a room that, despite only having been his home for two months, looked nearly as lived in as Fel's. He'd filled all Euphoria's old shelves with sheaves of blank pages and dozens of old books picked up at the various shops around town. The writing desk, normally covered with spells in various stages of completion, was instead rigged up with some of Martin's gear. A tin with some manner of scorched, strong-smelling black powder had been set on a metal stand over an alcohol burner. Beside it, a glass beaker filled with sticky gunk and a pitcher full of water stood ready to be deployed.

"A few weeks ago, I found one of the unicorn's hairs on my bed—which is what inspired me to start using reinforcing magic on the door, I'll have you know. But out of curiosity, I burnt the hair and mixed up a sample of ink, and it was surprisingly potent. Not as strong as the top-quality stuff, but appreciably close. So I tamed Parch and took some larger samples. A tuft of hair, some powder from the horn. Some hoof trimmings. Nothing he'd miss."

"Don't try harvesting Parch, Tome."

"No, no. Heavens no. Nothing to hurt the creature. But you'll be happy to know that the horn powder made very, *very* potent ink. Perhaps even more potent than the quality ink I spend a fortune on. That, coupled with the substantial amount of midquality ink I can make from Parch's shedding, suggests having a lesser unicorn around could reduce my ink budget to zero while leading to a net improvement in my spells."

"So long as you don't—"

A jangling drew his attention to the stairs below before he could finish. Two gleaming claws crested the steps and hauled the rest of the clattering contraption called Oiler to the top. Its expressionless, serpentine brass face managed to communicate delight quite effectively through the bob and angle of its head. Alternating claws and tail, it hobbled its way over and plopped its canvas pack of a body down at Fel's feet with all the loyalty of a trusty hound. After a moment, it spotted the curtain at the bottom of the door and pinched the end to lift it up.

"No, Oiler, we've been through this, there's no point in—"

Again he wasn't given a chance to finish. Oiler deftly gathered up the bits and pieces of wood and started precisely applying dots of glue from a needle-sharp fang that emerged from its slot of a mouth.

"Where do you suppose the glue comes from? I never see you refill it, and it never seems to run out," Tome said.

"I assume it's just a product of the contraption," Fel said, not truly interested.

"The production of material from nothing is a substantial act of magic. I hope we find those books so that your father can suss that sort of thing out. It could be of huge benefit to us if we can make the determination."

"Do me a favor and stop thinking about this little enterprise in terms of 'we' and 'us.' I don't intend for this to be a permanent partnership," Fel said.

Oiler finished piecing the broken section of door back together and slid it into the gap. It held the bits in place for a few seconds, then slowly took its claws away to reveal a completely patched hole. Precisely three seconds later, a soft clatter from within the room ended with an explosion of wood shards as Parch handily punched his way back out. Oiler spread its hands and waggled its fingers in excitement, then extended a claw and gingerly patted Parch on the head.

"I live in a circus…" Fel muttered.

"I don't think you should waste your breath complaining about such a thing when you're the one who invited the clowns."

"Fair point."

#

Vivian and Epiphany stood to either side of the assayers as they did their work. Each shopkeeper wore the convincing and entirely disingenuous expression of someone who was absolutely delighted to have their workday interrupted by two representatives of the Teskal nobility. The assayers themselves, a man and a woman, were at least quite professional, which was hardly something to be taken for granted. As often as not, the assayers comported themselves as though they were nobles themselves, worthy of borderline worship, rather than mere representatives.

It was clear at a glance that they were better funded and better equipped than the City Watch. Their uniforms, while perhaps not tailored to the officials themselves, at least lacked the "generational" quality that was an earmark of the Watch armor.

The male official held up a freshly repaired contraption with two rotating wheels on either side and asked, "And these wheels rotate constantly?"

"Yes. Since the repair, they have moved continuously without slowing," Vivian said.

He placed the box down on the counter and braced it against the table with one hand while testing the strength of the rotating wheels with the other. No amount of force could keep the wheels from rotating in the least.

"Cogged perimeter, extreme strength. Likely intended to power some larger machine," the woman said.

"I concur," said her partner. "You'll need to hand it over."

"As expected," Vivian said.

He fetched a small satchel from his waist and counted out a handful of coins in exchange for an inexhaustible power source of arcane origin. The woman paced along the carefully aligned rows of contraptions.

"Music boxes, suitable for sale… Puzzle boxes, suitable for sale… You seem to have a considerable infusion of inventory once again."

"Martin has made something of a breakthrough with regard to repair technique. I discussed it with your associates last month."

"Yes, we have it noted here," the man said. "You must have had a tremendous stock of devices awaiting repair, if two straight months have produced such a high volume of repaired contraptions."

"Dad never throws anything away if he can help it. We were up to our necks in contraptions we thought were hopeless. We also were fortunate enough to have a rather successful vault run near the Greater Lands Wall," Epiphany said.

"And this is the entirety of the repaired stock?" the woman said.

13

"Of course," Vivian said. "Though as we speak, my husband is working on more. Nothing likely to be completed by the end of the day. And if all goes according to plan, my boy will be making another run to the vault. Hopefully you'll be going through a similarly substantial set of goods next month."

The woman picked up an alarm box. "I've seen a lot of these in the wealthier stores and homes," she said. "Selling a lot of them, are you?"

"They are relatively common, fairly easy to repair, and in high demand. And they need to be reset here in the shop once they go off. They're some of our most valuable items."

The official turned the box over in her hands. "I hate to be the bearer of bad news…"

"Then you're in the wrong line of work," Epiphany said, before she could stop herself.

"Please don't tell me those aren't permitted any longer," Vivian said.

"It is too early to say," the man said. "But Lord Katritz is not entirely pleased at how widespread they have become. You'll recall what happened with the larger ballerina toys…"

"Yes. After he'd acquired three of them and his acquaintance wrote to us hoping to acquire four, he decided they were suddenly too dangerous to continue to sell," Vivian said.

"There hasn't been any change yet," the assayer said. "Not that we've been made aware of. But I wouldn't be surprised if this time next month we'll be acquiring what remains of your stock."

"With any luck, if such a change happens, it will be brief," the woman said apologetically.

"Then may luck be with us."

"Indeed. It looks like we're through here," the woman said. "But before we go, there was a matter that we were asked to bring to your attention."

"Oh?"

"A couple of months ago, there was the incident with the hippogriffs."

"Indeed, we were at the center of it."

"Yes, that is the matter at hand. That this shop was at the center spurred some discussion in Teskal about the possibility that contraptions were *also* at the center of it."

"Our lives center on contraptions. I don't think it should be a surprise that they were after contraptions."

The man leaned forward. "Which contraption precisely?"

"If you think for a moment I even entertained the idea of discussing the demands of a pair of thugs who, might I add, were rather transparently impersonating people with your authority, then you don't understand how the Maskers do business."

They nodded to one another. "I assure you, we'll be keeping an eye on the issue. We take improper usage of contraptions very seriously."

"As you should," Vivian said. "Though if I were you, I would devote your attentions to the northern fringe of Quarr and Shalia. It is no secret that's where the greatest violations are coming from."

"What can be done is being done in that regard. What we are hoping is to ensure it doesn't spread."

"Perhaps you should have done a little more than *hope*, because the barn door is wide open on that one," Epiphany said.

Vivian gave her a sharp look.

"… With all due respect," Epiphany added.

The officials dusted off their hands in a strangely coordinated act and hefted the crate of confiscated goods from the counter.

"I believe that will be all for this month," said the man.

"Same time next month," said the woman.

They marched out the door. Vivian put her hands on her hips and glared at Epiphany. "Epiphany Mason Masker, what has gotten into you?" she barked when the officials had rattled away in their wagons.

"They just rode away with four thousand duots worth of contraptions and paid us one hundred duots for them.

"Four thousand five hundred and eighty, by my accounting, and that's the price of doing business."

"It's too high a price. And now the alarms might go? It isn't…"

She went silent and turned in unison with her mother as they each sensed someone approaching. A tall, nearly gaunt older woman in fine clothing appeared in front of the shop and stepped inside.

"We'll discuss this later," Vivian said.

"Of course," Fanny said, offering a smile and nod to the customer before hurrying downstairs.

"Hello, ma'am," Vivian said. "Pardon the clutter, we've just finished our assessment from the assayer. How may I help you?"

"In a moment, one of my servants will be arriving with my silver. You've actually done a fair amount of truly exemplary work for me in the past, but this is the first we've met face-to-face. My name is Eveline Verfessa."

"Ah! Mrs. Verfessa. You'll be wanting your silver polished, then. As always, happy to do so. I believe my boy was there just a few hours ago to pick up your silver. I suppose the timing didn't align as well as it might."

"Oh, he arrived just when he was supposed to, but I decided there was some business that was best done face-to-face."

Vivian climbed to the top of a step stool to slip something onto a high shelf. "Something more than polishing your silver, then," she said.

"Indeed." Eveline stepped up to the counter and handed her the next item that needed to be stowed. "Contraptions. I've really not given them much thought, myself."

"People seldom do."

"Imagine my shock at my own ignorance when I discovered some of the foremost experts in their care and sale made their home just around the corner from my own, and were in fact the ones polishing my silver."

"Ours is not a highly lauded profession."

"So many professions not deemed laudable are nonetheless profoundly important in their way. I wonder if you would be willing to share your expertise."

"If you are interested in making a purchase, simply list your requirements and I shall find the perfect item for you."

"I have no doubt you could do so brilliantly, but it was a sale I was hoping to make, not a purchase. I wondered if perhaps you could help me set a price?"

"Mrs. Verfessa, you strike me as a rather savvy individual. I would be very pleased to look over your contraption if you were to bring it in, but that might not be the best thing for you. I am dedicated to providing a fair price—with the understanding that such a price would be set based upon our need to resell at a profit in order to remain in business. And that necessity for resale would take its toll on your own profit. You would be better served by a neutral party. Representatives of the assayers office aren't halfway down the road by now. I could send my son to—"

Verfessa raised her hand to silence her. "No, I think a private appraisal would be more valuable. I've done some limited investigation into the nature of the assayer's office's services already. I am confident your price assessment will be fairer than theirs. We are more interested in establishing a baseline price for future negotiation with hypothetical buyers beyond our fair city's borders. And, to speak more generally, my husband is not terribly fond of working with representatives from Teskal."

"Oh. I see." Vivian finished stowing the last of the top-shelf items and stepped down to Verfessa's level. "I get the feeling the bulk of this conversation has been between the lines."

"There are some matters best approached from oblique angles, the better to provide a healthy bit of separation should an indiscreet listener arrive at the wrong conclusion."

"It would be best to do such things outside of business hours. There are some matters of future inventory that I'll need to be a part of until then."

"I would never wish to interfere with the running of your business."

"Our hours run rather late into the evening. I can offer you an appointment near midnight, or tomorrow morning before six."

"It so happens my husband is something of a night owl. He does most of his business meetings in the wee hours. Either would suit us. Morning is preferable."

"Very well. And there will be a small fee for my services."

"No expert should ever ply their trade without proper compensation."

"Very well. Tomorrow then?"

"I shall be expecting you."

The door jangled. A weary-eyed maid stepped inside with a box of silver serving trays.

"Ah. Excellent timing. Our business is concluded. I look forward to the benefit of your expertise, Mrs. Masker."

"And I hope to be of use to you, Mrs. Verfessa."

#

Epiphany marched down through the house. She ignored Fel and Tome, who were engaged in their near-constant pastime of her brother loudly affirming something that their houseguest quietly contradicted. A few flights of stairs took her to her father's workshop, which was practically unrecognizable compared to what it had been just a few weeks ago. Where once the walls were utterly clogged with projects spanning years, now the place was half-empty. Anything that could be fixed had been fixed, and now was either for sale, sold, or being strategically stored with one or two pieces missing to avoid having to sacrifice them to the assayers just yet.

Her father was at his workbench, magnifying lenses in place as he pored over the notebook that had provided the precious access to the Greater Lands Wall.

"Fanny! Good to see you. I take it the assayers have come and gone?"

"They have."

"Did they take the cogwheel contraption?"

"Of course they did, Dad," she said.

"Ah, well. It never hurts to be optimistic."

"It seldom helps, either." She gazed at the walls. "I've never seen it this clean."

"Oiler is quite the asset. Though I find it doesn't quite grasp the proper functionality of a given device as quickly as it might. For the more complex contraptions, it does a better job at finishing reassembly than actual repair. But having another set of sure hands, and having the benefit of those books Fel brought back, has been nothing short of revolutionary. Now that the assayers have come through, I can finally unlock the doors to the storage. Keeping Oiler away from the nearly finished contraptions has been like keeping candy out of your hands when you were knee-high. Wily for a contraption, that one."

Epiphany plucked a slip of paper from where it was pinned to a board on the wall. It was the inventory of goods they'd held in reserve. "Three locks, prohibited complexity. Five spring traps, prohibited potential for violence. Four image projectors, prohibited complexity. Six echo-horns, prohibited for reasons of security," she grumbled.

"There are plenty of sellable items. The frame with the alternating image within. The flutter-bird egg. *Fifteen* music boxes. Another dozen alarm boxes…"

"They warned us the alarm boxes may be the next to go."

His brow creased and his fingers tightened about his pen. "They know best."

"Father, how much would those prohibited items sell for, if we were permitted to sell them?"

"I don't do figures, Fanny. I leave that to you and your mother."

"Right, so I'll tell you. Twenty-eight thousand duots, without serious haggling. Twice that if Mom or I get a chance to speak our piece. Even if we leave out the spring traps and the door unlockers—those I can accept we might not want in the hands of the average collector—that still leaves us with fifteen thousand duots, easily."

"Theoretical duots don't pay the bills."

"Precisely. And I'm through theorizing. I'm making the trip."

He looked up from his work. "We discussed this."

"We did. For weeks. I discussed it with you. I discussed it with Mom. I discussed it with Fel. I even discussed it with Tome. I debated it with myself. I have given it all due thought, and I have made the most carefully considered decision of my life. I'm going to meet up with Mr. Badgerweed and see about selling some of the more valuable items before the assayers can take them away."

"Do we even know if he'll meet with you?"

"I have exchanged three letters with him since he left Beffshire. It turns out it's rather easy to have letters reach him when you know what route the bazaar is taking. We'd already planned for me to take a trip south to see if I can acquire any decent contraptions. If I leave a day or two early, I can arrive in Brentmire while he is still there. With his dedicated attention, some samples of your handiwork, and no mercenaries breathing down my neck, I'm certain I can persuade him to buy some of our goods. The timing is right, you've already got the inventory, and on the off chance I'm stopped by officials, I can explain that I'd just *acquired* them during the trip rather than brought them with me, since that's the primary reason for the trip."

He scratched out a few more lines. "We seem to be doing a lot more deception as a part of our business these days."

"You certainly don't seem broken up about hiding Oiler. You've been hiding Wick for years. Where is he, anyway?"

"In Tome's room. I've been paying Tome to copy over some of our notes and burn them in Wick's flame so that he can provide them to you and Fel while you are out and about. But if hiding him set the example that led us to this, then I suppose I may have chosen poorly. I set a poor example. We try to be *honest* in this family. Barring the odd and necessary exceptions."

"Dad, we're not turning into thieves and scoundrels. We're not the Bolivan family."

"No. Not yet. But we've got more in common with them today than we did a few months ago. And we'll have more in common with them tomorrow when you head out to make yet another illegal sale. Not out of desperation, but out of… financial aspiration."

"You were going to say 'greed,' weren't you?"

"I don't have your and your mother's gift for instantaneous tact. The point is, it is my job to make sure we don't become what the Bolivan family did. Or, it *was* my job. You, your sister, and your brother are the future of the family. You're adults now. And I suppose that means making your own decisions."

"So I have your blessings?"

"'Blessing' is a strong word. You have my resigned acceptance."

She nodded. "Better than I expected, if I'm honest."

"Your father is old and tired now, Epiphany. I don't have the fight I once had. And if I'm going to send your brother back to the wall without a second thought, it would be unfair of me to keep you from tackling risks you feel you're a match for. But I want you to promise me one thing."

"What?"

"One of these days, and I'm thinking it will be sooner than I'd like, you're going to see your fortune opening out in front of you. Something far grander and brighter than your mother and I could ever have hoped to provide for you. When that day comes, just remember you've got a family here in Beffshire."

Epiphany tightened her lips and slowly shook her head. She took a step forward and placed a hand on Martin's back.

"I'm not going to do what Euphoria did." She gave him a kiss. "Fel and I are going to keep the Masker name on the map. Mark my words."

#

"Hello, Mariss, you're looking lovely today," Fel whispered to himself as he paced along the street leading to Divinity's Oven. "Hello, Mariss, you're looking *lovely* today."

Parch clip-clopped along beside him as he swung a bread basket and tested the greeting with every possible combination of inflections. His share of the money from selling the Bygone dagger meant he'd been able to afford a few extra trips to Divinity's Oven and thus see Mariss a bit more often. In his mind, every day he walked in and picked up a roll or a pie or anything else she might have for sale as though it were a casual afterthought, he took one step closer to making her believe that he was wealthy and important enough to belong in her part of town.

He reached Divinity's Oven and stepped inside. Nice as it would have been to leave Parch outside while he made his purchase and chatted, he'd paid for enough broken doors in the past few weeks to know it was just easier to get

19

dirty looks from shopkeepers for holding the door open for the beast.

"Hello, Mariss, you're a lovely looking day," he said.

She turned and tipped her head curiously, wiping her hands on her apron.

"I can't say I've ever been called that before," she said with a slightly baffled smile on her face. "Oh! But you brought the little cutie again!

Fel tried to keep the embarrassment of the fumbled greeting to a low, searing burn in the back of his mind. "Heh, I don't have a choice, at least until I train him a little better. He listens to commands fine, but if I leave him somewhere, he just comes and finds me. I swear, he's got a sixth sense for tracking me down. I'm lucky I can get him to stay home for my morning rounds."

Ever since the beast had returned to Beffshire with him, Fel had acquired an unwanted reputation around town thanks to Parch's constant company. Having the tippy-tap of little hooves beside him wouldn't have been so bad if lesser unicorns were a more common sight in cities. Such was not the case. Having Parch with him was roughly akin to choosing to wear a parrot as an accessory: baffling to some and irritating to most. But after a couple of months of doing his rounds with Parch at his heels, the city had at least come to accept the eccentricity.

"Here, here. I hoped you'd come. I saved these for you," Mariss said.

"Oh! Well, thanks, I'm happy to know you…"

Mariss set a basket down in front of Parch and dumped some apple cores into it.

"… kept Parch in mind," he said, hoping the disappointment in not being the target of her affections wasn't terribly evident.

She cooed and crouched to fawn over Parch as the little creature bleated and tucked into the treat.

"I know it may as well be a goat, but the little thing is just so much more *majestic* than a goat. That sparkly, glossy coat. That pearly horn. Cutest little lesser I've ever seen."

"You only feel that way because he's never eaten part of your bed."

"Little scamp," she said, giving him a pat. She stood and marched around behind the counter. "But what can I get you today?"

"It's stew night, so I thought a nice loaf of bread."

"Stew night again? Weren't you in here just a few days ago claiming the same thing?"

"It's *usually* stew night," he said.

"What will you have? Something rustic and crusty?"

"Whatever you think is best. You're the expert."

"Good, hearty brown bread, I think." She turned to look over their offerings. "So, I never asked before, but where did you find Parch?"

"You, um, you *did* ask before, but I'm happy to tell you again. It was on a trip down south. I went to the Greater Lands Wall.”

"Oh! Yes, yes. I remember now. You have such *adventures*, don’t you?”

"I do!” he said a bit too eagerly. He tried to rein in his excitement. “It, er, it isn’t anything special. Not for me, anyway. Just part of the job. Sure, I was chased by a dragon, but you’ve got to take some risks to make your mark in the world.”

“A dragon? Not a *greater* dragon,” she said.

“That’s the only kind they’ve got, down by the wall.”

“I don’t know how you could *stand* it, the sort of dangers down there. I’ve barely left my side of Beffshire. Have you traveled much? Gone many other places?”

“I’ve been all over Thayn. You name a site with a Bygone relic or ruin, and I’ve been there. And down south, into the wilds? That’s practically a second home. Hip deep in swamps. Roasted red by the desert sun. But I’ve brought back some astounding treasures.”

“It must be wonderful,” she said, setting down his bread.

“It’s what I was born to do,” he said, returning the old basket.

She set a yeast roll atop the loaf and tucked in a cloth to keep it warm. He paid the princely fee for the bread.

“I’ll tell you what. I’ll be taking a trip south in another day or two. I might be a few weeks, but when I come back, I’ll bring something special from the trip, just for you.”

“Oh, you don’t have to do that, Fel, but I’m sure I’ll treasure it if you do.”

“You have my word as a Masker that I’ll bring you a one-of-a-kind treasure. And I am a man of my word.”

She waved sweetly as he hurried out the door, a well-fed Parch in tow.

“Did you hear that?” he whispered to the unicorn. “You don’t have to do that *Fel*.” He leaned down to slap the creature on his side. “She remembers my name. After all this time she remembers my name. This is my way in. Of *course* she wasn’t going to take notice of me just because I was spending money like I was wealthy. Everyone she *knows* is wealthy. That doesn’t give me an edge! But I guarantee you, no one in her social circle has ever been to the Greater Lands Wall. None of her friends know what it’s like to club a thorn-lizard that stalked him through half a forest. This is it. This is the way to her heart. She’ll be dripping with Bygone jewelry before she knows it. No one else can give her *that*.”

Parch reared up. Fel gave him a few faux headbutts with his hand and another vigorous pat.

“Come on. Let’s drop this off and have some supper. Then I think it’s time for a visit to The Fox and Log. I feel like a night on the town before we head out for our next adventure.”

#

A few hours later, Allie walked up to The Fox and Log to begin her shift. She yawned and tried to remember what day it was. The owner of the tavern had long ago figured out things worked more smoothly when she was present, so he'd given her permission to choose whatever hours she would prefer, so long as she preferred to do more hours than any of the other servers. It was beginning to wear on her, but it was hard to turn down the extra money in her pockets. And though she loathed admitting it, there was something nice about being so utterly indispensable.

As tended to be the case when she was starting her shift past midday, things were sounding rather raucous. It was difficult to tell if she was hearing people enjoying themselves or getting ready to pummel each other. It didn't help that for half her patrons, those two things were one and the same.

A handful of crickets flew past her head as she stepped through the door. That wouldn't have been so odd, except they were roasted and salted already. She dodged another handful and marched to the bar.

"Oovay!" she bellowed with all the concentrated authority of an angry mother. "What did I say about cutting people off *before* they start throwing food?"

"It is not my fault!" bellowed a thickly accented voice from the back room.

"You're the one serving the drinks, Oovay. You're the one who gets to decide when to *stop* serving the drinks." She put on her apron. "And why are you in the back room? You're supposed to be on the floor."

"I am on break!"

"Then where is Dina?"

"I am on break too," came a second voice from the back room.

"The whole reason for there being two of you is so that one of you can take breaks while the other one is working the floor!" She pinched the bridge of her nose and took a breath. "It's fine. The tavern isn't on fire. It's better than it could have been."

She dusted off her hands and stepped onto the footrail that ran around the bottom of the bar. With the extra height raising her up above the crowd, she raised her voice. "Boys, girls, fun's fun, but you settle down or I'm going have to start thinning out the herd," she said.

The request was impressively effective, mostly because it was Allie who said it. She'd taken great care over the years she'd been working at the tavern to cultivate an atmosphere of "if Allie talks, it's serious."

"Allie!" came Fel's voice from the back of the room, where the grum games were usually played.

She trotted to the table and found him, rosy-cheeked and grinning, with a half-empty pint and the spilled remnants of at least two more on the table in front of him.

"Hey, Fel. Been here long?"

"Long enough to be up forty at the grum table and down fifty on booze," he said. "I'm celebrating."

Allie glanced across the room and mentally logged two drink orders, then turned back to him. "What's the occasion?"

"For one, I'm heading out tomorrow. 'Nother expedition. Should be a good one."

"That's two in three months."

"Barely two months."

"Does this mean I'm going to have mercenaries on winged steeds messing up my town again?"

He shrugged. "Probably. Seems to be the new thing."

"Hey, are you in or out?" said Tem.

"I'm in," Fel said. "So, here's the other thing, Allie, I'm—"

"If you're in, you'll have to wait and tell me the rest of it later. Oovay left this whole place a mess, and I can't clean it up if I'm lingering here listening to you spin a yarn."

He pushed down his pile of tiles and pocketed his coins. "Then I'm out. Because these boys are sick of hearing what I've got to say, and you haven't heard it yet."

"Lovely," she said, marching back to the bar to start filling orders.

He followed her over. She thrust an empty tankard into his hand. "Rinse those out, would you? Make yourself useful. Someone around here's got to."

Fel mechanically went about the task as she filled up fresh cups and set them on a tray.

"So I was talking to Mariss today."

"Not much different so far," she said.

"Right, right, but she called me by *name*. She called me Fel."

"Well, what do you know," she said. "That only took a couple of years."

"You know what it means?"

"Someone finally told her your name?"

"It means she's noticing me."

"Probably it also means that someone finally told her your name."

He scratched his head. "Did I not tell her my name?"

"Nope!" She hauled the tray to her shoulder.

"You want me to carry that?"

"Only if I want it spilled."

He set the rinsed tankards down and followed her. "How would you know if someone did or didn't tell her my name?"

"Because I talked to her."

"And she told you I never told her my name?"

"Yep. Grab a couple of baskets of crickets for those two tables."

He tromped back to the bar and delivered the crunchy snacks, then trotted back over to her. "How would she find out my name if I wasn't the one who told her?"

"I told her."

"When?"

"The same time I talked to her. Try to keep up, Fel."

"What were you talking to her for?"

"She works at the bakery, and I had a special order."

He went silent for a moment.

"Something wrong, Fel?"

"I kind of thought I'd done this on my own."

"You could have, if you'd told her your name. Honestly, Fel, it's like the mere thought of Mariss knocks fifteen years off your age."

A thump and a cheer drew her attention to the corner of the bar. Parch was standing on a table. A man with a helmet on backward was lying on the floor, the chair having flipped backward with him still in it.

"You brought your unicorn in here *again*?" she said.

"No, I came in here and Parch tagged along."

"Either get that thing under control, or tell those guys that from now on the house gets a cut on any unicorn-headbutt-based wagers."

"You'll make a mint if you do that."

She set down the drinks and noted three more orders. Fel almost tripped trying to keep pace with her as she doubled back to the bar.

"But don't let me interrupt you," she said. "You were sulking about me being the one who told her your name."

"Yeah, because I don't like needing help to do things that I decide I need to do."

"Everyone needs help sometimes, Fel."

"I know, and I don't like it. For years I've done these expeditions, and I had no one to rely upon but myself while I was out there. I don't like having to rely upon other people. It makes a guy comfortable."

"Being comfortable is good, Fel. Go break up those two. They're about to throw fists. Where's Davie?"

Fel grabbed one of the would-be fighters by the collar and dragged him away from the other.

"The idea is if I get too comfortable, then when the help is gone. I might not be able to handle things anymore."

"You'd been talking to her for years, and she didn't know your name. I'd say you already weren't handling things."

"I mean in general."

"Then I promise to only help you in specific and not in general."

"Just ask if I need your help before you give it."

"If I did that, you'd always say no."

"Exactly!"

"Exactly." She glanced back at him. "You can stop dragging Lou around by the neck, he's learned his lesson."

Fel dropped the would-be fighter. "Anyway, it turns out she's impressed by my expeditions."

"Sure. She lives in a world of silver cuff links and polished shoes. A little dirt under the fingernails is bound to catch her eye."

"I told her I'd get her something when I make the next trip to the Greater Lands Wall… At least I think I told her… I might have just planned to do it as a surprise."

"I'm sure she'll love it."

Parch trotted over and reared up for some head pats. From the wobbly stumble in his attempt to do so, it was clear something wasn't right.

"Is someone feeding this thing booze?" she asked.

"Everyone is feeding him booze. He's like the tavern's mascot."

"We've already got a mascot." She pointed to a rather inexpert piece of taxidermy over the entrance. "It's The Fox and Log. I don't want people giving that thing booze."

"Why not?"

"It's bad for it."

"It's bad for me, and you still let me drink it."

"That's because you're not a dumb animal. At least not until *after* you drink the booze. You know what you're getting into. No booze for the unicorn."

They made another round trip to clear mugs and replace them.

"Oh, since we're talking about mercenaries tearing up the town while I'm gone…"

"That was a couple of subjects ago. I'm impressed you can remember it."

"I'm not *that* drunk. But it reminded me that you really helped the family out when you gave us an alert when they first showed up."

"Oh, so you're fine with me helping your *family* but not you?"

"Yes. Especially when I'm not around to do it myself."

"It wasn't a problem. One of those 'specific' times when it seemed like help was needed."

"I should have asked back then, but is there any way I can say thanks? Properly, I mean."

"You already paid your tab. That's thanks enough."

"No, I mean it."

She stood up a chair that had been knocked over and brushed off the seat. "A music box," she said.

"Really?"

"Yes. One of those nice ones. You can make them play specific songs, right?"

"With a little work."

"If you can manage it, I've got a song in mind."

"You're interested in music?"

"Yes."

"I didn't know that."

"That's because I never told you."

"*Now* who's bad at telling people things?"

"I haven't been courting you for years, Fel."

"Your loss," he said. "But I'll set a nice music box aside for you. And you can tell Dad what song you want. He'll set it up for you. I'd do it myself, but I figure you want it to actually sound good."

She laughed. "Much obliged. So, what are you drinking?"

"Actually, I should call it a night. I'll have to leave early, particularly since this little critter will be the one pulling the wagon."

"What? Why?"

"Because my mother and father wore me down and won the argument. I just wanted to stick around long enough to tell you the good news and let you know I was heading out. Didn't want you to worry about me."

"You're heading to the Greater Lands Wall. I'm going to worry about you *more*."

"Then I wanted to stick around long enough to know you'd be worried about me."

"How thoughtful."

"Have a good night. Come on, Parch."

He marched out the door, a bit more steady on his feet than his four-legged companion. Allie watched him go.

"He better come back in one piece," she muttered.

Chapter 2

Bright and early the following morning, the Masker siblings stood before their respective vehicles and ran through their gear and goods for the journey. Epiphany likely wouldn't be leaving for a few more hours. She had a great deal more to load, including a small assortment of the older inventory that had been clogging their shelves for too long and might fetch a nice price elsewhere. She would also be carrying some of the items that were destined to be handed over to the assayers next month if she didn't have any luck selling them to Mr. Badgerweed. The special item, which she was instructed to take far greater care with, was the lantern. Fel had installed a new hook specifically to provide a safe place to mount it. It wasn't a sentry lantern, though the flame burning in it was indeed presently observed by Wick. It had been lit from his flame and, so long as it did not fully extinguish, would remain a valid point for spying and communicating. She had a supply of lamp oil and some candles to temporarily maintain the flame while she refilled it. In theory, Wick should be able to keep an eye on her and deliver messages for a month or longer before she'd have to worry about purchasing additional oil on the road. She'd loaded it all into the wagon Fel and Tome had purchased during their last adventure.

As for Fel?

"I cannot believe you were able to buy this back," Fel said, eying up the ancient two-wheeled family wagon that had been sold in order to help them avoid being spotted.

"It wasn't hard to find, and it was even easier to buy," Epiphany said. "Apparently most people aren't as willing to endure its bumpy ride as readily as you are."

"I hate to question the wisdom of the Maskers," Tome said. "You are, of course, the old hats at this particular set of enterprises, but why is the young lady taking the actual wagon, while we take this glorified chariot? Surely we are the ones who will, fate willing, be acquiring the greatest quantity of valuables."

"Time isn't a factor for you and Fel," Epiphany explained. "And you two are supposed to be going for quality, not quantity. If you bring back a wagon this large loaded with goods, people are going to start asking even *more* questions than they already are."

"And the decision to provide Parch as our steed rather than a proper horse? That seems more likely to be a source of questions rather than a means to avoid them."

"Parch eats roadside scrap, he makes up for his slower speed in that he's practically tireless, and we already have him, whereas we'd have to buy another horse," Fel said.

"There comes a point when frugality ceases to be an asset and becomes a liability."

"Fine. We'll buy a horse, and we'll take it out of your cut."

"I retract my complaint."

Martin emerged with the sentry lantern and hung it in its place on the family wagon.

"Fel, in the notes you'll find my best guess on where the library might be found within the wall. It is just that, a guess. I have also included an inventory of items and components that are highest value for us, now that our repair capacity has so substantially improved. And, of course…"

Martin grunted and hefted the pack from his back. Oiler was obediently tucked inside, only his multitool of a tail showing beneath it to suggest there was anything unique about the pack. Fel accepted the pack and loaded it into the back of the cart. He surreptitiously removed a small puzzle box from his pocket and dropped it beside the pack. Claws quietly emerged to grasp it, and the flap flipped up just enough to give the contraption a view of its treat as it set about solving it.

"Now, Tome. I have here a fresh book for you," Martin began.

"Wait. Dad, why are you giving *him* instructions."

"Because I am your partner," Tome said.

"No, no, no." Fel gestured to himself, his father, and Epiphany. "We are family. You are a tenant, who I'm bringing along because you need work."

"Don't mind him," Martin said. "Tome, if you do encounter the library, try to find some sort of index or catalog. Failing that, I want you to transcribe as many of the titles as you can so that subsequent trips can be more precise and fruitful."

"I could have done that, Dad," Fel said.

"He is a *scribe*, Fel. It is his specialty."

"A former scribe, but the talents have, I assure you, not atrophied," Tome said.

"I'd much rather you devote your time to the contraptions," Martin said. "Wick will be dividing his time between the shop, Epiphany, and you, so there will be substantial time when he is not observing. Be sure to keep him informed of anything worth communicating that may happen in his absence. And while you're at it, if you end up using the new contraptions I've prepared for you, do let me know how they function."

Fel climbed into the seat. Tome stepped up beside him. Parch, beneath the custom-made and downright comical-looking custom yoke, bleated happily and tip-tapped in place.

"Take care, and good luck," Martin said.

Epiphany stepped up onto the running board and gave him a hug. "Watch for me, I'll be passing you on the road in a few hours," she said.

"You dirty rotten rat monkey!" came a chorus from the rooftops.

"Yeah, yeah. I didn't forget," Fel said, reaching into his rucksack.

He pulled out some travel bread. The common wisdom was the stiff, dry, crunchy stuff stayed fresh longer while on the road, but Fel's personal theory was that it started the journey stale and simply remained so. He snapped a piece into four equal pieces and tossed them into the air. The harpies grabbed their share with the sort of coordination that would suggest they'd discussed who would get what before leaving their nests that morning.

"I'm honestly surprised we don't have a flock of those things by now," Epiphany said.

"I suspect they are defending their territory," Tome said. "They wouldn't want to have to share with any more harpies."

"Let's go, Parch," Fel said.

The unicorn bleated again, scrambled his little hooves, and brought the wagon to a merry little trot. A couple of months had given Fel time to train the beast at least well enough to no longer require the taming spells that had gotten them home. And now that he was moving of his own volition rather than due to a mystic compulsion, he seemed both happier and a bit faster. The pace was still barely half the speed of a decent horse, but it was better than the crawl they'd endured a couple of months ago.

As harpies crunched at their meals and Martin and Epiphany continued to load the wagon, Fel set his eyes on the road, waiting for the inevitable.

Tome clapped his hands and leaned back in the seat. "Now then! We've got a fine bit of time ahead of us. What do you say we pick something to discuss. Say… the wall itself, hmm? I've always been fascinated about the wall. Such *history*."

Fel wearily let the flood of words buzz around his head like a swarm of flies and daydreamed about the days when he considered loneliness a consequence of such a trip rather than a cherished memory.

#

Vivian checked the intricate watch she kept on her belt. It was the proposal gift from Martin all those years ago, and as a testament to both his skill at repair and the contraption makers of old, it had worked flawlessly since that day, keeping perfect time and reminding her when the tiny sliver of the day she didn't feel compelled to be in her place in the shop was nearing its end. As it was, she had three quarters of an hour before the formal start of the business day. She hoped that would be time enough to complete her business on this side of town.

She stopped in front of the address provided by Mrs. Verfessa. Two guards in their booths surveyed her with dull expressions.

"My name is—" she began.

"Mrs. Masker?" said the more alert of the two guards.

"That's correct."

He gestured with his head. "They're expecting you. Knock twice."

She nodded and paced along the path to the door. Two quick strikes with their ornate door knocker summoned a maid, who silently opened the door and pointed to the staircase at the far side.

"Just head down until you find him," she said when Vivian gave her a questioning look.

She walked briskly through the well-appointed home. Her mind tallied the endless sequence of priceless works of art and pieces of peerless craftsmanship as she went. This place told a lengthy and detailed story with the variety and quality of its furnishings. It was the home of a wealthy family, certainly. But she'd known that already from the silver she'd had to polish over the years. More informative to Vivian was the quality. There was a degree of ostentatiousness, but nothing at the level she would have expected. These people had taste, and rarer still, they made purchases with utility and quality in mind, not just value. Nothing on display seemed to have been purchased for the express purpose of impressing visitors like her. This place had a unified look, a curated look. It was assembled by people who knew what they wanted and expected to get what they paid for. Vivian respected that mindset far more than the wealth that facilitated it.

Another staircase brought her down to the cooler, deeper section of a house dug deep into the ground, not unlike her own home. This level was a bit more thrifty, decorated a shade more haphazardly with restored pottery and mosaics, and sporting only two burning candles to provide light.

"That'll be Vivian Masker, yeah?" came her host's jovial voice.

He stood beside one of the candles. At a glance, she would have assumed he was one of the groundskeepers. He was a large man, stout and strong. His hands were coarse, and his face unburdened by stress and anxiety. It was the look of someone whose job wrung every last bit out of him each day, so that he slept through the night and woke up fresh and new. Not the kind of face one expected from the lord of the house. But at the same time, he looked far too comfortable and at home in this place to be anyone but its owner. He marched up and held out a hand.

"Let me take your bag. Can't have my guest getting blisters hauling around the tools of the trade, can I?" he said.

With her hands freed, he clasped one in a shake that felt like it was designed to test the sturdiness of her shoulder.

"Donovan Verfessa, and let me just say it is nice to talk to someone who has been in business in this town longer than I have. An institution, that antiquities shop."

"We try."

"Been there for generations. That's more than trying, that's succeeding. I take it the wife gave you the short version already? Looking for an appraisal on some goods."

"Yes, I've been informed. And I presume she informed you there will be a fee."

"Right, right. Fair. Right this way."

"May I ask, how did you acquire these contraptions you want us to assess? Most such items that come through Beffshire come through our shop."

"I think you'll be able to work that one out on your own."

He grabbed a candle from its place on the wall and carried it with him, dragging the pool of light through the floor until he came to a large table carefully laid out with items. He handed her bag back to her and pulled up a pair of chairs.

"Let's see you work," he said, lighting two lamps to better illuminate the table, then sat down and slapped his hands on his thighs, his face beaming like he was anticipating a feast. "I live to see expertise in motion," he said.

She opened her bag and pulled on a pair of white gloves. The first items were a pair of identical bracers. They were creased and cracked with age, but at first glance they appeared too young to be an artifact of the Bygone Era. She sniffed the leather.

"Well worn. Recently oiled. Good maintenance, but this is a repair. Fresh leather. Maybe ten years old," she said.

She flipped the bracer over. A brass panel awaited her, rubbed clear of tarnish through regular use. She fetched two small hooks from the bag and gently ran them around the perimeter of the panel. It popped free of its home in the bracer and revealed an intricate internal face.

"It is inactive. There is a switch here." Vivian turned the piece about in the light and fetched a magnifying loupe. "There are markings here. Old, but newer than the device. I am not the first person to assess this device and its functionality."

She carefully read through the short sequence of etched markings, which were something of a set of instructions. When she was satisfied she understood, she slid up her sleeve, pressed the rear plate to her skin, and depressed the button on the front plate. She stomped her foot, but the motion produced no sound whatsoever. She depressed it a second time and stomped again, producing a loud thump.

"The bracers are relatively new, but this bit here is a Bygone Era contraption for rendering its user silent. This would be prohibited for sale due to obvious security risk."

"Granted. But how much is it worth?"

"It's worth what a buyer would be willing to pay for it, and no one would be permitted to purchase it."

"You know what I'm asking you, Mrs. Masker."

She gave him a measuring look. "Contraptions of this complexity, and with such pronounced effects, are exceedingly rare. Rendered even rarer by the Teskal nobility's policies of sequestering them. I would use the word 'priceless,' but as you are probably seeking a number, I would not accept a duot less than sixteen thousand for a contraption like this."

She set it down and gave its twin a quick inspection, this time simply testing it while still in its leather housing. "As a matched pair, forty thousand."

She worked her way through the equipment. All told, the table contained eighteen items, most of them in pairs. There were weapons for projecting needles, very likely tipped with poison. One contraption, through careful analysis, was revealed to be capable of snuffing out every source of light in the room. Individually, each of the pieces of equipment was impressive and worrisome. Taken as a whole, they were a set of gear that could allow a would-be infiltrator to penetrate nearly any defense and assassinate whoever they chose. All the contraptions were of the prohibited variety, and rightfully so. And none of them—should a buyer be found—would sell for less than ten thousand duots.

"I would place the value of the lot at a quarter of a million duots," she said. "And based upon the specific notation, I would say they were worked on by and were part of the collection of the Bolivans to the north. That would make possession of these items not only an issue with regard to the assayer's office, but a genuine danger. The Bolivans *will* attempt to reacquire them."

"I'm used to that sort of thing," Verfessa said. "But you're not done. I've got two more things here. Too big for the table."

He led her to a pair of trunks, each the size of a bale of hay. He clicked them open to reveal large, skillfully assembled saddles. They were stored upside down, revealing the telltale brass workings of their undersides, which betrayed their true nature.

She shut the cases again. "I don't need to assess them. I know what they are. The taming saddles that made the hippogriffs manageable. Utterly priceless. If they're still functional, a half a million duots each would be a steal."

"One of them still works," he said. "Don't ask how I know. The other one needs work."

"Owing to the rarity and potential of such a contraption, the lack of functionality only slightly lowers the price, though it does narrow the potential buyers to those with the skills to repair it or those with access to those skills."

"Could that man of yours fix it?"

"Given time, I'm convinced he could, but we would be exposing ourselves to enormous risk if we worked on a prohibited contraption without reporting it to the assayers."

"Only if they find out."

She tugged the gloves from her hands and stowed them in her bag. "I get the distinct impression that the nature of this consultation extends beyond applying a hypothetical price to these contraptions."

"That's because you've got a head for business and aren't a dullard like half the people I seem to talk to. Can I trust you to keep your mouth shut if I lay it out for you plain?"

"A degree of discretion is generally assumed when we work with individuals."

"Lookin' for a couple of degrees. Crank that discretion up to boiling."

"Your secrets will remain your own, sir."

"Good. Here's where we're at, then. I took these off the Bolivan boys. Not the mercenaries. They only had a couple of contraptions, and they were cheap and easy. Stuff I could get if I scrounged. I'm talking about the boys who got themselves into the Watch. Now first, I wanted those boys dead on general principle. They came here, put their dirty boots on my clean carpet, and didn't even have the decency to say hello before they did it. Can't let that sort of thing stand. But once I piled all this up, I got to thinking, maybe those Bolivans are onto something. If this is what they're willing to strap to their troops, just imagine what's sitting on their mantles impressing the neighbors? Good money to be made. And if you know your stuff, and I bet you do, then it looks like I was right. So now I'm thinking the best way to let those folks know they should have kept their dogs out of my yard isn't to put up a taller fence, but to… can't quite get that turn of phrase to keep going. Point is, I want to get into their business. And having some of the best folks in the field right around the corner from me? Well, it'd be spitting in the eye of opportunity if I didn't extend the hand of partnership."

"What exactly are you suggesting, Mr. Verfessa?"

"You call me Don or I'm liable to think you're going to rap my knuckles for sassing my teacher. What I'm suggesting is you keep doing what you're doing, selling things you can sell. But when you've got something you can't? Maybe you come to me. Let me know what sort of price I ought to be shooting for, and I'll make sure you're taken care of. Maybe I'll send some of my boys with yours to help dig up fresh ones. Maybe if your daughter wants to do some business in a rougher part of the world, I send some muscle along so she can keep her mind on the game. I'm offering partnership."

Vivian took a breath and considered his words. "Don—I would be lying if I suggested your offer wasn't enticing. But ours is a very old business. And we do not make changes lightly. Particularly not changes that could jeopardize the business. While I am willing to continue to offer our appraisal services, and of course I welcome any silver polishing your wife may have for us, I am just not yet willing to consider making a man like you my partner."

"A man like me."

She reached back to the table and picked up the bracer. "The sort who considers washing bloodstains off contraptions a part of the standard upkeep."

He took the bracer and ran his thumb over the seam, where a line of rust-brown betrayed the means of acquisition.

"I told that boy to scrub them good and proper. Going to need to chat with him." He set the contraption down. "Well, Mrs. Masker, I'd be lying too if I said I didn't respect that way of thinking. It's how you stay in business for a few generations. But you know what I respect most? The word 'yet.' One way or another, I think I'm going to be giving this business a try. I don't want to have to reinvent the wheel, but I won't let it get in the way of a good payday. I'll keep that door open for you to change your mind as long as I can, but don't expect it to be open forever." He thrust his hand into his pocket. "What do I owe you for this?" he said. "Keeping in mind the secrets you're leaving in this room when you walk up those stairs."

"The fee for appraisal is two hundred duots."

He snorted. "You came down here and told me I was sitting on over a million when I thought I was working with maybe half that? And you only want two hundred?" He cascaded a stack of coins into his palm. "Take a thousand."

She counted off her fee and handed back the rest. "The price is two hundred. I thank you for your generosity, but I'd prefer to keep the compensation commiserate with services rendered. Otherwise there might be some confusion over the precise services being offered."

He laughed. "Mrs. Masker, I admire your integrity. I don't envy it, but I admire it."

"Thank you. I do my best. And you can call me Vivian."

#

Martin helped Fanny load the last of the contraptions into the wagon. The vehicle was rather optimistically left half-empty, the expectation being that she would be hauling home a lot of goods for him to repair or for her to resell.

"There," he said, wiping sweat from his brow. "That's everything."

"Thanks, Dad!" she said, giving him a hug. "I should get moving."

"Just a moment," he said. "Your mother isn't back yet, and I wouldn't hear the end of it if I let you leave before she came back."

34

"You never know when someone might come with a special request," Epiphany said in a distressingly accurate impersonation of her mother.

"Someone who knows the price book should *always* be in the building, even if we're closed," Martin said, somewhat less accurately.

"That's the difference between a good shop and a great one," they said in unison.

"Besides," he continued. "It will give me a chance to double-check some things." He leaned close to the lantern. "Wick, are you in place?" he whispered.

"The flame is, and assuming continuity shall remain, a valid point of observation for me. I shall endeavor to spread my observational and communicative time equally among the two principle lanterns and the one temporary one," came the disembodied voice of the one-of-a-kind sentry lantern.

"Excellent. You keep an extra close eye on Epiphany here. If you need to spend less time here at the shop, so be it."

"I'll be fine, Dad. I've done trips like this before."

"You've done trips like this before, but never when the Bolivans were being as bold as they've been lately. I don't relish the idea of you traveling alone. I still contend it would have been better to send Tome with you than with Fel."

"Fel is heading to the fringe of the Greater Lands. He's going to encounter all manner of traps and beasts. He needs help more than I do. There's no threat in the other cities around here that isn't worse in Beffshire."

"True, but your family and friends are here to help keep you safe."

"I can handle myself."

His face, creased with fatherly anxiety, remained impassive.

"You aren't honestly going to try to persuade me not to go, are you?" she said.

"No, Fanny. This is how the business is done. But I think perhaps additional considerations may now be advisable. Stay right here."

He hurried inside and vanished down the stairs. A few moments later he returned with a burlap sack. He revealed the contents one at a time. "This is the dazzler. You should be well acquainted with its use."

"Of course I am. It's the main way we 'discourage' the rare attempt to rob the shop. It belongs *in* the shop, Dad."

"We have three of them now. One with Fel, one in the shop, and now one with you. Besides, I'm working on a superior replacement. Take it with you. And then there's this."

She squinted at the familiar shape. "Isn't that just an alarm box?" she said. "You don't need to give me one of those, I've got plenty for sale."

"No, no. This one is…" He paused. "I don't know if the word 'malfunctioning' or 'enhanced' is the better fit. But the sound this one produces is *deafening*. Don't let it activate without covering your ears, or you won't hear anything else for the rest of the day." He stuffed it back in the bag and handed the bag to her. "You have your boot blade and your knuckles, but I'd prefer an option that doesn't require you to allow someone to get so close."

He pulled a pocket-sized device—mundane, not a contraption—that she'd seen him tinker with in the past. It looked like someone had taken a crossbow and lopped off all but the trigger and the cradle for the bolt. A box behind the bolt sported a hand crank and was large enough to suggest some hidden mechanisms.

"You want me to take the bolter?" she said. "You wouldn't even let *Fel* take the bolter."

"Your brother's skills are numerous and valuable, but marksmanship is not among them. I built the bolter hoping it would solve the problem, but the last time he pulled the trigger on this device, it nearly cost him his foot. I suspect you'll be able to follow the instructions more thoroughly than he did. It isn't a matter of aiming it at something you want to hit, it is a matter of aiming it *away* from something you don't want to hit. Hold it out at arm's length when you fire it, and brace yourself. Anything generally in front of the weapon will be disinclined to continue hostilities. There are six bolts there. You slip them in here, turn that crank until it clicks, brace it with both hands, and don't put any part of your body past the point tip of the weapon. Understand?"

"I understand."

"Good. Here's your mother now," Martin said.

Vivian approached from down the street, bag in hand. Her expression was neutral, rigidly so. She didn't even glance in their direction as she approached the door.

"Mom?" Epiphany said.

The word seemed to shake her from whatever had seized her mind. "Oh! Fanny. Heading out?" she said, stepping up to her daughter.

"That's right. We were waiting for you, and Dad had some additional fretting to do."

"Your father's mind is peerless in the world at concocting ways in which things might function, which unfortunately means it is also peerless at concocting ways in which things might go wrong," she said, stepping up to kiss her daughter on the cheek. "Make the family proud like you always do."

"You looked a bit distracted, Mom. Did the consultation not go well?" Epiphany asked.

"It went fine. You father worries enough for the lot of us, don't trouble yourself," Vivian said, marching to the shop. "Bring me plenty of fresh inventory. And don't take a duot less or give a duot more than something is worth."

"I never do," Epiphany said.

"On your way then. Time is precious," Vivian said before slipping through the door.

"I'll be expecting regular updates through Wick. And be more careful about keeping him lit this time."

"I will, Dad."

He slipped into the shop and lingered behind the recently repaired windows, where he presumably believed he could not be seen watching anxiously as she snapped the reins and guided the horse on its way.

#

Farther outside town, Fel's fists were tight around the reins as Tome continued to muse aloud about the latest in a string of topics.

"… And then I started talking to Martin about the differences between—"

"Mr. Masker."

"Beg pardon?"

"Call him Mr. Masker."

"He quite explicitly requested that I call him Martin."

"He's my father. I call him Dad. Having you call him by his first name when I don't feels wrong."

"Surely 'Dad' is a much more familiar name than—"

"Call him Mr. Masker or stop talking about him."

"Fine, fine. *Mr. Masker* and I were discussing the difference between paper magic and contraptioneering. It seems that there is less room, and less requirement, for interpretation and improvisation when working with contraptions. It must be refreshing to know that once you've learned a procedure, that procedure will be unchanged if it must be done in some other place or at some other time. Such simplicity affords a more accessible degree of understanding."

Fel grumbled under his breath.

"Is something wrong?" Tome asked.

"Did Dad talk to you about how to operate the new contraptions he equipped us with?"

"He did not. I'd assumed the operation would be obvious."

"It's never obvious. Whoever made these things either didn't know how normal people would want to use them or was like you and just wanted to seem smart."

"It worries me that you characterize me in such a way."

"Then stop acting like it." He reached up and pulled a rod from its custom mount on the sunshade. "This is the dazzler. You twist this bit, a chain falls down. Pull it, the end spins up, and a blue ball of something loud and glowing shoots out the end after a bit. You get one shot every few hours. For some reason, every animal I've ever shot this past has turned to chase the ball. Humans? Shoot them in the face with it. It doesn't hurt, but it'll get their attention."

"I see. Why do you suppose animals—"

"Don't know, don't care. No questions, or we'll never get through this." He

37

thumped the seat between them. "Under here is the chaser. That one's easy to use. Pull it out, slap the top until the wheels spin, and it'll chase away little things and get bigger things to chase it. I've used this and the dazzler plenty of times. They've gotten me out of some tight scrapes. But Dad finished up some new things using the repair books." Fel paused for a moment. "Just a minute."

"What?"

"I said just a minute."

Before Tome could ask for more clarification, Oiler thrust its claw up and jiggled the puzzle box. Fel grabbed it and shuffled the faces before dropping it back down again to a chorus of contented clicks and clanks from within Oiler's mechanical head.

"How did you know it was about to finish?"

"I could hear it."

"You could hear that it was about to finish?"

"Yeah. The sliding faces start happening a lot faster. You didn't notice that?"

"I was a bit busy talking."

"Maybe you should cut that out, then. Anyway, I've got some more contraptions here. We should get through the list."

"Must we? I'm skeptical that we'll find use for all of them."

"The idea is, it's better to have it and not need it than need it and not have it."

"A policy to justify hoarding if ever I heard one."

"And what's so bad about hoarding?"

"Hoarding, by definition, weighs you down. I can get everything I need from this case right here."

"I notice you've been having stew with us every night instead of eating out of that case."

"Naturally there are some necessities that need to be acquired through other means. But I submit that having the flexibility to, at my very whim, leave with nothing but my case and the shirt on my back and thrive just as surely as I did before I left is worth every bit of comfort I might have drawn from a more anchored existence."

"So you'll be moving on, then? No more sleeping in my sister's bed?"

"When my fortunes twinkle more alluringly in other locales, then I shall seek them. As it happens I've found my exposure to your family and its specific expertise quite enlightening. Just last night Martin was—"

Fel glared at him. Tome rolled his eyes.

"Mr. Masker was suggesting some ideas for new spells that, frankly, had never occurred to me." He pulled a folio from his pocket and slipped a page from it. "This one for instance. It is a spell for creating light. I had, until now, always focused on the raw act of conjuring light. But he suggested I assign that light to an object. For example, a stone, so that it could be carried and transferred. A concept brilliant in its simplicity. And I've been tinkering with a spell for granting enhanced vision, such that I would not require an additional light source *and* I would be able to see great distances."

"Great," Fel said flatly. "And here I was using a spyglass and a lantern when I could have been spending hours a day writing out spells to do that stuff."

"You seem uncharacteristically surly of late," Tome said. "Which is quite a revealing statement, as your surliness is indeed very much one of your defining characteristics. To exceed even the lofty levels you typically display is an achievement. I would think you would be excited. This is your specialty, expeditions and the like. There are few things more enriching than having one's unique skills put to good use."

"It's fine. I'm fine. There's just a long road ahead, and I'm anxious to get to work."

"Mmm… I find I am quite the opposite. The preparation and anticipation are the parts I enjoy most of all. The bulk of a paper mage's craft is planning for what is to come. If we do our jobs correctly, then the actual application of our art is seamless. Though I suppose it would be wise to start preparing some simple spells to test the potency of the ink I've crafted from Parch's generous contributions."

"Will that shut you up?"

"By the high, I wouldn't be much of a scribe if I couldn't write while speaking."

Fel shuddered and his lip curled. "Great…"

#

Martin gazed out the shop window long after there was nothing for him to see. Vivian was behind the shop counter, preparing the books for the day.

"If you're going to stay up here, the least you can do is refresh the shelves," she said.

He nodded and moved mechanically to the shelf nearest the window. He shifted and adjusted each item on display with a speed and efficiency that spoke to the years he'd spent perfecting such minor tasks. For items with a best face, he put it forward. For items in which it didn't matter which way they faced, he rotated them to provide the semblance of novelty on the off chance the fresh perspective would catch the eye of a customer who hadn't found the other sides pleasing.

"When did our children grow so independent?" he mused.

"They've been going off on their own to run errands since they were four years old," Vivian said.

"There is a wide gulf between running to the bakery for some buns and leading an expedition to the Greater Lands Wall or running off to potentially negotiate an illicit sale."

"What a fine thing to talk aloud about in our shop, Martin," she snapped.

"I just thought I'd have a few more years of being needed."

"Oh, hush. We all have our jobs. Most of us have several. For you and me, we've had to keep the business running and raise three children. Don't get weepy over doing the second bit well enough you don't have to work so feverishly on the first bit."

"You can't tell me you don't miss being a mother."

"I'm still a mother, and you're still a father. Having grown children doesn't change that. Now stop moping. We've got things to discuss, and it's best to get it over with before the customers start coming."

"What's to be said?" he asked.

"My little appraisal revealed some concerning information. Through means I prefer not to dwell upon, Mr. Verfessa came into possession of the equipment the Bolivan family armed their agents with. I can be more specific another time, but suffice to say that they are risking profoundly valuable contraptions in their pursuit of the goods they hoped to steal from us. More valuable than I'd initially thought. If nothing else, they'll be sending people to retrieve them, and I really don't think that if they were willing to go that far on the first try, they wouldn't be willing to give it a second try."

"We've sold the dagger, and Oiler is with Fel," Martin said.

"For all we know they think we still have both. And even if they don't, they know we translated the map, and that we were able to acquire the dagger and Oiler. The real treasure isn't the contraptions, it's the *source* of the contraptions. I think they're going to do everything they can to get the information we have."

"I've armed Fel and Epiphany as best I could."

"I know. So that just leaves the shop. I know you've been working on the defenses since the 'griff riders, but we may need to enhance them further."

He nodded. "You *are* aware of what I'm working on."

"I am. And it may not be enough."

He raised his eyebrows. "How far, precisely, is far enough in your estimation?"

"Do you remember 'the thing' you did, back before the kids were born? The thing that convinced the Bolivan family that perhaps Beffshire and the surrounding areas weren't worth investing their time and effort into?"

"I remember quite well."

"Don't do that. But let's remind them of it."

The door jangled against its chime. An elderly man with a silver-headed cane stepped inside and adjusted a pair of spectacles to investigate the wares on display.

Martin turned to his wife. "I believe I can calibrate my response adequately."

"Excellent. Now if you'll excuse me, I need to help this good gentleman." She stepped from behind the counter and approached the customer. "How may I help you, sir?"

"An associate of mine, a collector, suggested there might be some value in acquiring some… er… what he called Bygone relics."

"Ah! Yes, of course. You've come to the right place. We have a full selection of—"

"Oh Vivian?" Martin said, sticking his head out of the hatch to the lower levels.

"Yes, dear," she said, the words brandished like a cudgel.

"You'll want to brace the dumbwaiter shut. Things may get noisy while I'm working."

She grinned. That was what she liked to hear. Martin was taking the threat as seriously as she'd hoped. When he got "noisy" it meant some of his more troubling innovations were being pulled out of storage. She did not envy the next Bolivan who tried to enter this place.

Chapter 3

Parch clattered along the ancient road, ears twitching and eyes constantly sweeping both land and sky. Fel was showcasing his impressive ability to sleep while the cart was in motion. If the two weeks they'd spent on the road were any indication, the little lesser unicorn would never be quite as well behaved when Tome was at the reins. Ever since they'd left the main road and begun their approach toward the Greater Lands Wall, though, his pace had slowed considerably and his posture had become increasingly anxious.

The sun was rising behind them. The wall loomed in the distance. At their present tentative pace, they would reach it in an hour or two. Or, rather, they would have, if Parch hadn't glanced in the direction of a lone tree surrounded by brush, flicked his ears, and bleated.

"No, no, no," Tome said, tugging at the reins. "Not now, we're so close!"

The unicorn ignored the tugging of the leather straps and hauled the wagon off the road toward the tree. He plopped down in the shade of the tree, glanced up past the yoke, and bleated expectantly. Despite the creature making virtually identical sounds throughout the journey, and the wagon producing a rattling cacophony as it rumbled across the uneven old road, this specific sound stirred Fel from sleep.

"Are we there?" he said blearily.

"Very nearly, except this unicorn of yours decided it was time to stop," Tome said.

"I'll get the bowl."

As the trip had progressed, they'd learned quite a bit about the little critter pulling the wagon. For one, he seemed to have a real zeal for towing a load. If he wasn't eating, drinking, or being scratched and pet, he wanted to be pulling the wagon or climbing on whatever architecture or geography was available. He also had a much different relationship with sleep than the humans. Rather than a typical creature, who slept either during the day or during the night, Parch seemed to decide at arbitrary moments throughout the day or night that it was time for a rest. Once the decision was made, it didn't matter what anyone said or did. Parch would totter off the road to find some shade or shelter, plop down, and munch whatever greenery was nearby while waiting to be given a bowl of water. Once he was fed and watered, he would drift off to sleep for a few hours and wake up with a spring in his step and raring to be put to work. All told, he probably slept about as much as Tome or Fel, but he did it in random chunks of time, which meant the travel could be happening at any time of the day or night. It necessitated a rotating shift of sleeping and guiding the wagon that Fel didn't mind in the least and Tome found utterly frustrating.

"Is now really the time for indulging that thing's poor timing?" Tome said. "As I recall, this is about the distance from the wall that you claimed to have encountered a dragon."

"This is where Parch grew up. He would know better than us what's a safe place to stop," Fel said.

He filled a bowl of water from their supply and set it down beside the unicorn. He rubbed his eye and winced.

"My eyebrow is still swollen," he said.

"You did take quite a blow to the face in that last tavern," Tome said.

"And *you* said you could cure it."

"I didn't say I could cure it. I said I could treat it. And I did. You've scarcely got a bruise."

"I don't understand how you can write a spell that *nearly* heals a black eye, but not one that *completely* heals it."

"No, you *don't* understand. Despite my repeated attempts to explain. For the sake of ease and simplicity, and to ensure that they remain useful in the most dire of circumstances, I focus my spells on treating the most severe of ailments. Minor annoyances will take care of themselves."

"If that was true, you'd have run along by now."

"It wasn't *my* fault that fight started, you know."

"*You were cheating at grum again!*" Fel snapped.

"Yes, but the fight started because you failed to distract the other player at the proper time, as I instructed. It was really a very simple plan."

Fel waved his hand dismissively at Tome and scratched the unicorn as he drained the bowl.

"If we stay here, we'll be in plain view of anyone and anything that comes along this road," Tome said. "The 'anyone' doesn't concern me, as I doubt we'll have any visitors this far from a proper byway. But the 'anything' is something I'd just as soon avoid."

While Parch yawned and Fel lifted the yoke off his back, the burly adventurer mulled over their current situation.

"Mmm… You're right. This wagon is a pretty big target if something was flying over."

He plucked Parch off the ground and set him down in the back of the wagon, then disconnected the yoke extension and tossed it in the back as well. A grunt and a heft pulled the arms of the yoke from the ground, and he hauled the cart forward.

"This is… this is astonishing," Tome said.

"It's light. It isn't even loaded yet. The reason my grandfather liked a wagon like this was how easy it is to move it around without a horse."

"Not that! You just lectured me about failing to perfectly heal your black eye. Meanwhile the unicorn, a creature whose *entire* purpose in this journey is to deliver us to the wall, stops well short of that destination, and you happily drag it *and* its load along without so much as a second thought."

"Yes," Fel said.

"You don't find that a *bit* hypocritical?"

"I like Parch better than I like you," he grunted, rolling the wagon over the roots of the tree and tugging it back to the main road. "Don't take it personally. I like most animals more than I like most people. Like I said last time. At least when animals are awful, they aren't doing it on purpose."

"And you submit that I am awful?"

"Yes."

Tome trudged along behind him. "And what of the fact that you are making not just yourself walk this last stretch, but me as well, simply because you don't wish to rouse a wild animal? Is *that* not a thoughtless, unpleasant act?"

"It's pretty bad, but then, I'm a person, aren't I?"

Tome glared at him. "So you do not exempt yourself from your own contempt."

"I'm just as irritated by myself as everyone else."

The mage considered the words. "You're consistent. That, at least, is admirable."

#

Epiphany arrived in Brentmire and stiffly hopped down from the wagon. She'd done more than her share of traveling, but she'd become accustomed to the much less onerous task of riding in a shared wagon. She'd never been at the reins of any wagon but the little one Fel had taken. When her mother had suggested she take the full-size wagon, it didn't seem like it would make a difference, but maneuvering it was a trial she was glad to be free of for a few days.

She fished a few duots out of her pocket and tossed them to the stable boy to handle stowing the wagon and seeing to the horse, then grabbed her lantern. While she lingered long enough to be sure he'd done the job properly, she took in the sights of the town. It didn't take long. The bazaar existed, in some ways, because of certain cities on the route. Epiphany liked to believe that Beffshire was one such town. Elsewhere, towns existed because the bazaar existed. That was certainly the case for Brentmire. Whereas Beffshire seemed to have at least two shops dedicated to anything someone might need, this town lacked even a general store. The place was like a bit of farmland around an ancient river, desperately waiting for the river to flood the land twice a season and give the fields a frenzied few days of badly needed vitality.

The town was dominated by a huge cobblestone courtyard. The wagons of the bazaar were just pulling into their places around the edge of the courtyard, but already people were lining up, shouting the names of items they needed or that they had to sell. In the few minutes it took for the stable boy to finish getting food and water for her horse, half a dozen people stopped to ask what she was selling and what she was buying.

"No, no. It will be antiquities. Contraptions and the like," she explained to a seventh would-be customer. "I'd love to quote you a price on your carving, but I need to talk to my buyer first so I know what sort of inventory is still mine to sell or trade. Thank you."

"Is that the good Miss Epiphany Masker?" asked a voice amid a wave of potent and rank smoke.

She turned to find the man she still knew only as Mr. Badgerweed approaching her from across the courtyard.

"You, sir, are a difficult man to get ahold of," she said, hurrying to meet him halfway.

"We can't all be fortunate enough to have a successful shop in a thriving town," he said. "Come, come. You must be exhausted from the road. There isn't much in this town worth seeing, but there is something you won't want to miss." He turned and pointed with his pipe pinched between two fingers. "Do you see? Just past the edge of town there? Follow me."

He marched forward. She followed a few steps behind, calculating precisely how far from the rest of town she was willing to go with someone she hadn't quite decided she fully trusted. Either as a happy coincidence or as good judgment on his part, the place he was leading her to was in full view of the courtyard, and indeed was quite near the purple wagon she knew to be his.

It was a pleasant little fountain, the sort fed by an underground spring that kept it merrily trickling water with just enough pressure to give an attractive cascade. The fountain itself was entirely covered in a chaotic and complex mosaic. It depicted a colorful landscape around the ring of the fountain, with the central spire representing the golden sun. Years of constant water had given said sun a green tinge despite obvious efforts to keep it clean.

"Do you know the story of the fountain?" he asked as he took a seat at one of the stone benches set up around it.

"I can't say I do," she said.

Badgerweed waved over one of the other vendors and tossed him a couple of coins in exchange for some manner of meat-stuffed pastry. He bought two, offering the other to her.

"If you let the locals tell you, they'll spin a yarn that will take twenty minutes of your life. The short version is that the fountain represents the continent, and each part of the mosaic is made with pebbles and such from that part of the world."

She leaned closer and observed that, sure enough, those parts of the mosaic representing the beach and sea were made of shells and wave-polished stones.

"Impressive," she said, sniffing the meal she was offered.

"A worthy distraction at least, but I imagine you would like to get to business." He waited until the vendor moved on, providing them with enough privacy to speak openly about things they might not want overheard. "I suppose it is too much to hope that you've tracked me down because your brother was able to secure the chain-filled pack and the mask."

"I'm afraid they haven't turned up, though Fel is, as we speak, taking another trip in hopes of locating them."

"That is good. I have been in contact with my employer, the person for whom these items are intended to be acquired. And to my great surprise, they were not overly displeased by the elevated price. I suspect, with some minor coaxing, I could persuade them to provide that same price for the remaining pieces."

"That's good, because I would consider that price to be the absolute minimum from this point forward."

He raised an eyebrow. "The minimum?"

"You'll note I've just said that Fel has gone on a *second* expedition. Our overhead is increasing."

"Your inability to deliver on a single trip is by no means justification to raise the price farther."

"On that point I must disagree. The rarity of an artifact and the difficulty in acquiring it are the two greatest factors in its price. But, and I say this to illustrate to you the transparency with which I prefer to comport myself, I want to set the proper expectations regarding the mask and the pack. There exists the likelihood that they either no longer exist or will not be found. My brother is extremely thorough and dedicated. If he failed to locate the items the first time, they simply may not be there."

"Mmm… Of course we have entertained that possibility. But I have in my possession the blunt dagger after your successful delivery. That one of the artifacts was precisely where it was believed to be is a strong indicator that the others shouldn't be far."

"And with any luck, you are correct, but my point is that it is hardly a mark against us if we are unable to find something that was lost to antiquity."

"Nor is it a mark in favor. But you didn't chase me down simply to warn me that you might not succeed."

"No, I did not. I came regarding our brief discussion about further business."

"I see. And you believe you have items that would entice my employer even more than those we requested?"

"Not more, but perhaps as much. And more to the point, we can provide these in steady supply and for a much more affordable compensation."

"And you are not selling these in your shop because…?"

"Don't be spurious, sir. We both know the answer to that."

"Mmm." He puffed the pipe. "If you truly want to open a long-term working relationship, one would think the goodwill engendered by fulfilling the initial request would be the proper place to start."

She pulled an inventory from her pocket. "I have it on good authority, from the mouths of the Teskal assayers themselves, that alarm boxes are being considered for prohibition. If that were to occur, then their price would escalate considerably among collectors who are willing to overlook such prohibitions. It would be a *very* good investment to purchase what I've got in stock before they become impossible to acquire."

"And you expect us to take you at your word that such a prohibition is being considered."

"You are free to believe or disbelieve me as you choose. But consider this. If you purchase them now and the prohibition does *not* occur, then you can simply resell them at their present value and you've lost nothing. If you *fail* to purchase them now and the prohibition occurs, you'll be cursing yourself as the goods you could have acquired are instead handed over to the officials and locked away."

He took another puff. "Tempting. But you'll forgive me if it doesn't compel me to empty my coffers into yours."

"Of course. A little caution keeps wealth from shrinking. But too much caution keeps wealth from growing. Sometimes boldness is required."

"Let's move on, shall we."

"As you wish. Perhaps, when I am back on my way, I'll seek out your employer directly. Removing a middleman should make for a smoother transaction and a better profit for all involved."

He chuckled. "You think you can find your way to my employer, do you? I assure you, pains have been taken to maintain secrecy and anonymity. And if you start trying to go over my head, I'm just as liable to find someone better suited to find my next artifact."

"You're welcome to try. But those items spent hundreds of years hidden from the world, and within two weeks of learning of them, we were able to return with one-third of them. I don't know how long your employer was looking for them, but I suspect it was greater than a few weeks. I'm confident that if there was someone better suited to find them, you'd have spoken to them already. So it really comes down to the most convenient and profitable relationship. Will that be with you, or without you?"

He puffed the pipe. "Let's discuss your inventory, then, shall we?"

"I thought you'd never ask."

#

Fel was dripping with sweat by the time they finally reached the wall. Considering how harrowing this stretch of the journey was last time, he'd expected to be more worried. And by rights, he should have been. But the small motivation of giving Parch a much-needed rest without delaying them any longer, combined with the massive motivation of seeing Tome beside himself with both frustration and anxiety for the hours it took to complete the trip, proved more than enough to keep him grinning for most of the way.

"This was an absurd waste of time and a pointless risk, and I think you know that," Tome said as he leaned against the locked gate separating them from the relative safety of the nearest alcove in the wall. "Your little pet could have easily put off its nap by two hours and done all that walking while ensuring that *both* of us were available to watch the skies and react should reaction be called for."

"And?" Fel said.

"And pointless wastes of time should *matter* to you if you aren't a complete oaf."

Fel set down the arms of the wagon and pulled a rag from his gear to mop his face. "Let's talk about pointless wastes of time." He pulled his cudgel from his belt and took stock of the rusted chain securing the gate. "When you decided it was time to stick your nose in my business and earn yourself a slice of *my* share of the money, this is right about where that happened, right?"

"A bit further south, if accuracy is a concern."

"And how did you get here to do that nose-sticking?"

Tome crossed his arms. "I know what you are getting at."

"You ran, didn't you? You ran *and* you were invisible. And you ran at least as fast as a hippogriff can fly. But here we were taking almost two weeks to make it here from Beffshire. You want to talk about wasting time, why didn't we just *run* with one of your little spells?"

"I suppose you think you're clever, asking a question like that."

Fel bashed the chain, breaking it cleanly with one blow, and pushed the gate open. "Oh, I know I'm clever."

"Not half as clever as you think you are, because the answer is very simple." Tome marched into the shade of the alcove as Fel hefted the wagon inside. "For *myself* to run here, invisibility notwithstanding, required nearly a pot of ink and a spell that took me the better part of several days to pen. For *all* of us to utilize that same spell would have required it to target not just me, not just you, but Parch, the wagon, and everything on it."

"Couldn't it just be Parch? He's the one doing the running."

"No, as it happens, it *couldn't* just be Parch, because if you were to cast that spell on Parch, then Parch would go tippy-tapping along, fast as you please, and the wagon would be torn to bits trying to keep up with him. It takes all of us. And a spell doesn't grow nicely to double the size when it targets two people, and triple the size when it targets three. I need to include a degree of specificity and nuance to make a spell efficient, and the *moment* it targets something *besides* myself, it would grow by a factor of ten. And another factor of ten when it grows to include the animal. And another factor of ten when it includes the wagon. A stack of pages becomes a stack of books, and the cost and time invested would have greatly outstrapped the benefits the spell would have provided. So *that* is why I didn't simply magic up a faster way."

"A likely excuse," Fel said.

"Extremely likely, as it is one hundred percent accurate."

Fel fetched his brush and handed it to Tome. "Clear off the markings above the door. Time to see if we really do have all the keys to this place."

"Gladly," Tome said.

The paper mage marched to the carved rear wall of the alcove and industriously put the brush to work while Fel cleared and filled the water trough that seemed to be a part of every alcove. He pumped water until it was clear, then rinsed a few layers of road grime from his face and hands. Behind them, he heard Oiler jangling at the chains. He looked to find the contraption carefully removing the broken link, splitting the next link, and easing the two ends together into a complete chain again.

"Oiler, you don't have to do that," he said. "We'll only have to break it again when we leave."

"I don't understand how sometimes that device listens to you and sometimes it doesn't. I thought machines were supposed to work consistently."

"Spoken like a man who has never had to maintain one." Fel picked up the pack and slid Oiler on his back. "Even mundane machines can have a mind of their own. Contraptions are another matter entirely."

"There, I've revealed the label. Shall I unlock the door?" Tome asked.

"If you think you can." Fel tossed him the book and took a step back. "Just remember, if you fail, you get to find out if the traps work as consistently as you would like Oiler to."

Tome flipped the book open and thumbed through the pages, eying each heading until he found one that matched the markings above the door. Beneath it was the page-filling list of procedures that would, ideally, open the door without activating its trap. Tome looked to the page, hovered his hand over the ring of tiles that made up the business-end of the locking mechanism, then shakily backed away.

"For both our sakes, I will defer to your expertise, if only to provide me with another demonstration. Your father is a brilliant man, and like most brilliant men, he struggles with terseness and clarity at times."

"Watch close. It's actually very simple once you get the hang of it," Fel said.

He worked his way through the instructions his father had traced out. One by one, rings of tiles rotated, and individual tiles transferred between them. He maneuvered the pieces into the indicated configuration, through the indicated set of steps, and double-checked that the final pattern matched what had been sketched at the bottom of the page.

As much as he would have liked to confidently press the center button and show Tome just how skilled the Maskers really were, his good sense finally overruled his sense of bravado, and he stood aside and pressed the button with the handle of his cudgel.

After a delay just long enough to convince him to take another step back, the door clicked harmlessly open.

"Ha-*ha*!" he crowed. "That proves it! That proves it once and for all. The Maskers have the keys to the whole Greater Lands Wall. Hundreds of years, Tome. Hundreds of years since the Bygone Era ended, and in all that time, as far as I know, *no one* has gained access to the wall. Not the Bolivans. Not the Graves. Not the Teskal officials or the nobles of Quarr or Shalia. Who did it? The Maskers. This wall is our personal vault now."

He grabbed the sentry lantern and held it up. The flame was flickering in the wind. "And Wick wasn't even here to witness it." He slapped Tome on the back. "Come on. Let's see what treasures await us, shall we?"

#

Martin tightened a fastener and leaned back to admire his work. His day-to-day tasks for the shop weren't as visible as Vivian's, but they were no less frequent or important. Restoring jewelry took a steady hand and a sharp eye. Resetting alarm boxes and replacing the melody disks in music boxes were rather tedious procedures that couldn't be rushed. But now that the bulk of the malfunctioning or unrestored contraptions were largely completed, he found the time between tasks could turn to what had in recent years been an extremely rare pastime.

He was making something *new*.

In fact, he was making several new things. Like a child with a rare and forbidden treat, he'd been nibbling at this cherished opportunity, dancing between three different projects in parallel and nursing them along, both to be sure they would function and to make the experience of working on them last. Now, with this final bit of tweaking, he'd completed the last of them, just as he'd completed the first two in the predawn hours. They weren't whole-cloth inventions, as he dreamed the contents of the Great Lands Wall library might facilitate. But they were certainly innovations the contraption makers hadn't intended.

"There we are," he said, holding up the latest completed device. "Rather more violent than I tend to prefer, but I am confident it does not technically violate any of the rules set forth by the officials, and likewise it will prove quite dissuasive to would-be intruders."

"Is it time to test them?" Wick asked.

"Oh. I apologize, Wick, I didn't realize you'd returned. I was thinking out loud. Any word from the kids?" Martin said, angling his contraption and testing its weight.

"When I left Epiphany, she was at the edge of the courtyard in Brentmire. She had located the intended buyer and had initiated negotiations. I last checked on Fel and Tome a bit more than an hour ago. Fel was pulling the wagon and being reprimanded by Tome, who was exasperated by his decision to personally propel the device rather than wake Parch to pull it for him."

"No obvious danger?" Martin asked.

"I would not call Fel's position one of pronounced safety, but there was no looming threat."

"Head back and check up on him when we're through here. But I suppose it would be wise to have you observe the activation of each of the devices. You might observe a malfunction or shortcoming that I would miss."

"This is a pleasant and fulfilling service I would be happy to provide."

Martin opened a drawer and plucked a palm-sized device from within. It was quite unassuming. At a glance, it would appear to be little more than a block of recently stained dark wood, but through the holes and slots drilled in the face of the block, a faint glint of metal was visible.

"I believe this contraption was originally intended as some sort of aid for administering medical treatments. Whatever its original purpose, it has sat on the shelf upstairs unsold for years, thanks in no small part to the fact that its only functions seem to be storing a small quantity of liquid or powder in this upper canister and, when activated, delivering them with alarming accuracy to the nose, mouth, and eyes of whoever is directly in front of the device. I've filled the canister with a combination of desiccant and ground pepper flake. I know from experience that individually these powders are extremely uncomfortable to get in one's eyes and difficult to remove."

He picked up a piece of chalk and traced a crude drawing of a man's face on the wall of the workshop. He held up the device, faced it forward, and depressed the button. The device hissed. Powder coiled through the air with a focus and precision that defied nature. The powder scattered across the eyes and nose of the drawing.

"I've yet to determine through what means the contraption is able to choose its target. There is intelligence enough to identify the eyes of a drawing, but not enough intelligence to dismiss that drawing as a pointless target. I suppose it goes in the same category of invention as Fel's sparker. That always seems to know what needs to be lit." He deftly opened the upper canister and funneled a fresh load of powder inside. "So many mysteries to be uncovered. Next, we have the modified music box."

He selected the second contraption. This one was visibly more cobbled together than the first. The base of it was one of the ornate music boxes that were so popular with the wealthy folks of Beffshire. Atop that he'd attached something that had quite obviously been scavenged from an entirely different contraption. It had a grid carved into its face.

"The officials forbid dedicated cranks, motors, and similar. But the music box turns its melody disks, and swapping some gears was sure enough more than adequate to increase the speed with a surprisingly small reduction in strength."

Again he angled the grid at the wall and activated the music box. It produced a tune played at an unrecognizably high speed and uncomfortably loud volume. Then the sharp twang of powerful springs kicked the box backward with enough force to stagger him. Something hissed through the air and slapped against the wall, producing plumes of dust when it struck. He waved off the dust and inspected his handiwork. A net composed of thin, twisted wires woven together had deployed against the wall. It was pinned there with darts at the end of each run of wire.

"The winding is enough to activate the net launcher with at least as much force as the prohibited power source."

He tugged at the darts. They'd been driven into the very stone of the wall with enough force that he needed to pry them free with pliers. He looked over the condition of the dart, then observed the hole it had left.

"I'll need to use this at a greater distance, or else I run the risk of doing more damage than I intend. In retrospect I believe I understand why Fel so frequently lists this as the contraption test he liked least."

A simple matter of levering off the face of the grid, stuffing the net back inside, and reattaching the face completed the reset procedure.

"That leaves the alarm box I altered."

The alarm boxes were among the less artful contraptions that were in ready supply. Unlike most of the relics from the Bygone Era, they clearly served no aesthetic purpose. They were *only* used for producing loud, difficult-to-ignore alerts when activated. Thus, his modification, though significant, did not seem to be out of place. It was a bit of cowling around the front and an additional lever on top.

"After digging through the inside of the broken box I provided to Fanny, I realized I could make a similar modification on purpose. The switch should allow me to cut the alert short, and this bit here should ensure the bulk of sound goes toward a would-be assailant."

He held the box out, rather awkwardly attempted to cover one ear with his free hand and block the other with his shoulder, and flicked the switch on and off rapidly. The sound was loud enough to rattle the tools on his bench. He shook his head and wiggled a finger in his ear.

"I may need to either improve the directionality or tone that down just a bit."

"It would appear great care has been taken to ensure these defensive contraptions are not overtly lethal," Wick said.

"I try to avoid overt lethality."

"Do you believe the Bolivans will take similar pains to protect your safety if they strike?"

"I don't know and I don't care. I know myself, and I know what sort of things I am capable of. The Bolivans know too. It's what kept them away for this long. After last time, it would be hard to forget."

"Last time," Wick said. "I do not believe I observed the event that you so frequently obliquely reference."

He shut his eyes tightly. "It's better that way. We were in the southwest. Ages ago. Just shortly after I was married. A new vault had been discovered and no one was able to get in. The Graves family had their go at it and nearly lost their son. The Bolivan hadn't sent anyone, or so we thought. So it was my turn. I was able to work out the code for the door and start loading up the materials within. It wasn't very well equipped, that vault. Not with functional contraptions. But the rare materials, cogwheels and the like, those were worth their weight in gold in the right hands, and near worthless to most others. Decades later and I've still got a fair amount of material left from that haul. Maybe a third of the goods we've sold in this shop were repaired with what I brought home that day. But I was wrong about the Bolivans."

He popped the alarm box open and inserted a tool to gently coax the innards back to a fully reset state. "It wasn't that they hadn't sent someone. It was that they hadn't had the people they sent try to get in. They were waiting. Waiting for me, specifically. Their timing was bad. I'd only loaded up two crates of goods when they struck. They claimed the crates, smashed up my wagon, and tried to kill me. I was able to get inside the vault and lock the door, but it was clear they had no intention of letting me leave. So I..."

Martin ran his hands through his hair. "Vivian likes to say I 'became as creative as the circumstances required.' There were many traps integral to the vault. There always are. And traps are meant to stop people from entering the vault. I modified them. Delayed activation triggers. Adjusted trajectories. I changed their intent. The creators didn't want people to enter the vault. My intention was to make sure no one *left* the vault. Then I issued a verbal warning and unlocked the door. When the dust settled… let's just say I faced no further opposition."

"How many Bolivan operatives were there?" Wick asked.

"The remains were not in a state that would facilitate an accurate tally." He shut his eyes tightly once more. "I'd prefer not to discuss this any further. Go check on the kids, would you?"

"I would be happy to fulfill this service."

\#

Tome held Wick's lantern high and gazed at his surroundings with a wide grin.

They'd been through two large sections of the wall's interior, and a few things had been made clear. First, the place had a highly regular structure. Both the sections they'd accessed matched the general layout of the section Fel had uncovered during his first visit. They'd taken to calling that first chamber the "barracks." The first door they opened during this visit had granted access to a room that precisely matched it, down to the mostly empty racks of equipment and the military pennants and banners. The chamber they were in now had been subdivided into smaller rooms via interior walls with locked doors. His father's notes didn't reference them, therefore providing no means to open them, but they were fortunately free of traps, and thus a solid blow from Fel's heel could pop them open.

This came as a source of endless delight to Oiler, who gleefully repaired the doors behind him each time he bashed through to a new room.

"Fascinating. Truly fascinating, isn't it?" Tome said as they stepped through another fractured door.

"There's nothing much *here*," Fel replied, sliding the tiles on yet another door.

This section of the wall looked to be some sort of living quarters, a bit more comfortably appointed than elsewhere. Bunk beds stood out from the walls in front and back. Most were in a state of disarray. Moth-eaten sheets hung from hay-stuffed mattresses. Smooth, noticeably less grimy bits of floor suggested there had once been a chest at the foot of each bed, but most were missing. The few that remained were open and had only a scattering of items at the bottom.

"Precisely, isn't that fascinating?" Tome said. "The door was locked. Firmly so. And there was no evidence that it had been defeated through force. This place is as it was when it was last used by the rightful residents of this room. Yet it is emptied. Stripped bare. These people left in a rush. Why? What could have chased them from so heavily fortified a position? There's no sign of violence. No bloodstains or damage—beyond what you've been doing along the way. Doesn't it set the mind aflame with curiosity?"

"I was sent here with a shopping list, Tome. I can waste time wondering what happened to the last guys once I cross everything off," he said.

He crouched and rummaged through one of the chests with some contents still remaining. The items within were probably abandoned because they had little value at the time, but each of them represented a small but appreciable price that could be earned at the antique shop.

"Some forks and spoons. Good repair. What is this, a locket? That'll fetch a good price. Ah! This here? You know what this is?" Fel held up a fist-size bronze gadget with a blue bead on its face.

"I couldn't hazard a guess."

Fel depressed two barely visible buttons on the perimeter, and the bead produced a sharp, focused light that cut farther into the darkness than Wick's flame, albeit in a way that cast a much smaller pool of light.

"Useful."

"Eighty duots, base price," he said, tossing it back inside. "Even cleaned out as well as this place is, there's enough here to make us a tidy sum. Enough to make the trip worthwhile and then some."

"So why aren't we packing them away?"

"Because these will be here waiting for us if we can't find the stuff on the list. This is the guarantee we didn't waste any time coming here. So we may as well dig and see if we can find real treasures." He smiled as he came to a slightly raised panel on the floor. "And you know you're getting close when you start running into traps."

Tome took a cautious step back.

"Hey, hey. Keep the light over here," Fel said.

"Forgive me, but my general policy is to keep clear of traps. Particularly when your chosen method for exploring involves bashing things apart like an ape instead of employing so much as a modicum of cleverness."

"Look, you want to earn your keep and learn the Maskers' line of work, you're going to have to start getting familiar with traps."

"I'd rather hoped my aid would come in the form of keeping a lookout."

"That is a service which I happily fulfill," Wick said.

"*By the high,*" Tome yelped, nearly dropping the lantern. "When did you get back?"

"A few moments ago," Wick said. "Fel's father wanted me to check on the two of you."

"So far, not much to see," Fel said. "How's everyone else making out?"

"No worthwhile updates from Epiphany yet, but your father has completed his new contraptions for personal protection and defense. He also recounted the broad strokes of his last clash with the Bolivans ages ago. It was a chilling insight into the sort of things his ingenuity can achieve."

"Mmm. The good news is, you're about to witness something important," Fel said. "I'm about to teach Tome something."

"It is a moment of particular note when wisdom flows in that direction," Tome said.

"This is probably the simplest trap trigger you're going to encounter in a Bygone site. It's a pressure plate. The only thing simpler is a trip wire, but mostly you don't have to worry about those because after a couple of centuries the little wires have snapped and the traps will have already triggered. That said, if you *do* encounter an intact trip wire, take extra care because those things are fragile enough that looking at them wrong could set them off."

"Noted," Tome said, his expression growing more concerned.

"A pressure plate will be set off if you step on it. Sometimes. Other times it'll be set off if there's something on it already and you take it off. But this one's clear, so it's going to be set off if you step on it."

"It is in the middle of what looks like a living space," Tome said. "Wouldn't it be terribly dangerous to simply have a random section of floor trigger a trap in a place like this?"

"I'm trying to teach you. Stop asking questions," Fel said.

"Knowledge is attained through questions, Fel."

"Not when the person doing the teaching doesn't know the answers. But you want a question? Here's one." He pointed to the plate. "How do you deactivate the pressure plate?"

"I imagine there is some sort of switch or lever somewhere that deactivates them."

"Maybe, but it's not going to be in here. It's going to be on the other side of a wall or on another floor. There's not much reason to put a trap somewhere if you can deactivate it without leaving the room."

"Now that's just silly. A trap is like a lock. It protects something. And locks are designed to be disabled at the whim of the person who holds the key."

Fel gestured around. "If you already know better than me, then let's see you clever your way to a solution."

"I didn't say I know better than you. I am simply implying that even a moment of thought would—"

"Either you know better than me, or I know better than you," Fel interrupted. "So prove you know better than me, or admit I know better than you."

"Have I touched a nerve, Fel?" Tome asked.

"You've been standing on it since I met you. Now get to it. Deactivate the trap."

Tome gritted his teeth and set Wick's lantern down. "Obviously you wouldn't have challenged me if it wasn't a relatively simple task. And if it is relatively simple, I should be able to manage something. Let me put some thought into it." He leaned low, then dropped to the floor and gazed along its expertly fitted stonework. "I imagine there are tools of the trade I should be considering?"

Fel dropped a canvas bundle on the floor and unrolled it, revealing an assortment of picks, pry bars, hammers, and other instruments tucked neatly into individual pockets. "Take your pick," he said.

Tome selected a thin pry bar. Fel slipped a stout crowbar from the roll and twirled it in his grip.

"What's that for?" Tome asked, eying the larger implement suspiciously.

"Do your job right and we won't find out," he said.

"Look, Fel. If your intelligence is feeling threatened, I shall tone down my rhetoric, but there's no sense acting so surly. We have different methodologies, that is all. You favor blunt force, I favor careful thought. Like this. The trap is quite subtle. We can therefore reason that its secrecy is a key aspect to its effectiveness. Thus, being aware of the trap gives one the opportunity to disarm it. You wouldn't have presented this test if such wasn't the case. You have informed me that this pressure plate has nothing on top of it, which means it is activated by downward force. It follows that it can be safely interacted with via *upward* force. I've spotted a gap just below the center of the leading edge, which I reason is used for precisely this purpose."

Fel continued twirling the crowbar. Years of playing grum had, if nothing else, taught him to keep his face still as stone at times like this.

"Obviously you wouldn't allow me to endanger my life or yours. Since you've not instructed me to stop, this indicates I am correct. Thus..."

He carefully slipped the pry bar into the gap and levered it upward. A dozen things happened in the moment that followed. A loud click sounded from beneath the plate. Stone tiles rattled in place as workings beneath them started to shift. Dust poured down from seams above them. What may have been chains, or perhaps gears, rattled unseen within the walls. Tome whipped around and cringed at a blur of motion near the ceiling. Then, with a loud metal-on-metal clank, all the motion came to a sudden end.

Fel stood a few steps back, beside the wall. He'd inserted the crowbar into a well-hidden track within the wall, and thus had jammed the mechanism of the trap as it was activating. The motion near the ceiling turned out to be the edge of a barred wall dropping down from above. It ran the width of the room, and if it had successfully dropped into place, it would have trapped Tome.

"The first step is locating the trigger. The second step is figuring out what the trigger does. Then shove something sturdy into the parts in between. That's how you deactivate a pressure plate." Fel shrugged. "Or just throw a brick at the trigger and hope you're far enough away. In this case, you were the brick."

"It would seem I underestimated how much thought you were actually employing."

"Yeah, it would. Just because I'm putting my boot through things doesn't mean I don't know what I'm doing."

"Point made," Tome said.

Fel pulled one of the bunk beds over and positioned it beneath the wall, then wrenched away the crowbar. The wall settled onto the top of the bunk and remained in place. "They wanted to trap someone in this section," he said. "That's a good sign. That means they were expecting someone to come through here with something they didn't want to leave the wall. Help me look for a hatch on the floor or in the base of one of the walls. I'll bet there's another strong room accessible through here."

"Right," Tome said, his hands shaking as he lifted Wick's lantern again. "It still begs the question. Why a trap in a place where people were expected to sleep? And why a hatch to someplace important in the same room?"

"Don't know. Don't care. Doesn't matter," Fel said.

"I wonder if perhaps we are observing evidence of some sort of a transitional period in the life of the wall. Besides the transition from active to abandoned, obviously. Perhaps the wall was built long, long before it was called to the purpose of housing soldiers and the like. It would make sense if these beds, these other uses for the wall, were installed by necessity, and the wall was never meant to contain them."

"Helping me look for a hatch doesn't require wondering about the history of the hatch. Just look."

"You know, I was talking to your father a few days before we left, and he shared with me his theory about—"

"I don't care what you and my dad were talking about!" Fel snapped. "Look for the hatch! It's going to be between the wall we jammed and that track in the wall up ahead, which would have had another wall if I hadn't jammed the first one."

The jangle of chains and the click of a smoothly shutting door signaled Oiler's completion of the repair of the bashed entryway.

"Oiler, over here," Fel said. "I don't want you fixing something I need to stay broken," he said.

Oiler thumped its way over to him, and Fel slipped the pack onto his back. Tome left the lantern in the center of the room and fetched the light contraption Fel had identified earlier. The pair worked their way along the walls, mindful of other triggers and searching for anything that might be a hatch. As it happened, Tome was the one to find it.

"Here, under the bed," he said.

They shoved the bed out of the way.

"Good news!" Tome said. "This one has one of those locks. That means high-value contents, correct?"

"Let's hope so." Fel flipped through the book and found the code that matched the markings on the door. "Do you want to try this one?"

Tome glanced at the wall propped up by the bed. "I think perhaps we'll leave the unlocking to you for now."

"Back away then. Give me some room."

Oiler gazed over Fel's shoulder as he moved and rotated the tiles. It was a very lengthy combination. When it finally clicked into place, he hauled the hatch open. A ladder led downward. Fel motioned for the lantern. Tome brought it over.

"Give me a hand, Oiler," he said, holding out the lantern.

The contraption helpfully extended its claws to clutch the light, leaving Fel's hands free for climbing down. When he reached the bottom, he crowed with excitement.

"Ha *ha*! We're in luck! Get down here, Tome. This is *exactly* what we needed."

The mage excitedly slid down the ladder. He was expecting to find shelves mounded with valuable contraptions or heavily laden bookshelves the likes of which Mr. Masker was after. Instead, he was greeted with a long, narrow, and otherwise empty corridor.

"I fail to see the cause for excitement, Fel," Tome said.

"What are you talking about? This is perfect!" he said.

"It is a dank tunnel. I was under the impression we were treasure hunting."

Fel gave him a flat look. "And you're supposed to be the smart one… It's not just a dank tunnel. It is a *long* tunnel. How many sections of the wall have we searched?"

"Two. Or, I suppose, part of one and part of another."

"And how many doors did we have to unlock to do that?"

"Three, so far."

Fel clapped his hands. A long, resounding echo reverberated through the tunnel. "How many locked doors do you hear?"

Tome pointed the light contraption down the tunnel. It ran so far that the end of it was lost behind the curvature of the wall.

"For a place with such an obvious dedication to security, this seems like an awfully large lapse."

"Oh, there will be locks keeping us out of the individual rooms, and there are bound to be major traps along the way, but this will speed things up. It'll keep us out of the sun, out of the shadow of any skyward meat eaters. And best of all, look over here."

He crouched down and held out Wick's lantern. A narrow, short side tunnel led off under the room they'd just climbed out of. Chains, linkages, and gears caught the light and sparkled blue, despite Wick's orange-red flame.

"What you see there is the mechanism of the trap. With any luck, we'll be able to disable the traps *before* we get into rooms rather than trying to work our way around them. Go make sure Parch is alright. Make sure he's got water and there's enough weeds and stuff in the alcove. Then get down here and let's see how much of the wall we can cover before nightfall."

Chapter 4

Fanny took a sip of tea and slid a small wooden case onto the table between herself and Mr. Badgerweed. For a person who had been haggling, wheeling, and dealing since she'd learned to speak, this was a rare occurrence for her. From the moment she'd arrived, she'd been giving Mr. Badgerweed the hardest of sales pitches. For any other would-be buyer, this much effort would have either scared them away or persuaded them to buy her entire inventory. But Mr. Badgerweed had been frustratingly immune to her most skilled and nuanced techniques. At first, he had been impassive, constantly deflecting to the two items she already knew he wanted and she already knew she could not provide. With aching slowness, he'd begun to show genuine interest. Now she'd made enough progress to unleash her secret weapon.

She opened the lid of the case and pulled a slip of paper from within. It had a stunningly well-rendered image of her own face.

"This, sir, was created with a contraption that was subsequently confiscated by the assayer's office for being too complex and self-motivated."

He took the page. "There are contraptions capable of this?"

"Indeed. My father was able to repair one, and having done so, he could do it again. I have it on good authority that no fewer than six such contraptions are currently languishing in a curio shop not far from here. Without my father's touch, they shall remain dormant, strange boxes among an endless array of other strange boxes. But once we acquire and repair them, we will briefly have in our possession a small fleet of these devices. They can produce, with exacting detail, the images and symbols on a page. Or, when depicting a human subject, can make intelligent decisions on how to ease away minor imperfections. I don't think I need to explain to you the multitude of ways in which such a device could be put to good use."

"Interesting… And you are willing to sell such devices despite the prohibition?"

"If we trust the purchaser, I think arrangements could be made."

"And am I correct in assuming that you are willing to overlook *all* prohibitions?"

She shook her head. "No. As a matter of fact we happen to agree with most of the assessments made by the assayer's office. We don't believe that contraptions with a clear military application should be made available to private collectors. We feel as though contraptions that may be destructive if misused should not be sold to the unwary. But that still leaves a wide gulf between the items in our inventory that we are willing to sell and those that the assayers prohibit."

Badgerweed puffed his pipe. "Treat these inquiries as they are intended. Simple idle musings that, perhaps, might turn into transactions under the proper circumstances. They are by no means binding contracts."

"Of course."

"I have buyers with an interest in the following areas. Communication. Stealth. Surveillance."

"Excellent. We've already discussed what an excellent investment alarm boxes are likely to be."

He took a particularly deep puff and breathed smoke out through his nose, stinging her eyes.

"You've demonstrated that you've had in your possession contraptions possessed of a rudimentary intelligence. Perhaps you might have had contraptions with a greater than rudimentary intelligence. Things that might, for example, observe. And even relay their findings."

She nodded. "I believe I know precisely what you are implying. Any student of antiquity is likely to have encountered tales of things called 'sentry lanterns.' These are items that serve the precise purpose you have speculated upon."

"Do they now?" he said. "And have you any such items in your inventory?"

"Sentry lanterns are the very definition of rare, sir."

"Rare simply means expensive, doesn't it?" he said.

"I can safely say that the Masker family has, at no point in its long history, had a sentry lantern for sale."

"I see. A shame. Because I am quite certain that I could find a buyer for such an item at any price." He puffed. "*Any* price."

"Then we can only hope that my brother's expedition turns one up. However, with regard to the subjects of stealth and communication, are you familiar with the translation mechanism? Because were you to have a pair, you could easily exchange messages without fear of any interlopers being able to read them…"

The minutes that followed were something of a breakthrough. She was able to tease out interest in at least five different contraptions that had passed through their hands in recent memory or were easily acquired. He was coy on the precise price he was willing to pay, but the low end was already comfortably within what Epiphany would consider worthwhile, and she was sure she could elevate it a bit before hands were shaken.

When she had her list composed in her mind, she excused herself and hurried back to her wagon. It hadn't accompanied her on this most recent session. She'd not been overly fond of the idea of the lantern smoldering there unsupervised, but to her great relief it was still lit and the wagon hadn't been damaged. Now all she had to do was prepare herself for a few days here, doing business, and awaiting the next opportunity to deliver a message via Wick to Fel. If he could locate some of the items this man was after, it would cement their reputation as people who could do things no one else could hope to achieve.

#

Fel and Tome had walked for miles inside the tunnel without serious mishap. In this case, "without serious mishap" meant they'd only triggered two traps. One of them had produced a burst of flame that had singed Fel's sleeve, and the other had provided Wick's lantern with a dent that would need to be hammered and buffed out. But the journey had been enlightening.

"Here, another one," Tome said eagerly, taking note of a placard along the way. "The third and fourth symbols are different, the rest are the same. And it matches the progression of the markings we were told to expect on the outside of the wall, but with an additional symbol. I would wager everything I have in my pockets that these symbols pair with some sort of a directory. That, I think, would be the true treasure of this trip."

Fel sniffed the air. "It smells a little moldy. And I hear water."

"We aren't approaching the shore already, are we?" Tome said.

"Not unless we've been moving a lot faster than we think."

The sound of running water became much more apparent as they continued on, and soon the stone of the floor was replaced by wooden slats. Fel crouched and held the lantern low.

"There's running water beneath us. There aren't any rivers that flow through the Greater Lands Wall. This must be an underground spring. That would explain where those water troughs are pumping from."

"Please take great care near open water," Wick said. "Flame is easily extinguished by open water, and I have been asked by your father to limit my gaps in observation."

"I know, Wick," Fel said. "Tome, try to walk near the edge of the slats. Wood, water, and time don't mix very well."

"You don't need to tell me twice," he said.

Fel waddled a bit, thumping along the edge of the walkway. Every so often the tunnel would open out into a larger chamber. Frequently these chambers existed specifically to permit access to more substantial mechanisms associated with traps in the adjoining sections of wall. This time, there seemed to be more to it. The wooden slats followed a shallow curve, swinging with the motion of their steps. The support came in the form of chains that ran down from the ceiling hidden in the darkness overhead. The wall they knew to be shared with the internal chambers continued downward. They already knew that some chambers had one or more levels beneath them, but this was the first time since they'd been traveling through the tunnel that they'd encountered a section that exposed the greater depths.

He slowed down and held out his hand to stop Tome from following.

"What is it?" Tome asked.

He narrowed his eyes and moved Wick's lantern in a slow circle. "There are too many chains here. One extra," he said.

He crouched and followed the extra chain. It looped under the walkway. He gingerly probed under the slats, then reached over to the other side and ran his fingers along a thinner chain, caked with filth. "Do you still have the light contraption?" he asked.

"Of course."

"Shine it there. Against the wall."

Tome produced the contraption and did as he was told. The thin chain ran to a small pulley, then up into a section of the ceiling a bit lower than the rest. That same section held the primary support chains for a platform at the center of the sagging bridge.

"It's a pitfall trap," he said. "A big one. If we'd swayed this walkway too much, I think the whole thing would have been dumped into the water." He pulled out a small pair of snippers. "The chain is slack, so cutting it should be safe."

"Should be?"

"We'll find out," he said, snipping the chain.

It swung down and slapped against the wall. Besides a terrified yelp from Tome, there were no consequences.

"All right!" he said, standing and dusting his hands. "Let's see what they were so interested in protecting. Stay a few steps back. There might be more triggers."

They carefully made their way down the rest of the slope. Sure enough, two more chains had been attached to the walkway and needed to be cut. The platform in the center of the odd elevated walkway was quite obviously a part of the pitfall trap, as rather than a standard connection to the stone wall and the threshold of the door, it had hinges. A larger plaque was affixed to the wall above the heavily fortified door. Fel handed over the codebook and set Oiler down on the platform.

"Tome, see if you can find what this door is. Oiler, stay put. Here, I'll scramble your puzzle box for you again. I'm going to check the rest of the walkway. There are definitely matching trigger chains on the other side, and it'll be easier and safer if I don't have a heap of chain strapped to my back while I'm dealing with them."

He moved with care along the walkway, Wick's lantern held low. Behind him, Tome shined his light alternately between the codebook and the placard. Fel snipped the nearest chain, then worked his way to the second. He had to take his time because he could see that it was quite a bit less slack than the others. Too much sway might set it off.

"Fel," Tome said. "I think… I think this is it. I think this is the research library."

"You're joking."

"It's one of the only pages where your father translated the markings rather than just transcribing them. The word 'library' is definitely here."

"That's fantastic!" Fel said. "Stay right there. I'll clip the last chain and head over to enter the code."

"The potential for an intact Bygone Era library," Wick said. "This is momentous."

"Yeah. I guess I'll believe it when I see it. The rest of this place is mostly cleaned out. We've got to imagine this place might be too."

"If there is even a remote chance that there is an intact archive, I respectfully suggest you leave my lantern outside," Wick said.

"What?" he said, setting the lantern down and very carefully reaching down to the chain. "I'm going to need light."

"Tome has a light-emitting contraption. That will serve the purpose without a fire risk."

"Don't be stupid," Fel said. "Dad would never let me hear the end of it if I set foot in the library and I didn't bring you to…"

Fel trailed off. The walkway was swaying. A moment before the chain would have gone fully taut and potentially dumped the walkway, he snipped it.

"Tome! Are you trying to get us killed?" he snapped, holding up the lantern.

"What? I'm here waiting for you," Tome said, still in front of the door with the codebook in one hand and the light in the other.

Fel squinted, then stood bolt upright. "Where is Oiler?"

Tome shakily pocketed the codebook and swept his light about. Fel held out the lantern. The pack of chains was conspicuously absent from where it had been left in front of the doorway, but it didn't seem to be anywhere on the walkway either.

A moment too late, Fel realized that a loop of additional chain had been wrapped around the walkway. Oiler was hanging beneath, where the trigger chain had been attached, and was extending one of his claws out toward where the severed chain hung. The compulsion to repair that which was broken was too strong, and before either Tome or Fel could dissuade it, the dutiful contraption pulled the trigger chain taut in hopes of reattaching its ends.

The instant the slack was out of the trigger, the chains holding up the walkway reeled out. The platform Tome was standing on hinged down, and he was sent tumbling into the water. Fel grabbed the walkway tightly, but when it reached the end of the slack, it came to a violent stop and he was torn free. He splashed down into icy, rushing water. The equipment strapped to his body that had saved him from being killed by half a dozen traps along the way dragged him below the surface. He scrabbled and flailed, trying to pull his tools free and float back to the surface, but the slippery stone beneath him dropped away and he was tumbling through the air. Sunlight was suddenly in his eyes, filtering through the droplets of water. He was outside. He was no longer sheltered by the wall. And he *knew* that there was no sluice or outlet on the Greater Lands Wall… at least, not on the *outside*.

The grim realization of where the water had taken him was the last thought to cross his mind before he plunged into a freezing pool of water and struck his head on the rocky bottom.

#

In the alcove on the safe side of the wall, Parch pleasantly munched at a bundle of weeds. With a stone arch and an iron gate between him and any would-be predators, the little lesser unicorn was perfectly at ease. Then, without explanation, he became still. One ear flicked and flopped irritably. He turned to the wall and snuffed out a breath.

Tome hadn't bothered tying him to anything when he'd refreshed the food and water. Prior attempts to do so had illustrated that anything short of a ship's anchor rope would be inadequate to keep the supernaturally strong creature from breaking free if he had the notion to.

He clip-clopped over to the door his friends had vanished through and pawed at it once or twice. He took a few steps back and lowered his head, ready to charge the door, but instead he paused, turned, and bashed through the gate. It swung open. He trotted out into the open. A few skillful jumps and uncannily sure footwork allowed him to scale the face of the wall with little difficulty. Once perched atop, he dropped his head low and sagged his ears, keenly aware of the unpleasantly exposed position he'd placed himself in. Nevertheless, he felt compelled to trot along the top of the wall, eyes dancing between the sky and the lush landscape beyond the wall.

#

Martin sat in the corner of the shop, bowl of stew in hand as he chatted idly with his wife. Normally at least one of the kids was home to share dinnertime or to take over at the counter to give Vivian the opportunity to head down to have a proper meal at the table. When they were both absent, Martin liked to bring Vivian's bowl to her and enjoy the meal in the spaces between customers. Much to Vivian's chagrin, today said gaps in business were more than adequate to make for a leisurely meal.

"Perhaps if we changed the items on display," Vivian said. "The window is the only real chance we have to entice people walking through town. It might pay to put something flashier on display."

"The flashier items sell for more, and thus are more likely to be stolen," Martin mused.

"So we watch them more closely and lock them up more securely during the off hours."

"You already spend more than an hour before open and more than an hour after close on such things, dear. If you add much more to your plate, you'll replace sleep entirely."

"If I don't keep my plate full, then pretty soon *this* plate will be empty," she said, tapping the bowl with the spoon.

The flickering lantern in the corner of the shop suddenly stopped flickering. The flame became perfectly still, and a normally cold and collected voice blurted something with uncharacteristic intensity.

"Something has happened," Wick said.

"What is it? What's wrong?" Martin said, climbing up to set the lantern down on the counter.

"Fel and Tome found what they believed to be the library."

"That's wonderful news! Was the code correct? What sort of books did they find inside when they—"

"Oiler, while unobserved, attempted to reconnect the trigger for a disabled trap, and they were all dumped into some manner of aquifer inside the wall."

"Were they hurt?" Martin said.

"I do not know. The flame in the lantern was extinguished when it struck the water. It did not appear to be a lethal distance, but the water was moving swiftly, and the outlet for the aquifer was unclear."

"This is… this is terrible," Martin said. "We need to do something." He stood. "I need a horse. A fast one. How does one charter a carriage? That would be best, wouldn't it? Quickest?"

"Calm yourself, Martin," Vivian said.

"Our son may be injured, Vivian. He may have been killed."

"Calm yourself," she said more firmly. "There is little you can do from here that will do any good, and nothing that can be gained by panicking."

"But Vivian—"

"Fel has done more than his share of solo expeditions. He has run afoul of traps before. Probably more than he's told us about. He has a good head on his shoulders, and he comes from hearty stock. He will be fine."

"We don't know that, Vivian. He could be—"

"Whatever his state, if you leave now with the fastest horse you can, you won't reach the wall for a week, and then you'll have to navigate all the same threats, and you aren't as young as you used to be. Meanwhile, I will be here alone in a town that may or may not be harboring Bolivan agents. I believe I can take care of myself, and the shop, by myself if I must. But spreading our already-stretched-thin family even thinner is not the solution. Fel is fine. He has help. He is tough. He is fine."

Martin blinked and tried to keep his breathing steady. His heart was racing. His mind was swimming with the thoughts that he might have sent his son to his death. But Vivian was steady as bedrock, and she spoke with an unshakable certainty. He knew she couldn't know, she couldn't *really* know, that Fel wasn't hurt. But the woman's will was so strong that Martin could almost feel the forces of nature bending themselves to align to her insistence.

"Wick," she said. "Keep trying to return to that lantern. At his first opportunity, he will relight it, and I want you there as soon as he does. We sent him with the only other artifact lantern for a reason. We knew there was a chance it would be extinguished."

"It will take me at least twenty minutes from the moment the lantern is lit," he said.

"Then I want you there in no more than twenty minutes. Don't keep him waiting."

"What about Fanny?" Martin said.

"She was in no danger when last I left her," Wick replied. "I came here directly following the event. I have not had an opportunity to inform her."

"Don't," Vivian said simply.

"If something happened to her brother, she deserves to know, Vivian."

"If something happened to Fel, she'll be no more able to help him than you will, but she doesn't have family with her to steady her nerves or talk her down. She'll drop everything and rush to the wall, and Epiphany has never been on an expedition. She's not experienced, not trained. I won't have her risking her life attempting to rescue Fel from a fate we aren't even certain warrants rescue. Don't tell her that Fel is in danger. Don't tell her anything we don't know for certain. It'll only worry her."

"Are we certain this is the proper course of action? Will I be withholding this information from Epiphany?" Wick asked.

"I should hope you've *always* avoided telling us things you don't know to be true," Vivian said.

Martin was silent as he considered her words. "Don't lie to her. But I suppose… I suppose this is best, until we know more… But I'm going to find him."

"Martin—"

"Vivian, he is our son. We sent him to the wall, and now he is in trouble. I have done expeditions, I can open the doors." He stood and set down his bowl. "Just need to prepare myself."

The door jangled. Vivian set her bowl aside. She glanced at Martin.

"Then go. Get ready. But it will be a long trip to find our boy with the situation in hand." She turned to the customer, her demeanor effortlessly shifting to the gleaming veneer of politeness that was a hallmark of all good shopkeepers.

#

Tome's head thumped and throbbed. He tried to take a deep breath. The air left in a violent cough that tasted of swamp water. He gasped and wretched until finally he could fill his lungs properly.

"What… where…" he murmured, rubbing muck from his eyes.

He wrestled himself into a sitting position and reluctantly took stock of his surroundings. His legs were nearly numb, submerged in rushing water. Every inch of his flowing outfit was saturated with water and stained with the brown and green of the riverbank. The area outside the wall was a dry field. He knew it well. And this wasn't it. The surroundings here were vivid and green, great towering trees that he was certain he would have remembered if he'd seen them in the distance. This was… the other side of the wall.

His hand instinctively went to the buttoned inside pocket of his shirt. It was secure. Inside he found the codebook for the wall and a copious amount of pulp that had once been his folio of prepared spells. He thumbed open the codebook and found it waterlogged but intact.

"I paid a premium for that paper, and Martin's book held up better…" he grumbled.

He stowed the book again and planted his hands in the muck to climb to his feet. His legs refused to cooperate and he fell forward.

"Fel?" he called, rolling to his back and crab-walking away from the water. "Fel we've got problems!"

There was no answer. He felt his head and his sides. He wasn't injured. Not badly enough for the pain to overcome the creeping terror of the realization that he was trapped in the Greater Lands. His heart started to race. Through sheer force of will, he was able to fight his way to his feet and remain standing on half-numb legs. He hobbled forward.

"Got to… I've got to… safe! Safe vantage. Get to a safe vantage, learn more. Learn more. When you know more, you can do more," he yammered, heading for a tree leaning over the water.

Calling upon skills unused since childhood, he scrabbled up the tree and huddled into the upper branches like the frightened animal he was. Thus hidden, he took careful inventory of what remained of his equipment.

"All right. All right. The prepared spells… worthless. My hip folio. What about my hip folio?"

He felt for his emergency supplies and found them relatively intact inside an oiled leather folio filled with twenty narrow slips of low-grade but apparently far hardier paper. It also contained a sealed bottle of the ink he'd made using

Parch's horn shavings and two salvageable quills.

"Bad paper, good ink… It's better than nothing. I can probably use some pages from the back of the codebook, if it isn't filled. I can work with that. It isn't enough for any major spells, but a dozen or so minor spells can make a difference. But where am I?"

He climbed a bit farther up the tree, now that his legs were more willing to cooperate. When he stood and poked his head out of the foliage, he instantly wished he hadn't. Wisdom may be a tool, but ignorance was bliss. Never was that more clear to him than when he glanced upriver, truly believing he would find himself in the shadow of the Greater Lands Wall, perhaps with a helpful ladder or staircase to bring him safely back inside. Instead, he discovered miles of twisting, turning river and a steep, treacherous climb up to a wall that was at least five times taller on the inside than it was outside. The Greater Lands was like a bowl, reaching up to the wall. And there were hours of hiking, at the very least, separating him from the rim.

Below, something rustled in the brush around the base of the tree. He huddled down.

"This is… not ideal…" he fretted.

#

Some distance away, Fel burst from unconsciousness to full wakefulness in a flurry of flailing limbs and swinging fists.

"What? Where? I'll break your jaw if you let me…" He blinked and shook his head. "What's happening?"

He looked down at his legs. His boots were packed full of mud, and long furrows in the muck led to the river. In the distance, he could hear the rush of rapids. Something tugged under his arms, chains jingled, and he slid another few feet along the shore. He also felt a jolt of pain in his shoulder.

"Stop, stop, stop," he said.

The loop of chain under his arms slipped away, and Oiler rattled around to sit on his belly. The contraption had seen better days. Water drizzled out of its head. Two fasteners were missing, and one was rattling loose. It reached up and grasped the loose fastener. It spun the screw into place and leaned close, slit-eyes in its serpentine mask adjusting.

"Okay… so you saved me from drowning," he croaked. "Don't think that means I'm going to automatically forgive you for being the *reason I was drowning to begin with*!"

Oiler continued giving him an inspection. Its head became still when it came to the shoulder that had been the source of the discomfort. Fel glanced at it and noticed what had probably given Oiler pause. Tumbling across the rocky bottom of the river had pulled his shoulder out of joint. Before he could work out how best to deal with that situation, both sets of gleaming claws grasped the shoulder.

"No, no, no!" he yelped.

The contraption shoved. Fel howled in pain and saw stars, but when the moment passed, his shoulder was back in joint.

"Well I'll be damned," he said, shifting his arm with considerably less pain and difficulty. "You did a pretty good—*don't!*"

Oiler froze and looked to Fel. It had discovered one of Fel's fingers was bent in a way that fingers shouldn't bend and had already gripped it to adjust.

"That's broken, I can tell. You need to be much more careful if you—*by the high what did I just say!?*"

Fel pulled his hand away and cradled it against his chest. The suspect finger was straight again, but with a good deal more pain and suffering than what someone with a better bedside manner would have caused.

"You need to learn to listen," Fel said. "Now come here. How are you? You lose anything important?"

Oiler extended one arm, then the other. All links were undamaged and intact.

"You've got a plate missing from the back of your left hand. We can probably hammer something out to replace it. It looked like it was just for decoration. The tail is fine. Alright. You survived. And besides the bad shoulder and the bad little finger, I'm in one piece. What about tools? Equipment? Help me up."

Oiler tumbled off and laced the fingers of its claws into a stirrup of sorts. Fel leaned on it and got to his feet. It felt like he was on the deck of a ship on unsteady seas. The lush foliage and creaking trees around him pitched and reeled. Clearly the more obvious injuries weren't the only price taken by the river ride. He nearly fell. Oiler dug its tail into the mud, reached up with its claws, and kept him from tipping aside.

"Good. Good. Thanks, buddy," he said.

Once he was moderately steady, he felt along his body with his good hand. His tool roll was nearly empty. A short knife he used for trimming leather had survived, along with a pair of pliers. The rope that had been looped over his shoulder under his jacket was still there. Everything else was gone. His other pack, his cudgel, Wick's lantern, everything. Even his pockets were empty.

"That river did a good job of cleaning me out…" he said.

He used the knife to cut away a bit of rope and trudged up to a tree to cut a green stick from it. When a splint for his finger had been tied, he leaned heavily against the trunk and rubbed his eyes.

"We're in the Greater Lands. And I can't see the wall, so we're pretty far into the Greater Lands." He raised his voice. "Tome!"

No answer. Fel turned to Oiler. "Did you see the other guy? Did you save him too?"

Oiler shook its head.

"Was that an answer to the first question or the second question?"

Oiler nodded. Fel sighed.

"Did you see Tome?"

Oiler shook his head.

"Did you… I guess that answers the second question. Alright. All things considered, we're lucky. We're lucky we got this far without dying. But my runs of luck never last long, so we've got to be ready for the debt collector when this all comes due."

He held his good arm down. Oiler turned and helpfully held up the appropriate strap. Fel hauled it onto his back and tore a half-rotten branch from the side of a fallen limb beside the tree. He hefted it in his hand and experimentally bashed the remainder of the limb.

"Sturdy enough for now. So we've got a weapon. Now we find if Tome survived, and we start heading for the wall. You watch my back. I don't want any more surprises. And for *both* our sakes, don't *fix* anything."

#

"This is wrong. This is *wrong*, this is wrong," Tome muttered. "I should be searching for Fel. It is the right thing to do. Fel could be hurt, and I should be searching for him." He dashed from the shadow of one tree to the next. "It isn't merely the moral and ethical thing to do, it is sound tactics. Fel is a bit of a brute and a bit crude, but this is a brutish, crude place and he's better equipped for this sort of messy, horrid work."

He checked his soggy pocket for the fifth time in as many minutes, ensuring his three freshly written spells were still there.

"But I am no tracker. How would I find him? It isn't as though there are two 'griff riders circling him like when I *last* had to find him." He glanced to the sky. "Are there?"

Nothing presented itself overhead.

"For all I know, he's dead. This is the proper thing to do. I go. I reach the wall. And I find help. Then we can come back and find him."

He trotted out to the slippery stone beside the rushing river. He'd reached the point where the slope was too steep for him to scale without putting his hands to work.

"But it will be days before we can come back for him. This is wrong. I have to go back. I have to find him." He took a breath and turned around.

Something was there.

Tome froze in place. The beast before him wasn't immediately intimidating, but it was a creature of the Greater Lands, which implicitly made it the most terrifying thing he'd ever encountered. It was a bird, though with the sleek and stout look of something more at home in the water than on land or in air.

It stood perhaps half his height, with a blunt yellow beak and a mostly white body with flippers rather than wings.

"Lesser or Greater. Lesser or Greater," Tome mumbled, slipping a spell from his pocket and backing away. "Think, think, think. You've read a dozen books about Lesser *and* Greater Mystics. You *must* have seen this. A water bird… what was it called? They had a name for it. Is it a selkie? No, no. That's something else."

It took a step closer. He tried to step back but nearly lost his footing on the increasing slope. "Is it… it could be a boobrie. But that doesn't make sense. A boobrie is…"

The feathers bristled and shifted. They seemed to flip up, rolling forward in a wave to reveal an unpleasant brown carapace. Its beak split into mandibles. Tentacles and feelers emerged.

"A boobrie is a shapeshifter…" he said shakily. "It sucks the blood of horses, devours livestock…"

Additional legs sprouted from the side of the thing. The tail snapped out into a horrid two-pronged claw.

"Hear me, boobrie!" he said. "I don't know if you are a Lesser Mystic or a Greater. I've never seen your like. But you should know, if there is wisdom in that head of yours, that you face no mere man. I am a paper mage. And if you threaten me, I shall boil your very innards with a spell conjured through ink alone!" He held the page up. "I urge you to back away. I do not wish to spill blood in this place. I simply wish to depart peacefully."

The thing clacked its mandibles together. As terrified as Tome was, he chose to interpret it as an act of war. He tore the page and tossed it at the thing. As it fluttered through the air, it burst into flame. The flames moved with a clear will, sculpted by the words on the page into a targeted swirl that coiled around the creature.

It shrieked, struggled, and was singed, but before any real damage could be done, the flames died away and the creature dove into the water. It vanished below the surface.

"That should have lasted longer," Tome said, digging out a second spell. For the moment, his fear was rivaled by the bruise to his ego. "I don't understand it," he said. "Were my hands shaking when I wrote it? Did I miss a line? It shouldn't have fizzled so quickly."

The water rippled. A great, horrid black bull burst from beneath the surface. Here and there, blackened carapace could still be seen sifting into its hide as the shape-changing creature finished its shift. Tome tore the second spell and hurled it. Now a bone-chilling blast of cold conjured between himself and the beast. The layer of water clinging to its hide frosted and froze, but barely a crust had formed when the breeze dropped away.

"Impossible! That was my first spell. I am a *master* of that spell." He turned and dashed for the trees. "I *know* I wrote it perfectly. It's this place. It *must* be this place. It's different somehow."

The ground behind him thundered. He tore the last spell and threw it. It should have conjured a choking, impenetrable smoke that could bring anything short of a dragon to its knees. Instead, the bull charged through, barely missing a step. Tome reached the trunk of a tree and scaled it. The black beast struck the base, nearly shaking him free.

He reached the relative safety of the sturdiest branch and held tight. His mind raced as he watched the bull paw at the ground and snort, its cold black eyes gazing up at him. He locked his legs around the branch and fumbled for his pen and pages.

"P-perhaps, if it stays where it is, I can quickly—"

It rammed the tree again. The shaking nearly sent his whole emergency folio tumbling to the ground. He clutched it tightly.

"I can't write like this… I'm going to die because this blasted land fouled my otherwise *perfect* spells."

The tree shook again. The branch began to splinter and sag.

"At least I die knowing it took the machinations of a malevolent land to best me. At least I die knowing it wasn't my fault."

The tree shook one last time. The base of the branch broke. He started to tip toward the maddened beast. It looked up to him. The rage in its eyes faded suddenly, replaced by a flash of fear. Above him, wings buffeted him. Great claws clamped onto his arms, squeezing them painfully tight, and he was wrenched free, drawn skyward out of the frying pan and into the fire.

Chapter 5

Fel thumped along the river, or as near to it as he could. With each step upriver, the question of just how he'd survived became more glaring. He had only just reached a bend in the rushing waters that gave him a clear view of where the flow of water left the wall. It was still miles away, and he'd been walking for a mile or two at least. Surely over that distance some combination of bouncing off the stones and being weighed down by his gear should have killed him. A more intellectual man might have questioned if perhaps there was more going on than he realized. A more religious man would have supposed it was the will of the gods, and that he might have some higher purpose to fulfill.

As it happened, Fel was neither of those things. Thus, what dominated his mind was simmering frustration at the long, muddy walk that was awaiting him and his concern over what had become of Tome.

"No remains," he said, gazing along the bank. "And I still haven't seen any footprints. Either he's farther up toward the wall or he passed us. And those rapids you pulled me clear of wouldn't have done him any good."

He felt a tug. Until now, the only sound he'd heard besides his own heavy breaths, the buzzing of insects, and the rush of water had been a strange clicking and ticking from Oiler. At first he'd thought it might be some sort of damage, but it became clear over time that the sounds he was hearing were the sounds of irritability and dismay. Oiler didn't like this place. But now that sound had been replaced by the telltale waggling fingers of Oiler's excitement.

"What? What do you see?" he asked.

Oiler reeled its head out and pointed a claw. Fel followed the gesture and poked at the mud with his toe. A bit of gleaming metal caught his eye. He crouched and pulled up what turned out to be the remains of the puzzle box he'd brought along to keep Oiler busy. He marched up to a drier piece of land and slipped Oiler from his back, then turned the box over in his hands.

"This doesn't look bashed apart," he said. "This looks pried apart. Like someone purposely busted it. These here look like claw marks."

He glanced up. Oilers eyes were intently fixed upon the box. Its claws tapped against each other anxiously, but it kept its fingers to itself.

"Oh, so you finally figured out not to fix things without being asked." He tossed it to the contraption. "Go to it. Fix it up."

The look of profound relief was an impressive feat for a creature with no real means of expression beyond body language. It hungrily tugged and twisted at the broken pieces, separating out the external plates and scrutinizing the broken insides.

Fel scratched his head as he watched.

"You don't like this place, do you? You've been more rattly than usual. Lots of clicking in that head of yours." He looked around. "I guess it makes sense. Whoever made you, made you to fix things. That head of yours is all about working out how things tick and getting them to do it again. But there's nothing around here but trees and stones and water. Nothing anyone built. I guess this is about as far out of your element as a place is liable to get."

Oiler merrily adjusted and straightened components. Fel crouched a little lower and ran his fingers over the dirt. There were bestial footprints. Fairly fresh. Nothing surprising about that. He didn't know much about the Greater Lands, but he knew it was a place teeming with all sorts of life. It was more than a little surprising he'd not encountered any. But what stood out to him was the odd smooth stretch of soil beside them. He followed it for a few steps and found a divot in the soft earth that held a bit of a woven pattern.

"This was a sack," Fel said. "Whatever these things were, they were dragging a sack."

He followed the footprints a bit more and scooped up a handful of dirt. He sifted it through his fingers. A trio of buttons revealed themselves. The same simple buttons he used to bribe the lesser harpies back home when he didn't have any food for them.

"Someone stole my stuff." He marched back to Oiler and slid it back onto his good shoulder. "Come on. We're finding the thieves who took my stuff. If Tome is out there waiting to be found, we'll have a much better chance of finding him if we've got my gear."

Oiler paid him little mind, far too busy putting its skills to good use for the first time in far too long.

Fel kept his eyes trained on the ground. The trail wasn't hard to follow if he kept his focus on it, but as they got farther from the river and the earth became less moist and malleable, it became increasingly difficult to find it again if he let his attention wander. He should have had Oiler keeping lookout, but the poor thing was contentedly working and it seemed a shame to cut that relief short. So the role of sentry went to his ears, listening for any motion that didn't seem like it was wind.

"Ah-*ha*!" he proclaimed.

He reached through the broken branches of a bramble bush and retrieved a palm-sized silver bit of kit. He held it up and depressed the lever. Sparks crackled at its tip.

"My sparker!" he said. "And it still works. Now I know we're still having a good run of luck, Oiler. I never, *never* leave home without my sparker. It's the first contraption Dad ever let me keep. According to him, it's the first contraption *his* father ever let him fix. I'll tell you what, if this thing found its way back to me, then fate's smiling on us."

He flicked it a few more times, producing more sparks. The flickers of light cut just a bit deeper into the shadowy brush. Something previously hidden caught his eye. He leaned lower and flicked the sparker again. A much, *much* bigger footprint was hidden in the brush. The branches around it were broken and still wet with sap from where they'd snapped. This was fresh.

"Or laughing at us," he said. "Stay on your toes, Oiler. We might have company."

He slid his improvised club from where he'd tied it to his belt and continued, with a bit more caution, along the trail left by the thieves. Evidently he wasn't the only one to have noticed the evidence of the large predator in the area, because after just a few steps the trail became much easier to follow. The claw prints were deeper, more frenzied. The dragging of the sack left bouncing dimples and dips in the ground. They were running now. And a second footprint from the larger beast blotted out a stretch of the trail.

They weren't just running. They were being chased. Fel paused to consider his options. Either whatever was chasing them caught them, in which case there was some question if there would be anything left of his stolen equipment. Or they got away, in which case the path would continue and he would find the thieves, the goods, and the safe haven they'd reached. There was really only one way that this could go wrong, and that was if he stumbled upon the hunter while it was still trying to get them. He gritted his teeth and tightened his grip on the club. He'd had enough games of grum go south to know which was the most likely outcome, but he was already in too deep. If there was a beast stalking around and looking for a meal, he wasn't going to beat it without his gear, so he had to keep moving forward.

He continued for a few minutes. The journey was uneventful, with the exception of the moment when Oiler finished repairing the puzzle box and waggled it in front of him in hopes of getting it scrambled. When nerves are ratcheted as tight as they can go, the sudden enthusiastic jingle of a shiny box is enough to stop a heart.

The forest was quiet, not a good sign, as it suggested a predator was near. But all things considered, it was preferable. At least it meant he wasn't tripping over a sequence of lesser threats in his watch for the greater one.

Oiler rattled with excitement. Fel whipped around, club held high. There was nothing. The contraption reeled out its head and pointed eagerly at a bush.

"We've got to find a less jarring way for you to tell me you've seen something, Oiler," he said, shakily affixing his club to his belt with a short length of cord and brushing the bush aside.

There was a scrap of rough cloth, the same sort of weave that had left its impression in the riverbank. It had been snagged on a thorny root, and a short distance away he found what had likely been the source of Oiler's excitement.

"The lantern. *The lantern*," Fel said triumphantly.

Wick's lantern had seen better days. Water ran out of it when he tipped it aside. The glass of the hatch was broken. A score of new dents and scrapes speckled its body. But the key portion, the portion that made it function, seemed to be intact. He fumbled for his sparker and clicked the lever a few times. Sparks delivered themselves to the wick of the lantern with surgical precision. In better circumstances, it would have taken one or two clicks to get the lantern lit, but the bit of cloth was waterlogged, and the sparks barely made a difference. A dozen clicks finally started to sizzle the end of the wick.

Fel paused to flex his fingers. Holding the lantern in his good hand meant clicking the sparker with his injured one, and it was beginning to inch him back to the point of discomfort. While he waited for the throbbing to go down enough for another attempt to light the lantern, he realized the silence was no longer quite so complete. In the distance, he could hear the soft chatter of some sort of small creature. It was far too small to be the predator, which meant there was a good chance it was one of the thieves.

He tied the lantern to his belt and gripped the club again. If not for the distraction of finding some of his gear, he would have known the thieves were near the moment he stepped clear of the brush. The mossy ground cover was torn up by a frenzied dash, and the moist earth beneath had yet to dry. They were close.

He followed the clear tracks. One more piece of his gear, a small pry bar, revealed itself among the moss. Then he came to a heavy stone slab in the shadow of an enormous tree. The leaves were so thick, even with the sun still bright overhead it was surprisingly dim. The slab was too rectangular, too flat to be something natural. But time and the elements had rounded its corners and coated it with a blanket of moss. A second, smaller slab had slumped against it, this one broken to nearly rubble. The two pieces propped each other up just enough to provide a small bit of shelter beneath. And it was at the mouth of this shelter that the trail ended. The chattering that had drawn his attention had stopped.

"Hey!" he said, rapping the top of the slab with his club. "I know you're in there. And I know you have what's mine."

No answer. He fished out the sparker and clicked the lever. With no clear target for the sparks to go, they simply fizzled in the air, producing a brief, flickering bit of light. In the flash he saw the glint of four pairs of large eyes but little else.

"Get out here, give me my stuff, and maybe we can help each other out."

He flicked the sparker again. One set of eyes closed, then the others.

"I'm going to give you the benefit of the doubt and assume you don't understand what I'm saying, because I can tell you're little and I've got a big club, so if you understood me, you'd be looking to make a deal."

Oiler rattled. Fel snapped his head around. A gleaming claw extended, pointing into the reeds around a small pond. Fel squinted, but the shifting shadows made it too difficult for him to determine what exactly Oiler was pointing at. One thing was clear, though. This wasn't the delighted "Oh, I've found something you'll like!" sort of point. This was much more serious.

Fel held his ground rather than going to investigate. He'd pressed his luck far enough already. Instead, he plunked the lantern down and started clicking the sparker again. Five clicks started the wet wick sizzling. Ten clicks and it started to smolder.

"Come on, come on," he said.

Another ten clicks and the tiniest, flickering flame started to claim the wick. It did a far better, far faster job of drying it out than the sparker had, and within a few seconds, the flame was growing to its proper brightness. He held it up. The light wasn't much compared to the sun, but directing it into the shadowy reeds revealed the leathery, ratty-bearded face of an old man. He was gazing with blue-gray eyes, stone still, and looking none too happy.

"Hey!" he called. "I see you there. Do these things in here belong to you?"

He heard a wheezy breath from the man.

"Look, no sense hiding in the reeds like a toad. I can see you. I don't know how long you've been watching me, but I'm in a bit of a fix, and if you can help me, I think it'll do us both some good."

The brows of his silent observer furrowed. The reeds shuffled and waved. Slowly he started to stand up… and the whole pond seemed to stand up with him. Fel's eyes widened as a few unsettling realizations presented themselves. The reeds were considerably larger than he thought, which meant the face among them was as well. The huge damp mound welling up behind the man wasn't earth or water. It was fur-covered flesh. The shape of the thing resolved itself, but Fel's mind was slow to conceive of it as a genuine creature. Great leathery wings shook the muck of the pond away. A massive, leonine body dripped pond water. The thing was huge, easily Fel's height at the shoulder. It had the shape of a lion and the bulk of a bison.

In what was surely an example of a divine being choosing to be entirely excessive, in addition to the bat-like wings and leonine body, a scorpion tail rose up behind it, bristling with a morning star of additional barbs beside its primary one.

"Any chance that man-face of yours means you're reasonable?" he said shakily, keeping his club low.

The thing grinned, the corners of its mouth stretching nearly to its ears. The jaws opened to reveal three full rows of finger-size teeth. It released a thunderous roar that sounded like a trio of war trumpets had been possessed by demons.

"And so the luck runs out…"

The monster burst forward. The gap in the slabs was too small for Fel to crawl through. He had no choice but to run toward the thicker trees. Brush snapped and branches crackled, but the thing after him was too big to navigate easily among the sturdy trunks. Fel wove between trees until the sound of the crunching and cracking was far enough behind that he was willing to risk a moment to get his bearings and see how much distance he'd gained.

It was desperately trying to claw its way between two trees, evidence that its unwillingness to reason with him was at least as much to do with its general lack of intelligence as its disposition.

"Right. Good. It's stupid. That'll help," Fel said breathlessly.

The scorpion tail struck, but it gouged into the earth well short of him.

"And that's its range. Good. Good. Maybe I can lure it somewhere, get it stuck. If I stay in the thick woods, it should be easy enough to stay clear of that stinger."

The tail pulled back. It curled down and flicked forward, lashing like a whip. Something hissed through the air, and a row of stingers prickled the ground between him and the beast.

"What?!" he yelped, scrambling back.

He looked to the tail and watched as fresh barbs sprouted to replace those it had hurled.

"What?!"

Fel didn't wait around to see what other surprises the thing had. He dashed for a rocky hill and slid down. The monster stalked around the thicket of trees and pursued. If Fel had known the area better, he would have known better than to pick this direction to flee. The farther he got, the more sparse the trees were and the quicker the beast could follow. He vaulted over a fallen tree and huddled behind it, club in hand.

As he shakily held it, ready to bash the first piece of the creature that came into view, he realized Oiler was staring right at the weapon.

"Oiler, I see you looking at the club," he hissed. "I know you don't like weapons, but that thing after us is a bunch of weapons all wrapped up into a beast, and if you try to disarm me at the wrong time, not only am I going to die, I'm going to die mad at you."

He heard the thing step closer. He huddled down. Something hissed through the air. Wood exploded in a cloud of splinters, and the stinger of the thing's tail punched through the log barely an arm's length away. The whole log slid back a few feet as the monster tried to withdraw its tail. Fel hopped to his feet and hammered madly at the tail head. If he could break it off, that would at least be one less thing to worry about.

Oiler clearly agreed. The contraption clamped onto the head of the tail and tugged at it. Fel continued to bash at it, each blow embedding more and more of its barbs into the head of his club. Finally the monster managed to tear its tail free of the log.

Unfortunately, Oiler did not let go.

Its chain arms reeled out. Fel was yanked off his feet. The pair swung in a wide arc over the beast's head. Oiler finally got the notion to release the tail at the very apex of the arc, turning the ponderous swing into a catapult trajectory. Oiler lashed its claws out and managed to snag a tree branch as they whisked past. It slowed their flight, but didn't stop them. Instead, the branch broke free and Fel, Oiler, and the fractured limb tumbled to the ground.

Getting tossed around didn't do Fel's aching shoulder and splinted finger any good, but he was alive and in one piece, which meant pain could wait until later. He climbed to his feet. The thing thundered toward him. Fel wasn't steady enough on his feet, and was too far from dense enough trees, to flee. Whatever happened next would have to end the fight in his favor, or it would be the end of him.

He flicked his eyes back and forth between the charging beast and the thick, jagged branch that had been pulled down with them. A thought came to mind. It was a typically bad one, but that had never stopped him from putting a plan into action before. He sidled forward, club held at the ready. The thing whipped its tail. He stepped aside and felt the stingers streak by him. The thing bore down on him, great paw rising for a swipe. He held his breath, bided his time, and dropped to the ground.

The monster slammed its paw down on the jagged branch, impaling it on the wood. He scrambled to his feet and brought the club down hard on the paw, pummeling it with the barb-studded head until Oiler decided the balance of power had shifted and grabbed the club to wrench it away.

"Damn it, Oiler," Fel gasped, backing away as the thing fought to free its paw. "I can't... you need to learn..."

He wavered. Something was wrong. His arm felt cold, he looked to it and pressed his hand to the source of the growing coldness. A shallow gash had been dug into his bicep. It must have been one of the barbs that had been hurled after him.

"It... I... poison..." he murmured, slumping against a tree and sliding to the ground.

The monster finally tore its paw free. Rather than continue to face the rare creature who could actually put up a fight, it spread its wings and fled.

Fel released a breath of relief. It was almost the only thing he *could* do. His limbs felt too heavy to move. His head was swimming. There was one mercy, though. Whatever had robbed him of his ability to move had also washed away the pain of his shoulder, his hand, and the gash on his arm.

Oiler wriggled itself free from his back, hauling itself up, and perched its pack on his chest. The serpentine head gazed down at him. Expressionless, it wasn't clear if the thing felt fearful, regretful, or anything at all. After a moment of studying Fel, Oiler dragged itself out of sight, then returned with the club. It placed the weapon in his hand and returned to its perch on his chest.

Some choice words came to Fel's mind, but he lacked the will and mobility to articulate them.

For a time—it wasn't clear to him just how long—he lay there, motionless. When he heard the soft crunch of footsteps on the brush, he half expected some little weakling of a creature to kill him while he was immobile as a final spit in the eye from fate. From the sound of the crunching, it was at least three or four creatures, but they were taking care to stay out of his limited line of sight. When they finally revealed themselves, it was all at once.

Four heads popped into view. They were reptilian, blunt-nosed and variously colored and accessorized. Two of them were gray, one was green, and one was blue. Their eyes, with slit pupils fixed on him, were large and contrasted with their scales. They stood upright on hind legs that weren't quite suited for that posture, leaving them to plop down on their stout haunches whenever they weren't walking. Stubby tails jutted out behind them, and cunning arms curled in front of them. They had decidedly nonreptilian ears, or frills resembling them, which flopped down on either side of their heads. The blue one had ruffled or serrated ends on its ears. Two of the others had "jewelry" punched through the ears, though they looked more like fishhooks than earrings. If Fel were standing, they'd be perhaps half his height, but with him stuck on the ground, they towered over him. One of the gray ones hefted a patched bag bulging with his stolen gear. It held the bag over its shoulder and had Wick's lit lantern in the other hand. The others were empty-handed. They inspected him, prodding his body with claws, poking him with their snouts, and flicking tongues over him.

A fresh new list of angry threats burbled to the surface of his mind. An attempt to utter one failed to produce anything but a string of *F* and *H* sounds. The creatures chattered back and forth in a rather animated conversation in some beast tongue. The argument ended with a firm point in his direction from the green one, who he assumed was the leader of the bunch. Claws found their way beneath his arms. The leader hefted his legs onto its shoulders, and he was toted off, helpless to object. Oiler simply rode on his chest, claws folded and expression, as always, blank.

The group of creatures dragged him rather uncomfortably through the brush. As they passed into the shade of another massive tree, Fel noticed the flame in the lantern gradually become still. A moment later, Wick spoke.

"Fel! I am pleased to discover you are unhurt," Wick said.

The lack of reaction from the creatures suggested the flame had limited his communication to Fel. He used his limited range of motion to glare at the lantern.

"It appears that 'unhurt' may be an overstatement of your condition. However, you are alive, which was by no means certain until this moment. The question I grapple with now is whether I should remain here and observe what happens next, or return to one of the other lanterns and inform the others of your relative safety."

Fel narrowed his eyes, then flicked his gaze aside a few times.

"As I see nothing in the direction you have indicated, I shall interpret your desire as a request to deliver news of your present state. I will do so and return as soon as possible, though your present location makes travel somewhat more difficult for me. Take care, Fel."

#

"No, no," Martin said. "This won't do. Not enough, I need more."

Beffshire was a place where, if you had the time and the money, you could get almost anything. Unfortunately, Martin Masker was short on time, and he had an uncanny ability to find the precise border of the word "almost."

"Martin, I'm offering you everything I have," said the elderly man at the mineral stall in the market district. "We don't have much call for this quality of bronze. We have iron, we have brass, we have copper. We've got some lower-grade bronze."

"No, no. It needs to be this grade or higher. The bushings wear out too quickly otherwise."

"Then you've got every ounce the city has to offer. I can put in an order. Three, four weeks and you'll have as much as you need."

"I don't have three weeks. I don't have three *days*." He drummed his fingers. "I'll have to settle for the low-grade stuff. As much as you can spare. I'll be burning through it."

The shopkeeper nodded and started to load the crate. "I've got some more in the storehouse across town. Do you want my full supply?"

"Everything you've got."

"Two hundred duots. I'll send the lot of it over in an hour."

"Two hundred fifty," Martin said, tossing down the coins. "Make it a half hour."

The shopkeeper raised an eyebrow. "You've never struck me as an impatient man."

"I'm not impatient, I'm in a hurry. In this case there is a rather significant difference."

The shopkeeper nodded and counted off fifty coins to toss back to Martin. "You've been my best customer for years. Half an hour. Just remember who takes such good care of you."

"Much appreciated."

He turned from the stall and marched out into the street. A side effect of the width and breadth of the goods available in Beffshire was the simple fact that different items were in demand at different times. Just two streets away, the stores were overflowing with runners picking up ingredients for the restaurants to serve a lunch, tailors were picking up their fabric to prepare for their appointments from the wealthy hoping to look their best for the evening's festivities, and a dozen other little transactions. But here at the edge of town where craftspeople bought their materials, the streets were nearly deserted. That suited him. He didn't want to have to dodge a throng of people on the way back to the shop. In fact, he decided to slip through the same alley he always did. The shortcut usually got him most of the way back home without having to encounter another soul at this time of day. He'd done some of his best thinking slipping through these back alleys.

He would not be doing his best thinking today.

His mind was too busy constructing horrific scenarios for what had happened to his boy, or what might happen if he didn't do something soon. With what he'd purchased, he would be able to construct a second bolter to replace the one he'd sent with Epiphany. He wouldn't be able to produce very much in the way of ammunition, but it was just one small part of the veritable armory he was preparing for the expedition.

"I should have prepared like this for Fel. I should have sent him to the wall as well equipped as I'm equipping myself. I failed my boy. I failed my…"

Martin stopped. Something was wrong. His mind—trained through years of careful procedure—dealt with the feeling of unease the same way it dealt with everything else. He rolled his mental to-do list back a few steps to see what he'd missed. He had all the materials. He'd made the plans. But there *was* something else. Something from before he'd learned about Fel. From before his mind was seized by that task.

"Ah, yes. The Bolivans," he muttered aloud.

Boots squeaked against the cobbles of the alleyway. Now that he'd named them, the person stalking him had little use for stealth any longer. She emerged from the darkness, dressed rather unremarkably. Clearly she'd been outfitted with the intent of blending as an average Beffshire resident. Aside from noticing her oddly puffy hat, he wouldn't have had a second thought about her, if not for the fact that she'd evidently followed him into the back alleys.

"Martin Masker, you are coming with me," she said.

He slipped his hand into his pocket. "You're young, ma'am," he said. "Young enough that perhaps you don't recall precisely why the Bolivan family has chosen not to cross paths with the Masker family for all these years."

"Oh, I've heard the stories. But that was a long time ago. You're not a young man anymore."

"No. No I'm not. And maybe if I were a soldier, that would make a difference. But I'm a contraptioneer. I assure you, my skills do not degrade with time. Quite the contrary."

"Get your hand out of your pocket," she warned.

"I really suggest you just go on your way. I've had time to prepare."

She reached under the brim of her hat and pulled a thick cloth hood down, covering her face and ears. "So have we," she shouted, louder than she needed to.

Martin's jaw tightened. "Well then… it seems this may not work for what I'd intended. But the sign of a good tool is its ability to serve more than one task."

She reached for something behind her back. He pulled the modified alarm box from his pocket and tossed it. His goal in designing it was to deafen and incapacitate the target. But a fist-sized hunk of metal hurled at one's face was a fairly effective distraction regardless of its higher purpose. She raised her arm and squeezed her fist. A thread, weighted at both ends, launched from inside her sleeve. She couldn't aim properly and dodge the contraption, so the twirling snare narrowly missed Martin as he dashed down a side alley.

Behind him, the box activated, producing the ear-splitting wail it was designed to produce. The sound didn't last long. His assailant managed to snatch it up from the ground and deactivate it, but it was loud enough for long enough that it drew the attention of the locals. Martin dashed out onto a busy street just as the flow of onlookers started to funnel into the alley he was in.

He didn't stop to see if he was being followed. His stamina wasn't what it once was, and depending on how dedicated this Bolivan agent was, simply being in public wouldn't be enough to keep him safe. They'd deployed hippogriff riders not three months ago. They would certainly risk a public deployment of illegal contraptions.

As he rushed toward home, knowing all too well that he had a long way to go, he felt certain he could hear the complaints of pushed-aside residents and the stomp of pursuing boots. She was after him.

He turned a corner onto one of the city's main streets. A press of people was blocking the way, forming the traditional "half-circle of spectators" that a lifelong city-goer knew to be a sure sign of a public fight either beginning or ending. Martin angled himself and wedged through to find the epicenter of the crowd to be a man being dressed down outside the door of The Fox and Log.

"Frollo, how many times do I have to tell you? You're not welcome here anymore," Allie said, flanked by two of the larger patrons. "You know the rules. I throw you out twice in the same day, you stay out. We're *barely* open and you've already started two fights." She glanced up. "Mr. Masker?"

He looked to her, she looked to him. An impressive amount of mental arithmetic played out in her gaze. She must have worked out the proper figures, because the next words out of her mouth were shaped like an invitation but delivered like an instruction.

"Why don't you come inside, have a drink?" Allie said, stepping aside and waving him toward the door.

He hurried inside.

"Fellows, do me a favor and watch the door while I set my friend here up with a drink," she said quickly.

Martin stopped just past the doorway. "Vivian," he said.

"Davie! Head down to the Watch and let them know someone's causing trouble at the Masker place. Mel, you and Lou head down to the antique shop and say hello to Mrs. Masker until Martin gets down there. Tell her he's here, catching his breath. When you get back, next three drinks are on the house."

The diminutive gnome Davie and the other troops, having been given their orders, dashed off to fulfill them.

"There you go, Mr. Masker. Handled. Have a seat. Let me get you a drink. You're a sherry man, right?" She sat him down at the bar and dropped a basket of roasted crickets in front of him. "What's got you running around in this neck of the woods?"

"What's got me *running* is someone I believe to be a Bolivan agent," he said. She set down the sherry. He knocked it back.

"So those boys are back in town again," Allie said. "You're sure?"

"Quite."

"I didn't hear you calling for help."

"Did you hear the alarm sound?"

"For a moment."

"That was my call for help."

"See, Mr. Masker, sometimes it pays to be a little more articulate than that."

He drummed his fingers on the table. "I suppose I'm unaccustomed to being in a position where aid is actually available when it is needed. Most of the trouble I've gotten into was rather remote."

"Congratulations on graduating to the local variety. If nothing else, it's more convenient."

Martin fished some coins out of his pocket and tossed them on the table.

"No, no. It's on the house," she said.

"I pay for my drinks. I don't suppose you can spare any more of your burly patrons for an escort back home? I'd much prefer to be with my wife if this hasn't scared off the Bolivan."

Allie smirked. "You're lucky there's so many day-drinkers in this town." She raised her voice. "Who wants to help this fellow back home in exchange for knocking a chunk off your tab?"

Three hands rose. Allie slapped Martin on the back.

"On your way then. And let me know how it all turns out."

#

"Thank you, boys! I appreciate it. And remember, if you ever need any antiques, you know where to find us," Vivian said as the borrowed muscle from The Fox and Log lumbered back to the tavern for their rewards.

She watched them go, then swept the street for any other potential customers or threats. Finding none, she turned to Martin, who was in the rear of the shop beside Wick's lantern. He held a crossbow in one hand and glared out the windows with a fierceness in his eye that she'd not seen in years.

"Well?" she said. "What do we think?"

"Something is wrong," he said. "This isn't like before."

"Before we got that map or before this morning?" she said.

"Before the map, the Bolivans knew to keep their distance. Once we got it, they clearly knew we had it, but they were aggressive and sloppy. Now they're… *informed.*"

"The Bolivans do traffic in information. Not as much as the Graves, but—"

"No. Not like that. Vivian, I modified contraptions that targeted the eyes, nose, mouth, and ears. I completed the first of them days ago, and word of their functionality didn't leave this shop. The moment I encountered this woman, she pulled down a mask that protected her eyes, her nose, her mouth, and her ears."

"Common enough targets."

"Not for me. Vivian, I *know* that mask was made in response to the contraptions I prepared."

"And what does this mean?"

"I believe it means that they have been spying upon us."

"Through what means?"

"I don't know yet. But these are the Bolivans. If we assume they have been entirely avoiding assayers and keeping the contraptions they've found, we have to assume they have capabilities far beyond what we've imagined. It must be a contraption they're spying on us with. It *must* be." He glanced at Wick's lantern. The flickering flame was beginning to slow. "Was Wick not present?" Martin asked.

"I don't check on him as frequently as you, but I did notice the flickering had returned shortly after you left."

"And he didn't announce his intention to leave?"

"No. One moment he was watching, the next he wasn't."

Martin focused on the flame, waiting for it to become perfectly still. "Wick," he said sharply.

"Martin," the sentry replied.

"What did I tell you about leaving without announcing yourself?"

"I understand that it is broadly against your wishes, but I suspected that under the circumstances you would have approved."

"And what circumstances are those?"

"I observed that the lantern in Fel's possession was relit."

"What's happened to him! Where is he?" Martin said urgently.

"He is presently a considerable distance into the Greater Lands. It is not immediately obvious to me how far, because my perception of distance is somewhat fouled once I cross the boundary of the wall."

"Is he hurt?"

"That was not immediately obvious to me either. His hand was bandaged, and there was an abrasion on his arm that did not appear serious. He seemed to be having difficulty moving, but it was possible he was responding in a subdued manner in order to avoid alerting the creatures in his company of the nature of the lantern."

"Creatures?" Vivian said, for the first time seeming to be as concerned as Martin.

"He was being carried by three subtly humanoid reptiles. My lantern was being carried by a fourth, who was also carrying most of Fel's gear. Oiler was seated on Fel's chest as he was being carried."

"And Tome? What of him?" Martin asked.

"He was not present. I did not linger long enough to learn his whereabouts, as Fel indicated through gesture that I should return and inform you of his present circumstances."

"He's got it handled," Vivian said.

Her tone wasn't as certain as it had been in the past. The statement was as much to reassure herself as Martin and Wick. Martin threaded his fingers through his hair and tried to steady his breathing.

"Too much is happening, and too quickly. This feels coordinated. This feels as though they waited for us to be spread thin. And all this could be a further sign of our being spied upon."

"Spied upon?" Wick said.

"Martin clashed with a member of the Bolivan family who was defended in a way that suggests she knew the way that Martin sought to protect himself," Vivian said.

"And if they were listening, then they could easily have been listening when we were planning the expedition, and Epiphany's trip as well. … Epiphany. Wick, you need to go to Epiphany right now. Immediately. Tell her the Bolivans attacked, that we are unhurt, but they are almost certainly planning an attack upon her as well. Tell her Fel is in the Greater Lands, but he is seemingly unhurt." He clenched his fist. "Blast it, just tell her everything we know about Fel. It isn't much. When you are sure that she is safe and as prepared as she can manage, get any message she needs to send and immediately go to Fel again until you are more certain of his situation. Only when *all* of that is done should you come back and update us."

"Understood, and I shall happily provide this fulfilling service."

The flame wavered and flickered with his departure.

"You realize you can't go," Vivian said. "You can't go to Fel now."

"No. Of course not. If this was all planned around spreading the family thin, then they're just waiting until you and I separate to attack us. That's why they waited until I'd gone for materials. No. I'm staying here, both to provide some safety in numbers and to tear this place apart until I find how they are spying."

"Get started on that now, then."

"You don't want me up here with you? In case there's another attack?"

"Of the two threats—attack and espionage—I'm more concerned about the espionage. But be ready if I need you. Now get to work." She pulled her cudgel from behind the counter and placed it on top. "It's still business hours, and I don't intend to lose any money over these hooligans."

#

Epiphany gathered up her things. One of the main skills she'd learned over the years was knowing when a would-be customer had gone as far as he was going to go. She'd gotten a handshake agreement on some contraptions he would purchase if she were able to acquire them, and before she left, she would be offloading a small selection of items he'd acquired for "his personal collection." In a few minutes, she would be moving on to the more conventional parts of the trade trip. But not just yet.

Another valuable lesson she'd picked up was that sometimes the best time to ask a question was when there wouldn't be much time to answer it. Something about knowing that it was the final word, and that there wouldn't be time to go into detail, meant that one was often willing to let slip some minor detail or another that they otherwise would have played close to their chest. She'd been holding on to this particular question since she'd arrived, and now seemed the time to try it.

"You know something, sir," she said, securing a chest and sliding it into the wagon. "When you provided that page, the one that earned you the first item on your list, and with any luck will earn you the rest of those items, one of the first things my father observed was that it was simply one page of many. He and I discussed why you provided that page and only that page, and I'm not certain either of us came to a satisfactory theory."

"Your father had the tools and skills to translate it," he said simply.

"You, or I suppose your employer, must have had some idea of what the page contained, as it sure enough led us to at least one item you desired. And, though I stand by my brother's work just as much as my father's, you've expressed some dismay that you didn't get *everything* you wanted out of the resulting expedition. Why didn't you hire us to simply translate the entire book and sponsor your own expedition?"

Mr. Badgerweed laughed. "Without revealing too many details, Mrs. Masker, you would have to pay my employer for permission to translate that material in its entirety. And though we aren't entirely pleased with how comprehensive your work has been, we are of the opinion that, as a whole, the combination of tasks was and is best served by the Maskers."

The flame of her lantern shifted and slowed. A voice became softly audible in her ears.

"Epiphany, your father and mother are well. As is your brother, in relative terms. But each has befallen some degree of misfortune. At present your parents are in particular concerned that you might be in danger of an attack by the Bolivans. They tried and failed to assault and/or kidnap your father, and there is the suggestion that they have been spying and might be well aware of your travel plans. If they are coordinated, their next attack may be forthcoming," Wick said quickly.

She didn't allow her expression to falter. "Mister…" She tipped her head. "You know, sir, I don't believe I've ever formally learned your name, despite our many communications."

"No, you haven't."

"You choose strange things to be cagey about, sir. But regardless, I wonder—for my own edification—what security precautions do you take? Over the course of a journey like this, you are sure to accumulate considerable amounts of currency and inventory. I've often wondered just how the traveling bazaar avoids being taken advantage of by brigands."

"You'll note that during this trip, and indeed in our meeting some months ago in Beffshire, you only ever did business with me, at least with regard to those traveling in my wagon. That's because my associates haven't been hired for their business acumen."

She looked them over. Both men did have the air of someone waiting for the opportunity to engage in violence. That was hardly a rare trait in people who spent much of their time on lengthy journeys. She always took particular care when her trading trips brought her to port towns. There were few people better primed for a fight than a sailor fresh off the sea. But a bazaar often had more amenities than the cities it visited, so their simmering, pent-up nature could certainly imply their status as bodyguards.

Epiphany weighed her options. "How much longer is the bazaar due to remain in this town?"

"Three more days. I believe a secondary caravan is going to be crossing paths with us to exchange goods."

"Is it, now? Well, I can't very well leave before that, now can I? I look forward to further conversation, sir."

"I'm sure it will prove mutually enlightening."

He paced away. Epiphany made something of a show of removing her chests again to prepare for a few more days of trade.

"Wick," she whispered.

"Yes, Epiphany."

"Tell Mom and Dad I'm going to stay with the bazaar for now. If there *is* an attack, I'd rather it happen while there are others to hunker down with. And if the Bolivans don't come along in a few days, it will at least give us time to make a better plan."

"I will do so when next I journey to the Beffshire lantern. My next trip will be to look over Fel. Before I do, would you like a more thorough account of what we know?"

"Right, yes. Let's have a proper update, now that I can talk without raising too much attention."

Wick dictated the details he knew. As she learned of what had happened, and surmised what had been kept from her until now, her expression became more dire.

"A couple of months ago, we wondered if that was the beginning of something or the end of it. I think we have our answer."

"It does appear a larger scheme is afoot, though there is no reason to suppose that Fel's own misfortune is a part of that scheme."

"Mmm… It makes me wonder if Fel would be facing Bolivan agents of his own if he hadn't found a way to get mixed up in the Greater Lands… Go to him now, Wick. I have a feeling he's going to need a lot more help than the rest of us."

#

Fel had been dragged over untold miles by the odd little reptile creatures. By now, it should have been worrying him that his strength had yet to return. Fortunately, the creatures had provided him ample distraction. That distraction came in three distinct forms. First, they took far less care where they were dragging him than he would have liked. It wasn't so bad while a single creature was carrying both of his legs. When they decided to switch and assign each leg to a different creature, however, his spread legs quickly started plowing up whatever odd bit of brush they trudged through. More than once they'd decided to go on either side of a tree, which hammered home reality that whatever venom he'd been injected with didn't make him *wholly* immune to pain.

Another source of distraction, not quite so unpleasant but just as constant, was the song. The creatures were downright musical. Hoots, growls, squeaks, and squawks filled the air, each creature's call gradually enfolding and mimicking the others in a sort of bestial round. The whole performance was almost unbearably merry. It would have been endearing, if not for the first issue, and the one that he was just now coping with. This last one managed to easily shove aside all his other concerns.

Wherever they were going required a *great* deal of climbing.

At the moment, he was dangling from his feet, hanging upside down while the other two creatures propped him with their little shoulders in a *very* poorly coordinated bit of tandem climbing. His dangling head treated him to a perfect, inverted view of a sheer cliff. If any of his escorts slipped, there was no doubt in his mind that his journey would end as a particularly unpleasant stain on the slate-blue stone of the cliff. Oiler would have fallen from his perch on Fel's chest ages ago if he'd not coiled his tail around to hold tight and patiently wait to see where this journey was leading.

The song reached a harmonious climax just as he heard the scampering of additional claws and felt himself hauled the last short distance up the cliff's face quite quickly. He was dragged to a section of flat ground and left staring into the blue sky, only for his vision to fill with the curious heads of half a dozen of the odd creatures. Three of them propped him up into a sitting position. Oiler slipped down to his lap. He finally got a view of what he'd been brought to.

It was sight enough to reveal his limited capacity for speech still had enough range for a single, slightly slurred word.

"Wow…"

They weren't at the very top of the cliff, as he could see that it continued far enough that the peak was hidden behind mist or clouds. The plateau before him was quite expansive, though. Three times wider than the street in front of this shop at home and following the contour of the cliff as far as he could glimpse in either direction. The entirety of the cliff face in front of him was covered with etched patterns and symbols. Some were crude, some were quite elegant. And all served to accent the yawning mouth of a cave that was quite clearly formed by pick and shovel rather than by nature. Iron torches with fluted tops smoldered with an unnatural white fire, providing ample light for what looked like a sort of open-air throne room. A long path of polished stone led to the throne in question, though perhaps the word "perch" would have fit more properly, as it was primarily a golden rod suspended between two sculptural holders. And balanced atop that rod was something Fel had only read about in dusty old history books. A greater harpy.

A far cry from the glorified crows that squabbled over shiny buttons and pastries in Beffshire, she was… she was precisely what one ought to picture when one pictured a harpy. She had a face, quite human, albeit with long and hawkish features. Her feathers were a gorgeous, gleaming onyx black. They flowed from her shoulders almost like a robe. Rather than hair, she had a crest of narrower, black-and-white-peppered feathers. Her eyebrows were a long and wispy match for them. She lacked arms in the traditional sense. In place were magnificent wings held daintily up on either side of her body. Her legs were powerful and ended in cruel talons. From its shape, Fel supposed she had a broadly human torso as well, but it was draped in some manner of silver mail tunic. She gazed at him with a cold, judgmental eye.

One by one, the creatures who had dragged him here approached her. Two quietly hopped to a pair of lower perches on either side of her. The others stood before her and began chattering at her. She observed them and seemed to understand their speech, but offered nothing in reply until they'd finished their account. When they were through, she hopped gracefully from the perch and plodded along the ground toward Fel. The creatures on either side of her scurried along to keep pace.

The harpy leaned down to look Fel in the eye.

"This, I believe, is the proper tongue, is it not?" she asked.

Fel's eyebrow twitched. Though she was simply speaking, her voice had an odd quality to it. It was sharp, yet not piercing. Like it was designed for song and was reluctantly lowering itself to the coarse act of speech.

She nodded. "I see recognition in your eyes. You are a stranger to these parts, so I suspect you will need this… state you are in explained to you."

As she spoke, she made the slightest motions with the tips of her wings. The two creatures on either side of her seemed to react to those motions as though they were commands. They poked and prodded him, lifting legs and pulling away the remnants of the less than ideal route they'd taken through the brush. They took special care to avoid getting too close to Oiler, however.

"That beast you faced? It was a manticore. A greater manticore, though I don't think that distinction comes as a surprise to you." One of the creatures pulled aside his arm to reveal the gash to her. "Ah, here I see. Quite a minor abrasion and still it laid you low. At least your kind are as frail as ours in the face of such a beast. And as fate would have it, you've brought along everything we require to relieve you of this malady."

The creature to her left raised his club, which had been hauled along with the rest of this things.

"The blood and venom of the manticore can be rendered into an antidote. It is a simple concoction and acts quite swiftly."

Her left- and right-hand creatures dashed away and returned with mortar and pestle. They pried one of the bloodstained stingers from the club and dropped it in the bowl. It was joined by a few leaves and a splash of water. When the ingredients were through being added, they started working the combination into a paste.

"This won't take a moment, and then the conversation can be a bit less stunted. Until then, let's clear away the… *thing*."

Two additional creatures tottered up and grabbed Oiler by the straps. They tried to haul it away, but each time they made it more than a few steps, Oiler extended tail and claw and dragged itself—and them—back toward Fel. They settled for leaving the pack beside Fel rather than atop him. The harpy observed it with a degree of distaste.

"That, stranger, is going to be a point of discussion." She turned to some of the other helper creatures. "Fetch the other one."

Two of the creatures scampered off. The harpy leaned down to inspect the contents of the mortar. She nodded. The creature to her left produced a smooth wooden spatula of some kind and scooped up a portion of the foul-smelling stuff. The creature to the right climbed onto Fel's lap and held his mouth open.

He did his best to resist, but the lingering effects of the venom were such that through supreme effort the best he was able to do was turn his head slightly to the left. A cunning paw to the cheek nudged his head forward again, and the spatula was inserted into his mouth. A concoction with what was handily the most pungent scent and horrid flavor he'd ever experienced smeared across his tongue. The results were immediate. He could feel the paralysis start to fade, beginning with his gag reflex. He tried to spit it out, but the helpful little creatures clamped his mouth shut and grinned at him until he, with no other options, gulped the stuff down. The harpy nodded, and they retreated to her side. He spat out the remnants.

"Where am I? What is going on?" he said, once he had enough control over his lips to enunciate it.

"You are in the Greater Lands. I should think that much would be clear. It takes enough effort to come here, I would like to think you couldn't end up here by accident," she said.

"Fel?" came a familiar voice.

He used his newly restored control over his neck to turn aside. Tome appeared from a small side alcove. He dashed over and crouched beside Fel.

"You survived!" he said. "Isn't this a fascinating, glorious place?"

Fel glared at him. "Are we in the same place, Tome?"

The difference in their experiences was evident, even at a glance. While Fel looked like he'd been pummeled by a wild animal and dragged through the wilderness, because he had, Tome looked better than he had during the trip to the wall. He was freshly bathed. His hair was tamed. Even the holes in his clothes had been patched. Tome took stock of this disparity.

"Right, er. You've had a rough patch or two. But the important thing is you're here now, and I assure you, these people will take good care of you."

"Bind his hands before he regains use of them," the harpy said.

"What?" said Tome and Fel at the same time.

"Tome, you are here because I assumed you'd know this man. It would be a vanishingly rare occurrence that two outsiders appear here in the same day and don't know one another. But your friend here is still an unknown quantity."

"Did they tie *you* up when you first got here?" Fel asked as he was gently tipped forward and his arms were crossed behind his back and bound at the wrists.

"They did not. But I am a rather more charming person than you are, let's not forget."

"Your disposition had little to do with it. Currently the matter at hand is your associate. Silence yourself or be silenced," said the harpy.

"Now, really. That—"

"Gag him," she said simply.

The gaggle of creatures descended upon Tome, looking a little too gleeful to have the opportunity to pull a length of fabric tight across his mouth.

"Alright. So you're not all bad," Fel said.

"Your name is Fel, correct?" she said.

"Yeah. Fel Masker."

Her nostrils flared a bit at the name. The assorted creatures looked to one another, as if expecting guidance about something.

"I am the Adept. I'm sure you have questions. And I'm sure you realize you are in a compromising position. I shall answer those questions I suspect are foremost on your mind, and then I shall ask some of my own. If you answer them to my satisfaction, you will be afforded as much freedom as is sensible to allow, understood?"

"Yeah, I got it."

She nodded appreciatively. "Your cooperation is appreciated. I'll begin with why you had to be bound. To be frank, I am rather concerned that you were able to fight off a greater manticore with a half-rotten piece of wood."

"I wouldn't call it a clean win."

"That there is any evidence of you remaining to be found is a far greater achievement than most who have clashed with the beast. Manticores consume their prey whole. I wouldn't have believed you'd actually faced the creature if not for the venom that paralyzed you. And, of course, that my left and right hand witnessed your actions."

"Your right and left hand…"

The creatures perked up and puffed their chests out proudly.

"I lack the dexterity for some tasks, Mik and Stix serve as my hands. You have my gratitude for rescuing them, and the others, from where they'd hidden themselves when the manticore approached. But someone who could best a manticore is someone I do not wish to have running free without some assurance you will not be a threat to us."

“I didn’t do it alone. Oiler helped,” Fel said.

“Oiler. That would be your contraption?”

“One of them. Your critters stole the rest of them.”

“Yes…” She turned and glanced to the throne area.

Her left hand—Stix, apparently—bounded off, grabbed the bag, and bounded back. She held it open. Mik pulled out the puzzle box and shakily held it up for inspection.

“What is the purpose of this device?” the harpy asked.

“It’s a puzzle. Mix up the faces and Oiler will solve it for you,” Fel said.

“Is that Oiler’s purpose? Solving puzzles?”

“Oiler’s purpose is fixing things and causing problems. It splits those two down the middle.”

She nodded. Mik set the puzzle box down.

“You will identify the rest of them. We will continue from there.”

One by one they emptied the sack and laid out the items while Fel explained their purposes. He was forthcoming, for the most part. The only exception was Wick’s lantern, which he simply identified as “A lantern that stays lit once lit.”

It was rather fascinating to watch her and her “hands” work. She didn’t seem to be instructing them. Their movements precisely matched what the harpies hands would be doing, based upon her desire and expression. The trio made short work of the contents of the bag. She stepped up and leaned over him while they tugged at his clothes to uncover the minor tools he was carrying. Last was the sparker. He explained its purpose.

“Why were you carrying this contraption on your person?” the harpy asked.

“It was the only one I found. And I always keep it in my shirt pocket. It’s a family heirloom, sort of.”

He winced as they shifted him about to make sure they’d not missed anything. The motion did not go unnoticed.

“Is there something wrong?”

“My shoulder is hurt, my finger is busted, and I have a hole in my arm. Now that you cleared away the venom, the pain is back.”

Mik reached up to cradle her chin, then scrambled to the Adept’s shoulder to brush her crest.

“My apologies. It is inappropriate of me to let you suffer, and I should have assumed you would have further wounds after your clash. Can you walk?”

“I have no idea.”

She glanced aside. “Help him. And take care of the bandaged hand, the abrasions on the arm and… forgive me, which shoulder?”

“The left.”

The cluster of helpers hefted him to his feet. His knees and thighs were not overly fond of the prospect of supporting his weight, but with a little help, he was able to stay upright.

"This way. We shall treat you," she said. "Tome, can you be trusted to hold your tongue?"

He nodded.

"Ungag him and bring him."

"Is it my turn to ask questions?" Fel asked, shuffling along with three reptiles cheerfully keeping him from tipping.

Oiler jangled along beside him. Everyone gave the contraption a wide berth, and two creatures quite conspicuously hefted clubs as they followed behind it.

The Adept marched forward, giving him a view of the fan of tail feathers that from the front had looked more like the train of a gown than a piece of anatomy.

"Not just yet." Stix held up a finger. "A final point that I feel is relevant, as it will color our relationship for as long as it lasts. To put it bluntly, we do not like contraptions. We like contraptioneers even less. And least of all do we like Maskers."

"My family has a reputation here?" he said.

"Your profession does."

Tome looked at Fel. "You didn't tell me it was an occupational surname."

Fel furrowed his brow.

"You didn't *know* it was an occupational surname." He turned to the Adept. "What is a masker?"

"If the profession is lost to antiquity, that is best for us all." She looked over her shoulder. "But it raises the question, what *is* your stock and trade?"

"I fix and sell contraptions."

"As I feared."

They'd moved far enough into the primary alcove to reveal that, just beyond where the sun reached, dozens more of the little reptiles were milling about. They were engaged in a dozen tasks. Sorting, painting, cooking, and otherwise doing the things that a community required to remain functional.

"That you came here, and that you carried so many of those contraptions and the means to repair them, would normally be reason enough to have you killed. We do not want your kind here. However. Your behavior is not that of a creature driven by malice and destruction." She addressed a handful of the creatures. "Treat him."

The creatures chirped and chattered happily and scampered over to him. They croaked and squeaked in their odd little language, clearly discussing him and what was to be done about him. Their treatment was not gentle, but it was swift and effective. They set about cleaning the gash and inspecting his hand and shoulder.

"You brought more tools than weapons," the Adept said, hopping onto the perch of a throne.

"I didn't come here to fight. I didn't even intend to come here at all. The plan was to claim some stuff from inside the wall, and Oiler here decided it was a better idea to set off a trap than leave it dismantled."

Her expression became subtly more intense. "Dismantled. You dismantled something inside the wall?"

"Yes. Is that good or bad?"

"In our experience, rare is the contraption which can be easily dismantled. Stix tells me she was able to break the puzzle box, which I see you have restored, but most of the things here require more destructive power to disable than we are able to achieve."

"When you know how to fix something, it usually means you know how to break it, too."

Stix hopped over the lower perch and drummed her claws on it while the Adept thought. She mulled over whatever was on her mind for nearly a minute while Fel endured the treatment of the creatures. They started to apply salves, manipulating the position of his finger with gradually decreasing pain each time.

"It should not surprise me that the first outsiders to come to this place in recent memory might have a grand purpose, but I had not supposed that such a purpose would be of benefit to us."

"Hey, I'll do anything you want if it means getting out of here in one piece."

"That decision is not mine to make. But you've at least earned an audience with the one who does make such decisions."

Stix tottered over to a bowl on a shelf and scampered back. She climbed onto the perch and held it up for her to drink.

"For the moment, I am satisfied. Your hands will be untied, and you will be free to move about the plateau, but you will be watched closely, and any indiscretions treated with the appropriate discipline. If you have questions, you may ask them now."

The bindings on his wrists were unfastened. He rubbed them and found, to his surprise, that the pain of his broken finger had reduced to an uncomfortable stiffness, and his slashed arm looked like it had been given several days to heal in just the last few minutes.

After having his head filled with questions and other more vigorous thoughts since he'd begun his indelicate journey, he found that it was difficult to select one. When a piece of roasted meat was thrust in his face by a grinning reptile, he accepted it and decided that was as good a place as any to start.

"What are these things?" Fel said. "Lesser dragons?"

All creatures in earshot produced a positively delighted squeal. The nearest one practically swooned.

"They're kobolds, Fel," Tome said. "Do you know nothing about the mystics of the Greater Lands?"

"Pretty much nothing," he said. "Are they greater or lesser? Because they kind of look like they could be lesser dragons."

Another wave of delight from the kobolds. He was handed another, larger hunk of meat from a kobold who fluttered its eyes and chirruped sweetly at him.

"What's this all about?" he said.

"Kobolds worship dragons. To be confused for one is a profound compliment," the Adept said. "And you'll get nowhere currying favor with them. As for the question of lesser versus greater, it isn't clear. Most of the Lesser Mystics have left the Greater Lands, so we must assume the kobolds are greater. But I know of no lesser version of them, even in antiquity. A bit of a mystery."

"Why don't you like contraptions?"

"Tomorrow you will be taken to meet Kazel. When you do, the answer to that question should become obvious."

"Who is Kazel?"

"Kazel is the dragon of this mountain and our master."

"A dragon, huh. I think I met him already."

"I assure you, you have not."

"If you say so. I guess the big question is, what are the odds we get out of this alive and get to go home?"

"I have a task in mind. If you succeed, I can assure you, not only will you survive, but you will be honored among us. If you fail? Unless you take action against us, I believe there is no threat in letting you live, perhaps without your equipment. No sense giving you rope to hang yourself with. But the question of you returning home, back past the wall? That may prove challenging."

"Why?"

"The wall is built to keep things in. And it does so quite effectively. But if you help us, we will make reasonable attempts to help you. However suicidal they may be."

"And what happens between now and whenever you take us to see Kazel?"

"You are free to move about the plateau and any of the caves and alcoves that are accessible. You will both be watched carefully, but you will otherwise be made comfortable. Your equipment will remain here, defended. All of it. Including Oiler."

"I think you'll find that Oiler isn't going to want to stay put. He's clingy."

"We will do what is necessary."

He looked at the contraption beside him. It was gazing about, fingers clattering together idly, simply waiting for what was next.

"Is there anything else before I return to my duties?" the Adept asked.

Fel took a bite of the meat he'd been offered. It was beyond gamy, but worlds better than nothing at all, which is what he was expecting.

"I don't suppose you've got something to drink. Something with a little kick to it?"

She raised her head, looking down her nose at him in an even more measuring look. "I'm not entirely certain the spirits we have won't kill you."

"I'm being gently held captive by an army of creatures I only vaguely suspected existed a couple of hours ago. And I'm in a part of the world that most people don't survive to return from. If the rotgut I've been living on for the past few years hasn't gotten rid of me, I'm willing to take my chances with whatever you've got if it means chasing off reality for a while."

She allowed herself a grin and turned to one of the other kobolds. "Fill him a cup. But watch him. I don't want him to die until Kazel has had his say."

#

A short time later, Fel sat on a stiff cushion in one of the alcoves near the throne room. It was directly opposite the barred section of the cave where his equipment was being kept, including Wick's flickering lantern. He'd finished the meat they'd given him, but was only halfway through a glass of what *they* called mead. If he were a smart man, he would have given up after the second sip, because the stuff kicked like a mule and every sip was a battle to get down his gullet. But at this point, it was personal. He wasn't going to leave this place knowing he'd been bested by a single cup of booze.

He glanced around. Five kobolds and Tome were all watching him like they expected his head to pop off his neck and roll down the mountain at any moment. He took another sip. One of the kobolds, the blue one with the frilled ears that was among his rescue crew, giggled and clapped. Another leaned forward, mouth hanging open.

"Is that stuff any good?" Tome asked.

"It's great," he said, the reply more wheeze than voice. Fel took a breath or two and hammered his chest until the burning stopped. "So… we're prisoners, yeah?"

"As incarceration goes, this isn't so bad," Tome said.

"I'm entertainment for a bunch of little dragon things."

The audience chattered happily. He raised the glass to salute them.

"Do they speak our language?" he asked. "I know they understand it, but do they speak it?"

"I've wondered that myself. The texts I read had nothing to say on the subject, but I believe—"

Fel mashed his palm against Tome's face in an overshot attempt at a gesture to silence him. He turned to the kobolds. "Do you speak my language?"

They turned to each other and chattered among themselves. There was much hand pointing and head shaking. Finally, the blue one reluctantly stepped forward. The creature's expression was that of a child who had been called to the front of the class to answer a question they hoped wouldn't be asked.

"No… talking. Hard… for… tongue… and… lips," the beast croaked in a voice that sounded like it was being wrung out of it.

The other kobolds slapped their orator on the back to congratulate them for the effort.

"Thanks, buddy." Fel fought down another sip, much to the mounting amusement of the kobolds. "You know, when I was a kid, my parents used to talk *about* my sister *in front* of my sister. She was little, so they figured she wasn't smart enough to figure out what they were up to. And I realized they probably did it to me. I *hated* that. But I'm drunk, and you critters are going to be listening to everything I say, so I guess I'm just going to have to get comfy about talking about you in front of you, even though I know you can understand me."

They nodded in unison, no suggestion that they had any opinion about it one way or the other. He turned to Tome.

"How many of these critters do you think I could take? You know. If it came down to it."

"Are you asking how many you could defeat in unarmed combat?"

"Yeah. You know. High end. I'm thinking I could take four or five."

The audience giggled and exchanged knowing chatter.

"Fel, I don't think it matters how many you'd be able to fight off, because the number you'd *have* to fight off is 'all of them.' Kobolds are swarm fighters, and they are fiercely devoted to their masters."

Fel held out his hand, estimating the nearest creature's height against his own. "I think I could take five. How many could you take? You with your magic and everything."

"Presently? Not one. Not yet, anyway. Setting aside that they've locked up my quill, ink, and pages, there's something off about this place. Something so thoroughly unlike the outside that my spells are a fraction of their strength, at least as written. I'll need to develop an entirely new vocabulary to craft a fully effective spell here. I'm speaking figuratively, of course. I'll be using the same language, but I'll—"

"You could have stopped at 'none.'"

"Mmm… On the other hand, there are plants here that I think could make particularly potent paper. Over by the edge of the plateau, where it begins to slope down into a cliff again. Very broad leaves. Very fibrous. And they have a quality to them that very much reminds me of the top-quality paper back home even *before* being processed."

"Paper. Great."

"I'm telling you I could cast *profoundly* powerful spells with this paper. That should be interesting to you. If we *do* get out of here, we should see about opening some sort of a trade for this stuff. I would suggest we find a way to grow it back home, but I have my doubts that would be possible."

"I'd ask why, but I don't care."

"It's because this place is so mystically different from—"

"I don't *care.*"

Tome crossed his arms. "You were a far more tolerable conversationalist during the trip."

"Guess this stuff is a good lip loosener."

He muscled down another sip, then leaned aside. The blue kobold who had demonstrated the difficulty of conversation was holding his sparker, contentedly watching the light dance in its shiny surface.

"Hey," he said. "Does your boss know you have that?"

The kobold looked up at him, then held the device close to its chest.

"Hey, little…" He turned to Tome. "Do these things come in the usual types? Boys and girls, stuff like that?"

"If I recall correctly, the ones with the serrated edges on those ear frills are female and the smooth-eared ones are males," Tome said.

Five of the kobolds nodded. One waggled a paw.

"Hey little lady," Fel said to the one with the sparker. "Wanna see a trick? Push down that little thing there. The lever thing."

She narrowed her eyes and tipped her head, distrustful. The others turned to observe. After a brief internal struggle, she squinted, extended her arms, and pressed the lever. A dazzling little spray of sparkles erupted from the top. Instantly she grinned ear to ear and held it close, flicking the lever again and again.

"You think that's good. Use it near something that'll burn. It lights things on fire. You know. Like dragons do."

She squeaked and held the device reverently before her. Two of the others attempted to snatch it, so she dashed away. They followed. The other three remained behind.

"I question the wisdom of teaching them to use that," Tome said.

"I'm drunk on magic mead. You're expecting wisdom?"

"Honestly, I was expecting you to try to pummel the beast and take the sparker back."

He shrugged. "Eh, let the little critters play. My dad let me play with it when I was their age."

"These creatures are probably our age or older, Fel."

Another round of nods.

"Their size, then."

With the thinned-out group of chaperons, he got a clearer view of the chamber with their gear. Or, at least, as clear a view as the booze would permit. For some reason, they'd neglected to extinguish Wick's lantern, and it was presently perfectly still. Wick was watching and listening. He didn't know how *long* he had been listening, but he was definitely listening now.

"All things considered," he said loudly. "I'd say we're being pretty well taken care of. No ropes, no chains. Healthy. They may even have a way out of here for us soon. Yes, yes indeed. If I had one bit of information I'd want to send home to my folks, it would be that we're safe and not in any danger right now. That's what I'd want them to know right now, without delay."

The flame shifted and flickered. Fel grinned, convinced that the message had been delivered with the utmost of subtlety. "I don't know about you, but I've got a good feeling about this," he said.

"The situation isn't ideal," Tome said. "But if I had to choose between stalking along for days and days worried two lunatics on hippogriffs would attack from above and sitting here surrounded by amicable creatures, I know what I would choose. I probably wouldn't feel the same if I were you, though. They were fairly clear about disliking not just contraptions but your family trade."

"Eh. I'm used to people hating my guts. At least these folks are open about it."

The female kobold streaked through the cave, holding the sparker in one hand and a flaming pillow in the other. She was squealing gleefully while three other kobolds chased her.

"I like these critters," Fel said with a chuckle.

Joseph R. Lallo

Chapter 6

"Fel Masker!" shouted the Adept.

Fel snorted awake and immediately regretted it. His mouth had the flavor and texture of the underside of a farmer's boot, and his head was throbbing so intensely that he was afraid his brain was trying to escape. Nevertheless, the powerful voice of the harpy, when sculpted to the purpose of anger and reprimand, had a way of motivating one to action.

"Huh, what?" he said, rubbing his bleary eyes.

The harpy was standing over him. Stix had the sparker in her hand. Mik had an armload of assorted charred items in his arms. The female he'd taught to use the sparker had soot smeared on her nose and was standing with her head lowered like a scolded child. The harpy's posture suggested she had planned to give Fel a talking to. Her expression was decidedly more confused.

"Is that... a lesser unicorn?" she said.

Fel glanced down to discover Parch nestled up against his side. "Oh, hey. How'd you find your way here, little fella?" he said, patting the sleeping creature on the side.

"You *know* this beast?" the Adept said, more out of fascination than accusation.

"This is Parch," he said. "Last time we came to the wall, this little critter was thirsty, and once I gave him a drink, he wouldn't leave me alone. He pulls the cart now. I don't know how he got here, though. We left him outside."

Parch, disturbed by the commotion, raised his head. He bleated and trotted up to perch rather uncomfortably on the still-reclining Fel.

"Easy with the hooves, Parch. I've sort of taken a beating."

The Adept crouched. Mik set down the burnt items and scurried forward to give Parch a scratch.

"We don't get Lesser Mystics within the wall much anymore," the Adept said, smiling vaguely as the unicorn was scratched on her behalf. "They don't last long here. The dangers are too great for so diminished a creature."

"I didn't even want him coming into the wall." He glared at Parch. "Which is why I left you with food and water on the other side and told you to stay put."

"It would take a tremendous connection, not only for a Lesser Mystic to cross the barrier of the wall of its own accord but for it to follow all the way here. We take care to leave few signs of our passage."

"Your kobolds dragged me across the landscape on my rear end. I think there's probably a path to follow," Fel said.

Mik lowered his head, Parch lowered his. The two playfully butted one another, though the kobold had to take a bit of care to avoid being hit by the horn too directly. Her skill at doing so suggested she had some experience with the game.

"I sense there is more to the connection than a willingness to follow a trail in the sand. Clearly my initial assessment that you are potentially trustworthy despite your contraptions was not wholly unwarranted."

Tome rolled from his own cushion and sat up. "Ah," he said with a stretch. "Another fine day. And how shall we fill it?"

The Adept looked to him, then back to Mik. The kobold scurried back and dashed toward the cubby that held their things.

"For now, you will fill the day with answers." Mik returned and held up the lantern. "What is this?"

"Like I said yesterday, it's a lantern that stays lit."

The harpy's expression hardened. "Tell me, Fel Masker. Are the rules different on the outside? Is something not offensive if one simply neglects to admit to the offense?"

He rubbed his face. Throughout his life, it had been very carefully hammered into him that Wick's lantern and its behavior were a family secret. He'd lived for more than twenty years without sharing the secret with anyone. Even as a child, when the whole point of a secret seemed to be to share it, he'd kept quiet about Wick. To tell someone else of him was to lose him, and perhaps cause the family a great deal of trouble. A few months ago, Tome had been the first person outside the family to be told of Wick. Now, so soon after, Fel had to decide if it was worth testing his host's knowledge. He might have attempted to be a bit more cagey if his head wasn't throbbing horribly. Simply talking was enough of a challenge, let alone being evasive enough to fool a harpy who seemed to know more about his own history than he did.

"It's a sentry lantern. The flame is still, which means Wick is here. Say hello, Wick."

"Hello, Fel and friends of Fel. It is pleasing to me to be able to speak freely in the presence of so many new people," Wick said.

Mik trembled at the disembodied voice. The Adept remained firm.

"Are you spying on us, Masker?" she asked.

"I wasn't even planning on coming *into* the Greater Lands. And these critters dragged me up the mountain, remember? None of this was my plan.

Wick is here to keep track of me, to deliver messages, and to learn stuff my dad might want to know. If you've got stuff you want to be secret, just keep him away from those, ask him not to talk about it, or extinguish the flame."

Mik slapped his paw against the wick, snuffing out the fire.

"Why didn't you tell me what this was when I first asked?"

"Because I'm surrounded by strange creatures who don't like me very much, and that's not a very safe place to be. If our situations were reversed, I think you'd do the same thing."

"Our situations would never *be* reversed. Because I have no desire to encroach upon someone else's land." She crouched.

Stix scrambled up to her shoulder. She ran her paw over the Adept's crest and scratched idly at the harpy's chin.

"I am the Adept. I am so called because I am the one expected to have the expertise necessary to operate this community from day to day. Rarely do I have any doubt or confusion about anyone or anything. Seldom do I have to change my mind. But since your arrival, I have had to change my mind, and change my plans, about you half a dozen times. You are a conundrum, Fel Masker. A disruption. And it is as frustrating as it is fascinating."

"I've been told I'm frustrating. Fascinating is new."

"I am not entirely pleased by fascinating things. They complicate matters."

"Yeah. I've been told I complicate things too."

Stix hopped down and held up the sparker.

"Why did you instruct Teya how to use this contraption?"

He groaned. "I was drunk, I thought it would be funny, and I thought she'd like to know, what with the fire and how kobolds like dragons."

"She set fire to quite a few things before we were able to stop her. And then she *hid* the contraption from me when I asked how she'd accomplished it. You are a bad influence. But like mead, even things with negative effects do not necessarily have no good use. It is morning. I let you sleep because, to be frank, three prior attempts to wake you failed. You really shouldn't have had so much mead."

"Yes, I'm getting that message loud and clear from my head."

"You are about to be taken to Kazel. All final decisions are made by Kazel, and thus what happens to you depends upon how well you acquit yourself before him. Be respectful, ask no questions unless prompted, and if I were you, I would attempt to be as helpful as possible. Depending on Kazel's whims, you will either be allowed to be a part of our community, be banished, be helped to escape, or be killed outright."

"Er… Am I a part of this? Because if I am, I would much prefer to be considered separately," Tome said.

"You will be permitted to make your own case, but all of you will be taken to be judged at the same time."

"All of us?"

"You, Tome, Oiler, and Teya."

"Why Oiler? And why Teya?"

"The contraption has the semblance of thought and motion, and cannot be simply banished as the sentry lantern could. Thus, it is subject to the judgment of our leader. And Teya used a contraption without permission and caused chaos. Punishment must be considered."

"No, no. It was my fault, I—"

Both Mik and Stix raised their paws.

"Actions have consequences, Masker. Save your pleas for Kazel. This matter is out of my hands. Now come. This way."

#

Martin removed a plate from the last piece of unfinished contraption in the current crate. Working in the workshop, five floors below the surface, had its benefits and its problems. One of the problems, which he seldom concerned himself with, was the lack of a reasonable way of knowing what time it was without looking at a clock. Despite the endless heaps of contraptions, most of which now stood in piles of dismantled parts around him, he didn't actually have a clock. He relied upon his family to beckon when he was needed, and otherwise he cared little if he was working into the night or the morning.

Another thing that he'd typically considered an asset of working so far below the ground was the constant coolness. Summer or winter, he found he seldom needed more or less than a light jacket. He kept his woodstove smoldering most of the time, as he did now, but all things being equal, he would rather be a little too cold than a little too hot. Alas, at the moment, he was sweating. Such was the feverish and harried pace at which he'd been pushing himself.

There was no telling what sort of contraption was being used to spy on him. Working with contraptions throughout his entire life, contrary to giving him the feeling that he knew all there was to know, had served only to underscore just how *little* he knew. He'd encountered the smallest fraction of the total variety of contraptions, and he understood the operation of a fraction of *that*. So a contraption capable of spying on him could come in any shape, any size. The only thing he knew for certain was that he'd kept close notes on the contraptions in his home that were in a functional state. It was the first and most important thing he assessed about any of the items brought in by Fel or Epiphany, or purchased by Vivian—did it work? If it did, he could take time to determine what it did and how it did it. If it didn't, he could take time to determine what it *should* do and why it wasn't doing it. But the first and most important skill he'd learned from his father was how to identify a contraption that was at least *capable* of operation. If he found something in an operational state, and it wasn't on his official inventory, then that thing might well be the keyhole that his enemies were peeping through.

All the intact contraptions were accounted for and dismissed some time ago. But contraptions were sometimes quite large, and something could be hidden inside of one. And then there were the antiquities that Vivian kept. All containers had to be checked. Heavy crates had to be moved. Floorboards had to be pried up. He was working himself to the bone, and still he hadn't found anything.

"Nothing," he muttered, pulling out the last large component of the contraption and peering inside. He mopped sweat from his forehead and muttered to himself. "So much more to do. Perhaps a bit more briskness will help keep me awake."

He opened his woodstove and spritzed water to extinguish the lingering embers. A spritz to his own face woke him up a bit. Before setting down the water sprayer—another vintage item that had been in the family nearly as long as the oven itself, he popped it open to inspect it. Nothing was above suspicion.

The last of the embers sizzled away, but the oven held its heat well. He decided to move up to the next floor and give the workshop time to cool down further. Upon arriving on the next floor, he realized it was even more crowded with dismantled items than the workshop. He decided instead to climb to the shop level. Vivian would want an update regardless.

He lingered in the stairwell of the shop until she finished with her current customer, then emerged.

"Anything worthwhile?" he asked.

"We finally sold that old painting that was taking up space on the shelf," she said. "Anything?"

"Nothing notable. But there are still crates and crates left to go through. And even if nothing turns up there, we still have to consider that there is some means to spy on us from a distance. Anything from Wick?"

"Nothing. Not since last night."

He walked to the counter and drummed his fingers on it, eyes fixed on the lantern.

"Something on your mind, Martin?" Vivian asked.

He picked up the lantern and turned it about. "How often do you talk to Wick?"

"Almost never. I tend to have my hands full with the shop."

"I talk to him constantly," Martin said, his gaze distant.

"I know. If I listen closely, I can hear you down there if I'm going through the inventory."

"It helps me gather my thoughts. And he remembers everything. But…"

"Don't dilly-dally. If you've got a concern, let's hear it."

"He helped the kids conceal their plans when they were working on acquiring the dagger and Oiler and such. And when I realized he might have something to hide, he spoke at *length* about reasons one might not want to know about things that others chose to keep secret. When Fel and Epiphany revealed they'd been…"

Vivian raised her eyes and glanced at the door to the shop. Martin realized almost too late that openly discussing their recent circumventions of the assayer's office in what amounted to a public space might not be the wisest option. It wasn't terribly intelligent to be discussing Wick so openly, for that matter, but what was going to be said had to be said.

"The point is," he continued. "I had assumed that the recent revelation was the secret he'd maneuvered me into keeping."

"But if he had one secret, you worry he may have others."

"Wick oversees the vast majority of this family's dealings. And we've been using him to communicate and observe over great distances for quite some time. His precise operation is what it would take to spy on us. Until recently, he couldn't have done so without me noticing, because there was no other flame for him to go to. He was always present in our own lantern, the flame solid and unmoving as illustration of that. But once we started experimenting with sending the children out with flames lit from his, his absence was possible, and expected."

"Is it possible one of the kids left a flame lit somewhere else? Either on purpose or by mistake? And our spy is listening through it?"

"It's possible there are flames elsewhere. But nothing in the considerable research I had to do to learn to repair the second lantern suggested it was possible to get information *out* of a sentry flame without the flame's participation. Wick would have to choose to communicate with someone."

"And you fear he may have done so."

"I've assumed he had some degree of loyalty to the Masker family. He's been with us for so long. But that loyalty has never been tested. And we now know he will keep secrets, and defend those secrets. I don't want to entertain the possibility, but I cannot discount it either."

Vivian looked to the lantern. "Then I suppose you and Wick will have to have some words when next he returns."

"I suppose so…"

#

The journey to Kazel was a strange one. It took them through twisting, turning paths cut deep into the mountain. Growing up in Beffshire, where most people built down rather than up, had given Fel a familiarity with the look of a passage that was mined rather than natural. These seemed to be a combination of both. The tunnels twisted and turned to follow the softest stretches of stone, or perhaps to follow a vein of something precious. Nature dictated the path, but hard work hollowed it out.

A surprisingly lengthy stretch of navigating the tunnels brought them far enough for a new, fresh wind to blow. Not far ahead, there must have been an opening to the outside. The tunnel gradually took on a more finished appearance. Rough slopes became carved stairs. Torch holders were installed with some regularity. And somewhere in the darkness, scratching and hammering suggested laborers were toiling away even now.

Those laborers revealed themselves to be two rather filthy kobolds with ancient, worn-down picks. They chattered a greeting as the Adept and the others walked past. Parch tippy-tapped over to them and received some cheerful pats.

"The unicorn should have remained with the rest of the kobolds," the Adept said, watching as they took a moment to fawn over the thing before getting back to work.

"I've got a bunch of broken doors back home that suggest it's just easier to let him do what he wants."

They came upon a small doorway, clearly designed for kobolds. The Adept managed to make slipping through it far more dignified than Fel would have imagined was possible. Especially after watching Tome nearly fall on his face in an attempt to avoid crawling. Fel just gave up and crawled, if only because having Oiler on his back meant that his balance wasn't at its best.

What awaited on the other side of the door was more than Fel was prepared for. It was a single massive room. The walls were perfectly straight, with scattered columns to keep the vaulted ceiling, at least two hundred feet high, from caving in. Massive doors nearly filled the far wall. They were the sorts of things that took a team of men to open, or would have if they'd not been a relic of the Bygone Era and thus likely able to move at the pull of a lever. He would have remarked out loud that the place looked precisely like the scattered vaults he'd encountered outside the wall, but he was too busy trying to avoid gasping at the sight of the room's occupants and contents.

Easily two dozen kobolds were present, engaged in all sorts of different activities, all in service of the most awe-inspiring creature Fel had ever witnessed.

He was a dragon, but one that looked as though he was designed by a fine artist expressly for the purpose of producing a mixture of fear and reverence. He was silver and gold. The colors weren't split simply between his body and belly. Instead, a principally gold belly was threaded with a delicate silver filigree pattern, too complex and artful to be natural but too perfectly incorporated onto his hide to be artificial. His back and sides were silver with inlays of gold forming larger, broader patterns. A row of scales down his back each curved up into a multipointed frill, leading down to a tail that had the overall shape of a weaponized fleur-de-lis. His head was broad and topped with a regal crown of gold horns. The beast was enormous, more like a building than something that ought to be able to live and breathe.

This was so clearly not the beast he'd encountered a few months ago. He was double that monster's size, at least. And many times the majesty. It was difficult to imagine that they were the same species. The grandeur and terrible beauty of the thing was such that it took several seconds for Fel to realize that the room was heaped with gold. It was mounded like sand in a desert, more than he'd ever seen in one place, or even dreamed of. The piles were sufficient to serve as a worthy perch for so grand a beast, with plenty scattered around to spare.

And then there was the feature of the room that explained much of what had occurred over the past few days. Shackles were affixed around the dragon's ankles and neck. The ones around his ankles were large enough to secure the massive trade ships at the port, and Fel couldn't picture anything to properly compare to the neck iron. Each of the shackles, each of the mounts, and all the links in the chain glistened with the deep blue light that Fel knew very well. The entire set of restraints was either one big contraption or a collection of interlinked ones. The chains were not taut. Fel estimated with the slack in them, the beast could access perhaps a third of the room.

Mik and Stix remained rigidly beside the Adept. Teya lowered herself to the floor in a bow. Tome elbowed Fel. He dropped Oiler to the ground, kneeled, and bowed as well. Parch took advantage of his position to hop onto his back, eyes very carefully trained on the dragon.

"Kazel, I bring to you the newcomers I spoke of," the Adept said.

"Humans," Kazel rumbled.

Fel held his hand to his head. Parch hopped down and huddled behind Fel, suddenly unwilling to face the beast head on. The beast was speaking softly, he could tell. It was almost a whisper. But at the same time, the intensity of his words rattled the air in Fel's chest and made his head feel like it was on the verge of shattering. A dragon was not a nice creature to have a chat with while nursing a hangover.

The Adept marched over to Tome's side. Mik tapped him. He stood.

"This human is named Tome Inkbrand the Fifth. He is a paper mage, or so he claims. I have seen no convincing demonstration of his skills," she said.

"It is a matter of—" Tome objected.

Stix jabbed him in the ribs. He silenced himself.

"We discovered him on the verge of being killed by a boobrie and brought him here to be questioned and to seek your council regarding what should be done with him."

She moved behind Fel. Mik tapped him. He stood.

"This human is named Fel Masker."

What followed was not a sound. Sounds were things one heard. The dragon's response was felt in Fel's rattling bones and throbbing head. If this was a growl, Fel didn't want to witness a roar.

"He claims not to be aware of the crimes committed by those who share his name. He does, however, admit to being a contraptioneer."

Kazel stood. Fel had to look away. The motion of so massive a being felt and looked more like a shift in the landscape than something animal. It triggered impulses in him demanding that he flee, but he managed to hold still. Silver eyes fixed on Fel.

"Through his actions he preserved the lives of four of your servants, including my left and right hands, when they were cornered by a manticore while collecting the contraptions he brought into our lands. Those contraptions, I should add, were numerous. While enjoying our hospitality, he has taken no direct actions against us, though his presence has not been without consequence."

Mik stepped over to Teya. She stood.

"Teya acquired a contraption from Masker. He taught her its operation, which enabled her to use it to create fire. She used it to burn, among other things, several pieces of furniture and a few minor documents. Nothing which cannot be replaced."

Mik moved aside and gave Oiler a poke. Oiler, who had been watching from beneath the flap of its pack, raised its head somewhat. It reeled out one hand and gave Mik a matching poke, only to receive an angry chatter in response.

"Finally, Oiler. A contraption that is capable of movement and thought. It has performed no significant deed against us and, according to Fel, was instrumental in the defeat of the manticore. He also claims that his presence here is due to the beast's compulsion to repair its fellow contraptions. Fel Masker had disabled a contraption that, once repaired, dumped Tome, Oiler, and Fel into a trap that left them floundering in the Silkstrand River."

"Disabled a contraption," Kazel said.

"Yes. It is a matter I imagine you will wish to discuss."

"And the unicorn?" Kazel asked.

"The unicorn entered the Greater Lands of its own accord. It has done no harm, and no good. Seemingly, it has a kinship with Fel. We have questioned all who were capable of answering. The humans state no desires within our land. They claim their entry was by accident, or more specifically by the machinations of those who constructed the wall. They further claim their greatest desire is to leave this place in one piece."

The dragon huffed a breath that nearly knocked Fel backward.

"I shall pass judgment. For the sake of the humans, I shall do so in their tongue," Kazel said. "For Teya, recompense must be made. Given the nature of your transgression, you must learn discipline in the face of temptation. You will thus be made the designated observer and guard for the humans, and Masker in particular. You will maintain this assignment, following Fel wherever he goes, until such time as he expires or departs."

Teya nodded and chattered something reverently. She shuffled behind the Adept and kept her head lowered.

"Tome Inkbrand, you do not interest me. You may do as you please and move freely among my people, so long as you do not take actions which may bring harm to them."

"Thank you, oh majestic dragon," Tome said.

"Fel Masker, you brought contraptions to this place, and tempted one of my servants with their use. I am sorely tempted to end you myself. The world is ill-served by your kind, whose machinations have trapped me here. But you may yet be of use. You will remain here, in my chamber, when the others depart. Your fate shall be determined by your value."

He glared at Oiler. "The contraption shall be destroyed," Kazel decreed.

"No!" Fel said.

All eyes turned to him, most concerningly those of Kazel. In the past, Fel had often earned a hard stare from people in his life. In the worst of those times, he could have sworn he could *feel* their gaze. This time was different. There was a tangible sensation to the dragon's glare. It felt like a fist being pressed into his chest. The raw force of it physically unbalanced him. He took a step back and braced himself like he was facing a gale-force wind.

"You do not contradict Kazel," the Adept said. "Your very existence continues only if he deigns you worthy."

"The contraption will be destroyed," Kazel repeated.

There was the slightest edge to the beast's voice. It struck Fel like a hammer. The splitting headache that had previously owed its intensity entirely to his hangover now throbbed anew, with a pain so powerful that tears ran down Fel's cheek.

Fel had a rebellious streak. It had gotten him into trouble before. And it had often been observed that he had a self-destructive streak. Beneath them all was something more virtuous but no less dangerous. And right now, all those elements were combining into a volatile concoction.

"That thing never did anything to you," Fel said. "And it saved my life. It's also almost gotten me killed a few times. But the point is, the only crime that contraption ever committed was keeping people from hurting other people, even when those people deserved to be hurt. What reason could you possibly have for destroying it?"

"Fel does not represent me or my people," Tome said quickly. "I am not only willing but *eager* to honor your judgment."

"You are a *coward*," Fel said.

"I've never claimed to be otherwise," he hissed. "And in light of present company, I would suggest the word you should be looking for is 'sensible' rather than 'cowardly.'"

"Silence," Kazel instructed. "Adept, take the mage and the unicorn. Leave the contraptioneer, the contraption, and Teya," he instructed.

The harpy nodded, and her "hands" went to work. One tugged Tome toward the stairs. The other gathered up Parch. The unicorn wriggled free three times, each time with an increasingly irritated bleat.

"Leave it," Kazel said. "And go. All of you."

The legion of kobolds obeyed. They filed out through the small door. When they were gone, Kazel flopped down. The motion sent a puff of wind that threw Fel to the ground and pelted the walls with gold coins like there'd been a freak hailstorm. Teya scurried over and helped him back up, then huddled behind him to escape the gaze of her master. Parch crouched behind Oiler, likely for the same reason. The contraption reeled its head out and inverted it to gaze down at the unicorn. It extended a metal claw and gently patted the beast on the head.

"Look," Fel said. "See? That's the thing you're so afraid of that you have to smash it?"

The intensity of Kazel's glare increased. Teya sidled away, eyes desperately searching for something to shelter behind that wasn't presently targeted for destruction by her master. She settled for a small pile of gold that had been scattered away from the rest.

"Masker…" Kazel rumbled. "You see these chains?"

"I do."

"Do you suppose I would wear them if I had the option to shed them?"

"I don't think anyone would willingly wear chains. Certainly not someone as big and strong as you."

"And yet I wear them. And do you know why?"

Fel opened his mouth to answer. Kazel didn't give him the chance. The dragon lashed his neck aside. A chain with links each heavier than a horse dragged across the ground and yanked taut. The links strained as he fought against them. Cracks began to thread themselves around pressure points. But through those cracks, blue light flashed, and the shadowy motion of gears and linkages clicked and shifted. The cracks pulled closed. Kazel relented.

"No amount of strength can break them. The full force of my breath cannot melt them. Contraptions are a blight upon my kind. A source of power too easily wielded by those who lack the wisdom to use them properly." Kazel uncurled his claws, indicating Oiler, who was now scratching under Parch's chin. "This trick. You think it should convince me? The tricks that contraptions can achieve are the very reason I fear them. You are a Masker. You should know just how dangerous a contraption can be."

"You and the harpy keep saying that like it should mean something to me. It is just my name," Fel said.

Kazel surveyed him with a measure of doubt. "If the work done by those who bear your name is truly lost to history, then we are all the better for it. But we are not here to discuss that. I am not cruel, and I am not unreasonable. My long life has taught me that anger is a poor map to plot one's course. It is for that reason that you were not killed already. Everyone can be of use. And anyone can be redeemed. But you… you will have to work for it."

"It wouldn't be the first time I've had to pay the price for something I didn't do."

"I am told you disabled contraptions within the wall."

"Disabling traps is the biggest part of my job."

Kazel grasped a chain link and slid it across the floor, placing it in front of Fel. "Can you disable this trap?"

Fel crouched down in front of the link. It was one of the smaller ones, but the link itself was still larger than his thigh. At this distance, he could see seams that separated the link into individual rings. There were visible fasteners.

"I can't make any promises. Some contraptions are made to be difficult to unmake," Fel said. "But I'm going to need a few things if I'm going to try. I'll need my gear. And that includes the sentry lantern. I don't know half as much about this as my father does. I'll need to use the lantern to communicate with him."

"You realize that anything you do which smells even remotely like treachery will be your final act."

"Yeah, I know."

Kazel glanced to Teya. "Fetch his things."

The kobold dashed through the door, not just eagerly but gratefully.

"I'm also going to need information. I need to know how the trap was sprung, and just as important, I need to know what's in it for me to unspring it."

"Your life shall be your reward."

"My life is the reason I ended up in the heart of a mountain, face-to-face with a dragon who hates me, all while nursing a hangover. Trust me, if my life is the only thing on offer, it's not much of a reward. Especially not right now."

"Kazel's expression shifted subtly. "You are remarkably self-aware," he said, a dash more respect in his tone.

"If I'm going to know anything, it better be myself. So what happens if I can help you?"

The dragon lowered his head, bringing it near enough to Fel's face that he could feel the heat coursing through the creature's veins. "Ask."

"You want me to make an offer?"

"I want to know what you desire."

Fel glanced at the heaps of gold. "I feel like this is a trap."

"This is a place of traps, isn't it? Ask."

"I'm not dumb enough to ask for your gold. That seems like it would be bad manners. Mostly what I want is to get back to the wall so we can get out of here. There's a bunch of stuff in that wall I was hoping to sell, and a lot of stuff I was hoping to learn."

"You don't strike me as a man who seeks wisdom without purpose."

"The wisdom is for my dad."

"Tell me what you value."

"I find, fix, and sell contraptions. That's what this whole trip is about."

"And if you find contraptions that satisfy your requirements, what will you do with them?"

"Bring them back home and sell them."

"You seek money, but you do not ask for gold?"

"Again, setting aside the fact you seem like you'd bite my head off if I asked for some of yours, I prefer to earn my way in life. With either gambling or hard work."

"And to whom would you sell such contraptions, and to what end?"

"If it is useful, whoever could use it. If it isn't, collectors. Collectors will buy anything."

"To accumulate that which has value. That, I can respect."

"Yeah, it seems like a dragon thing."

"All creatures gather that which holds value to them. Dragons merely have the time and the strength to accumulate the largest collections." Kazel swept his tail, splashing coins about and rumbling the vault around him. "There are some items, contraptions we have sought to destroy but which have survived. They have no apparent function, but I would just as soon be rid of them. If you are able to free me, and if you promise to take them along with all of your own contraptions and never return with them, I will provide these contraptions to you."

"How old are they?"

"Older than me."

"And how old are you?"

"Old enough to remember a time when there was no wall."

Fel shut his eyes and thought. The most valuable contraptions he'd ever encountered came from within the wall itself. And if these contraptions were from within the Greater Lands, and were beyond the capacity for even a dragon to destroy, the value might well be incalculable even if they could never be made to function again. Relics from the Bygone Era. Or even *before* the Bygone Era.

"That's a deal, Kazel."

"Not yet it isn't." The dragon pulled his head back. "I value honesty. And I will not allow you to accept an offer you do not understand. I offer you my word that I will help you to leave this place *if it is within my power*. I cannot guarantee that you can escape this place."

"As long as you accept I might not be able to un-spring this trap, the deal's still a deal. Now, how'd it get sprung in the first place?"

"You wish to know the tale in full?" Kazel asked.

"Seems like you and I are going to be in here together for a while. May as well give me the long version."

#

Long ago, not before the wall, but before any of those I now call followers were born, my dominion over this mountain, and much of this region, was complete and uncontested. There exists, far deeper inside this mountain, a chamber that was once my lair. Its entrance was well hidden, well defended. To this day, none have set foot there but those I deigned worthy. But the greatest threat of a large domain is the ease with which cracks in one's defenses can open. One must be vigilant. And so I was. This room, the one I now call my prison, had for years held nothing of interest to me. It stank of the work of contraption-makers. Of Maskers. It was a lesion in my territory, but it was, nevertheless, mine. To encroach upon it was to encroach upon my territory, and if I allowed that, even in the smallest measure, then it might have become the crack that could cause the rest to crumble away.

There was a creature... there *is* a creature, who is my kind, but not my like. By all reasonable measures, he is my inferior. A dragon called Duurth. Smaller. Weaker of body. Younger. More Brash. Unwise. And as the greatest symbol of his lack of wisdom, he valued the very things you do. Gold, silver, gems? Those things drawn from the earth and worked by the hands of skilled creatures, valued by all? He had no interest. This dragon sought to collect contraptions. He could not operate them. He did not care to. He simply wanted to possess them. And so, the stench of this place that held such contraptions was irresistible to him, even if it meant setting claw upon my land and daring my wrath.

As this place was so far from my sight, he came and went more than once without my notice. Enough times to all but clear this place. Enough times, no doubt, to construct a hoard that should have been enough to satisfy him. But his greed compelled him. And I caught his scent. When he crossed through the doors that now lay in pieces behind me, and offer me little more than a glimpse of the sun, I followed. There was a battle, though what happened that day is barely deserving of the term. He desperately tried to escape. I would not allow it.

I cornered him, wings spread, tail lashing. I approached. To this very patch of floor. The walls erupted with their shackles. Ensnared me. It was as terrifying to him as it was enraging to me. Neither of us anticipated the walls and floor themselves to hold the treachery of the contraption-makers as well. But they did. And so, I was trapped here. He escaped.

Teya had returned some time into the story, dragging the sack of Fel's goods. He'd gone straight to work, and as Kazel had slowly spun the tale, Fel had eyed the link of chain and tried to formulate a plan.

Now that the story was told, he slipped a tool from the bag and straddled the chain to start working on it. He grunted and worked at a fastener, slowly easing it out. Teya sat on the chain, eyes wide and paws clutched before her, reverent bliss on her face at the chance to be present for such a tale.

"And that's it? You've been here ever since?" Fel said.

"If not for my servants, my followers, I would have withered to nothing in this place. But now you know how I came to be here. What good does that do you?"

"It tells me this is going to be harder than just turning some bolts," he said.

He released the fastener. Slowly, it spiraled back into place.

"My father knows better than anyone how these things work. On my best day I can do maybe a tenth of what he can do. But the one thing we both know is how traps are sprung. Avoiding them is how I stay alive. And I've got to be good at it because I'm usually doing this by myself. I was just telling my helper up there about pressure plates. Just big buttons that activate traps, mostly. But they're tricky. You can't make them too sensitive, or a breeze would set off your trap, and what good is that? The best hauls I ever had, before we got into the wall, were when I'd get into a vault and the trap was already sprung. But you can't make them too stiff, either, or they'll never spring. Same problem. This trap was too stiff. The littler dragon didn't set it off. It got you because you were big enough."

"And how does knowing this help you?"

"It means I don't have to pussyfoot around. If it took something as big as you to set it off, there's no chance I'm going to be setting anything off." He abandoned the fastener and pulled Wick's lantern from the bag. "When you got here, before the little dragon started stealing stuff, this place was full?"

"Great displays of contraptions hung from the ceiling to the floor along the walls. Completely filled."

"And the little dragon emptied it out? He must have been doing it for years." He rummaged in the bag for the sparker. "This door I entered through. Was this always here?"

"It was dug by my servants to more easily serve me."

"So those big doors back there are the only way in?"

"Yes."

He found the contraption and used it to light the lantern, then slipped it into its dedicated pocket. "Strange. Everything you're saying makes me think this was a vault. The mother of all vaults, really. And the mother of all vaults ought to have the mother of all traps. That stands to reason. But why is it in the *back*?"

"Does the puzzle matter?"

"Not really. I need to go to the front. Where the original entrance is. Is that a problem?"

"Go. Teya, keep an eye on him."

Fel pulled Oiler onto his back and lugged the bag of his gear. Parch tapped along beside him. Whereas Fel tried his best to keep to the walls, away from the mounds of gold, Parch pranced and capered atop the cascading piles.

"No!" he shouted. "Get down from there."

"The creature can do as it pleases," Kazel said. "*You* are the one who must be watched."

"Fair. If I was locked up for as long as you, I'd probably have a grudge against the person who looks like the one who built the lock."

The many kobolds poured in behind him to resume their many tasks within the place. Teya balanced her time between keeping watch on Fel and gazing in awe and wonder at Kazel.

"Must be nice to be admired…" Fel muttered.

#

Tome huffed and puffed as he topped the stairs. He'd taken his time on the way up, which meant he was left alone for most of the journey. Teya had dashed up and back again before he'd reached the top, which was rather humbling. When he stepped through the door to the alcove, the Adept and her hands were awaiting him.

"Ah, you have arrived. I wondered what had become of you," she said.

"I'm not accustomed to this much climbing, oh noble Adept."

The Adept's hands gestured around them. "As before, you are free to live among us so long as you do not cause trouble," she said.

"Thank you, once again, for your generosity. I, er… I don't suppose you have any insight into how likely or unlikely it is that my partner down there survives this encounter."

"Kazel has great wisdom and greater patience. Your friend will be killed only if he deems it necessary."

"That doesn't answer my question."

She turned to him. "No, it doesn't. I don't have the answer to your question. I can, however, tell you that should your friend's death be made necessary, Kazel will inform me, and I shall choose the means."

"He won't just eat him?"

"Your friend is not deserving of a death by Kazel's claws or flame. Or, I

120

suppose, a far greater evil would need to be revealed before he would deem it so. Kazel's wrath is reserved for those who have threatened his people and dishonored his land. Fel has done neither to the appropriate degree, and shall not be given a chance to do so."

"That's a relief. He and I have only recently entered into something of a business partnership, and it is one of the better prospects I've had in quite some time. Even neglecting the general principle of a death at his age being a tragedy, I would hate for our partnership to be cut short so soon."

"Your concern for your friend is heartwarming," the Adept said.

"Tell me, have you ever been past the wall?" he asked. "I would not say that being flown here in your talons was the most pleasant way to travel, but now that I am prepared for it, you might possibly be the fastest means to return to civilization."

"I have no interest in what lies beyond the wall, and no desire to bear witness to it," she said.

"Even so, a little trip beyond the wall might prove enlightening. I'm sure we could work out some method of payment. If not for you, then for one of your winged associates."

"I have no interest in what lies beyond the wall, and no desire to bear witness to it," she repeated.

He tipped his head. Something in the delivery seemed curious. She said it precisely the same way each time. Not similarly, *precisely* the same.

She hopped up onto the throne perch. Her left and right hands hopped up beside her.

"There are precious few Greater Mystics on the outside," he said. "But there are some. I wonder why they left?"

"I have no interest in what lies beyond the wall, and no desire to bear witness to it."

"Fascinating," he said. "I wonder, do you have any paper? I have some thoughts that I would like to record."

She gestured. A kobold scurried off to a chest against one wall.

"You have behaved yourself until now, Tome Inkbrand. Your continued freedom depends upon continuing to do so. Remember that. We may not have much interest in, or regard for, contraptions, but we are quite well versed in mysticism. You will find that any attempts to use your magic against us will be fruitless. Our defenses are sound."

"I would not think of putting quill to page in anger against you or your people. You have been nothing but helpful. And besides, I have a measure more experimentation ahead of me before I would consider my spells worth the effort of casting here."

The kobold tottered back with an armload of blank scrolls. He accepted them and unfurled one to test between thumb and forefinger.

"Oh… Oh my…" he murmured.

Everywhere he went, and he'd covered much of the continent, Tome sampled every type of paper he could locate. Like so many other parts of being a paper mage, the precise features that made a page better for spellcasting were ill-defined. Even different pages in the same batch had a variance in their capacity to carry and deliver a spell with efficiency. He poked his nose into the mound of pages and took a whiff. He tore an edge and tested its texture against his lips, then chewed it. Everything about this paper sang clear and loud that it would be a superb vehicle for his craft.

"Thank you for your generosity. Is there anything I can do to offer compensation? You rescued me from danger. Fed me, treated me, clothed me. Surely I can be of some use to you."

She turned to him, clearly for the first time judging his value rather than his liability. "What languages do you know, Tome?"

"I can copy any language you please. I am, alas, only conversant in Thaynish. But I can read quite a few of the more ancient dialects. Including Bygone Common and South-Fringe Doggerel."

Her expression brightened. "Ah! Well then, I have a very important task for you, if you believe you are capable."

"I shall endeavor to be of use!"

She hopped down and marched forward. "This can be rather complex and difficult. The kobolds particularly dislike being placed in charge of the library."

"You have a library! Splendid. It just so happens my partner and I were hoping to encounter one. I'm sure yours will be quite differently equipped, but I am always happy to discover fresh sources of information. A hungry mind, you see."

"Dealing with hungry minds is the very reason we have the library."

She came to one of the few alcoves that had a secured door. Most were either open air or had gates or gratings. This one was thick, solid wood. A soft but undeniable din was filtering through the door. Stix reached up to the Adept's mail tunic and fetched a key from a pouch on the inside. She turned the key, and Mik pushed the door open.

Waiting inside the room was utter chaos. It was quite well lit, and a row of bookshelves was visible from the doorway, but between him and the precious volumes was a veritable melee of small kobolds. They ranged from puppy-sized to nearly as large as those milling about outside. They climbed and wrestled over one another, squawking and chattering as they ran amok.

"The children tend to be more manageable when they have had a story. Any of the books will do, but try to be interesting. It can be a trial to hold their attention."

"Eh… Childcare is not *precisely* my area of expertise, but I will do my best."

He waded into the room. For better or worse, they didn't pay him much mind, even as the door was shut and locked behind him. They were far too interested in scrambling over each other and attempting to outdo each other in cacophonous shouting.

Tome nearly made it to the shelves before one of the smaller kobolds, eager for some high ground to gain the upper hand on his siblings, clambered up his back, giving him a sudden and very clear illustration of just how sharp their claws were. When it dove free and into the pile of scrabbling claws, he hurried over to the shelves. It was clear to him that this place was more of a school than a library. In addition to the books, which were tellingly stored on shelves hanging from the ceiling where grabby hands were less likely to shred them, there were slates, lumps of chalk, and wooden blocks painted with assorted different creatures. The place was better equipped than most human schools he'd glimpsed in his travels.

"Children? Children!" he shouted.

They ignored him. He grabbed a piece of chalk.

"It has been some time since my days practicing on a slate, but this ought to be more eye-catching."

He traced out a few quick lines, then sketched a simple rendering of a kobold on the slate. A quick swipe through the first word of his rendering caused the rest of what he'd written to blacken and flare away. The doodle of the kobold hopped up and down and squawked. In a wave of fascination, all the creatures turned and marveled as it did a little dance, then vanished in a puff of chalk dust.

"Hello!" Tome said, trying his best to remain as animated as the conjured drawing had been. "I am here to read you a story, and I mean to do just that, but before we begin, I have a question."

The crowd of little ones responded with varying degrees of excitement and trepidation.

"How many of you know about the wall around the Greater Lands?" he asked.

They all quite vigorously indicated their knowledge.

"And how many of you know that there is a place beyond that wall?"

This reply was more subdued.

"How many of you have wondered what it would be like to leave this place and cross the wall?"

The children replied almost in a single voice. They spoke precisely the same sequence of chatters and growls.

"I don't *quite* know your language," he said. "But I suspect I know what you've just said. Let's get you a story, eh?"

He selected a book from the shelf, reasoning one of the well-worn ones would be popular.

"This one is called"—he glanced at the title—"with the cross mark below the serif, and the glottal stop at the end. … *The Clumsy Drake*?"

The little kobolds crowed with excitement.

"Wonderful! Let's begin."

#

Epiphany looked over her inventory. With the decision to stay close to the bazaar for a bit longer, she'd had the opportunity to work her magic on a few of the locals. Back home, she seldom enjoyed working the counter at the store. She would do it, and she would do it well, certainly. She took pride in it. But all things being equal, she found dealing with the same sequence of customers wasn't terribly stimulating. The same was not so of haggling and bargaining with people on the road. Different people every day, with different wants and needs, different weaknesses. In raw numbers she made much more money making big deals with other buyers, finding things for the shop or offloading excess inventory. But one of these days she'd have to invest in a proper bazaar wagon and join it for one full loop, just for the experience.

"And there you are, sir. I assure you, you've never had an alarm box as reliable as that. It will pay for itself the first time it chases off a robber. You need only send it to us and we will reset it, for a small fee, and send it back. The first two resets are free."

The customer nodded, feeling quite certain he'd gotten the better of her, and remaining blissfully unaware that he'd paid more than twice what he would have paid in the shop in Beffshire.

"Impressive," said Mr. Badgerweed, stepping up. "Though I should think you would have been able to sell him a second to use as a backup while the first is being reset."

She shook her head. "Not without lowering the price. A man only has so much in his pockets. And even *he* would have seen that for an upsell and left with a bad taste in his mouth. You've got to leave the door open for repeat customers."

"Not at the bazaar. You won't see that man for six months, at best. It would take a tremendously bad taste in his mouth to linger for that long."

Epiphany nodded. "I'll keep that in mind." She recounted the money and pulled out her ledger to record the sale. As she snapped it shut and pocketed it again, a shrill tone rang out.

Mr. Badgerweed smiled. "Seems like someone couldn't wait to test his purchase," he said.

Epiphany turned. "No… That's the one I buried last night," she said, reaching her hand into her bag.

Mr. Badgerweed's expression became stern. He motioned to his two associates. They not-so-subtly tucked their arms into their jackets. "You are sure you didn't bury it too near to the road."

"I know how to set an alarm. And that field right there is the only direction where someone could approach without being noticed by the rest of the town."

They gazed out over the field. It was broad daylight, and there was no sign of anyone.

"It must have been a false alarm, then."

"My dad reset and repaired those alarm boxes himself," she said. "They don't go off out of turn."

"But there is no one there. Perhaps a rabbit tripped the alarm."

A puff of dust rose up in the field. The alarm silenced.

"And did a rabbit shut it off?" she said.

"Button up!" Badgerweed shouted to his men. "We've got Bolivans, and they are overequipped."

She pulled her brass knuckles from her bag.

"If you've got anything in that wagon of yours that you can't bear to lose to the Bolivans," Mr. Badgerweed advised, "then I suggest you grab it and get into my wagon. It is more defensible than yours, and I very much doubt I am the only one they'll be after."

Epiphany was already grabbing the case of her most valuable contraptions. She reached for the lantern. It was no longer lit. The flame had been dancing not minutes before. Wick wasn't around, but there was more than enough fuel left in the reservoir to keep the lantern lit for days more without refilling. It hadn't burned out. Someone had extinguished it.

A thousand questions burst into her mind. Who had done it? When had they done it? How did they know to do it? These questions were simultaneously profoundly important and utterly meaningless, because regardless of the answer, she was now cut off from her parents and potentially at the mercy of an unseen enemy. Better to ask and answer the more important questions.

How could the Bolivans do this, and what could she do about it?

"Dad says military contraptions are always handheld or arm-mounted," she murmured to herself. "Most of them are on the left side so the right-handed soldiers can operate them more easily…"

She tightened her grip on the brass knuckles and pulled a contraption from the set she'd rescued from the wagon. It was what her father called a "duster," one of the contraptions likely to be confiscated by the assayers.

Confusion was beginning to erupt as locals and the people in other wagons saw Badgerweed and his men panicking for no obvious reason. Epiphany tucked herself in the narrow space between where two wagons had backed against one of the few buildings near the courtyard. There was only one place she could be attacked from, and it was directly in front of her. She dropped the duster on the ground and pressed its button. Air hissed from inside the contraption and started to kick up dirt into a thickening cloud. She kept her eyes trained on the cloud. The very moment she saw a strange void form in the dust, she burst forward, arm flailing. She'd intended to bash the attacker in the chin with her weapon, but from the meaty thud, her blow struck his shoulder instead. Regardless, a desperate punch with a hunk of brass hurt badly regardless of where it landed. Her full bodyweight was behind it, which was enough to bring her and her target tumbling to the ground. She shut her eyes and tried to envision the squirming body beneath her. Her fingers dragged down one arm and tore at a leather pad she found there.

Her attacker cursed, and she opened her eyes. Rather than a completely unseen form, he was shadowy and indistinct beneath her. She held tightly to the pad with both hands. He drove a knee into her midsection. Unseen hands wrapped around her mouth and neck, pulling her away. Her grip held, and the pad slid from the Bolivan agent's arm, rendering him fully visible. The instant he was visible, one of Badgerweed's men descended upon him. The results were not pretty.

Epiphany was dragged backward, still in the clutches of a second unseen attacker. She swung her brass knuckles down. She knew from experience that the corner of the knuckle would leave a welt if she wasn't careful and thumped her hand into it inside her bag. She wasn't sure which part of her attacker the cruel fob of brass caught, but he howled in pain. The other of Badgerweed's men tackled the seemingly empty space where the agent must have been, throwing him to the ground and knocking Epiphany away.

"In the wagon, in the wagon!" Badgerweed shouted.

She scrambled to her feet and dashed for his wagon. The sight of people appearing from nowhere was enough to cause the confusion to turn to pure chaos. She climbed into the back of the wagon and pressed her back against the sturdiest crate inside. Epiphany watched the door, brass knuckles ready to be deployed the moment the flap moved. Outside, shouting continued, and she heard the distinctive twang of crossbows.

Just as things were beginning to calm down, something slammed the crate behind her, hard. It tumbled over, forcing her forward and spilling her face-first onto the wagon floor. She tried to get up, but her arms were pulled behind her back and a gag was pulled across her mouth. With frightening speed and efficiency, her arms were bound. Someone grabbed her hair and pulled it back, and a familiar face with a scarred temple appeared beside her.

"Sit tight, Masker. I have some people who want a word with you."

He thumped her head down again and scrambled up to the reins. In seconds, the wagon was rattling across the open road with the dwindling shouts of Badgerweed and his men fading behind her.

Chapter 7

Fel had expected things to get easier when he found the mechanism he was looking for. He'd assumed, and rightly so, that if the major traps for the vault that now held Kazel captive were in the back, then the means of activating them and deactivating them would be near the front or outside the vault. All he had to do was locate them and, if luck was with him, he would be a button-press away from earning the gratitude of an ancient dragon.

Luck was not with him.

The door to the vault was massive. It had to be, if Kazel and Duurth had been able to pass through. It stood at the bottom of a long stairwell that was also large enough for a dragon. It even seemed to have been built with dragons in mind, as the human-sized stairs ran on either side of wide, flat steps that were nearly as tall as he was. Judging from the constant, brisk breeze swirling around them, the stairwell led to the mountainside, though it was far enough and had enough of a curve that he couldn't see its end.

What had once been a grand and sturdy wood-and-metal door lay in splintered, rusted ruins, likely broken by whichever dragon had decided to check the place out first. Most of the pieces had been pushed aside, and he'd had to shove and lever at them to clear enough room to search the walls and doorway. One would have imagined that deploying a contingent of kobolds to help would have been the obvious and wise decision, but help was not forthcoming. Even Teya didn't lend a hand. She spent most of her time sitting on a step and intensely observing Fel, with brief interludes of cuddling Parch and curiously poking Oiler.

When he'd finally revealed a sequence of five mechanisms beside the door, he discovered them protected by small barred hatches, each secured with their own tiny lock. Twenty minutes of bashing them proved fruitless. Bygone equipment was quite sturdy. He'd been forced to resort to a skill for which a person in the lingering fringe of a hangover was uniquely ill-suited. He had to pick the locks.

It felt like he'd been doing it for hours, but with his patience and no clear view of the outside, it could have been minutes. Regardless of how long it was, the flickering light of Wick's lantern had steadied while he was working on the fifth and final lock.

"Fel. I am happy that no additional harm has befallen you," Wick said.

"Wick!" he said, leaning back and flexing his fingers. "Tell my hands that. I feel like I've been trying to tie my fingers in knots."

"What is your current activity, and are there any services you need me to fulfill?"

"I'm just finishing picking these locks, but I'm going to need you to give everything a good hard look so you can tell Dad and he can help me deactivate a Bygone Era trap. Maybe even older. The short version is, there's a big dragon over there who hates contraptioneers and just about the only way I'm getting me and Oiler out of here in one piece is if I deactivate some big contraption shackles."

"I continue to be impressed by the sheer variety of predicaments in which you manage to entangle yourself."

"I'm good at finding trouble, that's for sure. How are Mom and Dad? And how's Fanny?"

"I did not have time to return to them before your lantern was relit and I returned."

"It feels like you should have had time. We're not *that* far past the wall, and it only takes you twenty minutes or so from there."

"It would appear a great deal more effort must be expended to seek out flames within the Greater Lands. Or else distance in the Greater Lands is more substantial than beyond the wall."

"I'm not going to try to figure out what you mean." The final hatch popped open. "Thank the high!"

He grabbed the lantern and held it up. Each of the hatches revealed a narrow slit in the metal plate installed in the doorframe. Ancient text was engraved around each slit, and each bore the same mark, something akin to a simplified ape face that was presumably the maker's mark.

"Do you have any idea what those say?" he asked.

"The dialect is extremely old. Give me a moment and I will attempt to decipher it."

"Gladly." He stretched, producing a serenade of crackles from his back, and paced back to where Teya was sitting.

The kobold shuffled aside a bit to put some more space between them. Parch kept rearing up onto his hind legs, and she didn't seem to know what to make of it.

"This is what he's looking for," he said, mimicking a game of headbutts with some well-placed slaps of his hand. "You wait until he tips forward and you sort of bonk him. Either right under the horn or on either side of it. Give it a try."

She held up her paw and gave a slap as instructed, much to Parch's delight. A grin lit up her face and she continued.

"So… Sorry I got you in trouble with the sparker," he said.

She shook her head vaguely. Her expression faltered a bit from the giddy glee at playing with a unicorn, but it didn't look like resentment. Fel dug out the repaired puzzle box from the bag and scrambled its faces. Oiler gratefully accepted it and started toying with the faces again.

Teya was distracted enough by the motion and actions of the living contraption that she lost track of the game and received a solid headbutt from Parch. She shook her head a bit, grinned, and returned to the game, now using her head rather than her hands.

"You must have a harder head than me. And that's saying something." Fel motioned at Oiler. "You know, you don't need to be afraid of Oiler. I know you've got some pretty good reasons to dislike contraptions and contraptioneers, but I assure you, we're not all bad. And contraptions are just tools. They're not good *or* bad."

Teya seemed to give the game of headbutts a bit more focus, as though she was actively ignoring Fel's words. Unfortunately for her, Parch had his fill of the game after a few more bops and decided to bound around the stone steps instead. For a creature that enjoyed scaling things so much, this was practically a playground. It made sense to Fel. Parch was a mystic, and this was where mystics came from, as far as Fel knew.

"I suppose I'm wasting my time talking to you. You're no fan of mine, and you can't talk back besides."

"Can talk," Teya said, her voice a good deal smoother than he'd expected based on how she chattered and squawked otherwise. "Just… hard."

"Oh. Still. I don't want you to trouble yourself. I'm sure your life is hard enough, being a slave to a dragon."

She glared at him and crossed her arms. "Not slave."

"Oh, come on. A whole legion of you serving a master. What would you call it?"

"Honor," she said, one paw over her heart as she lowered her head. "Great dragon. Great honor."

"Can you leave?" he asked. "If you want?"

"Can leave. No want." She made an encompassing motion with her hand. "Family."

Fel nodded. "Family. That I can understand. But you sure you don't want to leave? Strike out on your own? Especially if they're going to punish you and give you a lousy job like keeping an eye on me?"

She shook her head. "Stronger together."

"I believe I have a translation for you," Wick said.

Fel marched up to the plates on the wall. "Let's have them."

Teya pointed. "Shackle first, shackle… next first."

"The kobold is broadly correct. The first two plates say, in order from top to bottom, 'primary restraint' and 'secondary restraints.' Below it are 'main entryway,' 'midpoint wall,' and 'defenses.'"

Teya nodded.

"If you *knew* that, why didn't you say?"

She shrugged.

"You do understand this is what your master sent me to find, right? This is what will set him free."

She shook her head.

"What do you mean no? It says it right on it."

"No work."

"How would you even know that? The hatches were locked."

She hopped down from the step she'd been perched on and scrambled over the debris from the door. After a moment, she returned with a ring of keys. Fel furrowed his brow, then grabbed them. He inserted one into the open hatch. It turned easily.

"You had keys and you just let me fight with the locks for all this time?"

She nodded.

"Why!?"

She shrugged, then pointed at the slits. "Not work. Do nothing."

"Maybe you can't *get* them to work, but these things are the way we're going to get your master free. Wick, listen up, and then head back home and ask Dad for help." He cleared his throat and held his hands up to the slits, measuring them. "Five metal slits, top one is two hand-spans tall. The rest are one-and-a-half spans. All are four fingers wide." He held Wick closer and peered inside. With the other hand he inserted a probe. "I see… five tumblers, seven disks." He jabbed with the probe. "No motion on tumblers or dimples…"

#

Epiphany held still in the back of the wagon, as she had been for nearly an hour. She shuddered to think how a man earned such a skill, but Temple had managed to tighten the bindings on her hands and legs while single-handedly driving the stolen wagon as well. Horses, it seemed, could be trusted to stay on the road and running for at least the few seconds it took him to bind her more securely. Since then, he'd been driving the wagon and gloating. The ride had been a nearly unbroken string of threats, typically delivered with a glance over his shoulder, as if he couldn't enjoy them without seeing the look on her face when she heard them.

"… And after that? After that it'll be your father's turn. Oh, don't think I forgot about him. I'm going to break all his fingers. I'm going to make sure he

130

can't even *hold* a tool to work on those contraptions of his…"

She let him talk. She knew, for now at least, talk was all it was. If he'd planned on killing her, he wouldn't have waited. This wasn't an assassination, it was a kidnapping. And more importantly, he hadn't rendezvoused with anyone yet. Chances were very good the rest of the Bolivans had either been killed by Badgerweed and his muscle or hadn't been able to reach their transportation. If she was fortunate, Temple would be transporting her alone all the way to whoever had hired him. And he'd be doing it in a stolen wagon with a bright purple covering. More importantly she knew they were close to the border, and trading wagons tended to be checked quite thoroughly. It was something she'd always found frustrating, but now clung to as the best chance she'd have to be rescued.

"Mmm… the road is getting busy," he said. "I'll leave you to stew on what your future holds. Wouldn't want anyone to see you. I'd have to kill them too, and killing without a price attached is bad business. Torture, on the other hand? That's an acceptable pastime."

He climbed through the wagon and secured the rear flaps, delivering a kick to her side on his way. He then returned, secured the front flaps behind him, and continued.

For the first time since she'd been captured, he would have to do more than glance over his shoulder to see her.

With an uncomfortable arch of her back and curl of her legs, she managed to get her fingers around a well-hidden tab in her boot. A quick tug slipped a short, sharp blade from its hiding place. When she'd added the knife to her equipment, she'd assumed if it ever needed to be used, it would be under less restrained circumstances. Inverting the blade and working it against her bindings was a test of her dexterity, and took minutes longer than she'd hoped it would. But her luck held out long enough for her to get her hands free.

Thoughts and concerns that she realized had probably rushed through her brother's head a dozen times before started to crowd her mind. All she had was a small knife. The man at the reins was a trained mercenary. Even with the element of surprise, she very much doubted she would be able to best him. She needed a better weapon, and to pick her moment carefully. The two things she had in her favor were the facts that Temple wouldn't dare open the flap to check on her while he was on a busy road, and she was in the back of a large, well-equipped wagon owned by a man who collected contraptions *and* skirted the rules of assayers. If she moved quickly and quietly, there was the chance she could find something in the wagon that would either kill her captor or convince him that leaving her alone was the preferable course of action.

A more desperate person might have started rummaging through the boxes willy-nilly. But she was a trader, and so was Badgerweed. Paper was going to be far quieter to search through, and somewhere there was bound to be an inventory that would tell her just what was in the various boxes.

She found a thin leather portfolio tucked behind a strap against one wall and pulled it open. The first few sheaves of pages were of little use to her. Mostly they were filled with figures. She shook her head at the waste of him using pen and paper for doing figures when chalk and a slate was quicker and easier. Then came a travel itinerary. She almost abandoned it, but something on the page caught her eye.

Badgerweed had a full schedule of rendezvous. They were written in what was either a shorthand or a code, but the structure was unmistakable. Times, locations, agendas, names. To someone unfamiliar with Badgerweed and his workings, it would have been meaningless. Gibberish. But she'd done business with him. He was just as dedicated to secrecy when dealing with her as he was with whoever these people were. Thus, she'd been privy to the workings of his coding, his shorthand. He was clever enough to use a different shorthand for different people, but it was clear that the naive code he used was never intended to be seen in its various forms side by side. Alone, without his instructions, she probably never would have been able to break it. But with what she knew of her own version, she suspected her father could have it fully broken in minutes. Even her less keen translation and decoding skills revealed enough parallels for her to know that at least six other groups were in his employ, each looking for contraptions of assorted different types. The descriptions of the contraptions were barely coded at all, presumably because their locations and the individuals seeking them were far more sensitive information than the contraptions themselves.

Memorizing inventory was a skill that had been hammered into her. Almost without thinking, she ticked off the items that she was able to decode and logged them away. For the most part, they weren't terribly unusual. Most were rare, certainly. Only three or four of them had passed through the antiquities shop back home through the years. But if someone had handed her this list, she doubted it would have taken the Masker family as a whole more than four months to locate and acquire everything on it. She had a sneaking suspicion, like the code, the list had been broken into pieces not out of necessity, but to prevent anyone from getting a complete picture of what they were after.

The cart rattled on as she sifted through the pages. Fortunately, from the sound through the thick canvas sides of the wagon, the road had only gotten busier, and noisier. She felt a bit safer. Safe enough to risk levering open a small wooden case referenced on one page of the notes as "the records box."

The contents of the box were far less orderly than she would have expected. It looked less like a carefully kept archive and more like a hasty catchall for things that didn't belong anywhere else. Lengthy handwritten letters made up the bulk of its contents. She almost abandoned it and continued her search for the inventory that might lead her to a worthwhile weapon when she spotted something that drew her full attention. She slid a page from the box. It was a formal letter, quite ragged as though it was frequently referenced. No coding, no shorthand, though it was obviously part of a far longer sequence of letters, which may or may not have been in the case as well. The body of the letter described a number of artifacts. One was described as "a heavy canvas pack, which may or may not be a part of the contraption it contains. We have heard it referenced as 'a repair automaton,' and the descriptions claim it will have a serpent-shaped head, articulated claws, a body composed of chain and, most crucially, it is the simplest example of a contraption with rudimentary intelligence. Aside from its obvious utility for its intended purpose, study should help to reveal how such intelligence is achieved. It will be stored with its faceplate disconnected, which seems to be the most effective method of rendering it inert without special equipment."

"They knew he was looking for Oiler, not just a heavy pack of chains…" she said.

The very next entry was a description of what was clearly the Bygone dagger, which was somewhere in one of these boxes. They listed it not by its description but by its function. "The black dagger is a tool for removing the main fasteners of certain self-motivated contraptions. In addition to the mundane function of the dagger's tip, its direct contact interrupts the functionality of any complex contraption, simplifying maintenance on automatons."

A final passage referred, predictably, to the mask. The function of the mask was not explored, though it was made quite clear that it was the least likely to be found but the most highly prized. Twice she found warnings that the mask should not be acquired without also possessing the dagger. She read through the full description, which no doubt would have been of great use to Fel if he'd had it. It gave the measurements, the markings, the location of mounting points.

The final line, which she dearly wished she had context for, read "It is our strong belief that we cannot safely proceed with the search and utilization of the clockwork diamond without all three of these contraptions."

But all that was secondary to the thing that had drawn her eye to the page in the first place. The letter was addressed to Mr. Thaddeus Graves. The page folded together with it, featuring an incomplete reply referencing the acquisition of the black dagger, was in the same handwriting as the rest of Mr. Badgerweed's notes. Badgerweed was Thaddeus Graves. He didn't just *work* for the Graves family, the Maskers' competitors to the northeast, he was a member of the family. She knew the name well. Thaddeus Graves was the youngest brother to the patriarch of the family, and the uncle to the very man her sister Euphoria had married.

The revelation didn't have time to settle, as she could hear the rattling of a departing wagon and the muttering of Temple in the front seat. She slipped the top back on the case, dropped to the floor where she'd been bound, and restored the gag. Just as he pulled the flap open to check on her, she rolled to her back, concealing the arms that should have been bound.

"I'll give you this. You've got more sense than your brother. Behaving yourself. That's good. There's a cache of supplies I left for myself ahead a ways. I'm going to pick it up, we're going to make our way somewhere private, and you and I are going to have a chat. You keep behaving yourself and you might just survive this. If I'm feeling generous, that is."

He continued onward. Epiphany's mind raced. She was almost out of time. Once he pulled her out, even if she somehow was able to retie her hands, he would see she'd cut the bindings and know something was up. She had between now and when he found somewhere private to figure out how to either subdue him or escape. She moved with more care, gag still in place and ever-ready to roll back to the floor and pretend to be bound, and returned to her search.

After a few more minutes of search, which failed to turn up anything that might tip the balance of power in her favor, the wagon rattled to a stop. Temple slipped from the driver's seat and marched off to fetch the supplies he'd hidden. She gave him time to get a few paces away, then scrambled forward and stuck her head out of the flap.

"Where is it? Where is it?" she hissed, tugging open the cubbies and compartments accessible to the driver.

He'd taken her bag, and with it both her brass knuckles and the bolter. He hadn't had the opportunity to stow it anywhere else. It had to be here or…

She turned and gazed at him. The strap for her bag was dangling out of his pack. She cursed herself for not suspecting he'd do such a thing. Panic seized her.

"Think, think. What would Fel do? What would Dad do? What would Mom do?"

Fel would tumble out, fists swinging, and take his chances against the better fighter. Her father would have been equipped to the teeth with extra contraptions. Her mother?

Epiphany thought back to the shop. Then back to her own wagon. There was always a spare weapon just out of sight. She looked up, to the very spot on the sun shade where Fel kept his dazzler. Up above the strut she felt a leather strap, but whatever it had retained had been taken.

"Hey!" Temple shouted.

She turned to him. He was already reaching for his crossbow. Epiphany desperately reached to the other side of the sun shade, above where the driver's partner would be. A second strap, this one still securing its own crossbow, hung with a bundle of bolts beside it. She grabbed it with one hand and reached down to snap the reins with the other. The horses started to lumber forward.

It was a heavy wagon, and even with two strong horses, it likely wouldn't move fast enough to outrun the mercenary in a sprint. He would catch up with her. But that he'd not taken a shot at her proved something she'd suspected ever since he'd grabbed her. He was hired to capture her alive. That gave her a razor-thin edge, because she was not similarly constrained. But she needed to widen that advantage a bit. As she heard him approaching, she shifted her stance.

He jumped into the back of the wagon and rolled to his feet. She raised the crossbow to fire. His motions were impeccably trained, allowing him to shift aside and lunge forward. Before she could pull the trigger, he wrapped his arm around hers, pinning it to her body and wrenching in an earnest attempt to either disarm her or tear the limb out of its socket. She cried out and released her grip. The crossbow fell to the ground.

He scrambled for it and snatched it up, now armed with a weapon in each hand. "Did you really think you'd be able to—"

Regardless of his plans for the rest of the taunt, what followed instead was a bloodcurdling scream. Epiphany had used the time he'd taken to grab the fallen crossbow to retrieve her boot knife and drive it into his thigh. Before he could recover, she yanked it out and heaved her shoulder into his side, forcing him to the ground. The fall dislodged one of the crossbows from his grip. He raised the other one. She slashed wildly with the knife. It was a short blade, but it cut his heavy jacket enough times that he decided it was better to fall back and regroup. He tried to pull himself out the back. She caught hold of his pack with one hand and continued slicing with the other. Not until the pack was cut free did he finally manage to tumble out the back of the moving wagon. He struck the ground hard, dazed. She grabbed the fallen crossbow and fired. Her aim was about as good as one could expect from an untrained markswoman taking a shot from a moving wagon. The bolt dug a gouge into the ground, and Temple dragged himself into the ditch beside the road before she could hope to restretch the bow and fire another shot.

Epiphany shakily returned to the seat and took the reins. A snap of the leather straps got the horses back up to speed. Temple, out of anger or desperation, managed to fire two bolts at the wagon. Neither struck anything important. Three heart-stopping minutes passed without any sign he had been able to follow. Only then did she allow herself to collapse and let the wave of anxiety and panic claim her.

#

Martin sat at the dining room table, eyes staring intently at Wick's lantern. He placed it in the draft of the dumbwaiter, such that the flame was constantly leaning aside. The instant it began to stand against the breeze, he spoke.

"Wick."

"Martin, I am pleased you are present, I have a considerable amount of information to give you."

"Are the children in danger?"

"As of my last contact with each, they were not under any additional threat."

"Is any of the other information urgent? Any specific and immediate dangers I need to know of?"

"No specific or immediate instances of known impending danger. Do you have something pressing that I need to know prior to delivering my update?"

"No. I have something pressing that *I* need to know before your update."

"Then I hope to be able to do you the service of providing this information."

"Are you capable of telling precisely how many open flames are available to you at any given time?"

"Yes. All flames lit from one of my own are known to me, if not instantly accessible to me."

"And how many are there?"

"At present, there are only two. One of the points I was hoping to update you on was the extinguishing of Epiphany's lantern while I was helping Fel."

Martin's expression hardened. "So we don't have a way to get in contact with her?"

"Not through me, I am afraid."

"And you are certain that there are only two. This one and that?"

"That is correct."

Martin paused for a moment before he spoke again. "Wick, do you have any loyalty to this family?"

"I have a fondness for the Masker clan. My involvement in your lives over the years has been extremely fulfilling."

"I didn't ask about fondness. I asked about loyalty."

"I do not know how to accurately answer that question. By what measure is my loyalty to be judged?"

"Have you performed any tasks for anyone else?"

"Since being reignited, I have served only the Maskers and, more recently, Tome."

"And you haven't delivered any information to anyone else?"

"My presence was made known to certain members of the group presently hosting Tome and Fel. I have spoken in their presence, but I do not believe any information of value has been disseminated to them."

"We already know that you've lied to us in the past."

"I do not know that I have, Martin."

"You withheld information about what Epiphany and Fel were up to."

"Withholding information is not equivalent to dishonesty."

"Wick, we have reason to believe we have been spied on. Multiple times in the recent past, people have anticipated our actions and movements with an accuracy that I'm not comfortable ascribing to coincidence. It is my concern that you are either knowingly or unknowingly providing information to others about us and endangering the family as a result."

"I am not doing so."

"And how can I trust you?"

"I do not know. I do not know I can provide information to restore your trust, nor do I know if such trust is warranted. I am a contraption. My operation can be manipulated. I have not provided information to others, but I cannot rule out the possibility that information has been extracted without my knowledge."

"Are you withholding any information from me?"

"Not on this topic."

He hammered the table. "Are you withholding any information at all!"

"Yes."

"What are you hiding?"

"Untold volumes of information. Years of observation. Countless documents consumed in my flames. You do not have the time remaining in your lifespan for me to communicate all this information to you."

"What sort of information?"

"Information of every conceivable variety."

"You're being evasive."

"I am attempting to answer your questions as concisely as possible. I cannot interpret your intent, only your words."

"How did you get all this information that you cannot share?"

"Through my own inadequacy and failed fulfillment of service."

Martin hissed a frustrated breath.

"Martin, I apologize, but it I believe you would be more angry with me if I were to delay any longer in providing you the updates about your children."

He nodded, his jaw tight. "What do you have?"

"No additional information about Epiphany, and there shall be no more updates thanks to the extinguishing of her flame in my absence. At last observation, she was continuing negotiations with her buyer and endeavoring to remain close in order to rely upon his security in the event of an attack."

"The flame was snuffed out while we were waiting to see if there would be such an attack. That doesn't bode well."

"I agree. Hopefully new information is provided through other means soon."

"And Fel?"

"Fel has been recruited by a dragon who has been shackled by a massive contraption-based trap. He has provided a great deal of very specific information regarding its likely mode of activation and deactivation. His freedom depends upon successfully performing this service for the dragon."

Martin, after stewing for ages, worried about something he had no control over, stood and nodded. This, at least, he knew precisely how to handle. "I will get some paper and prepare my notes."

#

Fel reached the top of the stairs, Oiler strapped firmly to his back. Parch hopped and skipped around the steps while Teya tried to keep her delight tempered. Fel had, with some effort, explained that he wouldn't be able to do any more work for Kazel until he heard back from his father, and that meant he would need to hold on to at least Wick's lantern. They'd allowed him to keep Oiler as well, if only because the contraption kept trying to follow him anyway, and with Teya in constant escort, they were confident an alarm could be raised and punishment could come swiftly and savagely if the contraption proved more of a threat than it seemed.

He paced over to the alcove that he'd been permitted to spend the night in. Tome was already there. He was looking a good deal more frazzled than before, with some fresh tears on his outfit and a scrape or two on his face. He brightened at Fel's appearance.

"Oh! There you are. I'm pleased to see you again. Given your performance in front of the dragon, I wasn't confident I would."

"Mmhmm…" Fel said thickly. "Listen, I'm still working my way through the leftovers of this hangover. So if you could keep the voice down."

"Right, of course. I apologize." He grabbed a canteen from beside him. "Water?"

Fel took it and flopped down on the cushion.

"So what happened down there?" Tome asked.

"I made a promise to a dragon that I could get him free."

"And can you?"

"We'll find out in a few hours when Dad gets back to us through Wick. What have you been up to?"

"I have had an extremely enlightening time, as a matter of fact. I've learned four new fairy tales, at least one of which I have good reason to suppose is a firsthand account written by actual fairies, which is rather novel. I've also learned that it is possible to tell a fairy story *too* well, when your audience is an excitable collection of scamps with exceedingly sharp claws. Evidently my 'clattering, clanking sky-devil' voice is rather convincing. Even so, the kobold children didn't want me to go. If human children are half as easy to entertain, I suspect I may have missed my calling as a storyteller."

Fel shrugged. "You're good at bluffing. What's that if not storytelling?"

"An excellent observation." Tome glanced at Teya. "I learned a bit more, but I'm not sure I should attempt to communicate it in mixed company."

Fel gave a surly look to his escort. "I wouldn't worry about her telling anyone anything. Seems like she doesn't bother spreading the word about important stuff until people figure it out on their own. And get a palmful of splinters while they're at it."

Teya grinned and initiated a game of headbutts with Parch. It wasn't clear if her smile was pride at torturing Fel or contentment at having a new playmate. It might well have been both.

Tome lowered his voice. "I think there may be something deeper at play here, regarding our hosts and their relationship with the wall."

"Deeper than 'it's a wall and they can't get out'?" Fel said.

"I don't think it's a matter of capacity. I think it's a matter of desire. And I don't think it's natural."

"Tome, listen. I need *someone* here to talk sense. I was hoping that would be you."

Tome pulled a small slip of paper from his pocket and scribbled something onto it. The mage then looked to Teya. "You spoke my language earlier, if with some difficulty, correct?"

She nodded, switching to swatting at Parch's head rather than clonking it with her own.

"If you would do me the favor, would you please answer the following question in my language. I would truly appreciate it."

She whined irritably. "Don't have to."

"Certainly not. But I would greatly appreciate it. Now, would you like to travel to the other side of the wall one day?"

"I have no interest in what lies beyond the wall, and no desire to bear witness to it," Teya croaked.

Fel raised an eyebrow. Given the level of mastery she'd displayed so far, he would have expected a reply like that to take her half an hour to assemble. Then he looked down at the page, where precisely the same sentence had been scrawled by his associate prior to Teya saying it.

"How did you do that?" Fel asked her, before turning to Tome. "How did *you* do that?"

"I think there is something mystical at play. I think something is toying with their heads, keeping them from having the desire to leave this place."

"Is that true?" Fel asked Teya.

The kobold shook her head.

"And do you want to get past that wall?"

This time her answer came in her own tongue, but had the same wooden delivery.

"Every one of those children said it. The Adept said it. I don't think they even *realize* they are being compelled."

Teya shook her head. She pointed to her head and swirled her finger, evidently as a means to illustrate her opinion of Tome's theory. Fel palmed his forehead.

"Tome, I really don't have much of a head for puzzles. Don't add another one to the pile."

"Oh, come now. Isn't it fascinating? Doesn't it tantalize you to know that something is just beyond your understanding, waiting for you to unravel it? Your father and I—"

"I don't want to hear about you and my dad." He rubbed his throbbing temple.

"You seem to have a particular aversion to any time I discuss collaborations with your father."

"Yeah, and yet you keep bringing them up."

"Is this a raw nerve I should know about?"

"It is a raw nerve you should avoid. Like *all* raw nerves," Fel snapped.

Tome managed to hold his tongue for nearly fifteen seconds.

"I just don't understand why me mentioning your father is—"

"It's because it's easy for you!" Fel said. "You've met my sister. And you've met my mother. Fanny is just a younger version of mom. She latched on to everything my mom taught and hit the ground running. My eldest sister did the same. She ran a little too far, sure, but she became exactly the sort of person the family needed her to be. Now look at me and Dad. Do I strike you as someone ready to take over for Dad when the time comes? I don't know a tenth of what he knows, and the parts I *do* know, I know half as well, and they took me twice as long to learn. If I wasn't strong and willing to risk my neck, the family wouldn't have much use for me at all!"

"So you were destined for something else."

"No, Tome. I was destined for *this*. It is a *family business*. It's generations deep. Do you know what it's like to know you're the one who fumbled the baton when it was handed to you in a relay that's been running practically since the contraptions we sell were first built? No! You don't! Because you ran away from your family business after you figured out you were good for something else. Well I can't *cast* spells, alright? I can drink, I can gamble, and I can hammer on contraptions and such until they start working or stop working. Mostly stop working. Anything beyond that is an uphill battle. Then you showed up and went skipping up that hill faster than Parch!"

"Well how about that, then?" Tome said, his own voice rising. "I've never, *never*, found someone who accumulated friends and allies as quickly and easily as you. We wander out into the fields and find a unicorn that you are already friends with! You get attacked in your hometown and the whole *city* comes to your aid. Even the *vermin*. By the high, Fel, you represent everything these people hate, and by the end of the second day, they've assigned you one of their own as a protégé, and you're doing odd jobs for their master. You don't *need* to cast spells. You're charmed already!"

"I'm not charmed. I'm just not a frustrating loudmouth know-it-all."

"I speak very softly, and there is no shame in having a depth of knowledge," he said, chin raised and arms crossed. "In the spirit of compromise, I will admit that I tend to frustrate people, but it is a trait I am endeavoring to correct."

"Keep working on it."

"It isn't *my* fault other people aren't as enticed by the mysteries of the world as I am."

"Are you really blaming the fact that no one likes you on everyone else?"

"Why shouldn't I? *You* are blaming *me* for your own feelings of inadequacy regarding your ability to rise to the standard set by your family."

"I don't *feel* inadequate, I *am* inadequate," he barked. "If I wasn't, I'd be picking that lock right now and we'd be halfway to getting out of here."

"I'll have you know that you seem to be the only one who thinks you're inadequate. I've spoken at length with all but your eldest sister, and they have tremendous respect for and deem of greatest value your contributions."

"That's because *they* don't know how hard I've been *trying* and how little of what I *try* to do actually *works*."

"Fight!" crowed Teya.

They turned to her. She was sitting on her haunches, hands on what Fel supposed were her knees, and eagerly observing the rising confrontation between the two with a wide grin and wider eyes. Worse, the area around the outside of their temporary home was surrounded by other kobolds, watching with equal interest. They crowed, chattered, and squawked in agreement. Here and there, the more loquacious of the creatures would pepper in a suggestion.

"Do magic!" shouted one from the back.

"Do lightning!" squawked a little one.

"Punches!" shrieked another.

"I'm not going to hit him," Fel said.

"And magic is far too much work to waste on a squabble," Tome said.

The disappointment in their faces was just short of heartbreaking.

"One lightning?" Teya offered by way of compromise.

"No," Fel said.

The crowd dispersed with a few mopey groans.

"They were rooting for me," Tome said proudly.

"One of them wanted punches," Fel countered.

Tome rubbed his chin. "I really ought to try a lightning spell. With what's left of the unicorn-horn ink and this good paper, I might be able to produce something exciting… But that is beside the point. I was *trying* to explain that I don't know how valuable the aid of these creatures will be. Even if we grant them their every wish and earn their eternal gratitude, if it is our wish to be taken back to the wall, they may not be capable of granting it."

"Not wanting to go past the wall and not *being able* to go past the wall are two different things," Fel said. "And we don't need them to go past the wall. We just need them to take us *to* the wall. And there must be *some* of them that can go past the wall, because we got attacked by a dragon on the other side of it, and there are hippogriffs and all sorts of Lesser Mystics on the other side of it too."

Tome nodded. "Granted, further investigation is necessary. But if I were you, I'd be considering the possibility that we would be better off heading to the wall ourselves."

A motion at the corner of their vision drew their attention. Teya was shaking her head.

"Nope," she said.

"Are you saying we aren't free to go?" Tome said.

"You? Eh. Him? Nope. Need help. For Kazel."

"Am I correct, though? If he *did* gain the trust and gratitude of you all, would you take us to the wall?"

Teya chattered her way through the exact statement she did last time, indicating her lack of interest for such things.

"There, you see?" Tome said.

"I still need to get permission to leave. And unless you feel confident about venturing through the woods between here and the wall by yourself, you're going to need as much of a ride as you can get. So we're both stuck until we can get Kazel free."

"And how likely is that?"

"It involves breaking a contraption. If there's one thing I can do, it's that."

#

Epiphany pushed the horses for as long as she dared, but as the sun started to sag in the sky, she knew they needed to rest, and so did she. She wasn't familiar with the town she'd reached, but her familiarity with it didn't matter much. She didn't have any other options to feed and rest the horses, and the entirety of her interactions had been purchasing a quick refreshment. Since then, and until she got back to Beffshire, all her time would be spent in the wagon.

It had taken her only a few more minutes with Graves's papers to find the inventory, and from there a few minutes more to uncover where the more useful contraptions and equipment could be found. She'd liberated two more crossbows, giving her a total of three, though frustratingly they took bolts of two different sizes. Since then, she'd been splitting her time between anxiously listening for danger and going through the rest of the material she'd found.

Epiphany had read through the entirety of the records box. It had been enlightening. Given the relatively sparse nature of the personal communications she'd found, the more sensitive information had been destroyed rather than stored. Even so, she'd learned a great deal. There were three more references to "the clockwork diamond." And while nothing so much as hinted at what precisely it was or why they were after it, every mention was surrounded by warnings that it absolutely must not be sought until all proper precautions were made.

When she'd satisfied herself she knew everything the notes could teach her, she went through the contents of Temple's pack. It was considerably less information-dense. What he mostly carried was an assortment of hand weapons, some other survival gear, and a single folded mission brief. It called for the acquisition of Oiler, the Bygone dagger, and Epiphany. Considerable detail was given about the way Oiler would act, the potential usage of the Bygone dagger to both disable Oiler and to counter any contraptions Epiphany might be carrying, and the additional weapons her father had sent her with—those weapons that even *she* didn't know she'd be carrying until her dad had handed them to her. Yet he hadn't known about the boot blade.

She was squinting at the page for several minutes before she was able to tear herself away sufficiently to try to light the lantern and to continue reading. She grabbed it from its hook and felt around for the rather poorly restored sparker that was among Badgerweed's equipment, but something caught her eye. There shouldn't have been any light in the wagon. But now that the sun was down, what seemed to be a single ember of light was showing from a section of the wagon's wall she'd thought was solid wood. She ran her fingers over the wooden surface and found a gap. A bit of gentle prying pulled a thin plank free to reveal a very curious lantern. The light burning on the wick was minuscule, barely as bright as a tea candle. But the reservoir of oil beneath it was as big as a decent-size canteen. The inside of the compartment was lined with tin and caked with soot. She would have questioned why such a lantern would exist, too dim to be a useful light, too small to be a useful source of heat. But she had one not so different from it in her own wagon. The lantern that kept Wick's flame lit.

The flame flickered. She glared at it, uncertain if it had been flickering before. For the moment, though, that didn't matter. What mattered more was the scent the wind carried. Badgerweed.

She set the lantern down and used the sparker to light the larger one hanging on its hook. She took one of the crossbows in hand and waited until the lantern's glow revealed her own wagon rattling up. One of the two armed associates of her business partner in this little venture rode up. He had a weapon in hand.

"Put the weapon down," called the voice of the man she'd called Badgerweed until now.

"No, Thaddeus, I don't think I will," she said.

He stepped down from the wagon and into the light of the lantern. "As it happens, Epiphany, I was talking to my own man, not you," he said. He gazed at the papers, carefully sorted and spread around Epiphany. "You know something? One of the ways I'd rather enjoyed doing business with you was your willingness to respect my privacy. I see you've changed that policy."

"It started because I needed to find a way to ward off my kidnapper, but silly me, when I find evidence of treachery, it piques my interest. So, how's Euphoria?"

"Doing quite well. She's been an asset to the Graves family."

"And I imagine this is why we weren't invited to the wedding? Because then I'd have recognized any sneaky attempts to buy straight from us?"

"You wouldn't have enjoyed the wedding anyway. Interminably long ceremony, and my brother was terribly stingy on the refreshments. You say you needed a way to ward off your kidnapper. How aggressively did you achieve that?"

"He's still alive, but he'll be walking with a limp for a while."

"We didn't encounter him. But we did manage to kill two Bolivan agents, and we haven't been bothered by any others along the way. May I say, thank you for rescuing the wagon. Six months of inventory would be a terrible loss, particularly when said inventory includes the dagger."

"You and I need to have a conversation about what I've learned."

"Indeed we do." He stepped into the wagon and took a seat.

"First, what's this?" she said, holding up the lantern she'd found.

"I'd rather you not waste your time and mine by answering a question we both know the answer to."

"You have access to Wick?"

He laughed. "They'd told me the Maskers named it. It's always just been a voice to me."

"How long have you had it?"

"Let me be clear, and you'll find this both disappointing and difficult to believe—I don't have all the answers. The Graves family isn't like the Bolivan family. We aren't this sprawling syndicate with disposable members. We're not much larger than the Masker family. But apparently we're just large enough for there to be an inside and an outside, and dear Uncle Thaddeus is decidedly on the *outside*. Do you think I'd be sitting in this uncomfortable wagon trading as part of the bazaar for the bulk of my year otherwise? I'm told what they think I need to know to turn a profit, and that's all."

"So why did you have a *much* better description of the artifacts than you gave me?"

"Because I was instructed to give you no more information than you required, and you required very little. Your sister seems to think you're too good at figuring things out to be trusted with all the pieces from the beginning. Clearly that was a sound, if inadequate, precaution. But on the subject of withheld information."

He held out a hand. His bodyguard provided a slip of paper that was a perfect match for the one in Temple's pack.

"It seems these fellows were very well informed about you as well. In particular, it seems as though they expected you to have Oiler, or should I say 'the heavy pack, full of chain.' But you claimed never to have found it. And given the degree of detail they had, I don't think they were simply *guessing* about it. We've *both* been hiding information, haven't we?"

"Evidently. Tell me this. What is the clockwork diamond?"

He raised his eyebrows and took a puff of his pipe. "Listen, if you've read the stuff in the records box, you know everything I know."

"I don't believe you. There are gaps in the correspondences. You've destroyed information."

"Then we'd probably do better just to skip the accusations of dishonesty and the demands for information. Instead, we should focus on what we're going to do."

"We are four days from Beffshire if we go directly. I suggest we focus on keeping each other safe until we can get there, and then regroup," she said.

"A sound plan, since I don't think we'll be able to benefit from further usage of the bazaar while the Bolivans are after us. Any other thoughts?"

"Just one." She twisted off the top of the strange little lantern and blew out the flame. "My parents already knew my flame was out, so at this point it's more important to me that you don't have access to Wick for the duration of this trip than if I do."

#

"No, no. You bid on it. Bid. Like you say how much you want to pay for it, and other people have a chance to pay more," Fel said.

With nothing to do but wait until Wick got back, Fel and Tome had taken it upon themselves to make a simple set of grum tiles out of bits of wood and start teaching the kobolds how to play. Contrary to appearances, the little creatures were quite clever. Most of them hadn't fully grasped the game, but they were utterly fascinated by it. They had gathered around, sitting on mounds of firewood and supply stashes so as to get a better view of the show as Fel and Tome played a game with Teya and the one other kobold who had picked up enough to give the game a try, a male named Gru. In lieu of money, they were using piles of scales, a fact which did not sit well with Tome.

"I bid two for the milkmaid," Tome said, separating two scales from the rest of his pile. "If only to decrease the amount of discarded animal hide I have to deal with."

Gru passed the bid to Teya. Teya bid three. Fel bid four, and eventually the bid got around to Teya again. She had only four scales left to bid. But she looked herself over, scratched a bit, and managed to dislodge a scale to add to the bid.

"Yet another reason why scales were a poor choice of currency," Tome said.

Fel looked at the spread of hand-drawn tiles before him. "Any more bids?"

"Please, let this run end," Tome said.

The kobolds shook their heads.

"Drop the screens and let's see them," Fel said.

Everyone dropped the bits of bark they'd improvised into privacy screens. Gru had a fairly standard beginner set of tiles, in that there was one queen and nothing else of value. Tome had been bluffing, Fel had a run of carpenters and plowmen. As for Teya?

"Three kings and a red falconer," Fel said, smirking and shaking his head. "That's the win. Your third run of tiles, and the first one we didn't have to start over after one of you made a mistake, and you won."

Teya crowed and gathered up the winnings, then carefully counted them into four piles and started handing them back out.

"No, no. You keep those. Those are your winnings," Tome said.

Teya shook her head. "Play game. Play more game."

"The idea is you gather up other people's money until no one else can afford to play. That's how you win. And how you get rich."

She shook her head again and plopped down the balanced piles one by one. "Play. More. Game."

"Fel, I have finished discussions with your father," Wick said, suddenly present in the lantern.

The kobolds squealed and scattered, with the exception of Teya, who tensed a bit but stayed put.

"Anything good?" Fel asked.

"He reached a reasonably high degree of certainty that he knew the nature of the panel you described and laid out two possible methods for defeating it. Before that matter is addressed, it is worth mentioning two other developments."

"Oh? Am I going to want to hear them?"

"Quite likely not. First, we have lost contact with your sister. Her lantern was extinguished while I was observing you. There is no reason to believe she is in danger, but no way to be sure of that."

"She can handle herself. What else?"

"Your father, and possibly your mother as well, are of the belief that I have been used as a means to spy on the family."

"Have you?"

"Not to my knowledge."

"Good enough for me. Let's get down there and see if we can free the dragon and make some friends and earn some favors."

"I'll come along, if I may," Tome said.

"Seemed like you were in an awfully big hurry to get out of there last time."

"Now there's a bit of a riddle to be done, and the likelihood of some gratitude to be earned."

"Oh, I get it. You want to be there when I cut him loose so you can hog some of the glory."

"Don't care! Come! Fast!" Teya said, grabbing Wick's lantern and bounding for the stairs.

Fel hurried after her, snatching Oiler along the way. "What do we need to know?" he asked as they descended the stairs, struggling to keep in range of Wick's flame.

"Your father said that what you described sounded like what he called an 'inert contraption.' Much in the same way that the bygone dagger is able to make functional contraptions nonfunctional, there are contraptions which, themselves, are not able to perform their function without the proximity of other contraptions."

"Something that doesn't work unless you have another thing sounds an awful lot like a lock and key, which is what I already thought this was," Fel said.

"It is very much a lock and key, and Martin has provided a precise description of what that key would look like, but he also explained that contraptions like this cease to be inert when in proximity of *any* contraption, not just their intended key."

"That sounds like a terrible, ineffective way to lock something," Tome said, already huffing and puffing to keep up.

"The lock will not *unlock* simply because a contraption is nearby, but if the lock is picked with another contraption, it will unlock, whereas attempting to pick the lock without a contraption will fail regardless of whether the mechanisms of the lock are properly positioned."

"All right. Picking locks isn't fun, but I can do it."

"You are a fountain of unscrupulous skills, Fel," Tome said. "And in this case, it is admirable."

They approached the door. Teya was well in the lead and chattered with the kobold guards until they stepped aside, allowing the group into Kazel's prison.

Teya stopped and bowed her head in reverence.

"Fel Masker," the dragon rumbled.

"Kazel, we might have a way to get you free."

"Then go to it. And if you need any aid, it shall be given," the dragon stated.

The beast did not sound hopeful. The instructions Kazel gave had the feel of something he'd uttered dozens of times before. A formality before another inevitable failure.

Fel and the others kept to the wall and rushed to the still-unlocked hatches on the far side of the shattered door. He dropped Oiler and his gear. With his sparker in hand, he reached toward the lock. He had to just about insert the contraption into the slit, but once it was near enough, the interior began to glisten with the faint blue light of a contraption in operation. And the operation was quite evident. The tumblers started to shift ever so slightly, the disks bobbing in and out.

"Dad knows his stuff," Fel said with a grin.

Teya looked back and forth between Tome and Fel, guarded excitement in her motions. Fel inserted two probes while palming the sparker. With a bit of manipulation, and a lot of muttered profanity, the slit produced a soft click and a subtle flash of light.

"Was that it?" Tome said. "Nothing happened. Was something supposed to happen?"

"That was one tumbler. These bottom slits have three tumblers and two discs. I need to get them all," Fel said.

He fought for a few more minutes. Now and then, the lock would produce a flash. There was even a second in rapid succession at one point. But no amount of manipulation could do much more than put on a light show.

"This is not encouraging, Fel," Tome said. "Kazel is watching us, and you aren't doing anything useful."

"There are *three* tumblers and *two* disks and I have two hands, Tome. And this isn't like a normal lock. There's nothing for me to twist or lean on to get these things to bind in place. And they're moving, so I couldn't even wedge them in place if I had a means to do so. I need to do all five of them at the same time. I need three more hands."

"So should Teya and I help?" Tome asked.

"Help!" Teya said, grabbing a knife from the bag and scrambling onto Fel's shoulders to haphazardly jab it into the slit.

"No, no, no," Fel said, shrugging her off and taking the knife from her. "Setting aside the nightmare it would be to have to work together with a novice and another novice with a language barrier and only four fingers, there's just not enough room in the slit to get five tools in there. Maneuvering things into the right position would be..."

Oiler interrupted by poking its puzzle box up to be mixed again. Fel paused, then smiled.

"I have an idea." He took the puzzle box. "Oiler, I have a new puzzle box for you." He pointed to the slit. "Do you see inside there?"

Oiler reeled its head up and gazed into the slit. The blue illumination was far stronger once it had poked its nose inside than the sparker had achieved.

"Do you see those disks and tumblers? The tumblers go up and down, the disks go in and out. You will see a flash of light when one of them is in the right position. All five of them need to be in the right position to solve the puzzle."

Oiler looked at Fel, then reeled a claw up and stuck one digit inside. It tapped around until it found a tumbler and started to shift it up and down. There were flickers and flashes of light, but they were very brief.

"Move more slowly. It is a very precise position," Fel instructed.

Oiler's eye shifted. It leaned a bit closer and made finer motions with its claw. There was a clear, undeniable flash. Oiler withdrew its claw, almost as if startled, then waggled its fingers and jammed both claws into the slit. Flashes came slowly and irregularly. But after five minutes of manipulation, the flickers started coming in pairs, and then trios. Eventually, five quick flashes produced, rather than a click, a startling grind and a distant cacophonous rattle. The sound startled Oiler, who withdrew its claws and huddled into its pack like a frightened turtle. But the sound that came next was still more startling.

The dozens of kobolds, including Teya, produced an ululating trill of joy. The shackles about Kazel's hind legs had released and withdrawn into the walls. The dragon stood, one leg raised, and curled the claws of a leg with a rubbed-raw place hidden by his bonds for centuries.

"Again. *Again*," Kazel barked, his words rattling the very mountain.

"Next one up, Oiler. Same puzzle, different solution."

This one took longer to produce its first flash, but once the first one came, the others swiftly followed. Another rattling retraction of an ancient trap resounded. Kazel stood tall and thundered over his hoard toward them. Without the irons on his legs, he was able to reach nearly the midpoint of the room.

"Again. Once more and you shall know not only absolution for the crimes of those of your name but also rewards no human has ever known."

"This one might be tricky," Fel said under his breath.

"Why?" Tome hissed. "We're so close!"

"Because it's five tumblers and seven disks. Oiler only has four digits on each claw."

"… That's not going to work," Tome said.

"Probably not. Wick, what was the other plan to get this open?" Fel asked.

"Find the key."

"*I could have come up with that*," Tome said.

"Please tell me Dad has more information than that," Fel said.

"Your father was confident that the keys, all of them, would have been on display within the vault with which they were associated. He said locks and keys of this sort weren't meant to imprison, but to secure."

"What's the difference?" Fel said.

"Your father found one example of a trap and vault with a similar description in an old history book. The shackles weren't used to capture a prisoner; they were used to display a trophy."

Fel gazed at Kazel. "Whoever made this vault built it to capture something specifically to show it off?"

"Yes. In that vault, the key was made to be ornate, and was included in the display of the vault-keeper's wealth. Your father believes it is very likely that the keys were included in the vault."

"Does he know what the key would have looked like?"

"It would have been approximately square, scaled to the vertical size of the slit. The top front corner would have a serrated top, with serrations corresponding in position and number to the number of tumblers in the lock. There would similarly be a number of nodes corresponding to the position and number of disks within the lock. The serrations and nodes would be in constant motion, matching the motion of the tumblers and disks. A mounting hole would be on the center of the far side, and it is likely that there would be a decorative inlay of copper or more precious metals."

"Teya, did you get all that?"

The kobold nodded.

"Good, go ask everyone if they remember seeing that sort of thing."

She nodded again, then scrambled up to stand on Fel's shoulders and bellowed in her complex chattering tongue.

Fel wrestled her off his shoulders. "I said *go* and ask."

The contraption you seek was once within this vault," Kazel replied. "When I first came to this place, that very piece was on display."

"You're sure?"

"A dragon's memory is ironclad. This is doubly so for items of value. Even when that value is tainted by the whims of a contraptioneer."

"What happened to it?" Fel called.

"It, like most of the contents of the vault, was spirited away by Duurth before I discovered his trespasses."

Oiler retracted its claws and head, settling back down into its pack. When Fel gave him a questioning glance, the contraption merely shook its head and waggled the puzzle box again. Fel scrambled it and handed it back, adding a pat on the head for good measure.

"I can't pick the last lock, the one for the neck shackle. It's too much, too complex. I'd need two Oilers, and I don't even know if there *are* two Oilers or if they could work together like that. Is Duurth still around?"

"He persists," Kazel said, expression and tone making it clear that this was a source of endless dismay.

"Do you know where he is?"

The many kobolds nodded their heads.

"Then you're going to have to send someone there to get it back, if you want to get out of here. You've got enough kobolds, surely you can swarm him. Or send someone to sneak in when he's not there."

"My people cannot," Kazel said. "They cannot access his lair."

"Why not?"

The kobolds, again in near-unison, uttered the single phrase both Tome and Fel had heard often enough to recognize in their tongue.

"That is really unsettling," Fel said under his breath.

"Is his lair outside the wall?" Tome asked.

They all nodded. Kazel hissed a furious breath.

"Leave us. Leave only the outsiders and Teya. I wish to discuss matters privately."

The kobolds scurried out the door to the rest of the lair with remarkable efficiency.

"Approach," Kazel instructed.

Fel and Tome hesitated.

"You want us to climb on the gold?" Fel asked.

"*Approach,*" Kazel thundered.

Fel was briefly torn between the desperate need to do as he was told and the equally desperate need to flee screaming from the big scary monster that was yelling at him. Parch, illustrating that he might have a greater wisdom than the humans, launched himself up the stairs to what he considered to be a safe distance. When he regained control of his legs, Fel shakily stepped forward, treading on the shifting mounds of gold coins and bars until he was at the dragon's feet. Tome followed, a sensible three steps behind.

"If you're planning on roasting me or eating me, that's not going to get you free either," Fel said.

"If it was my intention to kill you, I would not have allowed you within my lair and its protections. The time has come for you to understand the deeper reason for the overall hatred for contraption-makers within the Greater Lands."

"It's more than just knowing we made the contraptions keeping you locked up?"

"Our distrust for you and your kind is universal among thinking creatures within the wall. You have observed the reply you receive when you inquire about the outside world."

"That is a point of great fascination," Tome said.

"Something holds sway over our thoughts. Something that, by its very nature, we are unable to fully grasp. It seems to effect only beings of the same general sort. Mystic creatures, and more specifically, mystic creatures with a degree of wisdom. Lesser Mystics seem to escape its grip, and beasts who lack the intelligence to conceive of it are likewise more weakly influenced. For most, it exists as a haziness of the mind that hangs over two portions of the world, one quite vast and one quite small. They are unaware of the influence, and seem even ignorant of the changes it makes to their behavior. Teya knows where she cannot go, and what she cannot do, but she does not know why, or even suspect that those things beyond her capacity are anything more than sources of distaste that she simply wishes to avoid."

Fel looked at his escort. Her expression was complex. Mostly she looked as though she was basking in the light of a diving being, enchanted by the mere fact that she was being permitted to be so close to her master. But around the edges there was a look of discomfort and confusion. One might imagine such a look in a person struggling with a bit of arithmetic or a riddle she didn't understand.

Kazel continued. "Beings of my age and wisdom are cursed with a deeper understanding. We are aware of the influence. But we are not immune to it. I cannot overcome the curse of being drained of drive and desire when I even *think* of leaving this place. But I am acutely aware that this behavior does not come from within."

"Astounding…" Tome said.

"And you think a *contraption* is doing this?" Fel said. "Because my family has worked with them for years, and with the exception of a few, everything we've found either makes noise, makes light, or makes things move. Our big moneymakers are things that play music or produce alarm sounds. If we could tinker with people's minds… well, aside from having those contraptions taken away from us, we'd probably be in a much loftier position in society."

"It is the work of a contraption. There is no doubt."

"You said there were two places you couldn't go."

"The first is the world beyond the wall," Kazel said.

"That's not 'a place you can't go,' that's everywhere but here. This is the only place you *can* go," Fel said.

Kazel lowered his head, bringing it once again close enough for Fel to feel the pulsing heat of his snout.

"It is comforting to know that ignorance of the nature of the world is not unique to Greater Mystics," he said.

"What do you mean?"

"You believe the Greater Lands to be a circle on a map, enclosed by your precious wall. I cannot force the truth into a mind without the means to grasp it. But if you do find yourself someday soon permitted to return to the wall, look upon its curve before you leave, and look upon its curve after."

"I know how circles work," Fel said, self-preservation barely able to keep the sharpness from his tone.

"You spoke about a second place," Tome said. "I assume that's where Duurth can be found."

"If you believe this place to be a circle of your own world, then in its center is an island. And on that island is a place I cannot know. A place forbidden from my mind. Within that place, Duurth resides."

"I guess that explains why you didn't just send people to kill him and get your stuff back," Fel said.

"None of my people can go there," Kazel said.

"Then how does Duurth go there?" Tome asked.

"Duurth is a curiosity. An oddity. From his scent, I know he is not a pure dragon. He does not share my nature. I believe him to be the offspring of a greater dragon and a lesser."

Tome tipped his head up. "I've seen drawings of a lesser dragon, and if we take you to be representative of the greater variety, the logistics of that coupling are something of a riddle," he said.

"You should do like I do, and just try not to think about that stuff," Fel said.

"Duurth escapes the bulk of the influence by nature of his dull, formless mind and his diminished mystic nature. He is barely more than a clever beast, free of the influence that chains us more securely than even the shackle about my neck."

"And since he's a dragon, I take it he's still got all that stuff mounded up somewhere."

"If the key has value, it is a part of his hoard."

Fel rubbed his forehead. "I don't like where this is going."

"If you wish for my aid, you must take the key from him and bring it here."

"Kazel, I'm not happy about having to deal with you and you're *reasonable*. Now you want me to go track down a dragon that's a wild animal?"

The words that followed should have carried the ring of desperation, of pleading. In essence, Kazel was begging for Fel's help that no one else could provide. But he spoke steadily and plainly, like he was patiently providing instructions to someone who didn't understand a simple task.

"You do not need to track him down. We will take you to the very edge of his territory. You will be given all the aid I can offer. I will send you with the Adept, with the best of my people. Supplies. Weapons. Whatever you require. You can remain distant, hidden, and enter only when the foul thing has departed. Duurth's fondness for contraptions has made him the enemy of all who reside in the Greater Lands. He must hunt at sea, or out beyond the wall to avoid clashing with our own. But none shall follow you into his lair to help you. They will not be able to."

Fel tried to work up the fortitude to refuse. He wasn't sure what Kazel would do if he did, but he seemed to be considerably safer to deal with than this Duurth creature. But the delay in his response lasted just long enough for him to realize something else. An old motivation reared its ugly head.

"You say this is an island?"

"Yes. Some distance offshore."

"So I'll need a boat, then. Do you have one?"

"Some of the kobolds go fishing. There are boats."

"How long will it take to get to the island?"

"The Adept will know. She will need to arrange for safe and swift passage. The swiftness depends upon the arrangements she can make."

Tome tugged Fel's sleeve. "You don't really think you can do this, do you?"

"I think it'll be worth my while to try."

"Then go. Explain to the Adept what must be done. Should you fail in service of me, know that your name shall forever be cleared of the stain of its past. And should you succeed, I pledge to you safety within my lands and my aid in returning to yours."

"I'll do my best."

Without being beckoned, the legion of kobolds returned in single file through the door.

Fel shakily slid from the top of the heap of gold. Parch pranced back up to him, and the whole group headed for the stairs to the upper lair.

Once they were through the door and a fair distance from Kazel's chamber, Tome tapped him.

"What are you thinking, precisely?" he asked.

"Do good! Help!" Teya said, with an encouraging slap to Fel's back that required a bit of a hop to deliver.

"Tome, do you remember when I said the closer to the Greater Lands, the better the contraptions?"

The mage paused. "Ah."

"If dragons *really* have an eye for value, we're being asked to infiltrate the lair of one who has cherry-picked the best items from a vault the size of a banquet hall. Even if the thing chose at random, there are going to be things the outside world hasn't seen since the Bygone Era."

Tome glanced at Teya, then back to Fel.

"But of course the *reason* you are taking this risk is to help the master of this land to be freed," he said with a rather transparent prompt for agreement.

Teya held up a claw. "Don't need lie. Don't care why help. Just help."

"I like your point of view, Teya. And you're getting better at talking," Fel said.

"Know how talk. Just make face tired. More practice, less tired. 'Til then, less words, better."

Fel rubbed his hands together. "Now we just have to hope that a dragon sleeping on top of it since the Bygone Era hasn't broken everything too badly."

"Since the Bygone Era..." Tome snapped. "I should have asked Kazel about the Bygone Era."

"What's to ask?"

"What's to ask? *Everything.* He was alive for it. And what was that about the curve of the wall? So many questions. I just wish either he was less intimidating, or I was as oblivious to danger as you."

"Brave. The word is 'brave,'" Fel said.

"Foolhardy, I would say," Tome countered.

"Both!" Teya said. "Even better."

"Shall I inform your father of your intentions?" Wick asked.

"You want to know if you should tell Dad that I'm planning to raid the lair of a dragon?"

"Yes," Wick said.

"I'd rather you didn't."

"You father is already having doubts about my trustworthiness."

"Then a little more silence couldn't hurt."

Wick paused. "As you wish. What shall I tell him instead?"

"Just tell him I'm looking for the key."

"I shall happily provide this fulfilling service."

Joseph R. Lallo

Chapter 8

Martin pulled the final plate from the final compartment of the final contraption he'd not yet searched. Despite his growing certainty that Wick was at the root of their spy problem, he continued his search. In part, it was because he still harbored some hope that he was wrong. Wick was a profoundly useful contraption, and Martin had come to think of him as not only a friend but also a member of the family. If he was now a liability, and a traitor…

"Nothing," he said. "Nothing but cogs, disks, and axles. No hidden contraptions. Nothing that could explain… what I already explained."

He pushed the dismantled contraption aside and cradled his head. Finding something besides Wick to explain the leaking information wasn't the only goal of the continuing search. In the Masker family, the task always came first. It was a family trait and a family tradition, taught to children and practiced like a ritual. When there was a job to do, the job was the only thing. Martin could throw his entire mind into any task, and he could stay focused upon it regardless of whatever else was happening, or wasn't happening, or might happen. But the very moment he dismissed this final contraption, the floodgates opened and he was forced to confront his looming uncertainties: that he had no clue where his daughter was or if she was safe; that his son was in a place that precious few adventurers had ever returned from, doing business with mystic creatures that could kill him with a flick of their tail. And though the kids had made their own decisions, it didn't change anything. He and his wife had willingly sent them off to these tasks.

He gritted his teeth and turned. There must be something else to search. He'd pulled up floorboards and checked the spaces between joists. He'd punched holes in plaster to search within. He'd even pulled the coals and dust out of the stove that normally heated his workshop. Nothing. In fact, the replacement of the vigorous, sweaty work of tearing apart the house with the meticulous work of disassembling the last of the contraptions had given him a bit of a chill without the oven smoldering. He grabbed a log and his sparker, but something in his head clicked.

Martin took Wick's lit lantern, its flickering flame indicating the sentry's absence, and held it up to the emptied and cleaned stove. He peered inside and ran his fingers along the base plate. It hadn't been this clean in years. Immediately, something felt wrong about it. It was quite smooth. Everywhere else on the thing had the rough texture of a casting. But this felt hammered. Flattened. Worked.

He knocked on the side of the stove. A dull thunk and a painful knuckle were the result. He knocked on the bottom. A tinny ring. He'd heard the sound a thousand times when adding fresh wood into the oven. He stuck his head inside and ran his fingers around the edge.

"Of course…"

Martin stood and grabbed one of his hammers. He stuck his head back into the stove and, with an awkward motion, smashed at the curve where the floor met the wall. What should have been metal chipped and shattered like clay.

#

"I came all the way down from the south edge of Quarr because I was told this antiquities shop would be able to restore it," said an aging man with a stopped watch.

"Whoever is advising you is quite wise. We specialize in devices of great complexity and age, and this watch is both," Vivian said.

"It is very precious to me. It's been in the family for generations."

"Then you are to be commended for the excellent care you have given it. Most devices I have seen of this age are barely recognizable. Though, of course, we restore them just the same."

"I hesitate to trust it to just anyone. There's a reason I brought it here personally rather than having it sent."

"My husband, Martin Masker, has the keen mind of an engineer and the steady hands of a fine artist. I can assure you without fear of contradiction that you could find no one in the world whose care would be safer than his."

The door and hatch to the rest of the house burst open, and Martin dashed up the stairs. He was caked with dust, soot, and sweat. The sleeve of his shirt was torn, and he seemed to have bits of clay in his hair and stuck to his face. He held a battered, blackened disk in his hand, about the size of a cake plate.

"I have it! I have it!" he raved, slamming it down on the counter.

"Thank you, sir," Vivian said to him, her expression unchanged by Martin's sudden appearance. "Do run downstairs and inform Martin that we have a very important, very precious piece of equipment that he'll need to repair."

Martin looked at her, then the customer, and finally at the condition of his outfit.

"Right, I'll just… inform him. He… won't be able to come directly. He's rather busy."

"Of course," Vivian said.

Martin crept rather sheepishly down through the hatch and shut it.

"My apologies for that," Vivian said. "We are having some rather significant work done on the house, and we may have skimped a bit on the price for the labor. I believe I can have this for you tomorrow. The price will be sixty-five duots."

"Mmm… Reasonable," he said. "Tomorrow then."

"Indeed, by close of business. Payment upon completion."

He nodded and left the watch.

She carefully boxed it for service, then turned and shouted. "The customer is gone, dear. I imagine you had something urgent to discuss?"

He emerged again, hair roughly tamed and freed of its dustiness but otherwise looking like a man who had been maniacally disassembling the house. Vivian picked up the disk he'd thrown down.

"What is this?" she said.

"That is the primary plate of a sentry lantern. It was hidden in a false bottom in the stove in my workshop."

"I see…"

He flipped it over. "This is where a flange would have to be very precisely etched with… I'm not sure what it ought to be called. With Wick's true name. The means to permanently assign a sentry lantern." Martin fished a magnifier lens out of his pocket and held it up to the flange. "This is not Wick's name."

"Are you suggesting there is a second sentry flame?"

"I am. And there are other elements of the contraption missing as well. I suspect it is the portion that maintains the flame without the need for fuel. Those components would be very difficult to replace, and a sentry lantern without it would be rather difficult to use. But with this plate in my woodstove, anytime I was heating my workshop, which to a minor degree was almost *always,* then the flame would be lit and burning. The flame would not be able to *see,* but it would be able to hear anything that was spoken. And, I hesitate to suggest it, but I believe it would also be privy to any pages I burned in the stove."

Vivian steepled her fingers and leaned her elbows on the counter, eyes facing the street outside. She snatched the plate and hid it behind the counter.

"Are we certain this is the means of eavesdropping?"

"Unless there is something in addition. But what concerns me is… that is to say, one of the *many* things that concerns me is, the question of when it was placed. No one but family comes into my workshop. Not even Tome has been allowed there. And anyone who might attempt to install it without my knowledge would have to defeat all our alarms *and* work through all five floors of a house that is never unoccupied."

"That is a puzzle. But what concerns me more is not who installed it but who has been listening."

"And furthermore, what is to be done about it," he said. "We may be out of our depth, Vivian."

"We may well be," she said.

"We may need more than the usual help."

She nodded. "You know that I've spoken to Donovan Verfessa, and he's offered a partnership."

"I do. And the thought had crossed my mind that we might be better served with his services and skills available to us."

"We don't yet know what sort of a price that carries. Financial and otherwise."

"So far, it is only through great luck and good friends that the price of the present dilemma was not our lives and those of our children. And we still don't know what's become of Epiphany, or where she is."

"Then what we need right now, more than protection, is information."

"Quite so. And if that is what we are after, I don't know that Verfessa will be of much help. "

She continued to stare out the shop window. "I don't have an answer, Martin. I don't know what should be done."

"Nor do I. But this is a family matter."

"Mmm… And until now, the family has always handled such matters itself."

"Until we know what precise help we need that Verfessa can provide, I think it serves us best to handle this personally."

"Information…" she mused. "The problem is that we lost control of the flow of information. We need to restore that control." Her eyes narrowed. One eyebrow cocked. "Would the sentry flame be aware it has been discovered?"

"Until it is lit again, it has no new information. Though, if I were the person monitoring for fresh information on the other end, I would be quite suspicious about the lengthy silence."

"Can the plate be reinstalled?"

"With some small effort."

"Then here is what I propose. Reinstall it, relight the stove, and continue your search. I'll be down after closing with a watch for you to repair. At that point, we shall have a discussion while you work on it."

Martin worked his way through her suggestion and paced it forward to its natural conclusion. He nodded. "A fine suggestion, love. I'll get to it immediately."

#

"So she just *flies around* all day?" Fel said, marching back and forth in front of the Adept's throne.

Teya nodded, as did Mik and Stix, who occupied their typical spots on either side of the throne.

"But she left her *hands*!" he said. "What exactly was she going to do?"

"She goes. Flies. Watches. Sees," Teya said.

"But surely she has people for that. She's in charge. Since when do people in charge actually do useful things on their own?"

"She likes flying," Teya said. "Flies just to… fly."

Stix and Mik both nodded.

"Why?" he asked.

"Wouldn't you?" Teya hugged herself and tipped her head back. "Fly. Like dragon."

"There is *work* to do," Fel said.

"I'm frankly not certain why you're in such a rush," Tome said, seated at a crate near the wall and scrawling on a page. "This is a terribly dangerous undertaking, and we need time to prepare."

"You need time to prepare. You're the one who has to predict what he'll need and write down spells for it. I just grab my gear and go. You don't even need to come along," Fel said. "You're not the one with a 'stained name' that needs to be cleared."

"First, I don't trust you to survive on your own. Second, dare I say there is some value in having a dragon owe me a favor. Third, there is *certainly* some value in whatever goods you're hoping to liberate from Duurth's hoard. And fourth… blast it, now I've lost track."

"Fine, come if you want, but I'm not waiting for you."

"Again, why the rush?"

"When you had a great big pile of chores or dirty jobs to do, some easy and some hard, were you the 'do the easy ones first' or 'do the hard ones first' sort of a person?"

"Fel, I copied books letter by letter starting before I could speak properly. I had only two chores. Copy symbols from page to page and refill inkwells. Both were dirty, neither was difficult."

"I had jobs. Sometimes the job was hauling loads of scrap metal from across town, up five flights and down five more. Sometimes I had to fetch a bottle of milk. I was *always* a 'hard job first' kind of person. That goes double for dangerous jobs. The quicker I get them done, the less time I have to lose my nerve."

"I never thought I'd hear 'fools rush in' codified as an official, well-reasoned policy."

Great wings fluttered in the distance, and the Adept swept up from below. She flipped in a graceful loop and fluttered down. "Fel Masker," she said evenly. "I suppose your presence here in the absence of my master should serve as evidence that you were unable to free him."

"As a matter of fact—"

Teya hopped up and down, interrupting him with a mad, chattering explanation. When she was through, the Adept looked up and began issuing orders.

"A map of the realm, and areas to the northeast and east. An inventory of all available weapons and supplies. Find out how many boats are in good repair and make them available. Talk to the seafolk as well," she instructed.

Kobolds peeled off from the cluster milling about to fulfill her orders. Stix climbed to her shoulder and ran her claws through the Adept's crest, wrangling some errant feathers from the flight.

"I feel remiss in my duties that I wasn't present to see the partial liberation of my master. I shall need to see it for myself. But one chain binding him after all these years—and your goal is to defeat that final restraint with an assault on the lair of Duurth."

"It's not an assault," Fel said. "We're going to rob him."

"The two are one and the same. A dragon will not stand idle when it finds a portion of its hoard has been tampered with."

"Then we'll just have to make sure he doesn't notice," Fel said.

"He will notice. He is a dragon. You could more easily fail to notice a missing finger than a dragon would fail to notice a missing piece of its hoard."

"I find that hard to believe," Fel said.

"I won't waste my breath attempting to convince you. Evidence will be forthcoming. You need to liberate a key, correct?"

"That's right." Fel held out his hands. "It'll be about this big, corner to corner."

"You are free to plan as much of the assault as you choose, but know this. The key is what matters. More than your life, more than mine. If it comes to sacrificing any of our lives for the key, those lives are a small price."

"As long as you don't grab it and run. I'd rather be there when Kazel is freed. Call me distrustful if you want, but this wouldn't be the first time someone tried to steal an artifact from me and the glory right along with it."

"If we had the means to acquire the key without you, we would not be having this conversation. I would be seeking it directly. I assure you, your contribution will be known. Now, I imagine your first question will be how long the journey to Duurth's lair will take. And the answer to that question depends upon how large a force you will be relying upon."

"Why?"

"The number of boats, and the means to facilitate their travel, greatly alter the speed at which we can deliver you."

"It'll be me and my gear," Fel said. "Including Oiler and Wick's lantern."

"This will be an intriguing thing to observe and report," Wick said.

Teya stepped forward and raised her hand with a chatter.

"No, no. You shouldn't be risking your life just because I am."

"She has been assigned to you. Until Kazel decides otherwise, she most certainly will be accompanying you."

"I don't think Kazel expected that assignment to mean she'd be risking her life."

"It is not for you to assess our master's intent. That is *my* task and I have done so. Who else?"

"I'm going too," Tome said. "My own equipment will be comparatively light. A sheaf of spells, some blank pages, and my quills and ink. All will be carried on my person."

"Wait, wait. I still haven't agreed to Teya, let alone you." Fel looked to the Adept. "Kazel said Duurth's lair is in one of the places you people can't or won't go to. What good is Teya going to be?"

"Irrelevant," the Adept said. "She must escort you as far as she is able. Do you require any additional aid?"

"I already have too much! My plan was to be sneaky."

"Then myself, my hands, Teya, you, Tome, your gear, and some defensive weaponry. A single boat will suffice."

Two kobolds arrived and spread a series of three maps on the floor. They were drawn with the utmost of care, so much so that certain individual trees were labeled and named. The maps were grids of something much larger, but they'd been placed in the proper relative locations.

"We are here," the Adept said.

Stix pointed to a rather impressively illuminated mountain on the map.

"Duurth's lair is somewhere beyond here."

Mik gestured vaguely at a blank portion of the northeast map. It looked as though someone had simply lost interest in illustrating the map for a blobby section somewhat larger than Kazel's mountain.

"You will travel by land from the mountain to the shore. I will fly ahead and prepare the transportation by sea. With a single boat, we should be able to reach the edge of Duurth's territory in less than two days."

Fel looked at the map. There was a considerable amount of sea between the shore and the island. "Just what kind of boat can travel that fast?" he asked.

"The boat is nothing special. But as representatives of Kazel, there are some seafolk who will be amenable to speeding our journey," she said. "How much time do you need to prepare?"

"Two days," Tome said.

"We can leave immediately," Fel said.

"Good, then gather your things," the Adept said.

She spread her wings. Mik and Stix shuffled into place beside her and raised their paws. She grasped them, one with each talon, and launched herself skyward.

"Come! Fast!" Teya said, trotting ahead.

"You know something, Fel? Most people, if given the option to have a skilled paper mage accompany them on a hazardous journey, would leap at the chance."

"Most people haven't lived with you for a few months."

Teya disappeared into an alcove and reappeared, struggling to pull an impressively large pack onto her back. It was bristling with arrows stuffed into one side of it, and once she had it in place, she fetched a rather lopsided longbow. The grip was closer to the bottom than the top, though the reason for it became clear when she held it up. The weapon was taller than she was. If not for the odd design, she would have to stand on a box to fire it.

"This way! This way!" she said.

Tome stuffed as much paper into a leather roll as he could manage. Fel pulled his pack to one shoulder, Oiler to the other, and grabbed his now-spiked club. Wick's lantern was strapped into its place on his pack.

"How can you be so *casual* about this?" Tome asked, awkwardly slinging his improvised folio across his back. "My hands are shaking so badly, I can scarcely write a spell, and you are charging forward."

"The way I look at it, this is the one job I've really been trained for. The one that I can do that none of the other Maskers can do anymore."

"Fighting a dragon?"

"We're not going to fight it."

"Fel, I'll admit I've not worked with you for very long, but I can say without any fear of doubt that if you end up within twenty miles of that dragon, we are going to end up fighting it."

"The *plan* isn't to fight it. The plan is to find our way inside a big, dangerous place full of contraptions and grab as much as we can. That's my specialty."

"A dragon has never factored into that recipe before."

"He's just a big trap. All we have to do is not trigger it."

"I refer back to my statement regarding the certainty of a battle."

"Fine. If you're so dead set on planning and preparing, then we'll split the work. I'll make the plan for if we *don't* face the dragon, and you make the plan for if we do."

"That's not what I'd call an even division of labor."

"For someone who insisted on coming, you're already spending a lot of time complaining about carrying your own weight. You're welcome to stay here and read more stories to the little scamps."

Tome winced. "I suddenly find myself without a word of concern or complaint."

"All I need is someone to take care of Parch. If there's one thing I don't need on this trip, it's that little critter to worry about."

#

Epiphany had ridden in silence as they continued toward Beffshire. She'd returned to guiding her own wagon. Inappropriately, but not surprisingly, they had gone through her things with the same thoroughness she'd gone through theirs. She, for the most part, had less to hide. The sensitive information was entirely in her head, and she'd run the bulk of her inventory past Thaddeus back when he was merely a prospective buyer. Nothing was missing. And now that they were at least ostensibly working together, she'd left the weapons

164

she'd found among their things with them. But that didn't lessen the load on her mind at all.

When they stopped to see to the horses and stretch their legs. The weight she was grappling with must have been rather obvious. The first words Thaddeus said to her as she stepped down from her wagon to take a seat around the campfire they'd started just on the side of the road illustrated that quite plainly.

"You look like a woman with some decisions to make," he said, blowing out a breath of smoke.

"Decisions must be made, yes. But I don't think I'm the only one."

"Oh?"

"Listen. If you had been clear with us, open with us, from the beginning, things might be different."

"Things *would* be different, I am quite certain. Because you would never have done business with me."

"You don't know that."

"I am aware of the bad blood between you and your sister."

"Bad blood and business are two different things. The Maskers wouldn't be in business if we had the freedom to turn down working with people who rubbed us the wrong way, or people who we rubbed the wrong way. We're contraptioneers. We start off on the wrong foot with most of the people we do business with. I'm sure it's the same for you. A compromise can usually be found."

"We sought one."

"You lied to me."

"I did not lie."

She rolled her eyes. "You concealed the truth for the purpose of misleading me, and did it to pursue your own ends. Spare me the semantic pedantry."

"Fine. But what's done is done. Where does that leave us?"

"It leaves me in a position of strength and you quite the opposite."

"Oh?"

"You clearly need the Maskers. The documents in that case showed that you have no shortage of other people working with you and for you, and despite knowing the friction that would result if you were revealed, you decided to work with us in acquiring what seem to be the three most crucial parts of this undefined plan. We are irreplaceable. To us, you are merely a buyer. And money isn't as rare as people like to think it is."

"Without embracing the truth or falsity of your statements, what purpose does establishing this serve?"

"It serves to explain why it would behoove you to be open with whatever information you have that remains hidden, so that I can understand why we're being targeted. Once I know that, I can better plan for how to get free of the focus of the Bolivans and, in the decreasingly likely chance I consider it worthwhile, how to see this shaky partnership through to a mutually beneficial conclusion."

"I've told you, I don't have all the pieces. I'm not trusted with that sort of thing."

"Then now would be an excellent time to tell me what pieces you do have, and what you know about them, so that perhaps we can assemble them. The dagger, Oiler, and the mask. Why do you need them?"

He rummaged through a pack and jabbed a metal stand into the ground to hang a teakettle over the fire. For the first time since she'd met him, he removed the pipe from his mouth and thumped it out over the flames before stowing it.

"You understand some of this will be speculation on my part," he said.

She nodded.

"Oiler has a purpose. A fairly obvious one that I doubt you need me to point out, but as you say, perhaps laying out everything we have is better than making assumptions. The Bolivans have a tremendous capacity for acquiring contraptions through surreptitious means. When they find new vaults, they bash their way inside—something that is rarely successful but very fruitful when it does succeed. More often, they leak the location of the vault, and someone like Fel Masker or one of our vault hunters finds their way inside and has to cope with an ambush thereafter. Ever since your father's now legendary 'self-defense,' such ambushes had until recently been our problem exclusively. They rob, cheat, and steal. If you spent more time up north, you'd probably hear about their not-uncommon raids of both official repositories of confiscated contraptions and antiquities shops across two kingdoms.

"We of the Graves family, on the other hand, have spent our time developing a substantial network of partners across Quarr, Shalia, and, as you now know, through Thayn as well. I won't go into detail, but we have found ways to… mitigate losses to assayers. But one thing that neither the Graves nor the Bolivans have is a contraptioneer who can repair and rebuild with half the prowess of your father. It is in the nature of a business enterprise to fill such gaps in skill. It has not been stated to me as such, but I believe the Graves clan has hoped to fill the role of your father with Oiler, a contraption that can repair other contraptions. I don't think I need to tell you the value of such a thing. Based upon your increase in inventory in recent months, I'd say you've been using Oiler to excellent effect."

"Mmm. And the others?"

"The dagger and the mask? As far as I know, they're simply items of particular value that can be combined to increase the value of other items even more."

"Do you know what the Bygone dagger does?"

"It stops contraptions from functioning."

"Is that all?"

"That's the only use we were able to find beyond tightening and loosening certain fasteners. Oiler can activate things, the dagger can deactivate things. There's value in symmetry."

"Having had to deal with it for some time, a means to deactivate Oiler would not be without use as well."

"Mmm… Synergy between those two items, then."

"And the mask?"

"My answer hasn't changed. Aside from the indication that it was of greatest individual value, as far as I know the mask has no function and is merely a precious artifact."

"What is the clockwork diamond?"

"Judging from the name, it would be a jewel with gears and a spring."

She glared at him. "Is it something to be acquired?"

"If it is, it isn't something they've decided to send anyone for. As you've seen, we have crews across the continent. No one has been sent to fetch it."

"Do you know where it is?"

"*I* don't know where it is. But I believe its location is known."

"I suppose there's value in not spreading that sort of information until you can acquire it with more certainty. And there is plenty of evidence that these items are important to acquire first." She crossed her arms and gazed off into the trees.

"You look as though you've got something more to talk about," he said.

"I do. But I don't think it'll do any good at the moment." She stood. "I'll be in my wagon."

"Won't you have some tea?"

"I'd prefer to be alone for now."

She paced toward her wagon. She hadn't learned much, but she had learned something. Thaddeus was more open with information than she'd expected. She'd imagined it would be a fight. And while he was most certainly still hiding something, she got the sense that what he'd said was honest. What concerned her now wasn't what he knew and she didn't, but the opposite. If they'd kept him this much in the dark, and they'd left him open to attack by the Bolivans, then that could mean a number of very unpleasant things. It could mean the Graves had more leaks than they realized, and that they'd been keeping the Bolivan informed without intending to. Or it could mean that Thaddeus was seen as expendable, which either meant her sister was in equal danger, or worse, that her sister was among those who deemed him so.

Too many questions. Too many riddles. She needed time to untie them.

#

The journey from Kazel's lair to the pass between his mountain and the next had been a harrowing one. The path, if one were to be charitable enough to call it that, was clearly made with wings and claws in mind rather than boots.

The stout, sharp claws of Teya's feet easily gripped the rough stone. Not so for Fel's and Tome's boots. Once they'd reached the pass, however, one of the more notable parts of an already legendary journey had been waiting for them.

Two greater unicorns had been summoned to the pass to provide transportation. Having lived and traveled with the lesser variety, seeing the "proper" counterpart was humbling. They weren't merely horned horses, as Fel had always pictured when he read about them. For one, they were quite a bit larger. These two were easily half again as tall as the average draft horse. Their proportions were elongated. Long, slender legs. An arched, delicate neck. Horn and coat alike shone with a pearlescent shimmer, and their manes and tails were of iridescent silver. The beasts looked to have been designed by a god determined to summon into existence creatures that would serve as a living definition for the words "grace" and "elegance." But the moment Fel and the others had pulled themselves to the saddle-free backs of their steeds, they learned that for all their slenderness, the beasts were not fragile. They moved with a terrifying speed, underscoring the raw strength that must reside within those legs.

A narrow trail traced a meandering path along the rocky mountainside toward the thin strip of forest between the mountain and the twinkling sea beyond. They raced along with a speed that left the crisp wind whistling in Fel's ears.

"This is astonishing!" Tome shouted, holding tight to the neck of his steed. "After a life of tedium, this is truly a moment deserving of a place in a memoir."

Fel, with his additional gear, found staying atop the beast a bit more of a challenge. It was made more difficult by the nature of their steeds. While they were unquestionably the passengers of these beasts, they were not the drivers. The unicorns knew where they were to go, and chose their own path and speed, both of which threatened to eject their riders at any moment.

"Ya-haa!" Teya crowed, straddling the unicorn's neck just behind its head, gripping the unicorn's horn for leverage, and having the time of her life.

"You know something. According to legend…" Tome began.

"Are you truly going to pontificate while riding a unicorn?" Fel shouted across the windy gulf between them.

He continued, ignoring Fel. "… Only a *virgin* is supposed to be able to ride a unicorn."

Fel glared at him. "What are you trying to say?"

"I'm trying to say that legends are plainly not the most reliable sources of information, naturally."

"Parch!" squawked Teya.

Fel turned. His eyes weren't as sharp as Teya's, but it didn't take him long to spot the bounding, leaping gray spot traveling down the mountainside. The smaller beast couldn't hope to match the speed of his larger cousins, but they couldn't match his nimbleness. Whereas the greater unicorns had to keep to the twisting path, Parch hopped and leaped directly down the steep mountainside. By the time the steeds turned and looped back one more time, Parch closed the gap and hopped to the back of the one carrying Fel.

"You were supposed to stay put!" he scolded. "What do I say? If I'm working, you need to stay home."

Parch bleated happily. Oiler reeled its head and one claw out of the pack to give him a pat. Teya awkwardly reached back past her own pack to try to do the same.

"Look at the bright side," Tome shouted. "Unicorns are supposed to bring luck. We'll need all the luck we can get."

Fel didn't have much time to consider just how Parch's presence might change his plans. It seemed like the moment they reached the forest, they were leaving it again. The unicorns were fast on the mountain, but they were the very wind in the forest. When they emerged, they found the boat waiting for them at a crude but sturdy pier. The boat was larger than Fel expected. It was an ancient but well-kept craft he was comfortable calling a ship. It had a mast with two sails, what looked to be at least two decks below the main deck, and three pairs of oars sticking off the sides. The nets and most of the fishing gear had been hastily off-loaded, and a raft more in keeping with what he would have imagined the kobolds would have made for themselves had been lashed to the rear. The Adept was waiting for them, perched on the edge of the meager crow's nest. Mik and Stix were perched on the yardarms to either side.

"I appreciate your haste," the Adept said. "Our master's freedom is close at hand. I do not wish to make him wait any longer than I must."

"Yeah," Fel said, shakily dropping from the unicorn's back. "Likewise."

"You brought your lesser unicorn along?" she observed.

Parch tippy-tapped along in front of one of his greater cousins and touched noses.

"He brought himself along. I don't know how he follows me so well."

"Again, Fel Masker, mystics in general, and unicorns in particular, can develop an affinity and fondness, a connection, that can lead them through the darkness toward what they desire. The beast sees something in you that I, at first, missed."

Tome dropped from his own unicorn. After another nuzzle to Parch, the pair of magnificent beasts trotted into the woods.

"I am not much of a horseback rider," Tome said. "Not *any sort* of one, if I'm honest. I would not have expected riding a greater unicorn bareback to be so achievable."

The Adept grabbed her hands and flitted down to the deck, setting them beside her.

"I would not recommend you attempt such a thing in any other circumstance," she said. "Those unicorns are allies of our realm and indebted to Kazel. They carried you at our behest. Should you have approached them without our word first, you would have likely been run through."

"Oh… I see," Tome said. He peered at the deck of the boat. "Er, I suppose it should at this point be addressed that, at this precise moment, my experience in riding unicorns exceeds my experience riding boats. Is there anything I should know? Are there procedures to consider?"

"Just get on the boat," Fel said, hopping over the edge.

Teya scrambled over and set her pack down. Parch hopped onto the boat and trotted over to Mik and Stix to be fondled. Tome hesitated, then stepped over the side and stumbled aboard. He widened his stance and held his hands out.

"It's moving," he said.

"That's the idea, Tome," Fel said.

"I expected forward. It is moving up and down."

"They are called 'waves,'" Fel said, pointing to the water. "I thought you were supposed to be the smart one."

"Understanding the theory of a thing is worlds different from experiencing the reality of a thing."

"I, similarly, am not fond of the preponderance of water surrounding us. There is a strong likelihood that the flame will be extinguished," Wick said.

"We'll keep you belowdecks if you want," Fel said.

"Settle these matters now. In a few moments, we will depart," the Adept said.

"Should one of us open the sails?" Fel asked.

"That will not be necessary until tomorrow evening. Until then, our ship shall be in the care of the undine."

Fel furrowed his brow. Tome's expression brightened.

"The undine? Spirits of water! Fel, the poetry that has been written of them. They are supposed to be creatures of breathtaking beauty."

"Never heard of them. Do they work for Kazel, too?"

"We do not 'work' for Kazel. We honor and serve him," the Adept said. "And the undine do not. However, they are amenable to negotiation, and we have acquired their services in exchange for favors that are of little concern to you. They will take us quite far. Better than four-fifths of the way to Duurth's lair. But from there we must use oars and sails, and likewise we must return the same distance through the same means."

"Why?"

"The creatures of the sea have borders just as surely as the creatures of the land do, and the sea around the island Duurth calls his home has been abandoned by all beasts of the sea."

"Why?" Tome asked.

"Their business is theirs. We do not meddle or pry."

Fel sat on one of the planks running just below the edge of the railing. In truth, he was as unsteady on his feet on a boat as Tome was. The only difference was, he knew that from three prior sea voyages rather than zero.

"Can fish?" Teya said, hopping up and down and pointing to the remaining fishing gear.

"Not during the journey. We will be moving too swiftly," the Adept said.

"Fish later?"

"It may be necessary. In the interest of time, we will be light on provisions. Supplementing them with fish during the final leg of the journey could prove useful."

Teya rubbed her hands together. "Fish, fish, fish," she said merrily.

Fel let Oiler slide to the ground. "What will we need to do during the journey?"

"Make whatever plans and preparations you deem necessary. Your role in this endeavor is entirely focused at its midpoint. You must acquire the key to Kazel's bonds through whatever means necessary."

Oiler raised its head and inspected its surroundings. It set down the puzzle box, gave Parch a pat, then reeled out its claws and raised the end of the plank Fel was sitting on. A squirt of adhesive and a few moments of clamping left it more securely affixed to its mountings. Oiler nodded its head and produced a soft, satisfied click, then scanned the rest of the boat. With an excited waggle of its fingers, it dragged itself about in pursuit of eliminating every lingering issue.

As it produced its fang to oil a pulley, something curious happened around the boat. The soft, random waves on which the boat had been bobbing eased away. All around them the sea and surf remained gently choppy, but for some distance in all directions around the boat, it was glassy smooth. Three figures emerged from the water, just ahead of the bow of the boat.

"Wondrous…" uttered Tome.

Fel shielded his eyes from the sun. The figures he was trying to catch a glimpse of were refracting a fair amount of that light. He'd been expecting mermaids, one of a handful of creatures he'd not only never seen the greater variety of but never seen the lesser variety either. But instead he got a being he'd not even known existed in any variety.

They looked to be composed of the water themselves, with no clothes and nothing to contrast features like hair or eyes. They weren't as well defined as a solid creature, with things like noses and ears either entirely smoothed away or little more than a subtle ripple. But their shape above the water was vaguely human, and even more vaguely female. If Fel had known the word "androgynous," he would have used it. Two of them were quite slender, arms blending into their bodies with the subtle suggestion that they were crossed on their chests. The third was the only one that Fel would have been confident enough to proclaim female, and only in her case because of a substantially plumper figure sporting what certainly looked like an ample bosom. Again, the lack of fine detail prevented the creature from having a scandalous or lewd appearance by Beffshire standards, but Fel found his imagination running in extremely juvenile directions.

All three nodded their heads. The Adept nodded hers. The two in front simply receded into the water. As they did, the odd stillness spread out before them like a carpet, tracing a glassy straight line that nearly reached the horizon. The plump one drifted behind the boat and pointed to where it was tied to the pier. Teya tugged out the knots that held the ship, and Fel helped her pull up the anchor. He put his boot against the pier and shoved. The boat barely budged, drifting slowly aside. The plump undine nodded and crossed her arms again. Rather than sinking down into the water, the water around her rose up to claim her. From the perfect smoothness, a swell nearly as tall as the ship's railing rose up. The ship tipped forward to coast along it, prompting everyone to grab something to hold on to. Ahead, the water dipped and curved into something of a trough. The prow of the boat nudged down and aside until it was in the center of the trough that was gently guiding its heading. Then the swell hoisted the boat higher and started to advance. The boat picked up speed until the wind was whistling in their ears.

Moving so quickly, and so smoothly, was like nothing Fel had ever experienced. It was eerie, but also thrilling. The Adept flitted back up to the crow's nest with her hands. All three sat stoically, watching the horizon. Parch wasn't entirely pleased with the sudden and swift movement. He chose to pace around behind Oiler as it continued finding loose or broken things to tighten or fix. Only Teya seemed willing to fully indulge in the exhilaration. She'd scrambled up the mast, midway between the deck and the first yardarm. Both hind feet dug into the mast, and one cunning paw held tight. She leaned out and held the other paw out to feel the wind, eyes shut and mouth in a gleeful grin.

"Ya-ha-ha-ha!" She turned to Fel. "Fun things, Fel! Glad Kazel made me watch!"

"It was intended as a punishment," the Adept called from above.

"Fun punishment!" Teya squawked.

"Teya. A little tip for you," Fel said. "If someone punishes you and you end up having fun, don't let them know. They'll probably just come up with a better punishment."

"Very bad punishment. Lesson learned," she shouted to the Adept, adding, "Ya-haaaa!"

#

Martin sat at his workbench, industriously reassembling those contraptions that had been in working order prior to his search for the spy. The oven was crackling away. He knew from years of working with Wick under what circumstances a sentry flame could and could not see what was going on. There was no way the mysterious second sentry flame could see what was going on in the workshop. Any spying while the oven was lit must have been done by eavesdropping. Thus, with a few muttered sentences here and there, he was able to make it seem as though he was still looking for the spy.

It had been hours since he'd revealed what he'd learned to his wife. His mind had been stirring since then, attempting to piece together the best course of action. He knew she was doing the same. Their minds worked best while they were occupied. It was something they had in common. Running the shop was second nature to her, just as repairing contraptions was second nature to him. Some of the best solutions and innovations he'd ever produced had been when he was working his way mindlessly through a task he'd done a thousand times. Indeed, he was so deeply engrossed in both tasks set before him that he almost didn't hear the thumping footsteps of Vivian's approach.

"Martin," she said, stepping through the door. "I'm afraid things are moving rather more quickly than I'd expected. I've decided it is simply no longer safe to keep that thing in the house. We should have sold it when we had the chance."

He nodded knowingly. It was clear to him what she was up to, and he knew just what part he needed to play.

"Vivian, the value is far greater than we were offered. Frankly, the chain-pack could usher in a whole new era of success for the Maskers."

She nodded back. They were on the same page.

"I don't care how successful it could make us or how much money it ought to be sold for. You were attacked. The Bolivans know we have it. It is only a matter of time before they corner one of us, or get through the shop. I believe I've found a buyer. The price isn't as good as it could be, but it's better than Epiphany's buyer, and this person is discreet and reliable."

"I suppose on matters of finance it is best to defer. What do I need to do?"

"Just have it ready to be sold by noon tomorrow. You can bring it to the square at the intersection of Axle Lane and Watt Avenue. We'll make the exchange there."

"As you wish," he said. "I just wish we had more time."

"There is a noose around our necks for as long as we have that thing, and it's pulling tighter all the time. I'm through pushing our luck."

"So be it. So be it," he said.

She placed a slip of paper on the workbench and walked back up the steps. He flipped open the paper.

Alive is better than dead, but I appreciate these things aren't always so simple to calibrate.

He folded the paper again and slipped it in his pocket. He would need a decoy pack that looked like Oiler, and whatever equipment he deemed necessary to counter the contraptions the Bolivans had. He couldn't use anything he'd discussed in the workshop at any point. They would be ready for that. But there was value in knowing precisely where and when a foe would attack. And, of course, being able to dupe them into preparing the wrong sort of defense.

"That much money… I'd best bring the dazzler. That's always done the job before. A good, reliable defensive contraption. Though it would be a sound precaution to do some preventative maintenance. It would be a terrible time for it to fail."

He pulled a crate from the bottom shelf and set about reassembling the first of three contraptions that would see their first real test tomorrow at noon.

Chapter 9

Fel and the others had traveled long into the night. Tome had busied himself with the spell preparation he'd moaned about not having time to do prior to their departure until he was tired enough to vanish belowdecks to find a place to sleep. The Adept spent as much time flying alongside the ship as riding it, and now slept soundly on one of the yardarms. Oiler had finished maintaining everything it could find that needed any care, and now was back to fiddling with its puzzle box. Parch had spent the time tottering back and forth among anyone with a notion to pet him, and now was sleeping on top of Oiler. Teya, no longer vibrating with excitement, was still utterly enchanted by the journey. She crouched on the plank on the railing across from Fel, eyes on the waves as they sparkled in the moonlight.

The only one who hadn't had anything to keep him busy or entertained through the journey thus far had been Fel. His mind, normally blessedly clear and unburdened, had been increasingly active as the hours ticked by. His concerns must have been showing on his face, because Teya glanced his way, then decided to hop over and sit beside him.

"Should sleep. Big tomorrow. Much to do."

Fel shook his head and rubbed his eyes. "I don't know how much sleep I'm liable to get."

"No try, no sleep. Try, maybe some sleep."

"I'm going to try to rob a dragon tomorrow. Even if I do sleep, I don't want to think about what sort of dreams I'd have."

Teya leaned over and poked him in the belly. "Try. Sleep, maybe win. No sleep, maybe no win. Win? Maybe Kazel free. No win, no Kazel free." She poked him again. "Do for Kazel."

"What exactly did Kazel do to earn this kind of respect? Sure, he's big and majestic and all that. But he's been chained up in a cave since before you were born."

"He is dragon," she said, eyes practically sparkling at the thought of it.

"That's it?"

"Dragon is enough," Teya defended.

"But what did he *do*?"

"Kazel is big. Scary. Greater Lands? Filled with big, scary things. Kazel is biggest. Keeps the others away."

"Even locked up."

Teya scrunched up her face, trying to fish up words that could articulate her thoughts without overreaching her capacity to speak.

"A land remembers. That mountain? Kazel's mountain. Has his smell. Has his stories. We tell stories. Others tell stories. What happened? It can happen again. Don't want it to happen to you. So you stay clear. But for us? No fear. Kazel is like… roof. Keeps the rain away. Shelter."

"So you hide in his shadow to stay safe?"

She nodded enthusiastically.

"And in exchange, you're what? A slave?"

"Not slave. Slave? No choice. Me? The others? Choice." She raised a claw. "*Correct* choice. We get much. Safe? Yes. Also, wisdom. Kazel teaches. We learn. We become better. More like dragon."

"What about Duurth? He's a dragon."

She narrowed her eyes. "*Bad* dragon. Worse dragon. Not *my* dragon. Like I said. Choice. Correct choice. And now? Loyalty. Family."

"Family," Fel said. "You know, there's something to this. Things must be so simple when the answer to every question is 'do what the dragon says.'"

Teya shook her head. "Kazel says, do this? Now it is… heavy. Important. Not easy. Not simple. Family? Family simple. Maybe I can't do. But family can do. Doesn't matter *who* does. Not always me. Sometimes us. Good to be us." She grabbed his hand and uncurled one finger from his hand. "This? Not do good. Not much."

She uncurled a second finger. "This? Better, but still not much." Finally she unfurled all his fingers. "This? Hold things. Build things. Do things." She slapped her paw against his hand. "This? Us. And you do this? You help Kazel?"

She stirred the air with a paw, encompassing Fel, the Adept, and herself. Then she slapped his hand again. "You are us, too. And us is good." She tipped her head. "But you don't like?"

"What do you mean?"

"Tome? You say, no no. Parch? You say, no no. You are very 'me.' Not us."

"Us is fine." He shook his head. "You've got me talking like you now. Being a part of a group is fine. Getting help is fine. But sometimes you just have to prove something to yourself. Or prove to someone else something about yourself."

She scratched her head. "Like learning lesson? Prove I fish good? Prove I shoot arrow good?"

"I guess it's like that. But it's more like… Imagine Kazel expected you to be able to do something and you just couldn't. You couldn't be what Kazel wanted you to be. Wouldn't you feel bad? Wouldn't you want to prove you were still good for something?"

She considered the question for a moment. "Nope," she said. "If not good for one thing, another. As long as *us* can do."

"And you'd be fine disappointing Kazel?"

"Not fine. Feel bad. Try to do better. But still *us*. Loyalty is two-way, not one-way." She scratched her head again. "Do *you* have a dragon?"

"I have a mom and a dad."

Her eyes widened. "Mom and Dad *dragons*?"

"No, no. But it's sort of the same thing. Living in the shadow. Trying to prove something about myself to them."

"Don't need to. Already family. Don't need to prove. And if family *and* need to prove? Only family if prove? Not worth proving. Not real family. Find better family. Find better us."

Fel rubbed his eyes. "I think we've reached the point where the thoughts in your head are too big to come out of your mouth."

"Maybe. So, you sleep? For us?" she said.

He stood. "I'll do my best."

"Good." She pointed. "Now go."

#

Epiphany had made a good deal more progress in her journey toward Beffshire than she had in her journey toward a solution to the problems buzzing in her mind. The first time she'd been asked to bring Wick along, she'd found it frustrating and invasive. But now the lack of a friendly voice and a link to the rest of the family felt far worse. Even if he was compromised, interrogating him might have given her something else to work with. Because right now, the avenues her mind was drifting down weren't filling her with confidence.

What did she know for certain? She knew the Bolivans and the Graves were after the same thing. She knew the Graves had a sentry lantern. And she knew the Bolivans were getting information about their plans faster than seemed possible. If Wick was a leak that the Graves had access to, then maybe the Bolivans had access as well. That was certainly one possibility. But given the amount of people the Graves seemed to have probing about, on the same payroll as her brother was a few months ago, then maybe the Bolivans had weaseled their way into being sent on a fetch quest and had simply followed their way up the chain. Or perhaps the Graves had hired them *on purpose*, believing they'd never find out who was pulling the strings. If they were willing to do that to Epiphany and the rest of her family, then why not the Bolivans as well?

She shut her eyes and tightened her hands around the reins.

This was bad. The longer she thought about it, the less safe she felt with them, and the less certain she was of anything that had driven her for the last few months. It felt like a snowball had been released at the top of a mountain. All she knew was that it was heading downhill fast, and getting bigger and more dangerous as it went.

#

Tome sat at the single table he could find in the whole of the ship. From the state it had been in when he found it, it wasn't used for eating, writing, or any sort of thing like that. This was probably where the fish they caught were cut and otherwise processed. It had taken him no small amount of effort to render it suitable to write upon, but now, aside from a lingering odor, he was more comfortable in his writing than he had been since leaving Beffshire.

"This is most certainly a human-scale table," he said aloud to Wick.

The flame was flickering, so Wick wasn't actually present, but it still felt better to voice his observations out loud.

"I wonder where this ship came from? Is it of human make and it ended up within the Greater Lands somehow? Does it predate whatever event separated the Greater Lands from the world at large? Perhaps it was copied from an existing ship and—"

"It was built within the Greater Lands by former allies of Kazel," said the Adept.

He turned to see the harpy hopping somewhat awkwardly down the stairs. Stix and Mik scampered down after her, arms loaded with leaves. Their rustling must have alerted Parch, who burst up from the lowest deck and sprang happily toward them. The kobolds dropped the leaves, and Parch happily munched upon them.

"I wasn't aware such provisions were on the ship," Tome said.

"They weren't. The unicorn was not a part of the initial plan. But there are smaller islands all around. I fetched some. It was only proper."

"I thank you on Parch's behalf," Tome said. "Now, you say this boat was built here in the Greater Lands?"

"Indeed. Your kind is not alone in your crafting skill. The difference is that within the Greater Lands, most beings know not to toy with things like contraptions."

"Since I've come here, I cannot say I've seen much evidence of what I would call—and forgive the implication—an advanced society."

"That would depend, I imagine, on your definition of 'advanced.' I would judge a society which allows itself to be destroyed by its innovations something less than advanced."

"Oh! Oh yes! I'd almost forgotten, with the looming task. You serve Kazel and speak for him, and he has lived since what we call the Bygone Era. There is some contention about just how the Bygone Era fell. I wonder if you have any insight."

"Contraptions, particularly those with a will of their own, are not to be trusted. That is the entirety of my knowledge of those events, and I have found that knowledge to be quite sufficient."

"Might Kazel know more."

"I imagine he does."

"Then when I return, I must make it a point to ask him."

He turned his attention to the spell he was crafting. Just as he was about to put his quill to the page, Stix scurried over and caught his wrist, lifting it up.

"One moment," the Adept said.

"One moment for what?"

The answer came in the sudden lurch of the entire boat. He was nearly thrown from his seat as the ship ceased its rapid travel with a worrisome creak. Had his pen been to paper at that moment, he would have ruined the spell he was working on.

"We have gone as far as the undine are willing to aid us. We shall need to ready the sails."

"Oh, yes. Right. I suppose I should see what help I can offer, as I believe Fel only recently managed to get to sleep."

"That would be best." She hopped up the steps in a decidedly avian way, her hands trotting up behind her. "I imagine you will require instructions," she said as they reached the main deck of the ship.

"If you can offer them."

"I am the Adept. I am expected to have at least a base level of knowledge in all matters relevant to the service of Kazel." Mik tugged a rope from a cleat. Stix pointed.

"Take that rope and begin feeding it out until I tell you to stop."

Tome hurried over to where he'd been directed. Both Mik and Stix went to work hauling at their own rope.

"How precisely do you direct them?" Tome asked, almost losing his grip as the tension on the line proved more than he was expecting.

"Direct whom? My hands?" the Adept asked.

"Yes."

"That is a curious question to ask. How do you direct *yours*?"

"Mine are a part of me. Yours aren't even the same sort of creature."

"I direct them in precisely the same way you direct yours. A notion or need arises, and they fill it."

"But how?"

"That's enough. The rope beside it, pull it until I say," she said.

He hauled at the rope. The sail started to shift and billow with the wind.

"Good, that will do. Another few hours and we'll see the land we're after. Now, as for an answer to your question, you would not be asking it if you understood kobolds."

"Oh? It is a function of their nature and not some mystic link?"

"Whether it is mystic is immaterial. All things are mystic, to some degree or another. But kobolds have an innate sense of the needs of a task. I've never encountered a creature with a keener capacity to observe and respond to a need. I have worked with Mik and Stix for many years. We are attuned."

"Fascinating…"

"You are easily fascinated."

"Of that I am most assuredly guilty."

She crossed her wings in front of her. Mik and Stix crossed their arms.

"You have prepared some spells?" she said.

"I have."

"May I see one?"

"Of course."

He pulled his folio from his pocket and selected one of the simpler spells. Stix took it and scrambled up on the plank by the railing to hold it up for the Adept's inspection.

"The phrases are unfamiliar, but I recognize the script and the words."

"Do you?" he said. "That's marvelous. Information regarding that language and its derivatives is vanishingly rare on the rest of the continent."

"It is quite prevalent in the library."

Tome's eyes lit up. "Library! What library?"

"Just as kobolds are born with teamwork and labor at the very root of their minds, dragons are born with a knowledge of value. Kazel's chosen hoard is traditional. Gold, silver, gems, what have you. But he has kept anything of value that he or his followers have come across. Among my many tasks is the cataloging of such things."

"We came here, or more precisely, to the wall, in search of a library!" Tome said.

"It was my understanding you came in search of contraptions to salvage and sell."

"That was, and is, a driving factor. But it was our greatest hope that we would find the library, a greater understanding of contraptions, of the era, of everything."

She narrowed her eyes and leaned low. "I would not expect you to listen, and it really matters not to me if you do. But I would advise against plumbing any deeper into the pit of contraption knowledge. As for mysticism…" Stix shook the spell. "Were you inclined, you might have a place among us. My personal aptitude is alchemical mysticism. Potions in particular. We have, if a pressing need arises, access to allies who have a degree of skill in spoken-word magic. We have no paper mages among us, and it is a skill set that would be quite valuable. Different beasts have strengths and weaknesses against different magics. A complete arsenal is always advisable. And the little ones have been quite vocal in their requests for your return."

"Have they?" he said with tempered excitement.

"Apparently few have told the old tales as engagingly. Despite a bit of a stumble with regard to the language."

For a brief and intense moment, he considered the possibilities. There were undoubtedly volumes of knowledge here that were available nowhere else. That, coupled with the availability of ingredients to make ink and paper of unimaginable quality, meant he could grow his knowledge and power by leaps and bounds. But doing so would require him to remain in the Greater Lands. Given the relative discomfort and significantly higher risk of death he'd faced here, it seemed much more reasonable to seek his fortunes in a place less teeming with horrid monsters.

"Tempting. But this place lacks some of the amenities to which I have become accustomed, and I hesitate to think what would become of Fel without my aid."

"Mmm… Provided you survive your clash with Duurth, we will revisit the offer. Though I would not expect you to remain. The Greater Lands is a place for greater creatures. Other sorts seldom remain."

Tome let the jab pass without comment. Now was not the time to argue. There were things far more deserving of his attention. He pocketed the spell.

"How is this likely to proceed, when we reach Duurth's lair?"

"That will be up to you. Our own involvement will be minimal. It has been some time since any under my oversight attempted to approach the lair. As I recall, we cannot progress much beyond the shore before…" She shuddered. "I have no interest in what lies within the island, and no desire to bear witness to it."

He raised his eyebrows. "A variation, I see."

"We can provide a means of escape. We can observe from a distance. But I suspect only you, Fel, and Parch will have the capacity to travel farther than the beach."

"And Oiler."

"I do not list that contraption among the living, and nor should you. But regardless of how you choose to count your forces, the question is not what our plan is, but what yours is."

The answer came from the stairwell, from a recently awoken and still terribly groggy Fel.

"We're waiting until Duurth leaves," he said. "Then I'm sneaking in and stealing the key and anything else I can carry. Then we're getting away."

"You're awake already?" Tome said. "I thought you'd only just gone to sleep."

"The ship practically turned upside down a minute ago. I assumed something was happening."

"It was merely the undines' final contribution to the journey. But if that is the entirety of your plan, you shall need to expand greatly if you hope to succeed," the Adept said.

"Seems pretty cut and dry to me," Fel said.

"You know nothing about dragons," she said. "We cannot rely upon him leaving anytime soon. A dragon does not eat the way you or I do. After a particularly successful hunt, a dragon might sleep for days, weeks, even months. Unless you intend for us to set up camp and remain indefinitely, you'd best produce a more nuanced plan for entry. And as for your escape? Start your count now. When we reach the shores, we shall need that time over again to reach the undines. And even with their speed, we will merely be a match for Duurth's flight."

Fel squinted at the horizon ahead. "All right, so if he's liable to be asleep, I sneak in, rob him blind, and sneak out."

"And if he awakes? Or if he *is* awake?" she asked.

He rubbed his forehead. "Depends on what he does. If he doesn't attack me, then I run. If he does, then I defend myself until he stops."

"If you have anything from his hoard, he won't stop until he has it back."

"He'll stop if I kill him," Fel said.

"It is not so simple to kill a dragon."

"I didn't say it would be simple. I'm sure it'll be really, really hard. And I don't particularly want to do it. But if it's him or me, you better believe I'm going to do what it takes to make sure it's him."

"Nothing would bring me greater joy than to return to Kazel not only with his freedom in hand, but with word that vengeance has been secured. But just how do you suppose you will kill him?"

"I'm a contraptioneer, remember? And he's sleeping on a big pile of contraptions. There's going to be something in there that'll convince him maybe this isn't the battle he wants to pick."

Stix drummed her fingers on the railing.

"I would prefer a higher degree of specificity. But I suppose if the high saw fit to send us a Masker, we should not be surprised that he would use a means only a Masker would."

"I am what I am."

"Fish, fish, fish!" crowed Teya, bounding up from below with a pole.

She baited the hook with something squirmy and cast it over the edge. The eager smile on her face lasted until she caught eyes with the Adept. She then took on a stern and serious look.

"Good punishment. Learning lesson," she said.

Her performance was only somewhat diminished by a not-so-subtle wink at Fel. The Adept glared at him.

"You are a bad influence, Fel Masker."

"So I've heard," he said.

She spread her wings and took to the sky. Mik and Stix watched her flutter away, then chattered with Teya for a moment. One fetched a net, the other an oar, and each idly sat while Teya teased at the rod.

"She says they have an instinct for teamwork. Born collaborators," Tome said. "Something that you could learn a thing or two from."

"What? Did you have a better plan?" Fel asked.

"As it so happens, I have been busy assembling spells. My little session as a storyteller gave me a chance to practice the location element of my spells. Which, in retrospect was far less of a concern than I'd thought it would be."

"Why?"

"Because I am now using paper *native* to the Greater Lands."

"Is that supposed to mean something to me?"

Tome rolled his eyes. "It would if you'd actually been listening to me during the ride to the wall. I am *quite* certain I discussed this at length."

"I try to ignore you, Tome."

"Why?"

"Because if I didn't, the constant, endless droning would eventually end with me wrapping my hands around your throat to wring a moment's silence out of you."

"If I were you, I'd listen this time. I can't be blamed for talking constantly if you force me to repeat myself. Each of a paper-mage's spells contain many complex components, covering virtually everything about the spell. I need to describe not only effects, but the time, the location, the person composing the spell."

"Fine, fine, fine. This part I remember."

"I can increase the potency of the spell and decrease its length by making something intrinsic to the spell representative of one of its components. Paper from the Greater Lands greatly decreases the depth of knowledge I need to have about this place and its nature. That can be done for many elements of the spells. There are even highly effective, albeit extremely unpleasant, ways to remove the 'description of the spellcaster' aspect. But I digress. With the usage of their paper, the location component, at least, is deemphasized. It might not get me all the way to the previous potency of a spell, but it should correct the horrid shortcoming of my spells while I was using my own paper."

"We've come a long way from wherever that paper was made. Is that going to be a problem?"

"Perhaps. But my intuition tells me the difference between one part of the Greater Lands and another is quite a bit less than the difference between Beffshire and the Greater Lands."

"That sounds about right. What have you got?"

"It so happens, you and I independently formulated similar plans. I have three variations on the strongest sleep spell I could manage. I've also completed the eagle-eye spell, which should help with scouting. I have one decoy spell. I didn't have the time or paper to create something complex, but once activated, the spell should create a reasonable illusion of the person who activated it. The illusion will remain stationary where activated. I also have the three spells I find most useful in a combat scenario. A fire spell, an ice spell, and an illusory smoke spell. I'm partway through a healing spell, and with any luck, I can have two more finished before we arrive." He placed a hand on his belly. "At least I hope so. I find myself feeling rather ill."

"The sea does that to some people."

"But I've been perfectly fine until now."

"Until now the undine were keeping the waves at bay."

"Fish!" Teya said.

She hauled back the rod. A rather meager-looking but very colorful fish flopped from the water to the deck. It was energetically netted and clubbed. Teya grabbed it by the head and used her claws with gruesome efficiency to gut the catch. She stuck some of the guts back on the hook, presented the fish to Mik, and cast for another catch.

Fel grinned and leaned on the railing.

"What's so funny?" Tome asked.

"We're on the most dangerous trip of any of our lives and they're just fishing. Teya is having the time of her life. I never knew much about kobolds before, but if this is the way they are, just able to go with the flow no matter which way it takes them, I think they might be the luckiest creatures in the world."

"Simplicity can be appealing at times."

"I didn't say they were simple. At least, not in the way you mean. They aren't dumb. I think there's a lot more going on in those heads than we can get out of them without knowing their language. But they're… I don't know… *clear*. Direct. They understand where they're going and they can focus on it. Enjoy the little pieces even of the big pieces are terrifying."

Mik loudly crunched at the raw fish. Tome put a hand to his stomach and leaned on the railing.

"Hey, I didn't take a look at much of the ship belowdecks. Is there someplace to cook?" Fel said.

"Don't tell me this is making you hungry," Tome said, his complexion a bit green as Mik slurped a tail into his mouth.

"You're not curious what a Greater Lands fish tastes like? The meat was decent."

"I haven't seen anything for cooking. Not that I could stomach anything even if I did."

"That's fine. I've got my shovel, and I'm sure I can sizzle something up on Wick's flame. Teya! If you catch a fourth fish, send it my way?"

"I catch four! For sure!" Teya said. "Two already!"

She pulled a second fish from the water. As the kobolds gutted and crunched at their catch, Tome leaned over the side and tried not to be sick.

"Gotta enjoy the little pieces," Fel said. "You never know when a big piece is going to fall right on top of you."

#

Martin paced down the street with a heavy pack filled with chain. It, naturally, was not Oiler, but even someone who had been spying on the Masker family for a number of months would have had a hard time making that determination at a glance. Martin had always been of the opinion that one should make replacement parts for any piece of equipment that was of any real value. Oiler's internal components, or at least those he'd been able to observe, were fairly typical and interchangeable with other contraptions. The serpent mask seemed to interact with them in novel ways, and thus the mask itself was a potential single point of failure, but he couldn't do anything about that at his current level of know-how. The bag, on the other hand, was entirely mundane and simple enough to replicate. He'd twice attempted to coax Oiler to swap to the new bag, like a hermit crab changing shells, but the mechanism had no interest in a refreshed outfit. So it had served as a simple pack for the weeks between its creation and this moment. Now, it served a far more important purpose. It was a decoy.

He approached the intersection of Axle and Watt. It was difficult to suppress a grin at his wife's cleverness. It *seemed* like the ideal place for an ambush. Though the streets were fairly wide, they were almost completely deserted. The buildings lining one side of the street processed some of the more unpleasant results of a large city. Every whiff of the air in this place had the stench of horse droppings and whatever horrid ingredients went into making the dye that was so prized in the textile district across town. It kept the streets clear and the neighboring windows closed. It also *seemed* like there was no shortage of places to hide and get the drop on a would-be victim. But Fel used to hide down here when he was a boy and didn't want to come home for supper. Between sturdy locked doors, unpleasantly filthy side alleys, and roofs with treacherous angles to them, there were a total of three places one could reasonably endure hiding for any length of time.

The first two of the possible ambush points had come and gone without any attack. If the mysterious spy lantern had been monitoring him as it should have been, and they'd been properly advised, there was but one place for an attacker to hide. Now was the time to be sure of his defenses. He reached back and slid out his dazzler from between his body and the pack. It was a smaller but functionally identical device to the one Fel liked to keep in the sun shade of the cart. Quite loud, quite bright, quite startling. And precisely what he'd claimed he would be armed with when making the initial plan with Vivian. Even the most stalwart person would flinch and recoil if this defensive weapon was discharged in their face. Really, the only way to endure an attack with it would be to wear some sort of dark lenses over one's eyes and some sort of protection for one's hearing. He slipped his other hand into his pocket.

"Hand over the pack and put your hands behind your back, Masker."

"Must we do this?" Martin said, turning to the source of the voice.

Sure enough, the young woman who had confronted him last time was there, and she was wearing a thick woolen mask. The sort that would filter the light nicely and dull any blast of sound.

"I have my orders," she said. "The pack first."

He raised the dazzler and leveled its end at her face. "This is really a very unpleasant device even *with* protection, though I can't help but wonder how you knew to *wear* such protection."

"That doesn't concern you. Don't waste your time firing that thing. It'll just bring people running, and we're far enough from anyone who matters that it won't do you any good, and it'll force me to do something more drastic. This doesn't have to be painful, Masker."

"I should be offering you the same warning."

"That weapon is no good and you know it."

"Indeed."

Martin pulled a strange, rattling contraption from his pocket. It had a brass nozzle on one end. He depressed the top of the nozzle. A dense cloud of some sort of strange-smelling substance hissed from the end and enveloped the would-be attacker. The attacker stumbled out of the cloud, producing a strangled, gasping cough and trying to pull the mask from her face.

"I'd yet to provide this for assessment because I honestly couldn't determine its intended purpose. All I know for certain is it causes cloth to constrict, and it has a terrible, choking scent," he said.

He kicked her legs out from under her and dropped his pack on the ground. "Relax. It won't kill you. I caught a lungful of the stuff when I was working on it a few months ago. It ruined my day, but you'll be fine." He pulled a short length of rope from his pocket and started to bind her wrists. "Quite a stroke of luck you were wearing that mask, or this wouldn't have been nearly as effective."

Chapter 10

What had been a dark spot on the horizon for hours slowly resolved itself from the mists. The Adept was circling high overhead, keeping watch for the dragon. Mik and Stix handled the ship quite ably, leaving Fel and Tome to stare at the approaching island.

"It's… not what I expected," Tome said.

"Yeah. I assumed it'd be a big mountain, or some caves cut into the ground."

The island that contained Duurth, at least according to Kazel and the Adept, was a far cry from anything the storybooks had prepared him for when describing the sort of place a dragon might call home. No forbidding black-stone cliffs. No smoldering fire-mountains. The island, even from this distance, looked like a bustling trade port, minus the bustling. Aging but still largely intact buildings clustered into a city that spread up along the slope of the island. The shore had a long, intact pier. A well-sheltered harbor even had some ancient boats still afloat. The place was eerie in its emptiness, but represented the greatest concentration of civilization they'd encountered since leaving the last city before the Greater Lands Wall.

In the distance, what looked like the Greater Lands Wall in miniature stood around something barely visible in the center of the city. A faint twinkling form, almost certainly the tip of something much larger, caught the light in a rotating display.

"You didn't say it was a city," Fel said.

"What city?" Teya said.

"There, right ahead. The whole island is a city."

She stared forward. Her normally focused and interested expression became dull and blank. When she looked back, her expression fluttered into sharpness again.

"Where?" she said.

"That's weird…" Fel said.

"A powerful enchantment. One wonders why it doesn't affect us," Tome said.

The Adept fluttered down and landed on the railing.

"No sign of Duurth. Either he is within his lair, or he is far enough away that I cannot see him," she said.

"Given that you can't see an entire city, I'm not very confident in your scouting skill around here," Fel said. "But at least we'll have plenty of places to hide." He took a breath and prepared his gear. "I'm going to do this in two passes. First, to see what's what, then, to do what needs to be done. How are you going to handle it if Duurth shows up?"

The Adept turned. Stix pointed.

"There is a second harbor on the east side of the island. It has considerably more intact vessels, some of which are quite a bit larger than this ship and clustered. We will anchor among them. It should provide us with a degree of concealment, at least visually, and is on the downwind side of the island. I am confident, at least while stationary, that we will be able to avoid notice. The greater challenge will be reaching the undine for the return trip. We were exceedingly fortunate to have reached the island without encountering Duurth. The likelihood of repeating this feat is exceedingly low."

"We'll cross that bridge when we come to it. Plenty of time to plan for that after we get the goods."

"Fel, it's entirely possible that the time between when we get the goods and when we need to escape will be a few terrified minutes while we're running through a ghost town being chased by an enraged dragon," Tome said.

"Even better. Fewer options, easier choice."

"… It may not be quite so much of a gift to be simple as I'd previously indicated," Tome said.

"For this first trip, I'm leaving Oiler and Parch here. Or at least trying to. I'm going to try to be sneaky, and neither of them is particularly clear on what that entails."

He pulled his pack of gear to his back, grabbed his club, and hopped to the pier. Tome, somewhat more reluctantly, followed. Teya bounded over the railing and practically bounced in place.

"Ready!" she said.

Fel gave her a curious look. "You can't come, Teya."

"Have to. Kazel said," she said, marching eagerly along the pier.

Parch pranced along around the trio. Not to be left out, Oiler hauled itself over the side and thumped forward.

"We go!" Teya proclaimed.

She marched along the pier and, for a moment, appeared to be every bit capable of joining them on the adventure. Then her steps began to slow. Her posture sagged a bit, and her serrated ears flicked. She paused and turned. From the furrow of her brow and the pensive look on her face, she didn't quite understand why she'd stopped. She turned again and managed a single additional step before turning back again.

Fel stepped up to her and crouched down. "Great try, Teya. But you can't go."

"Have job," she insisted.

"You can keep an eye on me when I get back."

"Maybe you don't come back," she countered.

"Tell you what. I promise I'll come back, and to make *sure* I come back, instead of watching me, how about you watch Parch and Oiler?" He took Oiler's puzzle box and shuffled it. "Oiler's easy. Mix this up whenever it's done and it won't be a problem. Parch? Well, if you figure out how to keep Parch under control, then let me know about it."

"You don't give job," Teya said. "Kazel give job. Or Adept give job."

Fel shrugged. "Fine. Then do what you want. But you're going to have to do it here."

He pulled his gear bag a little tighter to his back and paced past her. Parch tried to prance by. Teya watched the unicorn coming. There was a flicker of irritation and confusion, then the razor-sharp focus and enthusiasm popped back into place. She stepped forward and lowered her head. Parch instantly accepted the invitation, rearing back for a game of headbutts. Clearly if Teya couldn't do the job she was assigned to do, she was going to do whatever job she *could* do as well as she was capable.

Fel hurried along the pier while Parch was distracted. He could tell that Tome's interminable desire to fill the silence with pontification and chatter was straining at its chains. It was telling that the gravity of the situation was sufficient to convince him silence was preferable. Unfortunately, Fel wasn't able to enjoy the peace and quiet because he was too busy grappling with his mind's own reaction to the ludicrous task ahead.

Until now, he had been able to push off the fear and foreboding. But reality could only be denied by delusion for so long. As he stepped onto the cobbles of the street beyond the pier, his knees shook as though he'd stepped onto a flimsy rope bridge over a monster-infested valley. He gripped the strap of his pack tightly and braced the grip of his improvised club against his leg to at least plausibly deny that his hands were shaking.

"You watching, Wick?" he said to the lantern dangling from its strap.

"As always, Fel."

"Let me know if you see anything dangerous on the way."

"It will be a pleasure to serve this fulfilling purpose."

They crossed the street into the alleys of the city, and Fel focused on learning all that he could about his surroundings. As Tome suggested, his next trip through this town might be with dragon fire nipping at his heels. He'd best know where he was going.

The buildings were oddly familiar. Most were quite short. At least near the shore the tallest he spotted was two stories. They weren't so different from the oldest of Beffshire buildings in that way. But the actual architecture?

Every well-established town Fel had been to, and he had been to quite a few, had at least one building meant to show the wealth and importance of the town to visitors. Normally this building was built by a noble or lord. Someone with something to prove. It might be the mansion where some official or another lived. Often it was a grand hall. The most likely of all was a church. These buildings would be built of stone. Great columns would hold up an ornate arch over the door. Carvings, mosaics, anything that could be done to add a degree of grandeur and importance. Here, even the *least* of the buildings had some aspect of that. The island itself was composed of some sort of black, gritty stone and sand, but every brick and slab used in the city was of a ghostly gray color. He imagined a fleet of ships hauling in stone across the vast sea separating this place from wherever the quarry was.

Fel became aware of something else. He'd missed it until now because it wasn't something that was present, but some things that were absent. The silence that he was so rarely granted was much more leaden than it should have been. All he could hear was the periodic howl of the wind. In the forest, before the manticore attacked, the whistle of birds and chatter of rodents had vanished before the predator showed itself, but here there wasn't even the buzz of insects. And the answer to why that was soon became clear.

Nothing grew here. Not a blade of grass. Not a leaf of weed. It was utterly dead, devoid of anything but the city's remnants. The warm air should have been heavy with humidity, but the breeze felt strangely dry. It wasn't right.

Fel threw his shoulder against a heavy door. It swung open without resistance, almost sending him sprawling. It was a residence, and if not for the thick layer of dust on every surface, he could have imagined this place had only *just* been emptied. Cabinets hung open on the walls, empty but for the odd bowl or mug that was either far enough from the edge to be overlooked or of poor enough quality to have been deemed unworthy of packing.

"Just like the wall," Tome said softly. "This wasn't some sort of a disaster that killed the people. This was something, if not gradual, at least expected. This was an evacuation. I wonder what caused it?"

Fel glanced at him. "Do you suppose the *dragon* had something to do with it?"

Tome opened a cabinet and found some empty clay pots with some residue of the former contents.

"The whole thing seems more orderly than fleeing a dragon. They cleared out their food stores," he said.

Fel found the hatch to the lower levels and pulled it open.

"Lower levels, and they're intact. Wooden floors though. I was hoping for stone throughout. Probably every building is going to have these lower levels.

Deeper on the wealthier ones. Hopefully *they* will have stone.”

“I imagine you’re hoping for stone so that dragon fire will be less of an issue?” Tome said.

“Can’t slip one past you, can I. Let’s keep checking nicer and nicer homes until we find one with stone. That’ll give us an idea of where to hide if something goes wrong. If we can get into a sub-basement with a stone roof, we’ll probably be safe from the dragon.”

“But how will we leave?”

Fel shut the hatch and dusted his hand on his pants. “This is already more planning than I usually do.”

He pulled open a drawer in the single piece of furniture left in what must have been a bedroom. He grinned. “I’ll tell you this,” he said, pulling out some manner of medallion. “If we can solve the dragon problem, this is a place that’s liable to make future expeditions worthwhile.”

He held the medallion up to the light. It was a pair of silver rings that had a slip fit around each other. He tested the edges with his fingers until he found the activation button. When pressed, the rings began to rotate in opposite directions. Each one wrapped around a stained-glass disk in miniature. The shifting of one disk of glass against the other caused the bits of coloring to align and misalign, forming fleeting images before dissolving into dazzling refracted light and resolving again as a different image. He watched it cycle through three different scenes before it repeated, then happily tucked it away in his pocket.

“That one’s for Mariss,” he said.

“You don’t have any interest in planning our escape, but you’re perfectly willing to pilfer jewelry?”

“For the right price, I’ll go anywhere twice.” He grinned a little wider. “That rhymes. I should make that a slogan.”

“Can you take this seriously, Fel? I’d like to survive!”

“This is business, Tome. This is as serious as things get for the Maskers. But please. You tell me. How should we be spending our time?”

“I should think it would be wise to find the dragon.”

“He’s somewhere east of here,” he stated simply.

“Wild guesses don’t count as planning.”

“It isn’t a wild guess.”

“Then explain.”

Fel glared at him. “You never worked in a stable, did you?”

“Have you?”

“I’ve done every job you can do in Beffshire. I have lost a *lot* of money gambling.”

“And somehow working in a stable gives you an innate knowledge of where on an island a dragon is?"

"No, my nose gives me an innate sense of where a dragon on an island is. The wind is blowing that way, and I don't smell dragon dung, so the dragon must be that way."

"You didn't smell dragon dung in Kazel's lair."

"Kazel has servants. You saw what happened to Teya when she tried to follow. There aren't going to be kobolds here to clean up after him."

"And if Duurth is smart enough not to poop where he sleeps?"

"You've been living across the hall from a goat. How's that been?"

"Notable."

"And Parch is smart enough to hold it until he gets outside. A big animal takes work to not smell like a big animal. Unless you think Duurth is taking baths every day, he's that way."

Tome considered his words. "I defer to your superior knowledge on the subject. But there still remains the question of *precisely* where he is."

"You saw how low to the ground most of these buildings are. He's either going to be in someplace tall with a big door, or someplace short with a big hole."

"Mmm… Might it be wise to travel uphill, then? Toward the center of the island? A higher vantage point will help us scout the island more quickly, more thoroughly, and more safely."

Fel gave him a slap on the back. "See? I knew a plan would present itself."

#

Epiphany was shaken out of a near trance of runaway fretting and suspicion when the purple wagon ahead slowed and began to pull aside to a laughable little "city" that she'd never even bothered to learn the name of. And why hadn't she bothered to learn the name?

"We're not even half a day from Beffshire!" she shouted, hopping down from her wagon. "Why are we stopping? We used to snicker about this place whenever Fel talked about it, because if you were on your way to Beffshire, why would you stop when you could be there in less than a good night's sleep, and if you were on your way *away* from Beffshire, what could you possibly need by the time you reached this place that you couldn't have had there?"

"The horse is tired. It's slowing down. We rest here," Thaddeus said, turning with his pipe sticking out of his mouth.

"For how long?"

He puffed. "Until tomorrow."

"We are hours away from having the city walls, the City Watch, and my parents to keep us safe. An hour here to give the horse a second wind should be more than enough."

"We are staying here. I am hungry, my men are hungry. And judging by

192

your disposition, you could stand to have a proper meal yourself."

"Right now the only proper meal would be a bowl of my father's stew at my dining room table. You stay, I'm going," she said, turning back and heading for her wagon.

"I don't think that's wise."

"I no longer trust your judgment on what is or is not wise."

He jumped off his wagon and followed her. "I've got two armed men to protect me. What happens to you if they attack?"

"I had your men to protect me too, and I still got kidnapped, remember?"

"I seem to recall you being much more reasonable when we last spoke."

"When we last spoke you weren't, for some reason, stalling about getting to somewhere legitimately safe."

"What are you implying?"

"I'm implying there's still something you're not telling me, and if you want me to stay here, it is the last thing I want to do. It'll just lead to me getting captured by the Bolivans again."

"And traveling alone *won't*? If they can catch up with us here, they can catch up with us on the road."

"Unless you've arranged for them to be here."

"What!?"

"I'm not convinced you and the Bolivans aren't working together."

"I don't know what's happened to stoke your paranoia to this degree, but I assure you, it has taken you well past the limits of reason."

"You're both after the same thing."

"We are constantly being *attacked* by the Bolivans."

"So you say. And I think you'd agree that the only thing guaranteed to get me working together with the Graves family for certain would be a common enemy."

"You didn't find out we even *were* the Graves family until a Bolivan agent kidnapped you."

"You don't earn any points for virtue and trustworthiness by reminding me you were concealing your identity for months."

"Now you listen to me…" he fumed. He took an angry puff on the pipe. The moment he did so, his expression changed. "Go, go. Now!" he urged. "Men! Weapons up and ready. One man on reins, one on weapons. We don't stop until the animal collapses or we hit Beffshire!"

He climbed onto the running board of her wagon as she snapped the reins and brought it back up to speed. Behind them, seconds later, the thunder of hooves could be heard emerging from a well-concealed area of overgrowth just outside of town. It would have been an ambush. There was no doubt in her mind.

Two crossbow bolts hissed through the air. One tore a hole in the canvas of the purple wagon. The other killed the man at the reins. His partner scrambled over him to get the wagon moving, but their attackers were on horseback. Without wagons to pull, they would close the distance in no time.

"Take the reins," Epiphany said.

"Why?"

"Because someone needs to do something about the attackers, and I don't trust you behind me with a weapon right now," she snapped.

She climbed into the back of the wagon and fetched the bolter. She held tight to the strut holding her own wagon's canvas and raised the weapon. The purple wagon rattled aside. One of the horsemen peeled off to deal with it. The other continued after them. A familiar face with a look of fearsome determination gazed back from the saddle of the thundering horse. Temple.

It simply wasn't possible to keep control of a horse at full gallop and reload a crossbow, but if he kept up the speed much longer, he'd be able to board the wagon. She'd scarcely been able to defeat him when she had a hidden weapon and the benefit of surprise. She didn't want to think of what her chances would be if he caught up. She touched her finger to the trigger. Her father had said the weapon was best used at close range. But if there was one thing that Martin Masker could be trusted to do, it was overdesign and underpromise on effects. With that in mind, she braced herself a bit more sturdily before she pulled the trigger.

The weapon sounded like the mast of a ship cracking in a storm when it fired. What she'd assumed would be a wildly inaccurate bolt firing out the end instead left the weapon as a cloud of shredded wood and metal. The raw power of the weapon had shattered its projectile and knocked her back a half step. The assassin in pursuit charged his horse through the debris, much to his own and the animal's dismay. At this range, none of the fragments had enough punch left to them to kill, but a dozen painful gouges across a horse's hide were more than enough to make the animal think twice about obeying the man on its back. And the half-dozen fresh gashes across the arms and face of the rider didn't leave him in much of a state of mind to regain control. The animal shrieked and bucked. The rider tumbled off. He dashed after it, but the lingering limp from the last time they clashed assured he wouldn't be catching it until it decided to stop running, and it didn't look like it would return to its senses anytime soon.

"There's no one on our tail at the moment. But it looks like your two men are down, and the wagon has been taken."

He removed his pipe and tucked it behind his ear. "Tell me what happens next, would you? I had my doubts about this one."

"About what one?"

He put his fingers between his teeth and gave two quick whistles and one short one. Epiphany turned back and gazed at the purple wagon far behind. Black smoke started rolling from within. A moment later, brilliant flame consumed the rear of the wagon.

"Your wagon's gone up in flames," she said.

"I owe Euphoria an apology. I said she'd wasted her money buying that contraption. 'When would I want to burn my own wagon, and what is the likelihood that contraption will work?' I said. I suppose I should know better than to argue with a Masker woman."

"You're quite right. Which is why now might be a fine time to start answering my questions with a degree less evasion. Starting with, how did you know they were about to attack?"

"The voice in the flame," he said.

"I snuffed the flame specifically to silence its voice!" she said.

"Did you now?" He took the pipe from his ear and gave a puff.

"…You'd lit your pipe from the flame." She narrowed her eyes. "The pipe's *always* been lit from the flame, hasn't it?"

"A fine way to keep it with me. And to relight a replacement lantern if something goes wrong. Which I did."

"And just how did the *flame* know there was a coming attack?"

"I don't bother asking direct questions, because I don't get direct answers."

"Frustrating, isn't it?"

"Indeed."

"Now that it's down to you and me, and you've lost the one item I managed to secure for you, are you willing to stop hiding things?"

"I'll share a bit more, but you're wrong about that second part." He reached into his jacket and held up the Bygone dagger. "Once we switched back to our proper wagons I thought it was wise to hide the dagger just in case you'd try to take it back. A sound decision as it turns out, even if for the wrong reason."

"There's value in distrust by default, it seems."

"We've always found it useful to assume the worst. But if you can ask questions and keep an eye out for attackers, I'd suggest you do so. Once we get to Beffshire, my focus will shift to recovery rather than crisis."

She wrapped an arm around a strut in the back of the wagon and began the extremely lengthy hand-cranking process that would restore her father's weapon into firing position. "When did this search for the clockwork diamond start?"

"With the acquisition of the book that contained the page you were first hired to deal with."

"What else is in the book?"

"I will once again reiterate that I am not nearly as central to the decision-making processes of the Graves family as you give me credit for. I've seen perhaps three more pages than you have, and none of them were even translated to the limited degree that our people had been able to manage."

"Then what do you *know* about the book?"

"I know that it was either the journal of an explorer or simply a record. Either someone uncovering something *from* antiquity or preserving something *for* antiquity. We acquired it in something of a bid war from a merchant in the northern Quarr territories. It was part of a collection of books that otherwise had nothing to do with contraptions, which explains how it's evaded our grasp for so long, and we were only narrowly able to acquire it rather than losing it to our Bolivan counterparts. From that day, shopping lists began to be formulated."

"And you don't know the name of the buyer or the history of the book?"

"The bids were conducted remotely over a period of many months. I do not know if the buyer is a man, a woman, or even a consortium. I only know that they were in the territories and did business via a trusted courier who has since vanished."

"Convenient," she said.

"Given the value of the information they had, I could consider their aloofness singularly inconvenient."

"How many items on these shopping lists have you acquired?"

"Nothing unique beyond the dagger. Everything else was at best useful but general purpose."

"What other unique items would you consider crucial?"

"If you went through our files, you saw the answer to that question."

"I know. I'm giving you an opportunity to be honest."

"The only other items that, to my observation, are unique are a second map, which in my own notes is known only as 'more detailed and more extensive' than the first, and a badge of some sort. Or emblem? Purpose unknown. To me, anyway. I know that even if we were to have acquired all three of your items, whatever the next step is wouldn't have progressed until those were acquired as well."

"And to whom are those other crucial items assigned?"

He looked over his shoulder. "Your sister was handling them personally."

"I see." Epiphany dropped a bolt into the weapon. "Lovely."

#

The ship had settled into its hiding place. Sure enough, it was almost entirely hidden in the shadow of two larger, impressively intact vessels. Because of the division of labor that came with running the ship nonstop, the Adept and her hands had reached their limits and had to rest, leaving Teya on watch and unpleasantly alone with her thoughts.

She dangled her little feet over the side of the boat, fishing pole in hand.

But it was no use. The waters were completely barren. It was just as well, though. She couldn't devote much of her focus to fishing when Parch took every opportunity to wander off, and it was proving increasingly difficult to keep the little creature from tracking down Fel.

She raised a paw and gave Parch a playful slap or two to keep him distracted, then reached down and scrambled Oiler's puzzle for it. It seemed the only one who *didn't* get to have a distraction was Teya herself. And it was beginning to wear on her.

The kobold cast her eyes toward the city. For an instant, it filled her vision. Street after street of dazzling white stone. But it faded, unraveling into an incomprehensible jumble of shapes and lines. Somewhere deep in her mind she knew it was still a city, still precisely the place Fel had marched off to explore. But that sliver of thought was afloat in a sea of confusion, that alternately denied there was anything to see and insisted she look away. She could not will herself into the desire to go any farther than the pier any more than she could will herself to rise into the sky. That part of her mind was simply rubbed away like chalk on a slate.

But she wanted to… She so desperately wanted to go and do as Kazel had instructed. And, perhaps even more puzzling than the bizarreness of "wanting to be able to want something" was the fact that her orders from Kazel to escort Fel weren't her only reason for wanting to find him.

He was fascinating. She knew that contraptions were dangerous. There were heaps of singed and smoldering rags and pages back in the mountain to prove that. But not everything that was dangerous was to be feared. The sea was dangerous. But once you had a boat and a fishing pole, you could get a delicious meal out of it. She felt certain contraptions were the same. And Fel, he was the same too.

She took a deep breath. She *loved* living in the mountain. She loved serving Kazel, and serving the Adept. They'd taught her everything she knew. They were her friends. They were her protectors. Ever since Fel had arrived, and she'd been made to escort him, she'd done so much. Her first time in a boat in *ages*. Riding a greater unicorn for the first time. Playing with a lesser unicorn…

Parch.

She turned. The little thing was tippy-tapping his way down the pier. He had gotten much farther than she expected. She tossed the pole onto deck and dashed after Parch. Ahead, the boards of the pier and the city backdrop started to churn and unravel… but Parch remained solid and distinct. It was as though someone had dropped a stone in the surface of a lake, wobbling and washing out all the reflections but one.

Teya skidded to a stop in front of him. He bleated and walked around her. She kept focused on him. Though the world around him shivered and faded,

Parch remained a bright, vivid point. She didn't know if it was because he was a lesser mystic. She didn't know if perhaps Fel and Tome had done the same and she'd simply neglected to watch them go. It didn't matter. What mattered was this was an opportunity not only to continue to serve Kazel as he'd instructed but to help Fel and, just maybe, have a bit more adventure before her time with him was through.

She dashed back to the boat and pulled Oiler to her back.

"Have. Hold," she said, handing her quiver of arrows and her bow back to it.

After a moment of clicking, ringing consideration, Oiler stuffed the puzzle box beside its head in the pack and faithfully grasped the offered equipment. She squawked a warning to Stix that she would have to take over watch. Before the other kobold could question her or object, she grabbed a rope and hopped back onto the pier.

Parch had been on the move, but he remained just barely visible in the street ahead. She followed him like a guiding star, and when she reached him, she tied the end of the rope into a harness around him.

"Go, Parch," she instructed. "Find Fel."

The unicorn bleated and took a prancing leap forward. Teya hurried to keep up. The world around them was willfully disorienting. Sometimes dizzying, sometimes dull to the point of nonexistence. But Parch and the land around him were an oasis of solidity and sanity. Her mind tugged her ever backward, nudging her to turn away, to walk back to where things made sense. The rope tugged her forward, Parch dragging her onward.

She didn't know what she'd do when she found Fel. She didn't care. Each step was a step forward, and that was enough for her.

#

Fel crested the final steep set of steps to the base of the city's central wall. It had taken a tremendous amount of willpower to keep from picking through every promising new building along the way. The looming threat of his eventual clash with the dragon, it turned out, was most easily thrust to the back of his mind when he was using the rest of it to run numbers on just how much his mother and sister were likely to be able to charge for the treasures he was finding.

But those treasures could only be sold if he could bring them home. And he could only bring them home if he did this little task for Kazel. He'd discovered two buildings in a row that had deep, reinforced basements. That meant he knew what level of architecture would provide him with shelter if he needed it. Now he had to fully set his mind to finding Duurth.

He inspected the wall. Its construction was almost precisely the same as the Greater Lands wall, with two exceptions. The first, and most frustrating, was that there were no alcoves. He would have liked a little something to hide

198

in while he checked the rest of the city for Duurth. As it was, there didn't seem to be any doors or gates at all on the wall, unless they were on the far side of the ring it traced. The other main difference was the size. While it was a match for the height of the Greater Lands Wall, it had a comparatively minuscule diameter. Small enough that it couldn't have contained something any larger than a courtyard or a modest town square.

He shielded his eyes from the setting sun and scanned the city as Tome hauled himself breathlessly up the steps.

"I should have eaten that fish when I had the chance," he panted. "I am weak from hunger."

"Yeah, hunger. That's why you're weak," Fel muttered.

"What?"

"I said the shovel-fried fish was quite tasty. By now I'd have thought you'd have learned at least that much from me. Never miss a chance for a hot meal."

Tome leaned on the wall and gazed up along it. "The greatest wall the world has ever seen. Untold miles of the harshest wilderness. A vast gulf of unforgiving sea, and they still felt the need to build a second wall," he said. "What do you suppose is behind here?"

Fel shrugged. "I'd just as soon let it stay hidden. There's enough good stuff to be had out here."

Tome pressed his ear to the wall. "It sounds mechanical. I can hear motion. Gears and the like." He gazed up at the edge of the wall. "We're so close, and yet we had a better view of whatever is in there back from the shore. Something twisting and twinkling, remember?"

"Mmm…" Fel said, squinting at the city below.

"Aren't you the least bit curious?"

"I know enough things for certain about this place to form my opinion," he said. "I don't need to start wondering about the rest. Now help me look for anything large enough to house a dragon and his hoard."

Tome nodded and cupped his hands around his eyes. "There, perhaps? Beside that wedge-shaped intersection?"

Fel fetched his spyglass and raised it. "No. Too close to the way we came up," he said. "We'd have seen or smelled some sort of evidence."

"Evidence…" Tome leaned forward a bit, as though the extra three inches would make the difference. "What sort of a carcass is that? Beside the spire there?"

Tome pointed. Fel followed his gesture. There was indeed a very old and utterly desiccated husk of a creature. It was larger than a horse and looked to have had wings, claws, and hooves.

"It looks like a griffin," Tome said. "Or, what used to be one."

"I think you're right. And if that's where the leftovers ended up, then…" Fel pointed. "There. The church. That broken-out window looks big enough for a dragon to fit through, assuming he's not as big as Kazel."

"One moment, one moment. The angle is right, we can be sure," Tome said.

"How? I'm the one with the spyglass and I can't tell."

Tome reached into his shirt and pulled a spell. "Eagle-eye spell," he said.

"You waited until now to pull that out?"

"I don't know how long it will last. I wanted to wait until it would be of genuine use." He grasped and raised it up. "Do me a favor and hold my shoulder? I've only used this once before, and it was rather disorienting while it was in effect. I don't want to fall down the stairs."

Fel steadied him. He tore the page. It flashed into ashes. A twinkling blue light colored his eyes. He staggered a bit.

"By the high, that's effective," he muttered. "All right, all right. I can see… The dragon is inside."

"You can see that? There's not much of an angle."

"You see the intact window, just there through the broken one?"

"… No."

"Well, it's there. And I can see a reflection of the dragon's head. He's sleeping."

Fel squinted through his spyglass at the speck of a broken window in the distance. "You're sure you're seeing that?"

"Clear as day."

"That's a very good spell."

"It ought to be. It took me forty minutes to write it, and the ink and paper, if I were to purchase them beyond this place, would have cost a fortune. I can make out the color of the dragon's scales. They're… mustard yellow." He blinked and turned to Fel. "I know this—*gah!*"

He stumbled back when he looked at Fel.

"What? What is it?" Fel said, turning to look behind him.

"The human face is an unpleasant thing to look upon with eagle eyes. I can see every pore of your skin."

"Fine, but what were you saying?"

"I know—that is to say, *we* know—this dragon."

"I've only ever seen two dragons up close, Tome. One was Kazel, and the other was the one that attacked us outside the wall."

"That's right."

"This is the same one?"

Tome looked back to the church. "When you've seen a beast eat a horse, it finds a rather solid place in one's memories, and I am quite certain it is the same one."

Fel rubbed his face. "Leave it to me to come to the most remote place in the world and find an enemy."

"You make them as readily as friends, I see."

"Just that sort of man, I guess. Come on. If he's sleeping, now's the time."

"Give me a moment. I need to let the eagle eyes wear off. I'm surprised the spell has lasted this long."

"What about having particularly good eyesight makes you unable to walk?"

"Right now your face and the mast of the boat half-sunk in the harbor to the northeast are equally sharp, and it is rather difficult to make sense of the world like this."

"Then close your eyes and grab my shoulders so we can get going."

Tome nodded and awkwardly grabbed on to Fel as they began the trek toward their quarry. After the third near-fall during the descent of the steps, Fel shook his head.

"You were useful for nearly a minute there, you know."

"Magic is an art, not a science," Tome said.

"Don't drag artists down with you."

#

Vivian completed a sale and was logging it in her ledger when the door flew open and produced a particularly energetic ring of the entry bell. She looked up to see a red-faced, grinning bear of a man she'd met just once before, and under very uncertain circumstances.

"There she is!" proclaimed Donovan Verfessa with arms wide and a sack in one hand. "I tell you, Vivian, if I wasn't married and you weren't married, oh what a romance we would have."

"I beg your pardon, Mr. Verfessa?"

"Don! And I think you know exactly what I'm on about. Where's that husband of yours? Is he downstairs?"

"Yes. Working, as usual."

"All the best of us are. That's why I came down here. The alternative was having you or your man take some time off, and after recent events, I don't even want to suggest it. I heard what you did to those Bolivans. And here I was thinking you'd need my men to keep you folks safe, and that husband of yours trusses one up like a roast goose."

"We take the steps we must to keep ourselves safe."

"Right, right. But the victor is entitled to the spoils." He hefted the sack over the side of the counter to set it down beside her. "Your man earned this, and I think he deserves the right of first refusal."

She glanced uncertainly at the sack and Donovan. With a bit of well-disguised trepidation, she pulled the cord tying it shut and tugged open the sack. It was a small assortment of very high-quality contraptions, presumably confiscated from the Bolivan agent and awaiting appraisal from the assayer's office.

"You're going to hear a story about how the Bolivans have got someone in the equipment room at the watchhouse who stole these, but they don't. Or, at least, if they do, the dullard is unconscionably slow, because my boy got to them first."

"I see…"

"Now, I found myself a buyer for the ones we had. Quite the payday. I'd've been swindled if not for your expert appraisal, though. I'm going to have to keep you on retainer. That is, if you're open to it."

"Not so long ago, I would have denied any sort of partnership with someone in your very specialized line of work. But recent events have made me reconsider a bit."

He rubbed his hands together. "That's what I like to hear."

"I am not agreeing to any terms just yet. But I would be amenable to discussing them."

"Of course, of course. The best business partnerships have firm foundations. And in the spirit of firm foundations, I'll be honest. I didn't just come down here to provide your hard-earned gear. When I'd sold those contraptions, the price and the eagerness of the buyer had me convinced the equipment was as near to one of a kind as something was likely to get. But it seems the Bolivans just keep sending folks down here with that gear."

"Either the Bolivans have found an excellent source for that equipment, or they have been stockpiling for just this occasion," Vivian said.

"And that presents a problem. There's a few ways to get the better of someone who's got better gear. You can be quick. You can be clever. You can be sneaky. But the problem is, quick and sneaky only work once each, and I already burned sneaky. And clever? I try my best, but I think when it comes to contraptions, this here shop's got the market cornered on cleverness. If the Bolivans stay this bold and mean to put some roots down in my garden, I need someone with the right shears to clip them now and again until I can get my good gloves on to tear them out."

"You continue to have a lovely mind for metaphor," she said. "It is curious. You seem to be asking for us to provide protection when a degree of protection would have been my first request from you."

"A muddy mess the world has gotten itself into, eh?" he said. "Two of the oldest businesses in Beffshire coming to each other and looking for the same sort of help? Still, I've got brawn and numbers to offer, if you've got brains and tools."

"I'll have to take the matter to Martin, and ideally discuss it with the children as well. Both are away."

"When are you expecting them back? This sort of thing'll keep for a bit longer. After two black eyes, I can't imagine the Bolivans will be tripping over themselves to be the next to come down here."

"I trust my children to see to their business as quickly and efficiently as they are able. But I wouldn't expect a family reunion for a few weeks. But when they've come home and we've settled the books, I suspect you'll be hearing from us one way or the other."

"That's what I like to hear, Viv. That's what I like to hear."

#

One thing was clear as they drew nearer to the church they now knew to hold Duurth. Fel had been right about the smell. It wasn't foul, precisely. It didn't smell like a stable or a heap of manure. But the odor was potent, and had an earthy, *animal* smell that raised all sorts of alarms in their minds. This was the sort of scent their ancestors learned to avoid, because those who didn't learn that lesson didn't last long enough to produce offspring.

The closer they got, the more they found evidence of decades, perhaps centuries, of residency from the dragon. Bones of every size were scattered over the ground. Some had been reduced to little more than powder by sun, rain, and the idle crunch of the predator's comings and goings. Some still had the stench of rot and dried bits of sinew. Tome had, over the course of the journey, become accustomed enough to his stubbornly hyperprecise vision to walk on his own. Unfortunately for him, that meant he was treated to an unfathomably detailed view of the stomach-turning remnants of hundreds of dragon meals.

After having to climb over a heap of bones, they came upon the alley that ran behind the massive church. The slow, rhythmic hiss of a sleeping dragon's breath served as a constant, sobering reminder of just how close and just how real the danger was.

"From here, we must be silent," Fel said, his voice barely audible. "That goes for you too, Wick, unless it's important. I don't need to be startled by you."

"Understood," remarked the flame.

Tome nodded. Fel crept along the outside of the church. The dragon may not have had any use for them, but there were plenty of doors around the perimeter. None of those in the rear of the church were open, and Fel preferred not to test the soundness of a dragon's sleep by trying to bash through one. As luck would have it, the last to leave this place when it was evacuated must have done so through the door just below the shattered window, as it was ajar. Fel eased it open. His heart almost stopped when the stubborn hinges squeaked. He froze until he heard the next long hiss of slumber.

They slipped through the door. It led to a side hallway running parallel to the huge, vaulted main chamber of the church. The strange, wild scent was stronger here, and joined by a musty, damp smell. He kept Wick's lantern low. If nothing else, this was a moment that was worthy of being chronicled, so he'd best make certain the flame had a good view.

He made his way to the first arch that led to the main chamber.

By the high... he mouthed silently.

The mound of contraptions was taller than he was, swept into a surprisingly orderly pile. There were hundreds of items at least. Thousands, more likely. And in a testament to their build quality, those he could see were in near-pristine condition. Some had acquired a rather unfortunate patina of what Fel could only imagine was, in the best possible case, dragon dander. But they were worlds better than half of what Martin worked on day in and day out. The numbers floating through his head, representing just what he knew he'd be able to *carry* dwarfed even what they'd earned for selling the Bygone dagger. And there was just one obstacle between that glorious moment and this one.

Duurth.

Another hiss of breath treated Fel to the rotten-meat scent of the beast's breath, the same stench that had chased him into the safety of the alcove when he'd reached the wall months ago. If Fel hadn't met Kazel, this would have easily been the largest and most fearsome creature he'd ever encountered. Duurth was perhaps a third of Kazel's size, but he was still massive enough that the horse he'd eaten upon their second meeting was more than a mouthful but less than a bellyful. He lacked Kazel's majesty, less a work of art and more a work of grim efficiency. Armor-plate scales, muddy yellow on back and belly alike, though in two different shades. Tusk-like teeth jutted up and down from the front of his mouth, protruding while the curled lips offered just a glimpse of "smaller" teeth that were merely the size of carrots.

Claws the size of his arm clutched lightly around a pile of contraptions, firmly enough to be aware of their presence but softly enough not to damage them.

Fel realized he'd not blinked since he'd caught sight of the thing. He blinked his burning eyes and stepped back into the side hallway.

"We need to find the key," he whispered to Tome.

"I know," Tome replied.

"Any ideas?"

"None."

Fel pointed to Tome and silently instructed, along with copious hand gestures, *You, stay here. Use those eyes. See if you spot it.*

Tome nodded. Fel moved as swiftly and silently as he could back to the door, the absolute nearest place he could justify speaking out loud.

"Wick, there is a pile of contraptions that could fill our entire shop from floor to ceiling multiple times, and I'm looking for a specific one the size of a serving platter. One that, by the way, I've never seen before. It is going to take some time, and there is a dragon sleeping on the pile."

"So I have observed. I would be very interested in hearing what plan you may have privately devised for what appears to be an intractable problem."

"Wick, how long have you known me? Why would you think I'd have come up with a plan by now?"

He froze as they heard something shift inside. Fel stuck his head in the door. Tome had his back pressed to the wall, eyes wide and hands shaking. He made it clear that he had by no means made a sound. Nevertheless, the shifting of the dragon was far more than a simple toss and turn. Duurth was waking up.

"It would appear whatever precautions you've made against the beast picking up your scent have been inadequate," Wick said.

Fel raised his head and shut his eyes. "Right. Scent."

Tome dashed past him, heading for shelter. Fel tackled him to the ground and dragged him back into the church.

"What are you doing? What are you *doing*?" Tome hissed, still-enchanted eyes sparkling with a layer of terror.

"Church basement. At least two levels down," he said, helping him to his feet.

"The *dragon* is in the church," Tome said.

"The dragon isn't going to destroy his own lair, and the church is definitely the sturdiest place around here. Come on!"

The ground rumbled with an irritated growl from within the chamber. They dashed through the side hallway. Claws thumped onto the stone floor of the main chamber. A fearsome head dropped low and gazed through one of the arches. A claw flashed through. They barely avoided it and found a wide staircase at the end of the hall. The air rattled with an odd, crackling groan. They tumbled around a turn in the stairs. A brilliant orange light and a searing heat flashed behind them. Fel pulled Tome forward and threw him through an open door. He rushed in behind.

Fire swept around the curve of the stairs. Fel grabbed the door and heaved it shut, flames already licking around its stout wooden timbers. The door was thick and heavy, clearly meant to turn away would-be attackers or thieves. Once it was shut and braced, two more blasts of fire teased and licked at the wood. It produced a worrisome knock and shudder, but when the dragon's breath ceased, the door ceased its crackling and sizzling as well, heroically resisting ignition.

The pair held perfectly still, listening closely to the motions of the beast above. The floor thumped with his footsteps. The thing must have been pacing like a cat outside the shelter of a cornered rat. When a full minute passed with no flames and no shattered stone, they breathed sighs of relief and assessed their situation.

Fel held up Wick's lantern. The air here had an extra level of mustiness that he hadn't experienced before. The level looked like an archive, but rather than shelves of books or endless drawers filled with documents, it had carved stone placards. It was a catacombs.

"What do we do now?" Tome asked.

"First, we thank our lucky stars we didn't run into any traps on the way down," Fel said.

He pressed his palm to the door, then dropped to the floor and gazed underneath it.

"The walls are charred out there, but nothing's on fire. I think we can safely hide here," he said.

"For how long?"

"Until the dragon leaves."

The plodding footsteps above knocked some dust free.

"Until it leaves," Tome said flatly.

"Yeah."

"Fel, we just learned that dragons can sleep for weeks or months. You don't suppose they can wait a few days? Because *we can't*. Not without food and water."

"I've got some food and water."

"For what, another day? You've gotten us trapped in here! You and your stubborn refusal to come up with a decent plan!"

"I *can't* come up with a plan because I'm *stupid*, Tome," he shouted. "I thought you'd picked up on that. I don't plan more than one step ahead because I can't *think* more than one step ahead."

Tome opened his mouth, but paused. It was difficult to formulate a proper retort when the point had already been made. "Well you didn't have to drag *me* into it," he said.

"I didn't want you to come! I wanted to do this alone, remember?"

"If you'd told me, 'I don't want you to come because I'm going to be a blasted fool and get myself killed,' maybe I would have listened."

"I thought that went without saying!" Fel said. "I've only got three things going for me. I can follow directions and work hard. But following directions never gets you anywhere but where the directions tell you to go, and no one is going to give you the recipe for success and respect. Hard work can get you there, but only if someone gives you the space to do it. The other thing I've got is that *sometimes* I get lucky. And luck can get you anywhere. So I depend upon that one when it's really important."

"That is stupid."

"I just said that!"

The floor shook a bit and another burst of flame flashed behind the door. Tome clawed his fingers though his hair.

"You know something? You are impulsive, strong, and handy. I am cautious, cunning, and thoughtful. We complement one another precisely. In *theory* we should be the perfect team."

"My dad has a lot of theories. They tend to leave scorch marks on his workshop wall. Come on. Maybe there's another way out of here."

"Why would a catacombs have a separate entrance and exit?"

"Why is the city empty? Why is there a wall with no doors around some sort of contraption that's been operating since this place emptied out? If you're going to focus on the questions, we'll never get anything done."

"Should I inform your parents about what's happened?" Wick asked.

"No! First off, it's not done happening. Second, every time you go, you're gone for ages."

"Yes, I do apologize for that. The deeper you get into the Greater Lands, the more difficult it is for me to reach you. I have in my possession a fair number of maps of varying degrees of detail and accuracy. Knowing where you are and how long it takes to reach you has given me a fairly strong intuition for how travel time for me translates into distance for you. But clearly my intuition is flawed. Based upon the effort and time it takes me to reach you now, I would have supposed you would have left the area enclosed by even the submerged portion of the Greater Lands Wall."

"We *were* traveling for a rather long time at a very high speed in that boat," Tome said. "Do you suppose we've passed the edge of the undersea portion of the wall? Is that why none of the others can follow us?"

"I have not made myself clear," Wick said. "You are presently farther away than the far edge of the submerged Greater Lands Wall by a large margin. That is to say, it should have been faster for me to avoid the wall entirely to reach you. But I couldn't, because you are within the circle of the wall."

"You're not making any sense," Tome said.

"I agree," Wick said.

Fel handed the lantern to Tome and poked him in the chest. "You don't get to lecture me about not planning more than one step ahead when all it takes is two sentences to get you talking about maps instead of dealing with the dragon over our heads. At least *I* can focus on the *current* step. You can hold the lantern and argue about this, I'll look for a way out of here. Just follow me."

Chapter 11

Epiphany and Thaddeus hurried down the street, eyes darting all about as they covered the short distance between the stable and the antiquities shop. She heard the inevitable squawks and taunts from the lesser harpies aligned along the roof and dug a handful of buttons out of her pocket to throw to them without looking.

"Why are you throwing buttons to—" Thaddeus began.

"Because my brother is an idiot and he got them spoiled and now we all have to deal with it. Get inside the shop now." She shoved the door open and pushed him inside.

"Epiphany! You're home!" Vivian said.

Though the sound of relief was subdued in her voice, that her businesslike demeanor showed any cracks whatsoever while she was behind the counter of the shop spoke volumes of just how strongly she felt.

The older woman hurried forward and gave her daughter a hug, then cast a glance at the "customer."

"Thaddeus. I didn't anticipate seeing you in Beffshire without an armed escort," she said, her voice doing a slightly better job concealing her displeasure at his presence.

"You know him on sight?" Epiphany said.

"Of course. It was before your time, but we formerly had something of a working relationship with the Graves family, and Thaddeus was one of two men they sent to make deals. There was a period of several years when we thought better of our partnership. Then we made the regrettable decision to invite them for open trade once more, and they sent *the other* Graves man."

"The one Euphoria ran away with," Epiphany said.

Vivian's nostrils flared. "Which is why I question the wisdom of setting foot in this shop without protection." She turned and shouted, "Martin! Epiphany is home, and she brought a stray."

"Mrs. Masker, I assure you. I try not to go anywhere without protection, but at present all my traveling companions have been killed."

"Have they? And have you dragged *both* my daughters into whatever mess you've gotten yourself into?"

"We have not," he said.

"They have. They're the ones who sold us that page and bought the dagger," Epiphany said, glancing out the window of the shop.

Martin burst up from downstairs and rushed to his daughter. "My sweet little girl!" he said. "Things have been positively diabolical. I hope you've been clear of the worst of it."

"Briefly kidnapped, but I wasn't hurt."

"Kidnapped!" Martin and Vivian said in unison.

"It was one of the mercenaries from last time. The one with the temple scar. He caught a distant shot from your new weapon, but I don't think it's taken care of him. He could show up at any moment."

Vivian gripped her cudgel.

"And Thaddeus is a part of this," Martin said, his face stony.

"Right," Epiphany said. "It turns out he's 'Mr. Badgerweed.'"

Martin glared at him. "You're doing business anonymously now? Trying to trick the other of my daughters?"

"And doing business in stolen illicit antiquities," Vivian said. "But we can deal with that *after* we discuss this kidnapping. Downstairs. If he's got his own enemies, we don't need him dragging any more of them to the shop. We've got enough killers after us already."

She flipped a sign to indicate their absence, braced the door, and tugged at a few well-hidden chains to activate the freshly upgraded traps. She led the way, silently, to the dining room below.

"The kidnapping," Vivian repeated.

"The temple-scarred mercenary. He's working for the Bolivans. He captured me, but I used my boot knife to escape. Nothing untoward happened. But you should know that—"

"The Bolivans have access to a sentry flame," Martin said.

"What? No, the Graves family has access to a sentry flame."

"We found the key component of a sentry lantern in the stove in my shop and used it to set a trap for Bolivan would-be kidnappers," Vivian said. "Their response made it abundantly clear that they had full access to the flame. Why do you think the Graves family has one?"

"Because *he* has been taking orders from one for who knows how long. I'd assumed it was Wick."

"We'd assumed it was Wick, too. But unless Wick has been spinning very convincing tales of your brother's adventures from whole cloth, he's been away for too long to be responsible for this subterfuge. And we've yet to hear a voice from the second lantern."

"So… are there two sentry lanterns? Are there three? Does each of the contraptioneer families have their own?” Epiphany asked.

“It will be a difficult question to answer.” Martin looked to Thaddeus. “Unless *someone* has some insight to shed.”

All eyes turned to him. He puffed his pipe.

“Thad, it seems to me the Graves family have an enemy in the Bolivans, and the Maskers have an enemy in the Bolivans,” Martin said. “If either of us is to see a swift end to this madness, it’ll be with the addition of allies, not by adding additional fronts to the war. You need our help, and I’m sure we could use yours. You’ve lied to us, but truth now will begin to heal that damage.”

“We haven’t lied. We’ve merely—”

“I don’t do business with weasels, so save my time and what remains of your integrity by choosing to stop acting like one right bloody now,” Vivian said.

He puffed again. “I cannot speak for the Bolivans and their access to the lantern, but I can confirm that the sentry lantern placed in the stove was done by us.”

“You have been spying on us…” Vivian said. “For how long?”

“Since shortly before your daughter left.”

Martin shut his eyes. “She was the one who placed it, wasn’t she?”

“She was.”

“Years. *Years*. My own daughter…” Vivian jabbed a finger at him. “You Graves must be some of the worst businesspeople on the continent if you’ve been eavesdropping on us for years and you’ve barely managed *any* sort of real growth.”

“When you have ears in the shop of a rival, actions must be subtle lest you be revealed. Something that I suppose we can both feel fortunate the Bolivans didn’t take to heart. But if they’ve got access to our sentry lantern, which it is now clear is *not* yours, then the questions remain of how they attained it and how long they’ve had it.”

“There is one of them locked up in the watchhouse as we speak. You could have a word with them. Unless Verfessa has already decided to send a more thorough message about what happens to criminal enterprises that overlap with his own.”

“Questions remain,” Martin said. “If the Bolivans have access to your sentry lantern and you don’t know about it… the implications could be profound. Either for you in particular or for anyone who uses a sentry lantern. As far as I know, you can’t simply eavesdrop on someone else’s lantern. The flame must *tell* the information. So either your sentry flame is secretly providing information to the Bolivans, or the Bolivans have found a way to extract information from sentry flames.”

“Seems rather far beyond them. The Bolivans, in my observation, are not innovators.”

“Then you’ve got an issue, haven’t you? And so have we, potentially, thanks to your family's decision to insert a security leak into my husband's workshop," Vivian said. "We have a lot to discuss."

#

Like so many of the homes in Beffshire, the architects of this church had seen fit to dig far deeper down than they'd built up. Their search had brought Fel and Tome through three more levels of catacombs. This lowest one sprawled much farther.

"I really don't think we'll find a way out this far down," Tome said.

"You never know," Fel said. "And besides, we're farther from Duurth down here. That's an improvement."

Tome shut his eyes. "I'm glad I didn't write the bat-ear spell. I can still hear him thumping around up there. It would be turning my brains to mush if I could hear it any better. Though seeing this macabre place in pristine detail isn't much of an improvement."

"That still hasn't worn off?"

"Not yet," he said. "To be a paper mage is to understand that magic works differently in different places. I only hope that it isn't *so* different here that the spell is permanent."

"There are worse things than having good eyesight."

"There are better things, too." Tome raised the lantern higher. "Larger monuments down here. I think these are the more revered dead."

It was true. Whereas the other levels looked uneasily like the dead had been stowed in large stone drawers and labeled, this floor felt something akin to a museum. Large, artfully rendered plinths, busts, statues, and slabs of elegantly carved stone occupied carefully arranged rows and columns running along the sprawling level like city streets.

"Is it just me, or is the air fresher down here than it was on the last level?" Fel asked.

"It is. Almost not musty at all, at least relatively."

"That means some sort of ventilation. Maybe that will be our way out."

Fel alternated between watching where he was going and scanning the ceiling for some sort of an opening. He came to an intersection where one of the passages crossed another with no way forward. The monument blocking the path, however, caught his eye. A tombstone with a bit of brass inlay in the form of a clock escapement with an oddly shaped interior. Sort of a barbed double hook with a trapezoid above it.

"I've seen this before." Fel snapped his fingers. "Where was it… On Oiler. This is the maker's mark on Oiler's chin. Can you read what it says beneath it?"

Tome glanced at it. "I'm not familiar with the dialect."

"It says 'Tinker.' The proper noun, not the verb," Wick said. "And there is an epitaph. Shall I read it?"

Fel sniffed the air. "Do whatever you like. The vent is somewhere right near here. I'm sure of it."

He paced a short distance scrutinizing the roof, while Wick spoke.

"'Here marks the family tomb of the Tinker clan. Revered in the ways of contraption and innovation. Lifeblood of Clickspring.' I should at this point clarify that Clickspring is a proper noun, not a common one. A place name, I would imagine. Quite likely this very island. And what follows seems to be the address of the family estate to pay respects."

"They named a city after a conventional clock component," Fel said, doubling back to check in the other direction. "And they buried someone named Tinker in the sort of place reserved for kings. Why do I get the feeling I was born in the wrong era? If I'd lived here, I'd have been part of the social elite."

"Yes, you would have. You would have been buried beneath the monument to your right," Wick said.

Fel stopped. "What did you say?"

"To your right," Wick said. "Masker, proper noun. With the following epitaph. 'Here marks the family tomb of the Masker clan. May they forever be remembered as the visionaries who gave contraptions a voice.' And again, there is an address to a family estate."

Fel looked at the monument. It too bore an inlayed emblem, this one of silver rather than brass. The symbol was a circle. Within it was a face in profile, but the empty space opposite it had an eye as well, as though there was a second face staring out from behind the first.

"I had no idea our family went back this far," Fel said.

"Fascinating."

He thumped his finger against the portion that seemed to be the address. "I don't suppose it mentions Beffshire," he said.

"No. There is no mention of the city. I believe that would imply that it is this city," Wick said.

"It's a shame the island is in the thrall of a dragon. It might be edifying to visit the family estate," Tome said.

"Edifying nothing. Dad wants books teaching him how to build contraptions. This is apparently where the people who wrote them lived. Wick, remember those addresses, and once we get out of here, we're paying them a visit." He pointed. "And we *are* getting out of here. That's a… what do you call it. One of the vaults had one… a light shaft. And it's a big one. I think we can fit."

#

"Harold, if you throw one more mug, you're banned for good!" Allie shouted. "And Dana, you should know better. Get off that table!"

She doused a rag in clean water from behind the bar and swabbed her face. The Fox and Log was being particularly boisterous today. At least, if the word

213

"boisterous" could be expanded to include profanities being shouted in three languages and blood being drawn in two different tile games and a game of darts within the same five minutes.

"I swear, people. It used to take you until the sun went down before you all started acting like drunk toddlers," she growled.

"Excuse me," said a voice soft and polite enough to stand out amid the shouting.

Allie turned to see the flour-and-icing-speckled, pink-lace-apron-clad baker from Divinity's Oven. She carried a basket carefully tucked with a cloth and looked a bit put off by the enthusiastic revelry on display.

"Hello there, Mariss," Allie said. "If you're interested in some refreshments, I'll chase some of these drunks out of the corner booth for you. It's got shelter on three sides, so you shouldn't catch any flying debris."

"No, no, I was just wondering if Fel was here," she said.

"Still off gallivanting. Why?"

"I imagined such might be the case. It's been quite a while since he's been down to the bakery, and I know he likes to buy sweet buns for the family now and again. I thought it might be nice to bring some down as a gift, but the shop was closed. I know Fel likes to spend time here sometimes, so I thought maybe he'd come home and they were all here celebrating."

Allie paused. "The shop is closed?"

"Yes. There was no one inside. So, you know Fel pretty well, I suppose."

"Very well. You know a man when he's drunk *and* losing at tiles and you know the real man."

Mariss nodded. "I don't imagine I know the real man, then. He's been through the shop so many times, but I don't get the feeling that he's been *himself* all that often. He's sweet, but—"

"If you think he's sweet, he hasn't been himself."

"Oh?"

"I'm roasting him. He's fine. Just a little thick sometimes, and rough around the edges all the time."

Mariss smiled. "Phew. I was afraid maybe I'd judged him wrong."

"I'm sure he'd like you to have judged him wrong. If there's one person Fel doesn't have a high opinion of, it's Fel. Well, if there's *two* people he doesn't have a high opinion of, the second one is Fel. Because Tem back there probably tops the list. Just so we're clear, you're *sure* the shop was closed."

"Mmhmm! The door was braced."

Allie squinted and tipped her head aside. "Was it in flames?"

"No, silly," Mariss said with a cherubic giggle.

"Oovay! Keep these people from killing each other!"

She surveyed the room. At a quick glance, she knew the usual heavies she liked to rely upon for muscle were either absent or too far along their journey toward inebriation to rely upon.

"Davie! Take a walk with me, would you?"

Her diminutive runner, correctly predicting the purpose of his presence on the trip, grabbed a leather-wrapped lump of lead on a stick and scurried out to the street. Allie took Mariss by the arm and marched her back out the door.

"Is something wrong?"

"If they're closed at this time of day, very possibly. They've been getting a little in over their heads lately. We're just going to check up on them."

#

Fel grunted and heaved. The light shaft was *just* large enough for him to fit inside. That was a mercy. Another mercy was that it was at an angle rather than fully vertical. It meant if he slipped, he'd slide a short distance rather than plummeting back to the lower level. But those mercies weren't without their faults. The tight space meant once he'd reached the barred opening at street level, he had mere inches of leverage to put his tools to work, prying and hammering at them. Another problem was the simple fact that, like everything built in the Bygone Era, it was of a profoundly high level of craftsmanship. Nearly an hour of work had only just started to rattle one of the bars in place. And, of course, he wasn't alone. That was proving to be the most irritating problem of all.

"An angled light shaft is so fascinating, though," Tome said. "One imagines such a thing would be vertical, but with a moment of thought, it becomes clear that a vertical one isn't much better than an angled one. The sun doesn't spend any more time directly overhead than it does, say, at its midmorning height. I wonder if perhaps it was designed to cast light in a particular spot on a particular day. This city seemed so interested in mechanism and clockwork and the like, making their own catacombs a sort of timepiece could—"

"Tome, would you *please* be quiet. I've been listening to you muse over the design of this catacomb for so long that I'm beginning to wish I was buried in it." He turned to glare down the shaft at him.

"Well I hardly think that you need to focus on hammering. It doesn't strike me as an intellectually challenging task."

"The intellectually challenging task is keeping myself from giving in to the urge to come down there and bury this pry bar in your head."

"Really, Fel, you speak of violence so casually. That isn't healthy."

"One of us isn't going to be healthy if you don't quiet down and let me work."

He turned back to the bars. The downy gray muzzle of a lesser unicorn greeted him, poking his nose through the bars to excitedly bleat.

"What?!" Fel yelped, sliding back a few feet. "I thought I told Teya to watch you."

The kobold stuck her head into view and blinked at him. "Did watch! And now, watch you!" she said.

"How did you get here? I thought you couldn't."

She held up the rope tied to her wrist. "Parch go. I follow."

"Fascinating!" Tome called from below. "So how does that work? Do you—"

"Tome, I am going to drop this hammer on your head if you say one more word before we escape. Teya, can you tie that rope to this bar and get Parch to pull?"

"Yes, yes!" she said.

She pulled some slack from the rope between her wrist and Parch and tied it to the bar. There was some playful tippy-tapping, then the rope went taut. The incredibly strong little creature hauled at the sturdy bars. The stone Fel had been working at crackled and flaked, then finally shattered. The bars tipped forward and rattled down. The sound, after so much silence, was ear-splitting.

"Teya, quick, look that way. Is there a dragon coming?" Fel said.

The kobold looked up. She tilted her head. "Nothing anywhere," she said. "Let me help."

She was pulled aside by Oiler, who had set down her bow and arrows and was hauling itself, and thus Teya, toward the dislodged bars.

"You brought Oiler too?" Fel said.

"You told me! Watch Oiler!" she said.

He picked up the bars and tried to wrangle them back into the opening. Fel dragged himself out through the hole, which, at least briefly, persuaded Oiler to set the bars down and click and grind happily at the reunion.

Fel pulled a rope from his pack. Between keeping an eye on the church up the road, unraveling the rope, and fending off playful affection from Parch and Oiler, getting a line down to Tome to rescue him was far more difficult than it should have been.

Eventually, he tugged Tome and Wick up to the street.

"Duurth hasn't come out of the church yet. He probably thinks we're still down there," Fel said.

Oiler helpfully maneuvered the bars back into place and spat some adhesive onto the stone.

"Perhaps now is the time to formulate a plan?" Tome said.

"Yeah. I think it's probably time for that. Wick, do you remember those addresses?"

"I do."

"Good. Let's see if we can find the old family home. If we need to hide out, that's as good a place as any to do it."

#

Allie and Mariss reached the front door of Masker's Antiquities.

"Get out of here, you wretched bag of filth!" cawed Rudy the harpy from the rooftop.

"Rat monkey, rat pigeon, rat rat!" agreed Moody.

Mariss recoiled a bit as the four lesser harpies swooped down and looked up expectantly. "Oh dear," she said.

"They recognize the basket. Fel's got them trained, more or less. Or spoiled. Basically the same thing. You'll have to sacrifice a bun, I think."

"Gimme my boot back!" Toody croaked, almost sweetly as it gazed up at Mariss.

"Er… Do the honors. These things look like they could take a finger."

"Only if you're slow," Allie said, sneaking a hand under the cloth of the basket and snagging a bun. She tore it up and sprinkled it in the street.

"I'll have your guts!" Judy cawed gratefully.

The lesser harpies snatched up every last crumb of the bun and retreated to the rooftops once more. Allie looked through the windows of the antique shop. It was indeed entirely empty.

"I don't like this," she said.

"Is it really so odd for a shop to briefly close up? Perhaps they're on lunch."

"Vivian and Martin are 'lunch on their feet' sort of folks."

A series of deep, rattling, nonverbal caws started to rumble from the rooftops. Allie looked to the lesser harpies. They'd gathered, two and two, on the gutters on either side of an alleyway. Each glared down at something hidden within.

"R-a-a-a-a-at," uttered one of the beasts.

"I imagine they're trying to extort another meal?" Mariss said.

"They're not exactly turning on the charm, are they?" Allie said.

Davie gave his little leather thumper a flip and trotted toward the alley.

"Be careful, Davie," Allie said.

"Rat, rat, rat, rat," chanted the harpies.

Davie hadn't yet made it halfway to the alley when a frightening sight stumbled out. It was Temple. He was caked with dried blood and striped with gashes and slashes. He limped into the open, loaded crossbow in each hand. Davie took a half step back as their eyes met.

"You…" Temple uttered.

"Back again, are you?" Davie said.

Temple leveled the weapon in his right hand at the lightly armed little gnome. "It's bad business to kill without a contract. But I'm ready to start making exceptions."

"By the high!" Mariss squealed.

Allie shoved the baker into the narrow alley between two buildings and dove in after her. The twang of a crossbow and the clatter of stone suggested the mercenary's first shot missed its mark. The harpies erupted into squawks, shrieks, and the more colorful phrases in their limited vocabularies. Allie leaned forward and peered out to take stock of the situation. She spotted Davie wisely taking cover rather than facing the well-armed man head-on.

Temple staggered after him and fired another shot. Allie couldn't tell if it hit its mark, because the commotion had begun to stir up the people of Beffshire in the usual way. A small, thrill-seeking slice of the locals began to assemble at what they perceived to be a safe distance. The rest fled and sounded alarms. Temple turned back to the shop, and began redrawing the crossbows.

"Hey!" Allie shouted.

He glanced in her direction, clicking a string in place and slotting in a fresh bolt.

"Just what do you think you'll manage?" she shouted. "You know what you're in for if you try breaking into that shop! And you'll never get away with whatever you're trying to do."

He kept his eyes locked on hers, continuing to reload his weapons. She realized there was no sense trying logic on this man. There was no wisdom behind those eyes. Something in the pursuit, in the endless failures that were painted across his skin, had pushed him past the point of reason. He was at the ragged edge and wouldn't let the day end without spilling blood. The cold arithmetic in his expression suggested the only reason he didn't send a bolt in her direction was the likelihood that he'd need both to punch his way through the Maskers' defenses.

Temple turned his attention back to the doorway. He holstered one bow and pulled something from his belt. He flicked the top of it with his thumb, and it started to sizzle. "I know you're in there. I know you can hear me. On the count of ten, this is going on the roof of your shop. I'll burn this place to the ground. The only question is if you and yours are inside when it happens. Ten… Nine… Eight…"

The harpies flapped their wings and took to the sky. He raised the crossbow and fired. He failed to kill any of them, but a few shredded feathers fluttered to the ground, making it abundantly clear survival was down to successful dodging rather than poor aim.

"Seven… Six… Five…"

The door to the shop opened. Vivian emerged. Temple grinned.

"The old woman," he said. "The one person I haven't specifically been instructed *not* to kill. I wouldn't try anything clever or—"

Vivian didn't heed his warning. She raised an odd-shaped box. He drew his remaining crossbow. He had to aim. She didn't bother. Before he could pull the trigger, she activated the box. A wire net fired from the end. Temple tried to dive aside, but he'd barely begun the dodge when the net entangled him. He dropped to the ground. His crossbow fired uselessly into the cobbles beside him. The firebomb dropped and clattered along the street, slowly beginning to flare and splash with flame. Vivian slipped into the storefront and returned with a tin pail, which she overturned on the firebomb and placed a dislodged cobble atop.

The City Watch, perpetually a few steps behind usefulness, arrived in time to shoo away the lesser harpies, which were on the verge of taking an eye from Temple in exchange for the feathers. Vivian dusted off her hands and spotted Allie.

"Ah, Allie. Lovely to see you outside the smoky ruckus of your tavern," Vivian said.

"That was… really something, Vivian," Allie said, shaking her hand in greeting.

"We had a moment to prepare." She looked to Mariss. "And you are?"

"Mariss. I work at Divinity's Oven."

"Oh! Yes, yes. You'll be the one from whom Fel has been buying all those delightful buns. Lovely to meet you as well."

She shook Mariss's hand, then turned to return to the shop.

"You'll want to come inside. That fire contraption shouldn't explode, but it'll pop and hiss, and you wouldn't want to catch any licks of flame that escape the pail."

Mariss and Allie slipped inside while the less courageous of lookie-loos started to gather now that the violence seemed to be through.

"I don't suppose you young ladies are interested in any antiques or contraptions," Vivian said over her shoulder, the rosiness of her greeting already sliding toward her more measured customer-service tone.

"Oh, er," Mariss said, remembering she was technically the reason for the visit. "I just came to drop off these buns. Your son seems to like them, and since he hasn't been around, it just seemed neighborly. He's been such a good customer. I didn't expect, er, whatever just happened. I hope they haven't been too stirred up."

"The boy knows how he likes to spend his money. Much obliged for the gift. Epiphany's just home, and we've got some company downstairs. These will be well appreciated. And Allie? Have you just come to say hello? Or has it gotten so bad a young lady like Mariss needs an escort?"

"I'd say you've answered your own question," Allie said, glancing out to watch Temple as he was hauled away. Davie had reappeared and was not-so-subtly trailing the Watch. Evidently he had some business to settle with the mercenary. "But I dropped by because Mariss said she'd come by earlier to drop these buns off and you were closed. I can't think of more than a dozen times this place was closed while the sun was up without at least Martin loitering in the shop in case someone comes along."

Vivian clucked her tongue. "I hate to do it, but desperate times call for such things."

Allie leaned on the counter a bit conspiratorially. "So what's this all about, huh? I heard Martin had another run-in. Handled it himself this time. And now this?"

"I'm just happy we've managed to keep from killing anyone. Not always easy when the other party isn't as dedicated to the same end."

"… I'm sorry, what is this you're talking about?" Mariss said.

"The Bolivan family from up north has their eyes on some of our goods and, evidently, our family members. There have been attempts to kidnap both Martin and Epiphany, not counting this one. I suspect things will get worse before they get better, but we're taking necessary precautions."

"And what's Fel up to?" Allie said.

"A deeper expedition than he's accustomed to. I don't imagine he'll be back from the Greater Lands Wall for another week at least."

"So he *has* gone to the wall," Mariss said. "And there are… I'd heard there was some violence, but I didn't know it was Martin, and I didn't imagine I'd *witness* any of it."

"The Masker family gets up to some mischief, Mariss," Allie said. "That's the sort of thing you'll just have to get accustomed to if you're going to get tangled up with them."

"I'd… I'd rather thought Fel was exaggerating. He'd started telling these stories about dragon attacks and fights with assassins. There was the ring of truth to them, of course. I'd heard about the hippogriffs in town. But it's all true?"

"If Fel is telling it, more like eight words out of every ten are true," Allie said.

"He does have a gift for embellishment," Vivian said. "But one wouldn't have to add much seasoning to the telling to get something a bit too spicy for the average palate."

"Do you need anything? Am I going to have to hand out some more drinks to get some of the regulars down here to provide protection?" Allie asked.

"No, no. Dear. Thank you, but we have the situation in hand at the moment, I think. I appreciate the visit, but I've lost a whole hour to seeing to the guest downstairs. I'm sure Epiphany will be along to fill you in before too much longer."

"Looking forward to it," Allie said.

"It was lovely meeting you, Mrs. Masker," Mariss said.

"And you as well. Say hello to your father. It's a rare man who can make a bakery flourish like he has. Speaks well of the whole family."

"I'll send your regards."

Mariss and Allie stepped out the door, brushing by a distinguished gentleman with an old clock under one arm, clearly hoping for either a repair or an appraisal and not the least bit concerned about the borderline gang warfare that had been the undercurrent of the antique business for the last few weeks.

"Glad things are calming down, if just a bit," Allie said.

"That was things calming *down*? Such violence, such danger," Mariss said, eyes a bit distant as they marched along the street.

"Yeah. Fel? What can I say? Him and his family? They're not for the faint of heart. Again, I serve drinks to some rough customers. But they're amateurs. They do that stuff for a break from their lives. That's just life for him."

"It's terrible," Mariss said.

Allie smirked.

"And it's exciting," Mariss added. "It's… it's terribly exciting."

Allie's smirk faded. "You know you don't just dip in and dip out for this sort of thing. Trust me. I'm a casual accomplice, and it's led me to some places I wish it hadn't."

"Oh, I know, I know. But it's like this whole other world, and it's right next door." She clutched her hands. "What do you think Fel is doing right now?"

"He's either on his way toward or on his way away from something dangerous that should have been left alone, I imagine."

#

"Assuming the streets are progressing alphabetically, the Masker Estate will be to your left," Wick said.

Fel continued along. "Tome? How does it look?"

"I see movement inside the church. I think he's figured out we're gone," he said. "Also, I am relieved to say my vision seems to be sliding back to normal."

Fel quickened his pace. This section of Clickspring was unbearably familiar. It had the same feel of the neighborhood he spent a few mornings a week trekking through, collecting or delivering silver. Small, largely ornamental homes on suspiciously large plots of land for a city. Every last one of them would have a mansion's worth of floors hidden below the surface. Just ahead, an estate stood proudly with the same emblem on the column beside its gate as the gravestone had.

"We're here. Everyone stay back," Fel said.

"I don't think we should waste time outside, Fel. Duurth's got his head out the broken window now. I think he's sniffing for us."

"Tome, we're about to enter the personal estate of what was presumably one of the key contraptioneers of a contraption-obsessed city. What do you think that means for the main entrance?"

"Traps," Tome said sullenly.

"My thoughts exactly. Now stay back."

Fel crept forward, eyes sweeping the ground for signs of something that might serve as a trigger.

"But this place was evacuated. Do you really believe that they would set the traps before they left?" he said.

"I sure hope so."

"Why?"

Fel gingerly stepped on a stepping stone. It produced the faintest of clicks. Fel rolled backward. If he'd been any less cautious, he would have been skewered by the pair of spiked plates that sprang up and clapped together where he'd been standing. They started to retract, but he jabbed a pry bar into the mechanism, jamming it in the clamped position.

He huffed a breath and grinned. "Because if they set the traps on the way out, there's still something inside worth protecting."

Fel peeked into the exposed workings beneath the trap's hatch. A few thin chains ran in a shallow stone trough. He gave them a pull. Three more traps activated, sending a patter of darts, producing a startling flash of light, and opening a pitfall. He pulled a stone from the decorative path and wedged it in the chains to keep them taut and the traps in their activated position.

"All right. Everyone inside," Fel said. "Two steps behind me."

He sidestepped the traps and made his way to the front door. In what was likely a bit of hubris on behalf of his ancestors, the lock and brace on the door were rather lackluster. They must have trusted the traps would be enough to keep the place safe. A firm shove with his shoulder gained entrance to the house. The others filed in, and he shut the door.

Unlike the other places they'd swept through, the house looked like the residents had left just minutes ago. The foyer was a bit less ostentatious than the outside. Tastefully decorated. Pleasant. Parch immediately knocked down a table and sent the silverware atop it clattering to the ground.

"Hey! Be careful!" Fel said. "This place belonged to my family."

He crouched and pulled open the shutter beside the small window. The church was, unfortunately, not visible from the estate. But it didn't need to be. A shadow swept across the rooftops. Not in the correct direction, but the dragon was searching.

"Let's move farther down," Fel said. "He's on the move."

"Are you sure there's no more traps?" Tome asked.

"Nope. Let's go," Fel said.

"You have this horrible way of being casually uncertain in a very certain way, Fel," Tome said.

"This place. Nice place?" Teya asked, trotting along behind him with Parch's harness grasped firmly in her paw.

Tome stuck close to her and shuffled inside. Fel crept back outside and tugged the stone from the trap's workings.

"What are you doing?" Tome asked as he deftly avoided the triggers on his way back.

"If we've got traps we know about, we may as well leave them active."

Fel paced deeper into the house. Tome followed close behind him as they moved down to a somewhat more inviting, sprawling parlor of sorts.

"Nice place?" Teya repeated, awaiting an answer.

"It had three lethal traps before we reached the front door. It's not what I would call nice," Tome said.

"But look nice? Pretty?"

"I suppose that's a matter of taste. I do rather like the classic design. What do you think?"

"Can't see."

"What do you mean you can't see?"

Teya pointed and described things. "Floor? Yes. Can see. Parch, very see. You? Fel? See, but not very. All else? All around? Very *not* see." She swished her paw around. "Like… pull thread on cloth. Swirly. Make mind fuzzy. Want to go."

"How did you get here, then?"

She squinted at him. "No listen? Parch, very see. Follow Parch."

Tome shook his head. "So you're floating in a sea of half-seen confusion, and you came here knowing full well there would be a dragon? You came to a place protected by a dragon knowing you wouldn't be able to see where you were going?"

"Had to. Job. Also? Excitement!" She clapped Tome on the back. "Good fun!"

"Have a seat," Fel said. "I'm going to search the rest of the floor. And since you're so keen on planning, and so far *not* planning hasn't worked out, get started on that."

Tome looked to a dusty but otherwise sturdy set of plush leather chairs. He flopped down. Teya felt around until she found one she could be certain was actually there and scrambled up onto it. Parch hopped up and stood on the back of her chair, bleating curiously. Oiler jutted the puzzle box forward. She happily scrambled it.

Fel paced around the edge of the room. Paintings depicted people who had just enough of a resemblance to his father to convince him there might indeed be a family link. He pulled a book from a shelf and flipped it open.

"Give me Wick, would you? I need a translator. And why don't I hear you planning?" Fel took the lantern.

"Planning. Right. Right. We should start with an assessment of our assets. We have my spells. We have your tools. Your weapon. Teya, you have the bow and arrow. Can you shoot?"

"Shoot, yes! So much shoot! Aim? No," Teya said cheerfully.

"Lovely. What else have we got? Oiler? Useful if we need to fix something I suppose."

"Or disarm something," Fel said. "Us and them. Oiler doesn't like weapons in use."

"We have something more useful, though. We have time now. We have shelter. And we have knowledge. Two key pieces of knowledge. First, magic is *profoundly* more potent, when properly written. Second, Duurth is the exact creature we faced outside the wall."

"And what good does that do us?"

"We know that magic works on him. Remember? We attracted him when I was trying to distract the hippogriffs." He stood. "I need paper. There must be paper here. I'll write a few extra spells. Our focus is twofold. First, we need a source of prolonged distraction. Something that can keep the dragon away long enough for us to find the key. Then we need a way to find the key. Ideally the distraction will last long enough for us to escape, too. If not, we'll need a second source of distraction."

"Is this what planning is?" Fel asked. "Just listing off things we need."

"It's the most important part."

Fel flipped through one of the books. "This one's blank. Here."

"Why is there a blank book on a bookshelf?"

"The whole top row is journals."

"Exciting!" Teya said. "You learn? Learn about family?"

"Am I going to learn about my family, Wick?" Fel asked, holding the first book open.

"Unlikely. These appear to be technical journals."

Fel's eyes widened. "Even better."

#

The next two hours were uneventful, but quite illuminating. Tome completed three spells. The pros and cons of at least a dozen plans had been discussed. They'd found a rather potent collection of spirits that Wick had identified as Facture's Private Reserve. Most importantly, Wick, with Fel turning the pages, had dictated three of the journals.

"'Project Day 254,'" Wick read. "'The findings of Tinker and Mason seem correct. We have known for ages that the attentions of the contraptors can be turned to our tasks if and only if their interest and obsession can be turned to our cause. But how can one assess the interest of beings with whom we cannot interact? With whom we cannot converse? Tinker's masterpiece showed us that contraptions can be made to think. But the mistake lies within the word "made." They are not made to think. They are permitted to think. We are on the cusp of something. *I* am on the cusp of something. Diplomacy.'"

"Fel," Tome cut in, "you know that I lack the common skepticism about contraptions and their safety that is so pervasive within society today. But at the risk of upsetting you, the way your ancestor talks about them is making me rather concerned at his trajectory of discovery. It has the tone of a man less concerned about consequence than innovation."

"I'm just disappointed this is mostly him talking about what he's trying to do and not how he did it. I need to *learn*."

"I don't think you need to learn this, Fel."

"He said 'diplomacy.' What's wrong with that?"

"It's the overriding tone of obsession. Not to mention that at some point shortly after those words were written the entire city was evacuated. Context, Fel."

"Listen. Sometimes you start by building plowshares and end up building swords. Sometimes you learn from the sword maker how to make a better plowshare." Fel snapped the book shut. "We need to skip to the ending."

He pulled down the next few journals and flipped through the pages. In the second-to-last journal, on one of the last few pages, he found what looked like one of the reference diagrams his father used for assembly. "Here. Read this one," Fel said.

Wick recited the contents of the page. "'Project Day 832. It has been a long road, but a worthwhile one. The minister for Clickspring is pleased enough with my achievements thus far that he has decreed this shall be my legacy. No longer am I Felix Facture. Now I am Felix Masker.'"

"The day a family earned its name," Tome said.

Fel tapped the next page, where the second-stage diagram had been assembled into its final form. "It's an actual mask. A literal mask," he said. "My family is named after making some sort of contraption masks?"

Teya spat on the ground.

"You got something to say, Teya?" Fel said.

"Masks. *Bad.* You? Maybe not bad. But masks? *Bad bad.*"

"What do they do?"

She shrugged. "Don't know. Just been told. Bad, bad, bad. Masks, bad. Maskers, *bad.* But you? Maybe not bad."

"Keep going, Wick," Fel said.

"'The Ambassador has been of great value for the past few months. Far more valuable has been the Teacher.' It is worth pointing out that both Ambassador and Teacher are proper nouns, presented as names rather than occupations. It continues. 'The clashes have been becoming more intense, however. The completion of the Tactician'—another proper noun—'has helped to balance the battle. But a balanced battle merely assures continued losses for both sides. At the direction of the Tactician, and with my own reluctance, I have completed work on what shall be called the Soldier. I have requested that nullification tools be made available in all maintenance rooms. I have endeavored to attract contraptors with the appropriate disposition, but I fear that is precisely the problem. Tinker's maquette has been secured in a disabled state in the fourth-level workshop. There it shall remain until I am certain it will not be needed.'"

Fel turned the page. The final assembly diagram was there, along with three other completed diagrams with notations, probably indicating differences in the operation or maintenance. He flipped back to the previous page.

"Maquette. What's a maquette?" Fel said.

"A sculptor's model," Tome said.

"Something tells me that's not what it means this time." Fel glanced aside. "How much more time do you need?"

"Just a few more minutes, and then we can begin the plan." Tome flinched as the swoop of massive wings rushed by a bit too closely overhead for comfort. "And not a moment too soon. Duurth seems to be getting closer."

"We happy with the plan as is?"

"As happy as we're likely to get. I wish we had more time, and more ink. As it is, we'll be fairly limited in our options if things don't go well."

"Good enough. I'll be back."

Fel headed for the downward stairs. Teya hopped off the couch to follow.

The next floor was something like the bedroom level of the shop back in Beffshire, albeit at a far greater scale. Five bedrooms were present, each nearly the size of the whole floor back home. Beneath that were the servants' quarters and kitchen. And beneath that, precisely where he expected it to be, was the workshop.

Everywhere else in the house, there was comfort and order. Here, utter chaos. Or rather, the physical extension of the inside of an inventor's head. If not for the events of the last few months, Fel would have considered the contents of this room to be the greatest find of his lifetime: a comprehensive set of contraptioneer's equipment, no fewer than a dozen freshly completed contraptions, and another two dozen contraptions that Felix had likely purchased and relied upon rather than constructed. A row of seven leather-bound volumes stood on a shelf on the north wall. They were smeared with grease and heavily dog-eared.

"What do they say, Wick?"

"*Contraptioneer's Fundamentals Volumes 1 through 5. Advanced Contraptioneering Concepts Volume 1 and 2*," Wick said.

"Haha-ha! Thank you, Felix!" He dropped his gear pack and pulled out a sack. "Your descendants will make good use of your reference library." He loaded up the books.

"You like books?" Teya said.

"Not as much as my dad does."

"Family is nice."

Fel looked over the assorted equipment, trying to decide if it was worth taking any of it with him. "Do you have any family, Teya?"

"Serve Kazel? Family."

"But I mean literally. You have parents? Brothers, sisters?"

"No parents. Died. Three brothers, three sisters. Don't know. Maybe dead?"

Fel turned. "You don't know?"

"Probably dead. Didn't find Kazel."

"You don't sound upset."

She shrugged. "Tears dry now. Kobold, no dragon? Don't last. Lose family. Find new family."

Fel rubbed the back of his neck. "I need to hug my mom and dad when I get home."

He came to the workbench on the far side of the shop. Whatever Felix had been working on was waiting beneath a dusty cloth. He pulled it down. "… I think maybe you and Tome might be right about what Felix was up to being a little unnerving."

The cloth had concealed what appeared to be the head, shoulders, and chest of a statue. Everything below the neck was mundane wood and brass. The head was faceless. The missing face revealed the impossibly intricate internal workings of an incomplete contraption. The wheels and gears were stationary.

Fel rubbed a brass plate on the chest. "What's it say, Wick?"

"Tinker Maquette, Mk 2."

"I knew it wasn't a sculpture."

On the table beside the figure was a familiar tool. Fel picked it up.

"Another blunt dagger," he said. "We risked our lives to get it and it wasn't unique?"

He shook his head and tucked the dagger into his bag of equipment. Once it was stowed, he tipped the head back. It was attached to the body with a very simple mount, and the maker's mark on the chin revealed that the device was created by the same people who'd made Oiler. The Tinkers, evidently.

Fel scratched his head and mused for a moment. "If it was the last thing my ancestor worked on, it's probably worth taking with me, if only for Dad to study." He unfastened the mount and wrapped the head in the cloth to protect the gears.

"Fel," Wick said.

"Yes?"

"I recognize it is my purpose to provide services to you when asked, but I think it might be relevant at this time to offer one unbidden."

"Do you have something to say?"

"We are presently in a place left precisely as it was after some sort of unnamed calamity required the city to be evacuated. We've read a substantial portion of a set of journals that suggest your ancestor was working on something that even he found concerning. And you now hold in your hands an incomplete item from his workshop. If you are considering taking it with you, I might suggest you reconsider."

He hefted it. "Wick, you're not wrong. This is probably a bad idea. But in a few minutes, I am going to work together with a kobold who can't quite tell if the world around her is real, a unicorn with more strength than sense, a contraption who only ever wants to disarm people and fix things that I broke on purpose, and a paper mage who managed to render himself nearly helpless by having eyesight that was too good. Taking this head with me is not the most foolish decision I'm going to be making today."

"I see that you have given it thought. I shall respect your decision."

"Nah. You don't need to respect it. Just don't say 'I told you so' when it all blows up in my face."

"We are both aware I've advised you. There is no purpose in repeating it."

"Great! Then let's go try to rob a dragon."

Chapter 12

Epiphany, Thaddeus, and Martin sat around the dining room table. It was telling that Thaddeus had once again tapped out his pipe such that the discussion could proceed unobserved. The conversation had been heated, but such heat could only simmer so high for so long with Martin and Epiphany in attendance. Between Martin's predilection for logic and Epiphany's tendency to bargain and compromise, things had worked their way into a more comfortable, more reasonable tone.

"The issue at hand here isn't that you've been spied on, it is that *we've* been spied on," Thaddeus said.

"How precisely are you defining 'we,' Thad?" Martin asked. "Does it include just the Graves family, or the Graves and the Maskers."

"Er… Well, I'd meant just the Graves family. I recognize the subterfuge hasn't been ideal or appropriate, but we'd at least believed that it was fully under our control. There is a difference between a subversive act that's behaving as intended and one that's escaping control."

Epiphany crossed her arms. "Forgive me if I have difficulty finding sympathy for you."

"The Voice has been crucial to how the Graves family conducts business for ages. We aren't like you. Beffshire is a wonderland of constant fresh trade. If it wasn't for the bazaar, we might never have been able to keep ourselves afloat. The Graves family exists as an exceedingly diffuse network of trusted traders, linked by the rapid and secure communication of the sentry flame. Without it we will *crumble*. We will lose any edge we might have over the other traders in the region. It was a measured risk even losing the flame for the amount of time it spent here observing you."

"Again, don't expect my heart to weep for the hardships endured through your espionage," she said. "It is a problem. You caused it. And now *we* have to solve it."

"And in this case, I believe the proper definition of 'we' includes both families. The leak affects us both," Martin said. "*We* need to know how it happened. *We* need to know why it happened. *We* need to know what they know. And *we* need to know how to fix it.”

“This isn’t a decision I can make on my own. They don’t even like me to set prices on my own.”

“Then we send a message. One that doesn’t require a response, because there is only one reasonable way to respond,” Epiphany said.

Martin fetched the base plate he’d taken the trouble to remove from his stove again and dropped it on an old metal platter. He set Wick’s lantern beside it. Without another word, he lit the spy lantern. The flame flickered and fluttered briefly, then snapped to stillness.

“You’ve been found out,” Martin said. “After what happened to the Bolivans’ attempt to capture me and secure Oiler, that should be clear. Speak.”

“Those to whom I am permitted to speak are limited,” said the voice from the flame.

Martin shut his eyes. Epiphany tipped her head. The voice was not Wick’s, and yet it was. This flame spoke in a tone devoid of the interest and personality that seemed to flavor every syllable that Wick spoke. But the voice itself felt similar, to an uncanny degree. It was like hearing the voice of a previously unknown twin. On the surface they were the same, but two words were all it took for those who knew one to know it was not the other.

“And who permitted you to speak to the Bolivans?” Thaddeus said sharply.

“That is not a matter I am permitted to discuss,” said the Graves flame.

“Winslow, Carpenter, and Tender are dead. Bolivan attackers. Their blood is on your hands… so to speak.”

“That is not a matter I am permitted to discuss.”

“Let this be the matter you discuss, then,” Martin said. “This is the last message you will hear within the Masker household. Your scheme is revealed, and through it the Bolivan agents presently in Beffshire have been neutralized. If the Graves family is to survive, it will do so *only* if it sets aside any rivalry with the Maskers and combines resources to clean up this mess and solve our mutual problems.”

“I propose we have a meeting of the families. We will set up that meeting through means *outside* the flame,” Epiphany said.

“And if you wish to extend the hand of friendship, I can think of one representative above all others who would be an ideal ambassador between the Graves and Masker families. I want to speak to Euphoria. In person,” Martin said.

“I must concur,” Thaddeus said.

“The message shall be delivered,” the flame said.

“Then goodbye.”

Martin snuffed the flame. When it was certain that the wick was cold and they were no longer being overheard, Martin looked to Thaddeus. “How long will it take for them to receive the message?”

"They most certainly have already heard."

"Truly? Wick takes at least a few minutes to reach much beyond the borders of the city."

"We have seldom experienced more than a second or two of delay," Thaddeus said.

"Intriguing…" Martin said. "Having only dealt with Wick, I'd never considered there might be variance among sentry flames."

"What happens next?" Epiphany said. "Besides the obvious."

"For the sake of clarity, what precisely is 'the obvious'?" Thaddeus asked.

"If there are any lingering Bolivans in the area, they attack us," Martin said simply.

"All their targets are, as far as they know, in this very shop. The dagger, Oiler, Martin, myself. And if they want you dead, you as well. Obvious," Epiphany said.

"Y-yes… I suppose that is to be expected," Thaddeus said.

"But what happens beyond that?" Epiphany asked. "What do you intend to do? And how shall the Graves respond?"

"I shall remain in Beffshire and send some messages through some of our contractors. Those outside the circle of the family who know of and utilize the flame. In a week or so, I would expect a wagon to arrive and some trustworthy guards. Then I'll head north to regroup. I wouldn't expect any action and contact from us regarding this meeting for a month or more. The leak in our communications is going to have a ripple effect. We'll have to lock down and make some serious decisions. When the time comes, I imagine it'll be via a direct courier."

"So be it," Martin said.

"How safe are we in Beffshire? If there *is* an attack, I mean," asked Thaddeus.

"There are two places I would say are perfectly safe. Or at least as safe as we can make them. The first is this shop," Martin said.

"And the second?"

"The Fox and Log," Epiphany said.

"… The tavern?"

"The head barmaid is a good friend of the family. She's better informed than the Watch, and effectively wields a private army of thirsty patrons," she said.

"I see… Of the two places I could ride out a potential siege, I would be lying if I said the one that could keep my glass filled with brandy didn't appeal to me," Thaddeus said.

Martin stood. "I agree. Given recent events, a stiff drink is called for. I'll meet you there shortly."

#

Fel and the others stood in the shade of an alley. Tome and Teya each had small lanterns scavenged from houses. Fel had Wick's lantern. The three flames took turns remaining still. Duurth had been sweeping overhead in increasingly frequent searches. Had they lingered much longer, the upper levels of the Masker family estate probably would have been rubble. Duurth's animal intellect may not have been broad, but it was deep in this one area. He was a hunter. The moment they'd left the estate, he seemed to have known. He'd not spotted them, but they were at the center of his new circle of flight no matter where they went. Fel was increasingly convinced the beast knew precisely where they were, and was simply waiting for some sort of trigger to strike.

Regardless of why the monster hadn't struck, he had held his flame long enough for them to reach the poorer section of town where the buildings were closer and the cobblestone courtyards had turned to narrow, dim alleys. They'd selected one with a bit of an overhang, completely shielding them from view from above. The church containing Duurth's hoard was directly up the street, a lengthy but manageable sprint from their hiding place.

The dragon swept across the sky in the distance. His eyes were turned in their direction, but were searching. Teya gazed up with enchanted adoration. She chattered something in her native tongue. Before Fel could ask, she uttered it again in his.

"Dragon..." she said reverently.

"You can see him? You can see that far?" Fel said.

"Him, yes. Very see." She swept her paw. "Not around. Just him." She clutched her paws in front of her and grinned. "Dragon..." she repeated.

Fel gave her a suspicious look. "Is this going to be a problem? You're not going to switch sides, are you?"

She snapped out of it and crossed her arms haughtily, head turned aside. "Dragon, good. Not my dragon. Kazel better." She held out her hand. Oiler reeled out an arm and placed her bow in her hand. "Start plan."

Tome stepped forward with a spell and a piece of thread. He tied the spell firmly to the arrow. "This is a lure. When I tear the end, just fire the arrow somewhere far away. Into the water, if you can reach," he instructed.

She nodded. "Can see water. Can *only* see water."

"Are you sure this is going to work?" Fel asked. "Doesn't the spell burn or something to work? Won't it go out if you shoot it into the water?"

"This is the only part I'm *absolutely* sure will work. It's the only part I've tested. That dragon is highly susceptible to this spell. And it's been written with better paper, better ink, and with a better familiarity of the area. He will not rest until he's destroyed the lure, or it's consumed itself. I've taken care to ensure it consumes itself slowly, but once the mystic flame begins, nothing can extinguish the page until it is fully consumed. That means about fifteen minutes if he can't get to it. And I've got three copies, including that one."

"So she fires that one off somewhere. I run to the church, you run somewhere to stash a lure he *definitely* won't be able to get to, and that gets me up to a half hour to search for the key and grab whatever else I can carry, with the last lure to give us a chance to escape."

"No. To get back to cover and start scrounging for supplies to make more lures. We'll need a *lot* more of them if we're going to keep the dragon occupied for the half day it'll take to get back to where the undines can speed us up."

"Good enough for me." He pulled the straps of his pack tighter and planted his feet, eyes on the church doorway. "Ready."

Tome nodded. He tore the paper.

"Fire."

"Ah-ha-*ha*!" Teya squealed.

She jumped out into the open and raised her crooked bow. The page flared into a radiant blue flame. She pulled the bowstring back. Her short arms didn't make for much of a draw, but the bow creaked rigidly. It must have been a *very* stiff bow.

Teya let the arrow fly. Fel didn't wait to see where it landed. He dashed for the church. Tome rushed toward the town square. The air shook with an ear-splitting roar, and Duurth tucked his wings and dove toward the arrow.

The kobold's aim wasn't what it could have been. Fortunately, the sea was a very big target, and the bow's range was just enough to hit it. Unfortunately, to reach the sea, it had to take a high, ponderous arc. And Duurth was a very good hunter. He drew in a breath and heaved a brilliant tongue of flame that enveloped the arrow while it was still rising. A few seconds later the blackened, smoldering arrow sizzled into the shallow water at the edge of town. The spell that had been tied to it was a streak of ash fluttering through the air behind.

Fel ran for all he was worth. Parch followed, but tugging Teya along slowed him down. Tome dashed for city center, eyes set on a well. Three targets. One dragon.

"He's coming for you, Fel," Wick said. "Tome spotted him. Also, Teya is watching in delight and murmuring 'dragon' under her breath."

"I'm so glad she came along," Fel huffed, pouring a bit more effort into clearing the half mile or so ahead. "How close is Tome to the well?"

"Not close enough, I'm afraid."

Fel heard the flap of wings. He could hear the huff and smell the rot of Duurth's breath. Still so far to go before he reached the church. And the church didn't equal safety. The nearby houses were, by Clickspring standards, rather modest. They wouldn't have deep enough basements to keep him safe. And the dragon was gaining on him.

"Wick, I'm going to trust you to tell me when to jump," he said, eying up the progressively wider alleys between the gradually wealthier homes. "Too soon and he'll just get me where I land. Too late and he'll just get me."

"I shall happily fulfill this service."

He continued, legs burning. Fel was a lot of things. A runner, he was not. He could hear the crackling inhale behind him. He could feel the wind from the dragon's wings.

"Now, Fel," Wick said calmly.

Fel dove aside, bashing through the front door of the second-to-last house before the church. Fire crackled across the street. He dragged himself inside.

"Tome has dropped the active spell into the town well."

The effect was immediate. The flapping of wings became suddenly intense as Duurth attempted to reverse direction in an instant. Fel looked down. His boots were singed, and the cuffs of his pants were smoldering.

"Maybe a little bit sooner next time, Wick."

"Thank you! I shall do so."

Fel leaned out the door. Duurth touched down in city center and smashed the top of the well. He belched flames into it, but the distance and water were enough to protect the spell.

"Fifteen minutes, according to Tome."

Fel hurried back to the street. The blackened stones sizzled against his boots as he hurried up the steps and circled around to the still-open door from their first infiltration. The sun was lower in the sky, casting much less light on the hoard. But that was just as well. The one piece of the plan Fel had devised practically depended on it.

He hurried among the sconces and used Wick to light them one by one. As the darkness was chased away, Wick's view of the place grew more complete. So did Fel's. Without the looming danger of awakening a dragon, Fel was able to more fully appreciate the sheer size and scope of the hoard. Compared to the mound of gold that Kazel slept upon, it was rather meager, but if Fel had gathered together every contraption that had ever passed through the shop back home, it wouldn't amount to half of the heap. And somewhere in that pile, there was a key.

"I don't suppose you see anything, Wick."

"It is a great deal to take in, Fel."

"Tell me about it." He waded into the pile and started sifting.

"Dragons. Fly so fast. So strong!" shouted Teya from behind.

"Teya! Are you going to be able to help me search?" Fel shouted over his shoulder.

She squinted at the mound. "Not so much. Can't very see."

"Can you climb up and light the chandeliers?"

She looked up. "Where?"

He growled. "Just keep an eye out for Duurth and shout if he's coming this way."

"I do this!" she crowed.

Fel rummaged through the pile. With great effort, he was able to prevent his mind from running the tally of just how much could be earned by selling it all. He needed all his wits for locating the item that would earn Kazel, and more importantly *him*, his freedom.

"Teya!" he called.

"No dragon yet!" she called back.

"Not that. Drop Oiler. Let him come over here."

The thump of chains on the ground was followed swiftly by the jangling shuffle of the contraption hauling itself over to Fel.

"Oiler!" he said without looking. "Do you want another thing like the puzzle box? Another game? Somewhere in this pile is a key. About this big by this big. Find it."

The contraption stared up at him, then looked to the pile. It lowered its claws, pulled an ornate and complex jewelry box from the pile and pleasantly went about repairing it.

"No! I… never mind."

"Dragon still dig!" Teya said. "No fly!"

"Thank you, Teya!" he shouted impatiently. "Wick? Anything?"

"I have not yet identified the key as described."

He pulled at music makers, at devices for creating light of dazzling colors and patterns. He tossed aside things he'd seen in his father's books, things which could turn spoken words into written notes. Enormous things used for fashioning smaller devices. A veritable museum of contraptions. He was still digging through the pile when Tome breathlessly stumbled through the door.

"Did you find it?" he said.

"*Would I still be looking if I'd already found it?*" Fel snapped.

Tome climbed onto the pile and started looking. "We only have a few minutes left, Fel."

"You should get the second lure ready and find a place to dump it."

"Third lure. And that's for our escape. If we use that, we'll have to use the time it buys us to get to safety so we can regroup."

"We can't just keep making lures and searching. Eventually he'll catch us!" He threw aside a device with an engraved picture of a book on the side. "We either need to find it or find a way to take care of Duurth permanently. And I haven't found a single weapon in this pile."

"If you are looking for weapons, there is a cluster of them along the northwest side of the pile," Wick said.

Fel scrambled over. Indeed, a handful of enhanced crossbows, some oddly complex swords, and half a dozen different varieties of weapons he couldn't quite tease out the purpose of beyond "inflicting pain" had been mounded together at the very edge of the hoard.

"I don't know how useful any of these will be against a dragon. Probably some of them are potent, but we don't have time to figure out how to work them. And how did they all end up in the same place?"

Tome paused and stood up straight. "That is a very good question..."

"No!" Fel shouted. "No it wasn't! Don't stop and think, just look!"

It was too late, just like Oiler, Tome had gotten ahold of his favorite toy: a riddle. "Teya! What does a dragon do with its hoard all day?" Tome asked.

"So many things! Lay, lick, sift, count, sort—"

"Sort!" Fel and Tome said at the same time.

"We just need to figure out how Duurth was sorting. Now, they know value intuitively. Is it by value? Perhaps it was..."

Tome continued to spout possibilities. Fel gazed at the pile. Dragons were smart, but Duurth wasn't nearly as smart as the usual. As far as Fel was concerned, that meant it was far more likely that he'd come up with the right answer than someone with a more fertile mind like Tome's.

"Wait, wait!" Fel said. "He *sleeps* on it, right?" He pointed around the perimeter at individual sections of the pile. "Dangerous. Pointy. Delicate. Lots of corners. In the middle here all the stuff on top is round or soft. You ever play with building blocks as a kid? The flat, wide ones go on the bottom. That's where the key is. *Of course* it's where the key is. It's the worst possible place for it besides around the dragon's neck!"

He and Tome shoved their way through the top layer and quickly discovered a stratum of simple rectangular objects. Books, raw sheet stock of precious metals, and things of that nature.

"Duurth is flying!" Teya said, a bit more reverently than Fel would have liked.

"That was not fifteen minutes!" Fel said.

"It's an art, not a science!" Tome defended.

"Get out there and burn that last lure! We've nearly found it!"

Tome wiped sweat from his forehead and scurried off the pile. "Next time we fight a dragon, we're bringing at least one person who is used to *running*."

He dashed out the door. Knowing where the dragon was, and that it would be heading directly for the hoard, meant at the very least that he knew precisely where the dragon *wouldn't* be, so he could move without fear, provided he moved quickly enough.

Fel heaved and kicked his way down through the pile. As difficult as it was to excavate a dragon's hoard, the far greater effort went into trusting that someone else, somewhere else, could be relied upon to help him. If ever there was a time to put his need to work alone to bed, this was it.

The sensations he'd become all-too familiar with began to wash over him again. The sound of beating wings. The furious hiss of breath.

"Come on, come on, come on!" Fel growled, both at a pile unwilling to relinquish its prize and his unseen partner.

He heard Teya scurry out of the doorway. He felt the floor rumble as Duurth slammed down on the church floor after leaping through the window.

"So pretty…" Teya said dreamily.

Duurth whipped his head around. Teya and Parch scurried over the hoard and plopped down beside Fel, who had finally abandoned the search and brandished his club. The dragon stalked around them, eyes focused with raw predatory fury. Duurth raised a claw. His head snapped aside. He turned and leaped out the window.

Fel shakily slumped down onto the pile.

"Tome did good!" Teya said.

"Why didn't he roast me?" Fel said. "He had the chance."

"On hoard. Won't hurt hoard," Teya said.

"So I'm safe as long as I'm on the hoard?"

"No! Tail, claw, teeth? All very yes. Just not fire."

"Next time, tell me that."

"Next time?" she said excitedly. "We come back?"

He shut his eyes. "No. No. I just… never mind."

Tome hurried back in the door. "I dumped it down that light shaft leading into the catacombs. We have somewhat less than fifteen minutes," he said. "I suggest we use that time to get back to your family estate. Try to find some more ink. More paper. Try to get some more lures written."

"You want to go? Go! I'm not leaving until I find that key!"

"Fel," Wick said. "By your left foot."

Fel glanced down. He kicked aside a sheet of silver to reveal a rectangular contraption, two hands long, bearing the symbol over the main door of Kazel's lair. He picked it up.

"All right, then. Off we go." He paused and crouched down. "No. Wait."

Beneath the key was a thin, handwritten book, *Melodies of Clickspring*. He picked it up and pocketed it.

"I've got a friend who is interested in music."

#

They'd been moving as quickly as their stressed, exhausted bodies could handle. For Fel and Tome, that wasn't very fast. For Teya and Parch, it was quite brisk. Even with Oiler strapped to her back once more, she seemed utterly immune to fear and easily kept pace despite her stubbier legs putting her at a disadvantage.

"How long will it take you to write another couple of lures?" Fel asked.

"Having written three, I believe I've got the hang of it. I think perhaps I could write one in ten minutes now, provided I can find the materials."

"And how long could you make them work?"

"A very good question. The spell's potency is as strong as anything I've ever written. But I've never had to focus on slowing the consumption of the spell. I know this didn't quite push the duration to what I wanted. I can try something different. I have some ideas. I might be able to push it to a half an hour."

"And if the wind is with us, it'll take twelve hours to get far enough for the undines to help us."

"Twenty four pages of intricate spell. I will need a lot of ink and a lot of time."

"We've got a whole city to search and a whole city to hide in," Fel said. "So long as we get to someplace with at least two basements to keep us clear of his fire breath and to keep him from picking up our scent."

"Fel, there is a small problem," Wick said.

"What?"

"I can see through the window of the church, and the dragon has lost interest. He has raised his head."

Fel turned to him. "That wasn't even ten minutes."

"It's not a science," Tome said shakily.

The sound of a furious roar cut through them like a knife.

"Get in one of these houses. Start searching for ink and paper."

"But these are the smaller houses. They won't have enough protection," Tome said.

"They also won't have traps. And Duurth won't chase you." Fel held up his bulging sack of loot. "I'm the one with stuff from his hoard."

"But—"

"Hey, you said we should work like a team, right? This is how we do that. Don't argue, just go! Write something to keep him distracted!"

"Wait! The spells. Take what I've got!"

Tome pressed the stack of spells into his hands. Fel grabbed them and broke into a sprint.

"Where do I find you!" Tome called.

"I'm going home." He looked over his shoulder. "I have a plan!"

"Yaaaah-ha-ha!" Teya crowed, dashing after Fel.

It was astounding how much a dragon in pursuit could overcome the effects of soreness and fatigue. His brain kept tossing out dubiously useful instructions like "hide behind that garden wall" or "dive through that window." But as well built as these Bygone Era houses were, he knew Duurth wouldn't need more than a few moments to smash them to bits and roast them to cinders. He just needed time to get to the Masker Estate. As the dragon drew near, he cast a fleeting glance at the spells in his hand. He realized he had no way of knowing what each of them did, and with Wick in the other hand, he had only one way to activate them. And if he didn't know what any of them did, there was one way to be sure he'd activate a useful one.

"Get ready to learn some spells, Wick. And tell me when."

"I shall endeavor to time adequately this t—now, Fel."

Fel jammed the top of the spells through the broken hatch of the lantern. They fizzled to life. He threw them on the ground and dodged aside into a wide alley. Blue light fizzled and popped as all the spells activated at once. Duurth may not have been a terribly bright creature, but Fel very much doubted even Kazel would have known what to make of what came next. Three duplicates of Fel were produced in three different poses from his sprint. The dragon belched flame across the trio, but they remained. As Fel and Teya ran through back alleys, drawing closer to the Masker Estate, they could hear the sound of a dragon making a rather poor decision. Duurth touched down to more thoroughly deal with the strange illusions, and thus was subject to the other spells. Fel heard some crackling, some angry growls, and a lot of scrambling of claws before he bounded across the street and along the walkway of his family estate.

"Get inside!" Fel shouted, planting his feet on the walkway and turning toward the unseen dragon. "And stay off the walkway."

"I watch you!" Teya objected.

"Watch me from inside!" he shouted.

Duurth launched up from the street, appearing from behind the houses across the way. His snout was crusted with ice. Rage was in his eyes. Teya reluctantly retreated into the doorway. Fel tossed Wick's lantern aside. In one hand, he brandished the key. In the other, he brandished his club. Duurth crashed down into the street and glared at him. Fel smiled.

"That's right. That's right, you recognize part of your hoard. Of course you do. No pesky fire for you. You've got to fight fair." He twirled the club. "So let's see what you can do!"

The dragon took a step forward. Fel held his ground. Another step. Fel gritted his teeth. Duurth stalked toward him, lips peeled back, teeth fully bared.

"What are you, afraid?" Fel said.

"You hide too!" Teya called from inside. "You hide too!"

"I have a *plan*!" he growled.

Duurth thumped closer, head low and snarling. Fel started to step backward.

"You think you can take me? You think you can take a Masker?"

The dragon thumped forward until one of its heavy claws came down on a stone that made a soft click. Twin panels sprang shut, revealing spikes like a pair of chomping teeth as Duurth activated the first trap on the walkway. Duurth roared in anger and pain. The powerful trap pierced his scales. He pulled away, but it held tight.

Fel dropped the key to grip both hands on the handle of the spiked club. He scored two solid hits on Duurth's trapped leg, but the spikes thumped uselessly off its scales. Fel was strong, but he wasn't as strong as a contraption, and even *that* had only just managed to punch a hole in the tough hide. He reared back for a third swing, but Duurth's tail lashed around and struck his side. The blow sent him flying. The pack was thrown from his back. All of his gear and the goods from the hoard scattered around him. Duurth screeched and roared. With three claws planted on the ground, it heaved and tore at the trapped leg until both jaws of the contraption came free. Thick blood speckled the ground. The pieces of the ancient contraption rained down. Fel fought for breath and tried to pull himself to his club.

"Hey! Dragon!" Teya shouted.

Fel turned his blurred vision to the estate. The kobold sprinted out, Parch no longer tied to her wrist. She had something held to her lips.

She slid to a stop beside Fel. He expected some final, defiant remark from the creature before he and she were both crushed to a paste. She wasn't able to speak, however. Her cheeks were bulging with something. She pawed at his coat and pulled his sparker from his pocket. She looked up as the dragon's long neck coiled back, a serpent ready to strike. As it launched forward, she nimbly hopped, coming down squarely on the monster's snout. She held the sparker to her mouth and spat a mouthful of what turned out to be Facture's Private Reserve through the flickering blue sparks. The booze took to flame and sprayed across the dragon's eyes.

A flick of his neck sent Teya flying. She struck the wall of the estate. Fire wasn't much of a weapon against a dragon, but two eyes full of it were enough to blind and dazzle the beast for a few moments. Fel coughed, grabbed his club, and pulled himself to his feet. It took three swings at the distracted monster's injured leg, but he finally planted a cluster of four spikes into the wound. A fresh, furious screech shook the town. Stung yet again, Duurth retreated a few steps until the flames in his eyes started to fade. Fel hobbled toward Teya.

After a few seconds, Duurth was searching for the creatures who dared to oppose him. After a few seconds more, his injured leg refused to support him. A look of dim confusion, and even a flash of panic, painted the creature's features before he stumbled and slumped forward, four doses of manticore venom coursing through him. His eyes went glassy, he rolled to the side, and the once fearsome beast was reduced to a motionless, softly breathing lump.

"Teya!" Fel called.

He limped over to her. She sat up, eyes not quite pointed in the same direction.

"Is good? Is not dead?" she said.

"We're not dead. Neither is Duurth."

"Good. Both good." She rubbed her head. "Did you see? Breathed fire!"

"Yeah, I saw. Good job."

"Just like dragon…" she said softly.

"About how long do you think Duurth will be down?" he asked.

She blinked and looked to the bloodstained spikes on the club.

"That much? Small dragon? A day. Maybe two."

"Good. Are you all right to walk? Think you can find your way back to the boat?"

"Yes. Both yes."

"Good. Take the key and get going."

"You… kill Duurth?" she said.

"I get the feeling it'll take more than I've got. And besides. I hardly see the point of it for now. But I'm going to find Tome and then we're going to load up as much of his hoard as we can."

She nodded. "Good."

Teya grabbed the key and hobbled for a few steps until she became accustomed to the pain of the impact. She hopped onto the snout of the immobilized dragon and leaned down to look him in the eyes she'd so recently doused in flame. She chattered something in her native language, then seemingly translated for Fel's benefit.

"Sorry for hurt," she said, patting him between the eyes. "So pretty dragon. So pretty."

She hopped back off and pulled a dislodged scale from the tip of one of the trap's spikes, trilling happily to herself as she clutched it tightly and went on her way. Fel picked up Wick's lantern.

"Wick? You there?"

"Yes, Fel. And I am relieved that you are as well."

"You can head back to Mom and Dad. Tell them we're safe. Maybe skip the scarier details on what happened. Just let them know that if Dad as right about that key, we're headed home."

"I will happily fulfill this service, Fel."

#

"All right, Mr. Masker. I'm headed out. A girl's gotta sleep sometime. But now that Davie's back, I've got him and the boys keeping an eye out, and if you need some muscle to get you home safe, just let them know," Allie said, hanging up her apron.

"Much obliged, Allie. Much obliged," Martin said, reaching up to doff a cap that he realized a moment too late he wasn't wearing.

The patriarch of the Masker clan and the odd-man-out of the Graves family had been snacking on roasted crickets and drinking their beverages of choice for the better part of the evening. The amount of tipsiness on display suggested Fel's high resilience to strong drink had come from his mother's side, and for all his other vices, Thaddeus was a bit of a lightweight in the booze department as well.

241

They'd been given the "good" booth upon their arrival and hadn't left except to heed the call of nature. What had begun as a near-silent and extremely tense atmosphere between two rivals had devolved into something decidedly more silly.

"It's really so simple? You just swap out the disks, and they play a new song?" Thaddeus said. "That's how you do the music boxes?"

"I wouldn't call it *simple*. There are seven different types of gears that look pretty nearly identical but absolutely aren't. And the whole thing is *very* sensitive to speed. Wrong speed, won't play. Wrong set of gears, wrong speed. But once you get it all down, *and* you work out the engraving patterns for the disks, *and* you work out the best means for doing the engravings, *and*—"

Thaddeus raised his hand. "Stop, stop. Too many 'ands.' How exactly did you learn all this?"

"For the music boxes? A few comments in three different journals we turned up in expeditions and estate sales on top of a tremendous amount of observation and trial."

Thaddeus shook his head. "My father would kill me if he knew I was saying this, to you of all people. And my brother would probably help him do it. But when Euphoria decided she wanted to elope? We thought we were getting this."

"Getting what?"

Thaddeus waved his hand vaguely. "This. This 'observation and trial.' This intuition. I don't know. I supposed we'd ascribed some sort of mystical relevance to the Masker name. You're the only contraptioneers we deal with who have been at it longer than us. It conjures to mind some sort of rite of passage where the Maskers pass on their technical acumen. Don't get me wrong. Euphoria has been an asset to the family. She brought her own sort of intuition. We've… perhaps *doubled* our earnings year over year since she joined us. But that's mostly down to finding better buyers. Finding better loopholes in the assayer's rules. That. That's a big one."

He took a sip of his drink. "I've seen how the assayers run things down here. I don't know how you stay in business. No slack. We get away with so much more up north. But then, I *do* know how you stay in business. It's because of the whole family. We talk about contraptions. The Masker Family is a contraption. Fel, willing and able to hurl himself into the jaws of a deathtrap of a vault. You, able to turn a pile of rust into something worth selling. Your wife, able to turn duots into cenots with just a bit of talk. And your daughters, taking the business on the road. Each piece works together, and it makes the whole thing work."

"Surely that's every family. Every clan," Martin said.

Thad took a bigger sip and scoffed. "You don't travel up north much and it shows. The Bolivans and the Graves have their own way of doing things. The Bolivans are like a hammer. They smash their way through whatever is between them and their goal. Be it caches of goods or the ear of the best buyer, they'll leave a pile of rubble rather than give it up. Bribes, too. We've seen them come at us with goods that were confiscated from us by the assayers. Someone in that office is willing to let things walk out of their personal vault. Us? We make up for it by having a wider footprint. This bazaar? The one that comes down here? It's one of three we run. We've even got some ships. We cast a good, wide net to find enough buyers to sell to and goods to sell. We probably have three times as many, maybe five times as many contraptions pass through our hands as you do. But the *yield*. Pathetic. Half of what you produce. We just can't fix a fraction of what you can. And then we found out about that 'pack of chains.' Oiler. Fixes whatever it finds? By the high, that's a Martin Masker you can *own*."

"And what about the rest? The dagger and the mask? And what about all the rest of the items Epiphany says you were after?"

"You'll have to ask my brother, assuming this little meeting of the families happens. I just get shopping lists and marching orders. And I shop, and I march. The mask? Who knows. Maybe Euphoria got sick of the one she brought with her from here. She used to keep it on the mantel. Not anymore."

Martin tried to put his mind to work on the riddle, but the amount of drink made any real insight unlikely. Instead, his thoughts drifted to something else.

"The Masker family is not a contraption…" Martin muttered.

"What's that?"

"I say we aren't a contraption. A contraption ceases to function if it is separated from one of its key parts. And Euphoria is a key part of the family."

"Metaphor," Thaddeus said.

"Poor metaphor. But not as poor as it might be. We are in a fragile place right now. And I worry not just for my family but for the world. The skills I have are too rare." He pushed the mug away. "We need that meeting. Sooner rather than later."

He stood. "If there were any agents left in town interested in our necks, they would have made their move by now. Let's go. I'd like a word with Vivian and Epiphany."

Chapter 13

The journey back to Kazel's lair was uneventful. That a trip overseen by a greater harpy on a ship borne on the backs of three undines and ending with a ride on a unicorn's back might be considered uneventful spoke volumes of the nature of their adventure. The Adept was not happy that Fel had hauled six hefty sacks of choice contraptions from Duurth's hoard. But the presence of the key, and the promise of Kazel's release after so long, was a balm on that particular sore spot.

The sacks were left to be carried the slow way, on the backs of kobolds grateful to be serving their dragon in a new way. Though the Adept tolerated their presence on the ship, she had no interest in having them brought to the lair. The unicorns brought Teya, Tome, and Fel as near to the main lair as they could, while the Adept flew ahead to deliver the message of forthcoming freedom. From the moment Fel, Tome, and Teya stepped off the unicorns, their feet didn't touch the ground. A legion of kobolds—every one in the lair— carried them on their backs, straight to the door of Kazel's chamber.

Kazel stood, eyes wide and gaze sharp. He did not speak. He simply watched as they traced a respectful path around his hoard and through the broken door on the far side.

"You do the honors," Fel said, handing the key to Teya.

"Contraption. You do," she said.

"Look, if this works, I'm out of here. Seems like the person to set Kazel free ought to be one who'll stick around to get the glory," he said.

She hopped up and down, key clutched to her chest. "How? Quick! How?" she urged.

He walked up to the panel with its many keyholes and placed his palms on the wall, making a ladder of himself.

"Climb on up. That emblem should face the door. Slide it in the top keyhole and pray to whatever god you worship it still works after all these years under a dragon."

She scurried up his back and thrust the key into place. She heaved at it, and just as the claws on her toes were threatening to draw blood in Fel's shoulders, the key clicked into place. Something like thunder rumbled in the floor below. Then, with a terrifying rattle and clack, the final chain fell away.

The mountain trembled with heavy, plodding footsteps. Kazel emerged from a doorway almost too small for him to pass through. He turned and fixed Fel and the others in his gaze. Fel had just done battle with one of these beasts. But in this moment, locked in that impassive gaze, he felt smaller and more frightened than when Duurth's flames were at his heels.

"Follow," Kazel uttered.

The dragon plodded up the steps. Fel and Tome couldn't hope to keep up. Teya scrambled over the stone steps and vanished into the distance. When they reached the top, Kazel was standing in the open, eyes turned to the blue sky. The setting sun gleamed on his gold and silver scales. More than ever, he looked like something wrought by the gods themselves.

"I have not felt the sun on my face since before your grandfathers were born," Kazel rumbled without looking away from the open sky. "That I would owe my freedom in part to you, to a contraptioneer—to a *Masker*—proof that fate's games are a mystery even to the wisest among us."

He turned. Teya dropped into a chin-to-the-ground, arms-extended posture of raw worship. Fel and Tome knelt. Parch hid behind Fel.

"A debt is owed," Kazel said. "A debt that, even with my great wealth and power, I may never be able to repay. But I shall try. Speak. What can be done to balance the scales?"

Fel raised his head. "I know you talked about giving me some gear, but I've got everything I can carry already. Mostly I just want to get back to the wall. Get back home."

"You will be brought to the wall. As close as my people can manage."

"And my loot too? The stuff from Duurth's hoard?"

"I'll be happy to be rid of it. And what you ask falls well short of even the slightest of recompense."

"Well… If you *insist*. If I ever come back, I'll be sure to take those contraptions you offered off your hands. Claws. Whatever."

"It will be done. And you should come back. The Greater Lands needs more like you. And you, Mage. What do you require?"

"Seedlings or seeds of a handful of plants. I've prepared a list. And if they are available, some samples of kobold scale, harpy feather, griffin feather, unicorn mane. As much paper as you can spare. If you have any oak galls, kraken ink, if it exists, and…" Tome glanced up. "… And I think that'll do."

"Teya," Kazel said.

She shook. "Said my name," she whispered, trembling. "Said my name."

"Stand," he instructed.

She sprang to her feet and stood rigidly straight.

"The Adept has told the tale of your service. You went so far as to overcome the influence that keeps us from Duurth's lair in pursuit of your task."

"Did job," she uttered.

"You have served well. Exceeded what was expected of you. It is to be rewarded."

Teya shook her head. "Have dragon. Have friends. Family. Have home. Things to do. All I want."

"You also have my respect and my gratitude."

She covered her face. "Too much."

"Um, if I may?" Fel said. "I have a suggestion."

Teya turned and jabbed a finger. "No talk! Kazel talk!"

"Speak, Fel Masker," Kazel said.

"Talk now!" Teya urged.

He pulled the sparker from his pocket. "This is what got her in trouble in the first place. And it's what allowed her to save my life and get the key to you. I think you should let her keep it."

"A contraption," Kazel rumbled.

"All it does is make fire. I think you understand the value of something like that. She certainly seems to."

"Is important," Teya said, pushing the sparker back to him. "Is *family* important."

"Then take good care of it. If I come back, I'll swap it for a better one."

Teya looked sheepishly to Kazel. The dragon huffed.

"So be it. But use it with care."

Teya nodded and clutched the sparker happily.

Kazel spread his wings and gave them a flap. Teya and the others were nearly knocked from their feet.

"It's been too long. My wings are weak," Kazel said. "But soon I will soar."

The Adept swept down from above and placed Mik and Stix beside her. They bowed. Fel clutched his chest, at first thinking his heart was pounding in his chest. He realized when Tome did the same that it wasn't him, it was Kazel. He was speaking, not in their tongue but his. He realized that this was the same chattering language the kobolds spoke, but scaled to a dragon's size. It was like having a conversation with an earthquake.

It must have been a very efficient language, because the Adept nodded and stepped aside after just a few seconds of instruction. Kazel broke into a regal stride and swept down the mountain to get his first taste of freedom in too long.

"We will make an effort to gather your things for you, Tome. Fel, the sacks of your stolen items will be protected, should Duurth be foolish enough to encroach on Kazel's territory again to reclaim it. Teya… do not set anything of value on fire with that thing.”

“Careful!” she said. “I use smart.”

The Adept looked to Fel and Tome. “I want to be clear. Your contributions are truly appreciated. You did what I am confident that few others could have. We are forever in your debt. However, I intend to get you to the wall as swiftly as I am able, because I have no doubt that your continued presence here will cause more problems than it solves.”

“That’s pretty much how it goes,” Fel said with a nod.

“Then we are in agreement. I shall make the preparations immediately. You will be delivered to the wall by the evening.”

#

Vivian gave a knowing nod to the people manning the guard shacks on either side of the gate leading to the Verfessa home. She wasn’t terribly pleased. They’d become so accustomed to her comings and goings that the telltale alertness conjured by a potential intruder had vanished. That bothered her. But she supposed she was going to have to become accustomed to it, if things progressed the way it seemed they would have to. She marched up the walkway and knocked at the door. When it opened, the maid didn’t even inquire who she was or why she was there. She simply stood aside and allowed Vivian through.

The matriarch of the household, Eveline Verfessa, was waiting for her. A full tea set had been prepared. It was still steaming and complete with orange cake plated for three.

“We’ve been expecting you,” she said.

“Evidently,” Vivian said, eying the refreshments.

“Given the nature of your last discussion with Donovan, we thought it proper to have some of our people linger in your part of the city. We were told you were headed in this direction, and we suspected there was only one reason for you to leave your post. Please, have a seat. Donovan will be along shortly.”

“Now that Epiphany is home, I can spare some time. And we’ve had a rather detailed family meeting and come to some conclusions,” Vivian said.

“Please, save them for when Donovan arrives. I would hate for you to have to repeat yourself.”

She sat. Eveline poured her some tea.

“Normally I don’t like to be present for business of this type, but I suspect you and I will have rather more contact with each other than most of Donovan’s associates.”

“Oh? And just what type of business have I come to discuss, do you suppose?” Vivian asked.

Heavy boots thumped on stairs leading up from below.

“We shall soon see, won’t we,” Eveline said.

"Vivian!" Donovan said triumphantly as he approached and sat in the third chair. "I was hoping it would be you. Nothing against your husband. He's a capable man, but you and I, I think, run our minds along similar lines."

"I'm pleased you would consider me a peer in that regard," Vivian said.

He laughed. "No need to lie. I know you don't have much love for my sort of business. But you don't always get to choose your alliances, do you?"

"It all depends on what you are willing to risk and what you are willing to sacrifice. As it happens, for the time being, I have had my fill of risk, and thus I must sacrifice a bit to balance the scales."

"Cost of business, Viv. Cost of business. Let's start with what you need."

"We need to know there won't be a blade against our necks if we walk down the wrong streets in our own town."

"Protection. You'll need to help with that. If these were just the run-of-the-mill thugs, I'd have had them stomped into paste weeks ago. But the Bolivans can make themselves invisible and all sorts of other tricks."

"There won't be many more who can do that trick, but I've had a word with Martin, and he is confident he can rig up a passable means to detect those concealed by contraptions. He's spoken at length with a friend of the family who has a firm grasp of paper magic, and the two believe they can combine their talents in that regard."

"Contraptions *and* paper magic." Donovan turned. "What have I said, dear? Innovation. We've let ourselves get too stiff. Gotta get more flexible. Where'd you get yourself a paper mage?"

"My son brought him home. Another of the boy's strays."

"Well, that's a keeper. Send him down. If he'd like to make an extra bit of coin, I could use a man like that on staff."

"I'll suggest it to him. But if we could stay on topic."

"Organized, focused. I like it. Yes, if you can make sure we can see them, we'll make sure no one sees them for very long. What else?"

"Our primary avenue for sales that bypass the assayer has turned out to be rather less reliable than we had expected. Should we continue to wish to expand beyond entirely legitimate sales, we would benefit from access to any buyers you've been able to secure."

"Of course, of course. And what about the assayers themselves?"

"What about them?"

"With you and me both starting to work the gray area they're supposed to sniff out, they're going to start sniffing extra hard."

"We're accustomed to navigating them."

"You're accustomed to navigating them when you aren't doing anything wrong. If they stick their noses in deeper than usual?"

"We will adapt."

"I'll just come out and say it. My boys will be keeping an eye out for the assayers and nudging them off our scent. You and I work together, they'll be nudged off your scent too."

"No violence in that regard."

"Viv, what sort of a man do you take me for?"

"The sort who would discuss stomping rivals into paste over tea and cakes."

"We don't do that sort of thing on people with the blessing of the nobles and the kingdom. Too much trouble. Blood like that stains the hands deep. No. This will be strictly finesse and, if needs be, financial encouragement."

"I imagine there is value to that."

"Anything else?"

"This is not an open-ended partnership. There will come a time when we will no longer require protection, and our trading network will solidify. At that time, I would very much like to part amicably."

"I'm always willing to renegotiate, provided you are as well."

"Then that concludes my requirements from any potential partnership."

"Here's what I'll need from you, then. I'm already starting to get shipments of contraptions, some intact, some broken. I'll need your expertise in setting price and repairing what needs to be repaired. Daily appraisal appointments, and two days a week dedicated to repair and restoration on our goods."

"Two appraisal appointments weekly, with additional appointments negotiable. Priority given to your repairs one day a week."

He grinned. "Three appointments. Priority repairs two days a week, and access to Martin to train one of my associates to do simple repairs."

"There are no simple repairs, but that is otherwise acceptable to me."

"And then there's the matter of my cut."

"You mean beyond what we've just discussed?"

"I'm offering you protection, Viv. In my line of business, that carries a very specific connotation. You kick up, oh… ten percent of what you make at that shop, and I make sure nothing bad happens to it."

"As I understand it, 'protection' of that sort is usually protection *from* the person demanding the fee."

"Turns out in this case it's against someone else. Which makes the whole thing feel a lot more legitimate, if you ask me."

"I don't think that is negotiable," she said.

"You're right about that, Viv. Nonnegotiable. I get my slice."

She set down her tea. His expression became ever-so-subtly less jovial.

"We've gotten along well enough, but we both knew what sort of a man I am. What sort of a business I run. It was always going to come to this. My men will be risking their lives to keep you and yours safe. So far all you're offering is to do a little of your regular business on our behalf. That's not balanced.

This isn't a charity. I've got overhead. I get ten percent. And like you say, you can pull out at any time. That's a better deal than I'd give most of the people I work with."

She picked her tea back up and stirred it. "Ten percent commission on any sales made to buyers you introduce us to."

He whistled. "*Fortitude.* It takes *fortitude* to make an offer like that. Ten percent on everything."

"Donovan, we both know that each sale to one of your buyers will be at a price many multiples of what we make on sales through the store. You're getting the lion's share of what you'd have made overall. And I have no intention of showing you my books for you to check my accounting for the shop, but with your buyers you can check up on your own."

"Thirty percent on sales to my buyers."

"Fifteen."

Donovan leaned back and crossed his arms, face contemplative.

"What you are offering us is convenient and secure, but nothing we can't find elsewhere," she said. "What you are getting from us is access to a set of skills that exists nowhere else in the world."

He extended a hand. "Fifteen. And that's five percent better than anyone could have got out of me, Viv. You're a professional and I respect that."

She shook hands. "May all future business be as pleasant and equitable as this."

"I don't think you're foolish enough or curious enough to want to find out how things look around here when they get unpleasant."

"And I suspect you've looked into the Masker family and learned just how unpleasant we can get when backed against a wall."

He filled his tea, topped hers off, and raised his glass for a toast.

"Here's to staying hungry, staying scrappy, and teaching our lessons well enough that we only need to teach them once."

She raised her glass. "I'll drink to that."

He held his hand up. "No drinks just yet. Anything to add, my love?"

Eveline, who had been quietly observing the exchange, gave the question some thought.

"I would suggest that anyone capable of so ably negotiating with you, particularly with full knowledge of what you are capable of, is an asset to have as an ally. My only question regarding her judgment is the failure to partake of the cake."

Vivian grinned. "Business before pleasure."

"Then I wouldn't dream of prolonging business any further. And the pleasure is all ours."

#

It took a few hours, but Fel and Tome were delivered to the base of the

251

wall, along with all their things. Watching the influence of the wall affect the others was really rather fascinating. The kobolds, with the exception of Teya, started to peel off and wander back as they got to the point where the wall became steeper. The Adept made it a bit farther, but soon the focus and intellect drained from her eyes, and she retreated, with her hands, a short distance back. By the time they reached the base of the wall itself, their traveling crew had reduced to just Fel, Tome, Parch, Oiler, and a *very* distracted Teya. Fel had Oiler, his gear pack, and two more sacks across his shoulders. Tome struggled to carry two sacks of his own. Teya dropped hers and fixed her eyes on Fel.

"No more. Everything swims. I turn back now," she said.

Fel crouched. "Hey. I want to thank you for your help. Tell you the truth, if it was you tagging along with me on these adventures instead of Tome, I'd be a lot happier."

"Hey!" Tome objected.

"And you? Contraptioneer. Bad, usually. Masker? Bad always. They teach that. But now? I know you. They teach wrong. Some Masker, good. I watch you? I see so much. Do so much. I thank you." She held up the sparker. "For this." She held up the dragon scale, which she wore around her neck. "For this? For much. I thank you. Come, I give."

"No, no. I've got enough already. Kazel gave—*ouch!*"

Teya jabbed her claw into his leg, drawing blood.

"What was that for?" he asked.

"Scar. Good for remembering."

Fel tugged a bit of bandage from his replenished gear and tucked it into his pants to stop the bleeding. Teya turned to Tome.

"I give," she offered.

"No, no! I've got quite enough to remember you by already."

Teya nodded. "Goodbye." She pointed. "You come back. Visit."

"I just may, as long as you promise not to give me any more presents to remember you by," Fel said.

She nodded again and scampered away. Fel rubbed his leg and gazed up at the wall. From the outside, it was a bit more than two stories tall. Not insurmountable but more than enough to keep just about anything without wings from crossing. From the inside, thanks to the steep drop-off, it was more like six stories, and lacking any decent handholds.

"Now we just need to figure out how to climb this thing," Fel said.

"Fel," Tome said, gazing aside, his voice a bit shaky.

"Yes?"

"Do you remember what we were told about when we returned to the wall?"

"Nope."

"It was something about... I forget the words, but it doesn't matter.

Whatever they were, they were right."

"I don't need riddles right now, Tome."

"Just look along the wall, Fel."

He gazed left, then right. "By the high, what is going on?"

The wall was curved, as it should be. It traced a huge circle, and thus it was a very subtle curve. Yet the wall managed to vanish after a certain distance. Not lost in the lush overgrowth. Not fading into mist or darkness. Hidden behind itself, obscured by its own curve. It was curving *away* from them. As though they were on the outside rather than the inside of the circle it traced.

Fel gritted his teeth. "I am ignoring this. I am fed up with things not behaving themselves. We are climbing this wall, we are climbing down the other side, and when we do, we'll be back in the dry field and that will be that. *Parch!*"

The unicorn bleated and looked up to him. Fel pulled the end of a long bit of rope provided by the kobolds. He tied it into a harness. Parch seemed to understand the game and scaled the almost perfectly vertical wall with goatlike ease. When he reached the top, Fel tugged at the rope and Parch locked his little legs, ready for a game of tug.

"When I get up there, I'll secure the rope and call you. Tie the rest of these sacks to the line so we can haul them up."

"But the wall! What if it means something!" Tome said.

"I don't care! We're going home! Didn't you get attacked by a berry or something not so far from here? Do you want that to happen again?"

"It was a boobrie, and it was a half mile farther down the river, but fine. Point taken. Get moving."

Fel pulled himself up, planted his boots on the wall, and started to climb. Parch was more than willing to pull against the extra weight on the rope. The powerful little creature shuffled a step or two back every few seconds, and finally Fel came to the top of the wall.

He gazed left and right. The curve of the wall was certainly away from the Greater Lands, and the drier land on the other side seemed to be ringed by wall. As he stepped toward the far side, dragging the rope behind him, the wall seemed to straighten. He didn't feel a whisper of motion. There *wasn't* any motion. But nevertheless by the time he reached the far side of the wall and peered down the shorter distance to the bottom, the curvature had changed. Now it curved toward the Greater Lands, enclosing them.

"Ignore it, ignore it," Fel said, pulling the harness from Parch and fastening it to one of the crenellations along what he rigidly refused to think of as anything but the outside of the wall. "Tome, I'm going to pull up the sacks, then lower the rope and pull you up. And I swear, if I hear *any* observations or theories from you, I'm going to throw you back in the river. Now let's go. We've got a long road ahead."

Epilogue

Three weeks later…

The moon was just inching past the low row of rooftops on either side of the street. Fel hadn't checked the time before he left his home, and the closer he got to The Fox and Log, the more concerned he was that he'd waited just a bit too long to head down to pay his visit. He wrapped the end of the sack around his fist to keep it from dangling as he quickened his pace.

As it happened, a rather weary Allie was just stepping out of the tavern when he turned the corner.

"Allie!" he called.

She turned and scanned the street until she spotted him. A smile lit up her exhausted face. "There you are. The ol' wayward wanderer. We're breaking in a new server. His name is Fenton. He'll be closing out the night, so go easy on him."

"No, no. I'm not heading in for a drink. I just had to drop something off. You're done for the night? Headed home?"

"That's right. It was a long one today."

"I'll walk you home. It's been a while. I kind of wanted to catch up. It'll be easier without a bunch of drunks shouting for orders."

"Sure. This way," she said.

He trotted up to her and matched her pace as they made their way down the street.

"So. You just get back?" she asked.

"Been back for a week," he said.

"And you didn't come and say hello? The boys were starting to take bets on if you'd survived."

"Anyone betting against me?"

"Just Tem."

"Of course he did," Fel grumbled. "Nice to know that me not getting killed has cost him some money, then."

"What have you been doing for a week?" she asked.

"The usual. Loading up the loot we got, patching up the sore spots. And I had to work on some gifts." He opened the stack and pulled out the contraption medallion. "Here," he said. "What do you think of this? You think Mariss will like it?"

Allie held it up to the half-visible moon to put some light behind it. He tapped the button, and the pieces started to rotate.

"I engraved her name around the outside and polished it up," he said.

Allie dangled it back into his hand. "I think she'll love it. But tell me this, did you risk your life for it?"

"Allie, there were dragons involved. More than *one* dragon."

She nodded. "She'll like the story even more. Turns out your girl has a taste for danger."

He raised his eyebrows. "Does she? I know Mom said she was nearby when the guy with the scar nearly got the better of her."

"You ought to head down there and bring it up. I think she'll be swooning over what you've got to say. It's a shame we've only got a short way to go. I'd love to hear what sort of bone-headed things you pulled."

"I'll be down tomorrow, and I'll make sure I'm good and thirsty. But here. This is for you." He pulled a small, tasteful brass box from the sack. "You open the top there and twist the tab in the middle to start it up."

She tipped her head and opened the box. "This is a music box, isn't it?" she said.

"Yeah. You said you wanted one, didn't you? I didn't just dream that up, did I?"

"No, but I didn't tell you what song I wanted."

She twisted the tab. The soft, lilting melody began to play. A contraption music box, contrary to its more mundane cousins, didn't simply produce a tinkling, single-instrument tune. The music it produced was haunting and complex, the sounds almost mistakable for true instruments. There was even a wordless "voice" that dreamily wavered through what would have been the vocals.

"This is… this is the song I would have asked for," she said.

He shrugged. "Doesn't take a genius to figure out you'd want the song you hum to yourself while you're behind the bar."

"You noticed that, did you?"

"How many years have I been gambling away my wages at your place, Allie? Stuff is bound to soak through even a thick skull like mine if you give me enough time."

They reached the door of her home. It was one of the taller buildings, three stories. At some point in history, it had undoubtedly been an inn. Now it seemed the individual rooms of the place had been shifted to more permanent occupancy.

"Oh, before I head back. Seeing as how I know you're into music now…" He fished the final item out of the sack. "This is a music book I found in a city called Clickspring on the far side of the Greater Lands Wall. Sorry if it smells a little funny. It was part of a dragon's hoard for a century or so."

She took the book and flipped through a few pages. "A dragon's hoard."

"Yeah. I needed to find a key, and I knew it was in the hoard. It's a long story. I'll tell it when I'm halfway through whatever bottle of booze you're looking to get rid of tomorrow, but after I found the key, I found this just underneath it. I thought of you, you know?"

"So, you're robbing a dragon, and my hobbies just happen to be flitting through your mind."

"There are only so many pleasant times in my life, Allie. You're there for most of them. It puts you near the top of the memories I like to think back to when things are rough." He shrugged. "Hopefully you find something in there that tickles your fancy. Have a good night."

He turned to leave. She stopped him with a hand on the shoulder. When he turned back, she hugged him.

"I'm glad you made it back without too many new scars," she said. "The Fox and Log isn't the same without you."

He smiled. "It's nice to be missed."

She opened the door and slipped inside. "You make sure you stay sober enough to finish telling me the good parts of the story tomorrow."

"No promises," he said.

She shut the door. He smiled to himself and headed back the way he'd come.

#

The last week had been frustratingly busy for Martin. As he worked by the steady light of Wick's lantern, he found himself glancing to the top shelf where the reference volumes were waiting to be perused. Having dreamed for decades that he might someday find such a thing, knowing that he couldn't indulge himself until his task was through was maddening. And it had been *quite* a task.

He'd cataloged the loot that Fel had brought home and restored the items that wouldn't be of interest to the assayers. One full day was lost to repairing a taming saddle for Donovan Verfessa. Sacrificing some of his time to fix up items for someone outside the shop was a change that would take some getting used to. Then came the repair of the assayer-prohibited items that he knew how to fix, something that Oiler had been of particular use in completing. There had even been a bit of a repair to Oiler itself, as there were some missing plates and fasteners after its adventure with Fel.

But finally, with the click of a well-fitted panel, he was done with the week's work. He smiled and turned to the portion of his workshop reserved for his pet projects. A heavy cloth rested on top of the current focus of his interest.

He made sure his hands were scrupulously clean, then moved Wick's lantern over for both the light and the company.

"Pay attention to this, Wick," he said as he pulled down one of the reference volumes. "One of these days I'll have to have Tome transcribe these and then burn them for you. But until then, I want you listening to what I say and double-checking my work."

"It will be a pleasure, Martin."

He opened the book and flipped a few pages in. His mind did the swift work of translating the ancient text into something he properly understood.

"Let us see… The first and most important task of a contraptioneer is to determine the point at which the contraptioneer and the contraptor's interests overlap. A contraption exists for two purposes. To function according to its design, and to capture the interest of the contraptors such that indulging themselves produces the intended effect. The interest, and the intended effect, must always be developed in concert when designing, improving, or maintaining a contraption."

He looked up. "The intended effect," he mused, looking at the cloth-covered project.

He pulled away the cloth to reveal the faceless head that Fel had brought back from the ancestral home of the Maskers.

"Well, then. Let's just see if we can determine what you were built to do, shall we?"

* * *

From the Author

Thank you for reading! If you liked this story, or perhaps if you found it lacking, I'd love to hear from you. Leave a review, or contact me directly on social media or via email. You can find the relevant links (as well as my newsletter sign-up) at bookofdeacon.com/contact

Discover other titles by Joseph R. Lallo:

The Book of Deacon Series:

Book 1: *The Book of Deacon*
Book 2: *The Great Convergence*
Book 3: *The Battle of Verril*
Book 4: *The D'Karon Apprentice*
Book 5: *The Crescents*
Book 6: *The Coin of Kenvard*

The Big Sigma Series:

Book 1: *Bypass Gemini*
Book 2: *Unstable Prototypes*
Book 3: *Artificial Evolution*
Book 4: *Temporal Contingency*
Book 5: *Indra Station*
Book 6: *Nova Igniter*

The Free-Wrench Series:

Book 1: *Free-Wrench*
Book 2: *Skykeep*
Book 3: *Ichor Well*
Book 4: *The Calderan Problem*
Book 5: *Cipher Hill*
Book 6: *Contaminant Six*